The Heaviness of Things That Float

The HEAVINESS *of* THINGS THAT FLOAT

JENNIFER MANUEL

Douglas & McIntyre

Douglas & McIntyre (2013) Ltd.
PO Box 219, Madeira Park, BC, V0N 2H0
www.douglas-mcintyre.com

Editing by Barbara Berson
Copyediting by Shirarose Wilensky
Text design by Shed Simas
Cover design by Anna Comfort O'Keeffe
Printed and bound in Canada

Douglas & McIntyre acknowledges the support of the Canada Council for the Arts,
which last year invested $157 million to bring the arts to Canadians throughout the
country. We also gratefully acknowledge financial support from the Government of
Canada through the Canada Book Fund and from the Province of British Columbia
through the BC Arts Council and the Book Publishing Tax Credit.

Cataloguing data available from Library and Archives Canada
ISBN 978-1-77162-087-1 (paper)
ISBN 978-1-77162-088-8 (ebook)

For Nick
I love you more.

Author's Note

Although Tawakin and all its residents are fictional, this novel arose from the years I spent—first as a treaty archivist and then as a teacher—on the lands of the Ktunaxa, Tahltan and Nuu-chah-nulth peoples.

In this book, there are Nuu-chah-nulth words. In most cases, I have opted for informal spellings—for example, *chumiss* over the formal spelling of *çamus*. I received the spelling of these words, as well as the descriptions of mythological creatures, from Kyuquot elder Kelly John. I am grateful for his support and his teachings.

In 2010, Kelly John adopted me and gave me the name *aa ap wa iick*, which means Always Speaks Wisely. I am unsure I deserve that name. As I wrote this novel, I did not see this name as a label. Rather, it has been an aspiration. A hope that I will contribute something honest and compassionate to our discussion of First Peoples–settler relations in Canada.

This is a novel about understanding privilege. I am privileged by history. I am privileged by my heritage. And I am privileged to have known Kelly John, who passed away during the editing of this novel.

A note about the nurse's job in Tawakin. Generally, nurses rotate, whereas I chose to depict the nurse's posting in the Tawakin outpost as permanent, much like a teacher's. Her decades of duty allowed me to examine the nature of belonging, the limits of knowing one another and the stories of arrival that tangle with the stories of contact.

"Stories of contact" is a phrase that sounds as feathery and constructive as God's touch upon Adam's fingertip, when in fact these stories have been violent and corrosive. Weeds choking plants of sustenance. These are the stories of every person on the Tawakin Reserve and on every traditional territory in Canada, of every person who'd never arrived because they were already there.

I do not know anything about contact.

I know only about arrival.

And the dangers of presuming too much.

I have only four lines of sight:
  How I see me.
  How I see you.
  How I see you with me.
  How I see me with you.
Our different ways of seeing are neither right nor wrong.
But if you lay your lines of sight over mine, there
is a hidden map of understanding, and the invitation to
believe something new.

—Bernadette Perkal

(Found inside three bottles washed
up on the shores of Tawakin.)

1

Each morning, I walk the short perimeter of my island and listen for the stories in the wind and the water. A long time ago, Frank said the stories grew here along the coast, like organisms all their own, life upon life, the way moss grows around poplar trunks and barnacles atop crab shells, the way golden chanterelles spring from hemlock needles. They spread in the cove with the kelp and the eelgrass, and in the rain forest with the lichen, the cedars, the swordferns. They pelt down inside raindrops, erode thick slabs of driftwood, puddle the old logging road that these days leads to nowhere.

It might seem preposterous that I'd even considered this to be possible, but the world was full of strange phenomena. I'd read about boxes containing cats both at once dead and alive, photographs of frozen water crystals purportedly shaped by the words spoken to them, ancient sounds recorded in the grooves of prehistoric clay vases, and I wanted to know if this was also true, if our stories could be grafted like cells onto this world and grown into something that might remain long after we're gone. Besides, I wanted to believe in Frank, still.

So far I'd heard nothing like words on my walks, though the sun seemed to speak to me. Its rays bounced off the windows across the cove on the Tawakin Reserve like heliograph messages written with tilted mirrors. Bright glints that questioned my decision to leave the people who lived inside those houses, the people for whom I'd served loyally as outpost nurse for almost forty years. The people with whom I'd shared my life. At this point, it had become less of a departure, really—more like an extraction. The pulling of an old tooth deeply rooted. The unravelling of a cedar strip that had been woven tightly into a basket. Something that would cleave and render me useless.

*   *   *

Then one night I heard it on the VHF radio from the outpost: Chase Charlie was missing on the water. The report startled me from a deep sleep. At the sound of his name, I gripped the bedsheets tight enough to crack open a clamshell. Bolting upright, I planted my feet onto the cold tiles and turned up the volume on the radio. Nobody in the village on the Tawakin Reserve had seen Chase or his trawler since the late afternoon, and now it was the black of night and the wind was bending the cedars sideways. The radio crackled. People arranged who would search and who would stay. Somebody had a hunch he might be up north near Cougar Point, where the rugged coast of Vancouver Island turned to ivory-coloured sand, or maybe around the Janis Islands, where the fog often closed like curtains between arches of rock. Nobody knew for certain why he'd headed out on such a blustery day, northwesterlies topping thirty knots. Storm clouds scribbled on the edges of the sky.

Over the radio, Chase's wife, Patty, brayed, "He's been out there for almost seven hours. He left the house at exactly four o'clock. I know it because Oprah was starting, and I wasn't about to miss Oprah on account of him wanting fish for supper."

After scrambling into some clothes, I clipped the radio onto my belt and went to the bathroom, where I pulled my hair into a loose ponytail. I noticed, as I didn't usually, the mural of the rain forest Chase and I painted twenty years ago, when he was thirteen, during those precious months he lived with me. In the mirror, the cedars framed me, the green against the silver of my hair.

In the medical examination room off the living quarters I went to the window and pressed my hands against the cold glass. After forty years of living alone here on Hospital Island, this wasn't the first time I'd watched a convoy of boats and skiffs and silver punts motor away—lit at the front by yellow beams on the ends of sweeping flashlights—as those left behind in the clapboard houses on the Tawakin Reserve turned from braying to praying. But I'd seen enough tragedy in Tawakin to last four lifetimes, let alone decades, and if I was going to retire next month—well, it might not be joyful, but at least it could be peaceful. Without grief. Without guilt. Yet here I was, roused from my sleep and wearing my sweater inside out and staring at my ghostly reflection, worried not only for Chase's safety but also that I was to blame for his disappearance.

"He's got flour all over him," Patty said over the radio.

"What? Like daffodils or something?" It was my good friend, the ever-cheerful, always helpful Sophie Florence Joe.

"Not even," Patty said. "The cooking kind. A whole tub of it. And it's not whole wheat, it's white, so he should be real easy to spot as long as it don't rain."

"What's he got that on him for?" Sophie Florence asked.

Patty's mother, Loretta Joe, came on the radio: "Real dumb, she already told you. He wanted fish for supper. If my daughter is too lazy to make fish for supper, she don't have to make fish for supper."

This sort of talk was not common on the Tawakin Reserve. If anything, there was a peculiar abundance of kindness and generosity and, despite those previously mentioned tragedies, laughter in our community. Ernie Frank, one of our elders, told me just the other day that it was a First Nations thing to be like this. "It's not something you see with the white people in their white cities," he said. "It's not in them to be this way. They don't know how," a comment to which I took offence, until I considered the possibility that he no longer saw me as a white person. Still, I suggested, "Perhaps it's the size of the cities that are to blame, not the people inside them." By way of rebuttal, he then informed me that I was, in no small measure, real nutty.

How Patty endured a mother like Loretta was beyond me. Loretta could find a way to blame Patty if she felt a draft in a closed room. "What you got to blink your eyes so damn hard for all the time, Patty? If I catch cold from that draft, it's all your fault." Loretta could find a way to blame God, the Lord Almighty Himself, for her own sins. I could picture her entry through the pearly gates, screaming at Him until her face turned red. Hurling cherubs across the firmament like bowling balls.

From the supply drawers I retrieved compresses and rolls of dressing, plus tubing for a warm-fluid intravenous. I stacked additional blankets on the bed, where Chase had sat yesterday with blood caked on his shirt and in his eye and along the brim of his greasy green cap. The gash was wide though not deep, and I'd cinched it easily with two butterfly bandages. I'd watched his pupils respond to the beam of a small flashlight and checked his balance, which was steady as the horizon, as well as his memory—did he know his name, the date, where he lived?

He did.

"What's your daughter's name?" I asked him.

"Hannah," he said.

"And your wife's name?"

"Patty," he said, which I of course heard as "Petty," since she often showed signs of becoming a milder version of her insufferable mother. Small doses now and then of being short tempered, all knowing and irreproachable by everybody except Loretta. Just last week at the market, she'd complained that "Hannah would be a straight A student if them teachers did their jobs right," ignoring the fact that her daughter plugged the school toilets with pages of her textbook whenever she got an answer wrong (which, according to the teachers, happened often, since she never listened in the first place).

Patty's metamorphosis from being the sweet child who used to braid my hair into somebody more brusque was hardly surprising, given her mother's tight grip. Of all the Tawakin families—the Jimmys, the Sams, the Charlies, the Henrys—the Joe family was the most influential, the matriarchal head of which was Loretta Joe. A cold tide who decided which sands of truth and which shells of lies spread across our shores. Even among people kind and generous, there were lies. There are always lies.

"Tripped," Chase told me yesterday from his seat on the examination bed. "Split my forehead on the kitchen counter. But people do that sometimes, don't they, walking around their house?"

"No, not really," I said, knowing full well he was fibbing. The cut was too thin, too clean and straight to be made by any countertop.

"Got one for you, Nursema'am," he then said, his eyes bright and a mischievous expression on his face. "What do you call someone from Tawakin with one leg shorter than the other?"

As I brushed his hair gently off the small bandages, a pain wrenched in my chest. Is this what it would feel like, this ache in my body, when I soon left Tawakin forever? Had Chase imagined yet what it would feel like when he could no longer find me across the cove? Of course he had. This kidding around only masked his pain. I smiled at him and, despite having heard the joke several times before, played along. "I don't know, Chase. What?"

"Not even."

I mustered a small chuckle.

"Do you get it?" he asked.

I nodded.

"It's a good one, huh?"

"Not even," I teased.

Now that I thought about it, I wished that I'd found out what really happened to his head. I bet Hannah had done it, which was probably why I hadn't pushed the issue at the time. Chase would never admit anything that might cause their fifteen-year-old daughter any more trouble than she already faced on a regular basis. An impulsive girl without a clear sense of personal boundaries, altogether too rough and with little conscience to stop her. The cut might have happened by accident or on purpose, in a moment of horsing around, or as a means of testing the waters, or even as a joke. Hannah was hard to handle at her best, and at her worst—well, even a father as patient as Chase needed to get away for respite now and then.

This past summer, she had tried to burn down one of the abandoned houses on Toomista Island. Shortly afterwards, I asked Chase, "Have you ever thought of getting some help for her?"

"What sort of help?"

"Like a doctor maybe."

He wrinkled his nose. "What's she need a doctor for?"

"To help you understand her better—"

"Nobody understands her better than me."

"No, I know. Of course not. But there are ways of helping her behaviour. They've learned all sorts of new things about kids like Hannah."

Chase gave my shoulder a reassuring squeeze, then shook his head as if to say he knew I wouldn't understand. "She doesn't mean anything by her mischief. She's only testing."

"Like testing the boundaries, you mean?"

"Testing to find out what she can trust."

"Oh."

He smiled. "She'll stop testing when she finds some peace and quiet, and she'll find some peace and quiet when she finds something she trusts."

"Surely she trusts you," I said.

"That don't count. I'm on the boat with her."

"What boat?"

"It's like she's always floating on a boat in the ocean. She needs to test the land until she finds where it's safe to moor. And a special kid like Hannah? She don't just check the land. She's got to test the boat, the dock, the rope, everything," he said.

I thought of him out there now, on his own boat. Yesterday, he'd shown no signs of a concussion, but maybe I'd missed something. I worried now about pressure in the head, ringing in the ears, dizziness, loss of consciousness, and I imagined him, out there alone with two plastic butterflies on his head, tossed between cold gusts of open water, dusted from his greasy cap to his rubber boots in flour. Battered, like a piece of halibut.

"What was Chase wearing?" I asked into the radio.

"Patty told you," Loretta said. "Flour. White. All purpose."

"No, I mean what kind of—"

"Enriched. Pre-sifted. Quit hogging the radio channel."

I paced in front of the window. He shouldn't have gone out on the ocean after injuring his head. Maybe I should've kept him at the outpost overnight for observation. No, there had been no need. I was overreacting. How many false alarms had I seen over the years? Cases when we'd searched for days only to discover that the person had gone hunting or fishing, or even to town, without telling anybody.

I asked, "What *clothes* was he wearing, Patty?"

"How should I remember?" Patty said.

"Was he wearing layers of clothing? Or just his big coat?"

"Ay-ha, I don't know."

"Did he seem confused today?"

"Not really. Do you think there's something wrong? Is it his head, you think? Do you think he's—" Patty's voice trembled.

"Did he say anything about a headache? Dizziness?" I asked.

"Quit badgering her with these questions," Loretta demanded.

I squeezed the bulb on the blood pressure monitor until the arm cuff hanging beside the bed filled with air. "I'll contact Port Hardy," I said, "and put them on alert to send a helicopter if there's a medical situation."

*   *   *

There were no roads to Tawakin. The small community could only be reached by air or by water. One hundred people lived on the reserve, plus five in the three teacher trailers up the hill beside the school and another dozen who returned each summer to stay in the handful of fishing lodges and cabins scattered on the small islands around the cove. We were a long way from any other place. Our cove of coloured houses interrupted miles of green and grey along an otherwise uninhabited stretch of coastline. There was no RCMP posted here, no doctor. Only me, Nurse Bernadette Perkal.

Services from the outside came either sporadically, for example, the RCMP, or according to a schedule, like Dr. Thompson, who visited twice a year if we were lucky, and the counsellor, a lovely Dutch woman by the name of Katarina who came once a month on the mail plane. And then there were those who came to work and live in Tawakin, the countless teachers who'd come and gone over the years, the turnstile of numerous band managers, the handful of social workers back when the government bothered to send them and once, for a brief spell, some sort of justice officer, if I remembered correctly.

I decided long ago that these folks, for all their good intentions and initial enthusiasm, always fell into one of three categories: there were the Users, who came because they needed a job to get a better job somewhere else; the Runners, who came here to get away and hide from something else; and the Savers, who came here to feel good about rescuing the First Nations people.

✳   ✳   ✳

Voices, muffled by static and the whistle of the wind, exchanged information with faraway authorities on the radio. I recognized them as belonging to a few men in the community who served as auxiliary coast guard volunteers.

"We're heading to the Stannani River."

"We'll check Cougar Point."

"Watch that wind. It's picking up. Thirty-five knots."

"Yup. Heading to the dock now."

While I trusted that the searchers would leave fully prepared, it was Chase out there, and I couldn't help but give instructions. "Take some dry clothes. Can somebody send a thermos down to them at the dock? Coffee or tea. Even hot water will do. And blankets. Somebody bring them blankets."

"I will get the blankets!" Patty declared this bravely, as if she were volunteering to rescue a baby from a burning building.

"No, you won't," Loretta said. "You shouldn't have to do it. You've got too much to worry about. Nobody should be asking you to do a thing. I'll get the blankets."

But I knew that Loretta would soon be standing at her closet, straight faced and a little bored without the public performance of the VHF radio, picking her oldest, most threadbare blankets for her son-in-law. The ones she wouldn't mind getting soiled with flour or stained with salt water. So I said, "Each boat should take some blankets. Can somebody else also bring blankets down to the boats?"

"I said I would do it," Loretta snapped.

Sophie Florence came on the radio. "Me and Rupert are going to look around Yellow Cedar Bay."

"Yellow Cedar?" Patty shrieked. "What you got to check there for? He ain't that stupid. He knows the tide's turning."

"Me and Rupert are going to Yellow Cedar," Sophie Florence repeated.

"Oh, my poor Chase!" Patty cried out.

"Don't worry, bebba, we'll find him."

It was Frank Charlie. I couldn't help but smile when I heard his voice.

Wind rattled the outpost door, startling me, while leaves blew from the poplars and sprayed against the window. The small examination room, big enough for the one bed and a perimeter of supply cupboards, was cast in long shadows. I supposed it was the thought of soon leaving Tawakin, but lately, I wished for company. In my younger years, the solitude was an adventure, a badge of honour, and when my city friends predicted forty years ago that I'd go mad as a loon living by myself on the edge of nowhere, I'd gladly quoted Thoreau. Living deliberately, I said. But these days, the only essential fact of life I fronted in the woods was how shrunk and shrivelled my existence had become, solo. So low. So what—I clutched a rectal thermometer in my hand—what did my narrow concerns matter when Chase floated alone on the ocean in the black of night?

Out the window I could see that the smaller skiffs were already turning around and coming back into the cove. On the radio, a voice, quiet and monotone, asked: "Is my dad found yet?"

It was Hannah.

"No, bebba, not yet," said Frank.

"But there's boats coming back. I seen them," she said.

"We'll find him soon. It's too windy for the skiffs is all."

"Real dumb," Hannah said flatly. "They're stupid. And dumb. Stupid dumb fucks."

Patty came on the radio, shouting: "Daughter! Where are you? You down there in the basement? Get off the radio this minute. Why you always got to be saying stuff like that? You better watch it or the Basket Lady will come and steal you tonight. You're real mischief. I don't know what's wrong with you."

But she did know. Everybody knew.

✳   ✳   ✳

The hours passed, and the wind moaned under the outpost wharf as though all the drowned voices in the Pacific had resurfaced from their lonely depths. Across the cove, the lights inside the houses speckled the night air with amber dots. The tree-cloaked mountains that rose behind the village had vanished hours ago, shrouded in blackness, and I envisioned the rain forest and all the creatures lurking there at night. Not the creatures I sometimes watched from my window—the black bears and the occasional cougar or wolf that stalked the shoreline of the larger island on the other side of the channel—but the creatures that haunted the children's nightmares. The *alth-maa-koa*. The hairy *puukmis*. The Basket Lady. The creatures the children would tell me about when I went to the Tawakin Market or when I went to the school to check their heads for lice. The creatures that dwelled in the places never visited by the people, except in their stories. Stories I'd been told so often they'd seeped into me.

Branches snapped like brittle bones and fell past the window. The lamp flickered several times, and then went out. I stood in complete darkness. All the lights in the windows on the reserve had also turned to blackness, the electricity down. Only the dots of flashlights could be seen on the dock across the cove. I clipped the VHF radio back onto my belt and fumbled around for the flashlight I left hanging beside the door. I put on my gum boots and went outside to start up the generator. It could take days for the hydro company to repair the damaged line.

My small island belonged to the government, and the outpost, a government agency, had been built here rather than on the Tawakin

Reserve, as the reserve was intended for the band's use. It could've been situated on the main island, somewhere above the reserve in the rain forest, I suppose, but that wouldn't have been practical in an emergency. It was much easier and quicker to travel the small cove than to traverse the old logging road. Plus, this way I could see the village and they could see me across our half circle of shared water. There'd been many winter days when I'd enjoyed seeing smoke waft from the stovepipes, a small reminder that I was not alone.

The outpost consisted of a one-storey building with an examination room, a narrow waiting area, and an office attached to the living quarters. It perched on a sloping face of granite and shale above the shoreline of the island, the short perimeter of which could be circled by the slowest of walkers in a quarter of an hour. Nothing else existed on my island, except a dense patch of trees and ferns, the rodents and insects residing in the layers of forest decay and the occasional colony of sea lions barking on my wharf.

On the west side, the ridge overlooked another small island, appropriately named Fossil Island, with thick woods and black shores of Precambrian scallop fossils, now appearing as a hint of a black shape in the darkness. Somewhere in the woods on Fossil Island were the bones of a woman and her baby in a cedar casket. She and her baby were a local mystery. Nobody except the oldest elder in Tawakin, Nan Lily, knew who the woman was, or why she and her child were never buried in the ground, or how long they'd been there, and Nan Lily guarded the secret tightly. Local lore said there was a treasure in the casket, and because of this, children sometimes boated to the island with the intention of searching for it. But the woods were thick and tangled, and anybody brave enough to enter the trees not only risked the ire of the elders, who said the dead were not to be disrespected in that way, but they also gambled their future, because those who looked at the woman and her baby were said to be doomed to a life of misfortune. Whether this idea of a curse was created to stop kids from searching, or the curse was linked to the woman's death, I didn't know. I had never entered the woods, but I'd developed a strong attachment to the woman over the years, and I often spoke to her from my kitchen window or when I walked in the mornings.

The cedars thrashed their branches above my head, pitching their small scales of foliage and their pea-sized cones at my raincoat. I unscrewed the fuel cap on the generator and pointed the flashlight into the tank, the sheen of gasoline reflecting in the beam. A strange noise rattled nearby, a jaw-clacking sound, and when I turned, the strands of my hair whipping around my face, I saw it was only my canoe tapping against the outpost, rocked by the gusty breaths that shifted the deckled edges of darkness around the trees. I screwed the cap back on, pulled out the choke on the generator and tugged the motor cord, but it was stubborn to start. A loose skin of orange tarpaulin ruffled and snapped over the woodpile. Across the knuckles of rock that fisted the outpost, long grasses rustled and a watering can tumbled off the ridge to the shoreline. I could hear the *knock-knock-knock* of my boat, hollow and metallic, against the wharf below. Off to my left, it was too dark to see the narrow sleeve of water that separated my small isle of rock and trees from Vancouver Island on the east side. All these years, and still I worried one of those bears or cougars or wolves might one day swim from the opposite shore over to the outpost, and wouldn't that be just the way to end forty years of seclusion?

A life of chopping winter wood and hauling supply totes had kept me trim and strong, and eventually, I got the motor started with a yank that would have thrown out the backs of many women my age. I thought of Chase out in this darkness, the wind lifting everything not tied down. Now and then, voices buzzed from the radio on my belt to report no sign of him or his boat. The ocean swells, half as high as houses they said, were getting too dangerous to continue the search. The voices grew fainter with each report, and I couldn't tell whether it was a weakening of the VHF reception or a weakening of hope.

It was too early to become frightened, and although the thought crossed my mind, I refused to consider the possibility of him drowning. I couldn't bear the image of his panic, his terror in that lonely darkness, this young man I loved like a son. Helpless. Clawing desperately for air. Knowing with brutal suddenness that the end was inevitable. No, I blocked it out. But the cold. That was something I couldn't keep out of my mind. The cold, if not slow, was at least measured and predictable.

His skin would be the first part of his body damaged by hypothermia. I remembered him as a thin-armed boy with nubbly knees, his dark skin during those summer days of swimming off the dock. He'd wave at me until I stopped the boat to watch his cannonball splash. He was thirty-three now. But even a man—especially a man as trim as Chase—couldn't survive long in the cold of the Pacific. There would be violent shivering, his teeth hammering together, the paralysis of his arms and legs as his body pulled its last reserves of warmth to his core. The peripheral pulse in his wrists and thumbs would weaken and disappear from those hands that carried my boxes of medical supplies into the outpost. From those hands that always picked blackberries with me in late summer beside the school playground, that every year, for my birthday and Mother's Day—even though I wasn't a mother to anybody—carved wood into smooth feathers and small paddles and tiny masks of West Wind with abalone-shell eyes. No, I wouldn't think of it. The human body can be well preserved at low temperatures, and there are numerous cases where people presumed dead from cold have been resuscitated.

Had I ruled out every possible sign of concussion? I hurried back to my office, a tiny closet of a room beside the examination area. Inside the filing cabinets was the medical information of every person who'd ever lived in the community for the past six decades. It was the one thing I hated about my job—all these files. Over the years, my knowledge of the Tawakin medical records had been a heavy burden. Out of embarrassment, people had often avoided me at community dinners because of the information I held in these files. Others probed me at times for information that did not concern them. I had no one to help me carry the weight of my role in the community. Empathy, advice? I went without. Who could I ever talk to about my job? I used to talk to my younger sister, Anne, on the phone, and Anne had visited Tawakin now and then, which had helped, but even to her I could not divulge everything without compromising the privacy of my patients.

I envied those nurses in cities, and even those in small towns, who had other nurses to commiserate with, to share their frustrating, trouble-some, sorrowful experiences. Or those who went home to spouses and gossiped on their pillows at night, turning patients into anonymous char-acters with false names. Never mind that I had no spouse, we were all fish here in a small globular bowl. Privacy was difficult and anonymity impossible. To make matters worse, my patients were also my friends, my neighbours, my community. They were practically the only people in my life, yet I was separated from them by my knowing their private medical matters and their knowing that I knew. I was, in short, the secretary of secrets in a place that often seemed too small to hold secrets, in a place where secrets were squeezed so tightly they oozed out the cracks.

In a week, there'd be a new nurse arriving for orientation, a period of shadowing me to learn the ins and outs of the job. My permanent replace-ment. A woman I'd never met before by the name of Wren Featherstone. It made me squirm, the thought of somebody else caring for the people across the cove, caring for the private information contained in these files. She didn't know them like I did, that went without saying, but what if this Wren woman wasn't kind? Or loyal? Or discreet? She might do things differently. Do things wrong. Then again, she might do things better. And that would be good, right? Yes.

I located Chase's file and set it on the desk. Even though I'd had the file open just yesterday, I felt the same tug of hesitation I've always felt with his file, a warning from deep in my belly telling me not to open it again. Memories, it occurred to me then, were mutable things. Over time, they could be cloaked by other experiences, and as I grew older—was I really turning sixty-five next year?—I would, as many of us do, I suppose, continue to change my perception of the past. I lifted the folder and found myself staring at the start of Chase's life. Here, my memories were trapped on the page, labelled and documented. His birth record was not merely a piece of paper; it was a record that forever preserved the moment of a shocking discovery and a terrible loss for me. It archived the end of my ideas of what goodness and loyalty meant.

*   *   *

Chase's birth had been a difficult one. His mother, Miranda, arrived at the outpost with nerves frayed. Since Miranda's husband, Jimmy, had gone to town to buy propane tanks and wouldn't return for several days, Jimmy's brother, Frank, drove Miranda across the cove in his trawler. I was happy to see Frank, because we were deeply in love and I relished the chance to share with him the deeply intimate experience of bringing a new life into this world.

But things unravelled quickly. When Chase came out, he was still inside the amniotic sac.

"My baby's born already drowned!" Miranda screamed.

A wild southeaster had blown all day and into the night and the rain plummeted at sharp angles, making it impossible for the helicopter from the Port Hardy Hospital to land.

My own panic rose like a wave. En caul births were rare, and I'd only ever seen pictures in clinical books. With nervous, unsteady hands, I sliced the amniotic sac open and peeled the shiny membrane off the baby like a cocoon. It now brought to mind those plastic bags Chase was always bringing to the outpost, filled with slippery white lobes of halibut. The tip of his tongue poking out from the missing tooth in his grin. The smell of ocean air on his black hair as he gave me a hug, then pulled back and cocked his head sideways to say: "Got you a present. They're real good coated in flour and fried in butter, Nursema'am."

Nursema'am. As if it were one word. As if it were actually my name. It was what he'd called me ever since he was a small boy. It echoed in my head.

Nursema'am.

Nursemom.

Mom.

A slice of the moon peeked through the clouds for a moment, casting a brief glow on the Tawakin Reserve and on the neighbouring Mitchell Island, a narrow strip of land that scarcely sheltered the houses from the violence of the Pacific. Hints of light flashed in the distance. The larger boats were coming back into the cove.

I read aloud from the file: "The baby was very hesitant to leave the womb and come forth into a world in which things are never what they appear." Although it seemed unlikely that this was my professional opinion thirty-three years ago, so unscientific and bitter, there it was in my own handwriting.

"How joyous it must be to deliver so many babies and see them grow!" my sister, Anne, once said to me. For the most part, she was right. To be part of such a precious event deepened my ties to the community. No doubt about it. I've shared many tears of joy with friends, mothers and fathers, uncles and aunts, grandparents, even great-grandparents. But the birth of a baby can also bring anguish, if you ask me. Sometimes it reveals painful secrets. Other times, it promises a lifetime of struggle, as was the case for Patty and Chase's child.

The rain fell hard the night of Hannah's birth, too. It fell as if the sky knew the little girl needed to be cleansed even before she was born. Patty and Chase, both just turned eighteen that year, came in a small kicker, a shallow boat with a tiny outboard motor. With Chase's help, Patty staggered into the examination room and fell back onto the bed, soaking wet and moaning. Forty minutes later, Hannah slipped out. Easily, with that undersized cranium. I could feel the heart murmur even without using the stethoscope. I recorded it in the medical record, along with the weight and length and sex. I took note of the small head, the small upper jaw, the smooth upper lip, the narrow, wide-set eyes with the epicanthal folds. Not surprising, considering how much Patty drank in those days. With grave concern and a feeling of helplessness, Chase had previously confided in me that Patty stole alcohol from the houses on the reserve whenever anybody travelled to town. She'd sneak it to one of the small islands where nobody would find her. "I begged her to stop," he'd told me, "but she don't ever listen."

One day, Sophie Florence and I, after searching all afternoon, had found Patty nestled between logs of driftwood on Toomista Island. As we walked alongshore towards her, a frantically thrown bottle hurtled through the air end over end and crashed in the adjacent woods.

Sophie Florence called to her, "Bebba."

Patty stood, only two months pregnant then, not yet showing. It hurt to see her like this, swaying a little with tipsiness, and I couldn't help but remember how she used to hold my hand as a child when we came to Toomista Island to search for glass balls.

I pleaded, "It's early. There's still time. If you stop now, you could have a healthy baby. You could become a great mother. You *will* become a great mother, Patty."

"We care about you, bebba," Sophie Florence said.

Patty stared at us without expression for several moments. Then she pulled the hood of her sweatshirt over her head and said, "Please, don't tell my mother," a drowsy heaviness in her voice.

"We won't," Sophie Florence reassured her.

"*You* won't," Patty said to Sophie Florence as she narrowed her eyes in my direction.

"I won't." I placed my palm over my heart. "I promise."

"Maybe you won't tell Mother," Patty's intoxicated words were stones rolling over one another at the bottom of a river, "but Chase... You and him always talk. You're always talking, talking, and if you tell him—"

She took a small step backwards and fell onto the sand. Sophie Florence and I rushed forward to help her up.

"Don't touch me!" she yelled, climbing to her feet quickly and brushing bits of dried seaweed from her pants. "Leave me alone. Just leave me alone!"

And so we did. As Sophie Florence always said, you can't make a person do what they don't want to do.

According to Patty's wishes, the night she gave birth, Chase and I buried the placenta behind the outpost with three strips of cedar so that Hannah would become a good weaver of hats and baskets. The rain soaked me to the bone and the soil clumped under my fingernails, and as I glanced over at Chase and saw his proud face in the darkness, I swore to myself that I would look out for Hannah from this day forth, keep up with the latest research, do everything in my power to not let the circumstances of her birth taint her destiny.

Often, I thought about how some people's lives rose out of their circumstance like a short and straight line, whereas other people's lives arced high above it, and after moving to Tawakin, I found myself, on many occasions, trying to puzzle out my own trajectory. Was I moving along or away from what might have been prescribed for me?

I was born in 1951, in Victoria, British Columbia, a place of Garry oaks and harbour breezes, provincial museums and endless souvenir shops, sailboats and polite tourists, cabinet ministers and stone-grey government buildings. Named after Queen Victoria, that proud imperialist who brought eternal sunshine upon Britain's global expansion, it was a city replete with symbols of colonialism. Each morning on our route to school, Anne and I walked past the Empress Hotel, also named for Queen Victoria, the Empress of India, with its Bengal Lounge and Kipling's restaurant. From here, we cut diagonally across the road past the BC parliament buildings, a structure in the styles of neobaroque and Renaissance Revival, topped with patina roofs and a gold statue of Captain George Vancouver. On the front lawn was a statue of Queen Victoria herself, while inside, politicians worked to keep her legacy of colonialism firmly rooted in law. I gave no thought to any of this back then, of course. I was just a child. But its significance was not lost on me when I moved to Tawakin years later.

2

The air smelled like salmon and salt water, and the grey light softened the shadows on the Tawakin Reserve the next morning. Here and there, the Pacific Ocean appeared between the houses as I made my way with a container of shepherd's pie to the back corner of the reserve where Chase and Patty lived. It was a Saturday, but there were no children playing outside. Probably everybody, even the children, had sat by their radios all night long, and I imagined they were now sound asleep or reclined on their couches clutching video game controllers. I was exhausted, and as I turned onto the back loop of dirt road, I balanced the container in the crook of my elbows and squeezed my hands into tight fists to get the blood going.

Everywhere in my body, memories were stored. Some were cached under my breastbone and some in my head. I could feel good memories of Frank still residing in my heart. What about Patty, though? Compared with Chase, who resided across those lines in my palm that mapped my head, heart, my love, my life, my fate, Patty's memories occupied only a small part in my extremities, a light touch on my fingertips. But they were there, nonetheless.

I pictured Patty when she was eight years old, skipping alongside me. She chattered breathlessly about the dewy ideas inside her morning-fresh mind as we walked along the shore of Toomista Island. She moved towards me, sticking to my side as though drawn to me. A tiny pin pulled onto a magnet. Now and then, she stopped to stoop for a blue or green piece of beach glass, which she then pressed into my hand.

"It's for you," she said. "A present."

"*Klecko, klecko*," I said. "Thank you, thank you."

"Are you going to keep it forever?"

"Of course I am," I said.

She smiled at this, and then narrowed an eye at me.

"Where you going to keep it?" she asked.

"On my windowsill."

"You're probably going to lose it."

"I'll be careful."

"I bet you won't," she said.

I was always surprised by these small ways that Patty challenged me. I never knew when they were coming. They sprung up out of the blue and for no reason, as far as I could figure. I used to think it was merely a child's need to test the boundaries, except that once grown, Patty never stopped. This mystified me. But I now thought about how Chase believed Hannah would stop testing when she found some peace and quiet, when she found something she trusted. Was Patty also searching for peace and quiet? For something to trust?

As I passed the clapboard church with walls the colour of dried mud and waved to Ernie Frank coiling rope in his front yard, I tried to remember who else was there that day we'd pulled cedar on Toomista Island twenty-five years ago. Sophie Florence, definitely, and Gina Joe, with that steel thermos of hot coffee she always brought. Margaret Sam, who always lagged behind to collect abalone shells for beading. Miranda? Maybe. Never Loretta. She'd always scoffed whenever Sophie Florence invited her. But Patty loved to tag along.

When we all left the shore and clomped into the forest to search for a good tree from which to pull cedar bark, Patty turned quiet and timid. Patches of the green canopy above our heads opened and closed like eyes waking and blinking, and Patty looked around nervously. Even on the small islands like Toomista, surrounded by dark depths of water, the strange shadows of the forest held the terrible possibility of hidden creatures: black bears, cougars, wolves, the *alth-maa-koa*, the hairy *puukmis*, the horrible men made of tree bark. Patty was most scared of the Basket Lady, old and ugly, with yellow-nailed toes, a body of hair, and a cedar basket full of stolen children. As Sophie Florence and Gina prepared the bark for pulling, and the breezy branches shifted the dust-moted air into amorphous shapes, I felt Patty moving towards me, her small hand slipping into mine.

She'd always swung back and forth in this way, drawing close to me and then retreating, but always drawing close again, and although she seemed to have drawn close less and less over the years, I believed that, after all the years we'd known one another and all the time we spent together when she was a child, she'd eventually draw close once more. At least, I hoped she would.

*   *   *

When I reached Patty's house, I found her leaning against the porch railing with a pair of binoculars pointed at the ocean. She turned briefly to glance at me, and then went back to peering through the binoculars.

"I brought you and Hannah some supper," I said.

She didn't say a word.

"I'll just put it here." I set the container on the warped picnic table. Underneath the table was a prawn trap; its circular steel frame covered with black netting made me want to smile for what it suggested about Chase's deep love of his coastal home.

Patty said, "I've been doing some thinking. About Chase being confused and dizzy and him going out hurt. I had nothing to do with it."

"Of course you didn't."

She lowered the binoculars but continued to stare out at the ocean. Her face in profile, with its bulbous nose and soft, round cheeks, appeared young and innocent. Like Chase, Patty was thirty-three years old. Unlike Chase, she was not born in the outpost. Loretta stayed in Port Hardy for an entire month before her due date, declaring to everybody, including me, that she didn't trust delivering her baby in the outpost, not in a million years.

"You put them small bandages on his head yesterday," Patty said, her voice wilted with exhaustion. "You made him go home. You told him he could go out in his boat."

"No, I told him to rest."

A gust of wind tipped a bucket over behind us. It rolled back and forth.

Patty faced me. "This is *your* fault."

My jaw tensed, but part of me couldn't help but wonder if she was right.

"You're upset," I reasoned. "You've had a rough night. Everything's going to be okay. I know him, he's lost track of time is all. He's off hunting."

"Is that what he told you?"

"No, but—"

"What did he tell you?"

"Nothing."

Patty twisted around and searched the windows. She lowered her voice. "I know he told you something, he always does."

I shook my head. "He didn't, believe me."

"Why should I ever believe you?"

At first, her tone stunned me. Then it dawned on me: stress. She was worried. And worn out. I only needed to look at her face to see that. Darkness circled her sleepless eyes. Her mouth pulled downward. Her skin was pale. There was no point in taking any of it personally. None of this was about me.

I said, "You should believe me because I've never lied to you."

Patty said nothing. She headed towards the patio door, stopping momentarily beside the container of shepherd's pie on the picnic table. I expected her to pick it up. Instead, she looked at it, hooked her wrist around one side of the container and sent it sailing off the table. It crashed onto the wood planks of the patio. The lid popped off and flipped up into the air. Chunks of mashed potato and pebbles of ground beef, diced carrots and peas scattered everywhere. Patty marched into the house, her socks squishing potatoes along the way, and closed the door so hard the glass shuddered.

The Heaviness of Things That Float

I was shocked. My eyes fixed on the mess made of my neighbourly gesture. It disturbed me how much Patty had sounded like Loretta just then. Patty had shown traces of Loretta in the past, but I'd often found it hard to fault her for mimicking the mother she was desperate to please. This time, her rudeness crossed the line. Sleepless night or not, that was no way to treat somebody. I stomped across the patio, the rotting planks bowing underfoot and threatening to give way. Bending, I snatched the plastic container, turned it upside down, and rapped it hard against the patio until the remaining clusters of beef unstuck from the corners. I snapped the lid in place and stormed down the road. Like a child, I punted stones angrily into the tall fringe of grass.

One time after returning from pulling cedar, Patty and I sat together on Sophie Florence's front porch and put the coils of cedar into tubs of water to soak. Patty was nine. She started to braid my long blonde hair as she told me the story of the Yellow-Cedar Sisters. I twisted a strip of cedar into a rose while I listened.

"My auntie told me this story. My auntie is from up island," Patty first explained. "One time, Raven saw three young women on the beach drying salmon and he wanted it all for himself, so he kept trying to scare them away. First, he asked them, 'Are you scared to be alone on the beach when there might be bears?' They said, 'No!' Then he asked them, 'Are you scared of the wolves?' They said, 'No!' Then he asked them, 'Are you scared of the owls?' They said, 'Yes!'" Then Patty paused the story, holding long sections of my hair, and whispered in my ear, "Owls mean death and ghosts, in case you don't know."

I nodded.

Patty finished the story. "Raven hid in the forest and made owl sounds. The women got real scared and ran far away to hide. They hid on the side of the mountain until they turned into yellow cedar trees. And that's how come yellow cedar trees are so pretty and smooth, because they used to be pretty women like you."

Just then, Loretta walked past. She jutted her chin at my cedar rose and said, "Your petals are all loose. Real ugly. You work cedar like a *mamulthni*."

Patty dropped my hair onto my back and took off after her mother like a shot. At the edge of the grass she stopped and turned back briefly, running close enough for me to hear her whisper, "I think your cedar rose is nice." She looked at me with what I thought was pity, something compassionate and kind, something wholly unlike her mother. Only once, many years later, had I ever seen anything that soft and vulnerable in Loretta's face. It was a rare glimpse made possible by the fact that she was asleep in a bed I'd helped her into, her body crippled with grief and bone-sagging exhaustion. In that moment, Loretta seemed to be a child, much like Patty, searching for peace and quiet.

3

News of a discovery came over the radio the next day. Chase's small trawler was found north of Tawakin in Ootanish Inlet, anchored and bobbing in the tide. The people who discovered the boat searched the surrounding waters, as well as the shores of the inlet. Between the bearded trees and over ancient totem poles that lay there on the ground hidden in moss, they trekked into the forest calling his name. There was no sign of him. They scoured the trawler for clues. Sophie Florence asked the searchers, Is there a note? No. The boat radio, the searchers said, had been left on full volume, the microphone dangling from its coiled cord. Then one of the men pointed out that the rowboat and the set of oars were missing from the top of the trawler.

The people around the cove always left their radios on the community channel day and night, which gave the effect of one never-ending conversation between everybody. It was as if we all lived in the same house, calling out to each other through the walls. That afternoon, the radio buzzed with wild speculations.

"Ootanish Inlet? That's near her hut."

"What's he doing up there?"

"They checked her place. Nobody was there."

"No sign of his rowboat?"

"Nope, no sign of hers neither."

"He could be visiting his brother's resting spot."

"But where is he now, then?"

"Somebody needs to check her place again."

"Yup, I bet that's where he's at."

"No, he's not gone to her place," I said. "I know it for a fact."

Of course this was not a fact at all, but I knew Chase so profoundly it might as well have been. For years, he swore to me that he'd never set foot in his mother's place. "My brothers are dead on account of her," he'd said on more than one occasion. There was no reason for him to change his mind now.

The fact that his trawler was found in Ootanish Inlet near his mother's place didn't change my thinking that he was out hunting. It was a good area for hunting. Not far inland, the mountains next to the shore of the inlet rose into two thickly forested domes. Plenty of deer there. Bears, too. Ever since he was a child, hunting and fishing had always soothed Chase and lifted his spirit. He had run away many times in the past, for various reasons, ever since he was five. It was therefore a solid theory, one that put my mind at ease. When you lived in the remote wilderness, tragic scenarios could spread like a thick fog in your mind. Head down that path of what-ifs, and you might never find your way back.

To everyone's relief, however, Chase visited Loretta Joe that night in a dream to let her know he was alive and he would be coming home soon. Patty went on the radio the next morning to say it was just like on *Oprah*.

"See? If you go inside for your journey, it will be dark and you'll have to look real hard for the light, and then you'll see all the things filling your inside."

"Ay-ha, what does that mean?"

"Was Chase in her dream, yeah or nah?"

"Yeah," said Patty.

"For real?"

"Real as rain."

Already I knew that everybody would believe Loretta, because we all remembered the other time one of her dreams came true. I didn't think for a second that Chase, if given the choice, would ever willingly populate Loretta's dreamworld—though I had seen the outcome of her other dream with my own eyes.

It happened on a beautiful day following a vicious storm. Patty, seventeen years old then and not yet pregnant, was babysitting her six-year-old brother, Theodore. Ted, or little Teddy, they called him. She was taking him in their kicker to look for glass balls on Fossil Island.

"Make sure he wears a floater," Loretta had told Patty. That was the summer little Teddy declared himself a great swimmer, jumping off the dock with the older kids but not entirely good at estimating how deep or cold the water might be.

Certainly Loretta loved Patty back then, though not as much as she loved Teddy. That was obvious. Teddy was delicate boned and always smiling, generous, thick haired, affectionate, and Loretta treated him as if he were the Second Coming. A real chatterbox, and a charmer, he had a habit of calling out compliments about his mother in the middle of the Tawakin Market. One time in particular stood out for me. It was a mail day, and a crowd of people hovered around the post office counter. I was on the other side of the room waiting to pay for my groceries, trying not to roll my eyes noticeably. I'd always assumed that Loretta put Teddy up to these declarations.

"My mother is the most bee-yoo-tee-full lady in the world!"

A few people smiled politely.

"Isn't he real precious?" Loretta asked no one in particular. She sat on the large freezer by the window eating a Creamsicle.

"Not just him thinks it," Patty told her mother. "Me too. I think you're the most beautiful lady in the world."

Loretta had flapped her hand at Patty, like you do at mosquitoes on summer evenings, and looked away.

When it was finally my turn at the cash register, I added a candy bar to my purchase, which I then slipped into Patty's pocket. "I think *you* are the most beautiful lady in world," I told her.

Patty blushed, and smiled.

The ocean was fairly calm the afternoon that Teddy and Patty went to Fossil Island, with small crests glinting like glass as far as the eye could see, the steady breeze occasionally pushing a foamy wave over the rocky outcrops. Teddy was eager to look for glass balls, but first Patty had to pee. According to what she told us later, she sent Teddy searching along the shore to look for tooth shells while she went in the forest.

"Please don't go in the woods," Teddy said, "the woman in the box with the baby is in there, and if you see her, you'll have bad luck the rest of your life."

And so Patty had promised her younger brother that she would not go far into the woods. She later told everybody that she could hear him from where she squatted in the ferns, jabbering to himself and flinging handfuls of pebbles into the water.

Moments later, his cry for help came. It was so jarringly distressed that Patty wet the heels of her sneakers in surprise. Quickly, she pulled up her pants and tried to scramble through the trees and bushes, but something stopped her. It was, Patty sobbed hysterically, the ghost of the woman in the box with the trees.

"I heard her," she said, "laughing and laughing, and everywhere I ran, she tangled the branches so I couldn't get out of the woods in time."

In my report to the RCMP, I referred to the "dark waters" in which the drowning happened and to the abrasions the boy suffered. As far as I figured, he must have waded too far into the ocean, to where the undercurrents of the tide hooked his legs and tugged them out from under him like rope. It must have been an incredible undertow, I told the officer, because he was found two hundred metres out. Pressed against the rocky outcrop.

The community was heartbroken. They prayed in four directions, from the north, east, south and west ends of the reserve. They cut their hair in mourning.

"Loretta dreamed about this," Sophie Florence told me the day after it happened. "She dreamed that her son was trapped inside a dark, wet blanket, his whole body wrapped up like in a cocoon. I was in Nan Lily's store when she told it to Nan Lily. She wanted to know what Nan Lily thought it meant. That was two weeks ago."

"What did Nan Lily say?" I asked.

"She said it meant that he might drown."

"Was Loretta upset by it?"

"Not even," Sophie Florence said. "I don't know why she bothered to ask in the first place. She don't ever listen."

For several weeks following the accident, I could hear Loretta screaming in anguish from all the way across the cove, calling for her son from the end of the dock. Not by name. Just, son. Son! Sometimes she formed no words at all, only sounds. The sort of indistinct wailing that rises from the most primitive depths of the heart.

Chase took Teddy's death especially hard, which didn't surprise me, given how sensitively he reacted to the more common events of life. Squabbles with his cousins, bad dreams, minor troubles at school—these sorts of things always seemed to linger in his mind, weighing on him heavily. At least that was how he once put it to me when he was in grade five. He used to visit me after school back then, which was not unusual. When it came to being social, the children in Tawakin never set the adults apart. Frequently, they'd walk up the hill to the teacher trailers and hang out with their teachers, or tag along with the adults on excursions to the islands, or boat over to the outpost and ask me endless questions about the supplies behind the glass cabinet doors, or how many times people had puked on the floor, or what it was like the day they were born.

On this particular day, Chase and I were fishing after school in his little rowboat off the shore of Fossil Island. We sat facing opposite sides of the boat so that our lines wouldn't cross, and we'd been in that position, silent in our own thoughts, for nearly twenty minutes when Chase turned and spoke with fierce indignation.

"So Teacher finished reading *Charlotte's Web* to us today. Read-aloud time is dumb. The books are dumb. They're too stupid and sad, and then I cry at the end and I have to put my head down on the desk or else Tom and Derek will tease me, and then Teacher gets mad because she thinks I'm sleeping and not paying attention."

I reeled in my line a little. "That sounds frustrating."

"Uh-huh." He impaled a tiny silver fish onto his hook for bait, then winced and sucked in his breath as his finger pricked on the hook. He sucked up a dot of blood.

My rod tugged. Something nibbled on my bait.

He pointed to the bend at the top of my rod. "You got something on your line." His voice sounded so sad that my heart bristled as if it were sprouting antennae, a thousand tiny feelers oscillating and stretching out for the boy.

"Did you know that if a baby is in a big hospital room full of other babies and she hears another baby crying, she will cry too?" My voice strained as I pulled back hard, the weight of the fish bowing my rod. The boat jostled a little. "You see," I continued, cranking my reel, "the other baby's cries sound the same to her as her own. And so she thinks: that sound must be my own sadness. And then if another baby hears her crying, that baby will cry too. And so on, and so on, until all the babies are crying. It's like they all share the same heart."

In the next instant there was lightness in my hands.

"Your fish got away," Chase said.

"It did." I reeled in my empty line.

Shortly after Teddy's death, Chase sat in the outpost kitchen poking at the sandwich made with the salmon he brought me for our usual Saturday morning visit. He was only seventeen, but already he'd become a top-notch fisher. In the summers, he was starting to earn good money by taking wealthy Americans who flew in on private float planes out fishing on the ocean.

I said, "You're not eating. You always eat."

For several minutes, he gazed out the window in the direction of Fossil Island, the tip of it visible from the table. Finally, he looked down at his plate and said, "Me and Patty. She's sort of my girlfriend."

"Oh." I took a small bite of my sandwich.

"We've been keeping it a secret," he said.

I nodded.

"Because they'll say we're cousins."

I swallowed a piece of crust.

"But we're not even that close of cousins," he said.

I gulped down some water, then set the glass back on the watery ring it had left on the table. I nudged the triangular halves of my sandwich around, rearranging them on my plate. When had Chase started keeping secrets from me? Him and Patty? I'd had no idea. He was right, though. The elders might tell the teenagers they were too closely related to date. Hard to say for sure. Every spring, I joined the women and the girls at the fishing lodge on Mitchell Island for the girls' retreat. The women taught the girls that they were the givers of life and explained who was closely related to whom to prevent this very problem. No matter how closely I listened, I could never keep track of it all, the family trees branching and crisscrossing well beyond the shores of Tawakin.

"I'm worried about Patty," he said.

"Because of her brother?"

"She started drinking lots."

I frowned. "It's the grief. And the guilt. She needs someone to talk to. Counselling. I'll phone Katarina."

Chase lowered his chin onto the table and gazed at his sandwich from very close up. A buckle of noise came from his throat. Then he covered his face and sobbed. Loud heaving sobs.

I rose to my feet and placed a hand on his shoulder. "It's okay. It's okay to cry." His sadness felt like my sadness, and it was indeed my sadness, too, for Teddy's death had darkened the cove with a heavy blanket of grief. I also started to cry.

Two months later, Patty announced she was pregnant. Teenaged pregnancies were certainly not encouraged in Tawakin, but when they happened—and they happened regularly—the new parents were always given a royal treatment, and the baby was cherished and celebrated and cared for by the whole community. Even Loretta appeared somewhat pleased, though her positive reaction didn't ease my worry. I wasn't keen on the idea of Chase and Patty being together, scared of what Chase would endure if Loretta ever disapproved of him. Chase's own reaction to the news of becoming a father at the age of nearly eighteen was not one of worry or shame but pride, joy, optimism. "Nurse ma'am!" he cried out. "Isn't this just the best thing you ever heard?"

It wasn't. But I didn't say so. I just smiled, not wanting to burst his joy.

4

Frank Charlie's boat sliced a line through the misty water, opening the black surface like a zipper towards the outpost. Behind him, smoke rose from the stovepipes on the reserve and from the sheds where salmon hung over cedar sticks and from the boats at the dock where people gathered in groups for another long evening of searching.

Grey clouds swelled low above the treetops, fraying at their fleecy edges. As I watched Frank's progress from the couch where I was arranging seashells inside a wood case, I felt how much I wanted to mend things between us before I left. Although our relationship had ended unexpectedly, and with great shock and pain, we'd managed to rebuild pieces of our friendship over the past few decades. But I craved a deeper reconciliation than that, something that would renew trust—not to reincarnate our love but to give that time of our lives meaning, a sense that it was not all for nothing.

Back in our twenties, when we were first in love, he'd visit me every day here at the outpost, sometimes several times a day. Once, after he'd spent the night at the outpost, he drove across the cove only to turn back around the second he reached the reserve. I'd been watching him, as I always did, from the window. He burst through the back door and took my face in his cool hands. "I missed you already," he said. "Give me something that's in your heart, something I can keep."

This embarrassed me, because as romantic as it seemed, I wasn't sure what he meant. Thank goodness he elaborated before I had to ask. "Tell me something else about you so that I can think about it when I'm out on the ocean all day." It took seven years for me to tell him all the things I thought my heart contained, and I'd asked him once, after we were no longer together, a question he never answered: "What are you going to do, Frank, with all those things I gave you from my heart? Where are you going to keep them now?"

Letting myself fall for Frank had compromised my original plan. I'd come to Tawakin for two reasons: money and independence, which you might say were the same thing. In my teenaged years, a high school English teacher had given me a tattered copy of *The Feminine Mystique*, and by the time I headed to the University of British Columbia, I'd read it three times, plus everything by de Beauvoir, Steinem and Greer, and I'd become determined to start my adult life as an independent woman. By taking the job in Tawakin, I was not only going to earn my own living, but I was also going to exercise maximum self-reliance, without any help from a man, far from the comforts of the city, far from my friends' matchmaking services and my mother's desire for grandchildren. Maybe I'd even write an article about it and send it to the National Organization for Women, though I was aware that becoming a nurse was hardly breaking new ground. This was the mid-1970s, however, and with great pride, I was refusing to fulfill expectations—that I transform eagerly into wife, mother, housekeeper, tending to the needs of others, serving whenever service was required, nursing ailments while ignoring my own. I eventually came to see the irony in this.

A sea gull took flight across the water as Frank bumped his boat hard against the wharf below. He choked a rope around a piling and marched up the ramp in what looked to be a fearful hurry, searching the windows as though he expected to find me standing in one of them. I returned a speckled conch to its tiny chamber between thin slats of pine and went to the examination room. Through the wall, I could hear him stomping up the steps along the outside of the outpost.

He opened the door shouting, "You got to go talk to her!"

In the doorway dividing the examination room from the waiting area, Frank appeared, his face shining with sweat. Huffing heavily, he said, "Please go talk to her." And then, "please," and "please" again, between gasping breaths.

"Slow down, Frank," I said, taking him by the arm and guiding him to the bed. "You can't be getting worked up like this. You've got to be more careful."

Two years ago, Frank suffered a heart attack. It happened, fortunately, during a trip to buy boat parts in Port Hardy. I couldn't bear to think what would have happened if he'd been in Tawakin and had to wait for the helicopter.

"Unbutton your shirt," I told him, retrieving a stethoscope from the drawer.

"She won't tell us—"

"Your shirt, Frank." I unbuttoned the top two buttons for him, and then stopped. My face flushed. It felt too familiar.

His shaking hands fumbled with the remaining buttons. At sixty-three, Frank looked a fit man, with a slight build and strong muscles braided like rope. Tight and impenetrable, invincible, except for his unreliable heart.

I pressed the stethoscope against his chest.

"She won't talk to nobody," he said.

"Frank, quiet. Just breathe."

As I listened to the *thump-THUMP, thump-THUMP*, I stole glimpses of his smooth torso, the muscles snaking around his ribs, the dark nipples of his hairless chest—still taut, though his skin sagged a little with age— hip bones poking out from his jeans stained by a life outdoors. As the nurse I knew the location of every wart, mole, scar and freckle around the cove, but Frank's was the only body in Tawakin I'd ever touched as a woman.

"Sounds good." I hung the stethoscope around the back of my neck. "But you're going to have to manage your stress better."

Frank's face was full of dread. "Please go talk to Miranda."

I flinched at the sound of her name, of him uttering her name.

I asked, "What for?"

"There's something wrong. This morning she shot at Sophie Florence."

"She didn't!"

"She did."

"Where's Sophie now? Was she—"

"She missed her by a mile," Frank clarified. "And then some of the women—Sophie Florence, Margaret, Gina—they all went back up there a second time in the later morning, and she shot at them before they reached the rocks, so they turned the boat around and came back. And then I went up there to see her for myself, and she came out of her place with her shotgun pointed, and so I got out of there real quick."

I held up my hand to Frank. I needed a moment to process all of this. Rubbing my forehead, I gazed at the dull linoleum. I was surprised to hear that Sophie Florence, Gina and Margaret went to see Miranda without asking me along, even more surprised that they hadn't told me about it the second they returned.

"Did you call the RCMP?" I asked.

"What for?" Frank shrugged.

I knew it was a foolish question. The police were mistrusted and rarely called for anything. Whenever they came in on the RCMP boat there was a feeling of intrusion shared by almost everybody, as if the officers were nothing more than interlopers who needed to mind their own business.

"I think Chase is up there with her," Frank said.

I looked at him doubtfully. "Do you know that for sure?"

"Not for sure. But I feel it in my bones."

"Did somebody at least see his rowboat by her place?"

Frank shook his head. "Maybe they hid it."

"Maybe," I said. "But why would they do that?"

"Please, Bernie," he begged. "Go talk to her. See if he's there."

Through the window, I could see the boats leaving the dock to search for Chase and his little rowboat. Apparently, not everybody believed he was safe and sound in Miranda's hut. And Loretta's dream, as Ernie Frank pointed out this morning over the radio, only showed him to be alive and on his way home soon—"He could be hurt and with a difficult journey ahead of him," Ernie said. Along the distant horizon, a ribbon of blue sky underlined the grey clouds. A good omen, I hoped.

I said, "He'd promised himself he would never go there. I know him, Frank."

"He might have changed his mind."

"He hasn't seen her in twenty years. Why would he now?"

"People change, I don't know," Frank said. "They get new ideas about how things should be. About how things might have been, I guess."

"So what if he is up there?" I asked. "He's a grown man. He can choose to visit his mother if he wants."

"Please, just see if he's safe," Frank said.

I studied his eyes, now staring straight at me, and his mouth, too, how the corners tugged downward. "You make it sound like he's in danger."

He looked down and buttoned a hole that he'd missed. He said nothing.

How much he reminded me of Chase—the dark eyes, strong hands, warm vulnerability.

Finally, he said, "No good can come of him seeing her."

I considered the possibility that Chase had in fact changed his mind about his mother. Part of me refused to believe it. He would have talked to me about it first. Still, I would keep an open mind. "Maybe it's exactly what he needs. Maybe he wants to reconcile the past," I said.

"I just think—" Frank paused. "I just think there's stuff in the past that does nobody any good digging it up. You start digging and you find something, and then you can't stop digging and next thing you know, you're at the bottom of a dark hole all by yourself."

"Dark hole? What are you on about, Frank?"

A barrage of heavy raindrops burst sudden and hard against the window. Streams of water ran down the pane, blurring the cove.

"You're the only one she might talk to," he said.

"I don't know how to talk to her anymore," I said.

"Please try."

"I have tried. I've gone up there before to patch things up between us, but she wants to be left alone. I've even brought gifts—food and tea and all sorts of supplies—but she ran off into the woods every time. I've given up. It just doesn't seem to be within my power to draw her back out into the world. Who knows? Maybe she doesn't want anything to do with me. Maybe she sees me as some kind of threat, just another creature who might harm her."

"Please, try again."

"There's no point anymore, Frank. Too much time has passed. Too much has happened between us." My voice was rising to a crescendo, and I couldn't seem to stop it. "Too many things have happened to her. She's been living a life beyond anything I could ever understand. She carries hurts that—thank God—I could never fathom. I just don't know what to say anymore. I don't know her anymore. Besides, she shot at the other women. What if she shoots at me? I wouldn't feel safe heading up there."

"Miranda could hit a squirrel spiralling up a tree," he reasoned. "If she'd wanted to shoot me or the women, she would have. She was just trying to scare us off. You know she'll listen to you."

I laughed. Miranda listened to nobody. The more you tried to help her, the harder she pushed you away.

"You don't even need to talk to her much. You just got to see if Chase is there safe," he said.

It was hard to imagine anybody staying safe in that thin shell of a house. It stood several miles north of Tawakin, a small exoskeleton of wood on the shore. It was a home, though not much of building, with a cedar-shingled roof, some wood planks and boards along the bottom half of the walls and sheets of blue and orange tarpaulin covering the top half. Fragile shelter on a violent shore. Miranda lived alone there, far from any other living person, next to the place where her oldest son, Chase's older brother, Stan, died along the shore there twenty years ago. Once in a while, somebody took a boat up the coast to check on Miranda, bringing her fresh fruit and a box of tea bags, and when Miranda's second-oldest son, Ronnie, died the year following Stan's death, some of the men from the Tawakin Reserve buried his body near her hut. Otherwise, everybody left her alone.

I'd ended my friendship with Miranda the night Chase was born, and although she and I eventually arrived at a civil understanding, I was under no illusion that she would ever listen to me. On top of that, hearing Frank talk about her now was dislodging a pain, a sliver of grief deep within me, one that had been buried and mostly forgotten. Did we have anything left to say to one another before I was gone for good?

Nothing in this world, if you asked me, could ever motivate a person more than the feeling of scarcity. Scarcity of money, time, land or opportunity. I sensed a door closing. Would I regret leaving Tawakin without taking the chance to talk to Miranda one last time?

"I'll go see her," I said.

Relief softened Frank's face. "Thank you, Bernie."

The rain drummed against the metal roof and transformed the room into a small music chamber, dim and hollow and sombre.

"You haven't said a thing to me about my leaving Tawakin."

"I will," he said.

"Forty years," I marvelled. "How wrong you were about me."

Frank conceded with a smile.

*   *   *

The first time I searched the beaches for treasure in Tawakin, a week after I'd arrived, I found a sun-bleached seal vertebra, a pocketful of beach glass and a man. His long black hair reached his waist, and he wore a headband that said *Red Power*. He was sitting on a log of driftwood. He said hello, then opened his hand and held it out to me. Two narrow shells, slightly grey and about the size of my pinkie finger, lay on his palm. He smiled, a large bright crescent moon across his dark face. He said his name was Frank.

"Know what these are?" he asked me.

"I don't." I set my knapsack on the sand beside the log.

"Dentalia. Indian money. It's real hard to find. You got to be patient. Some people have an eye for finding it. Some people don't." He lifted his gaze from his hand and said, "That's a tall walking stick you got there."

I looked at the stick in my hand and agreed. It was a tall walking stick. Golden, smooth. I looked at him and said, "That's an interesting headband. What's it mean?"

Pulling it off his head, he read the words aloud, as if he'd forgotten what it said. "Red Power." He smiled and turned it around for me to see again. It was red, yellow, white and black, and in the centre was a silhouette of a First Nations man wearing a headdress, except instead of feathers, there were fingers shaped into a peace sign. He put it back on his head. "It means the land should go back to the Indians. It's American."

Admittedly, I was surprised back then in my naïveté that from this far-flung spot he had any connection to, let alone an awareness of, a civil rights movement in the United States. At the age of twenty-four, I was easily swayed by anybody who swam against the current, and this appealed to me, the idea that he was a rebel—that he, like me with my women's lib, wanted to change things in some way, if only for ourselves.

I scooped beach glass from my pocket and dropped it into the front pouch of my knapsack. A crow landed on a nearby log and eyed the shiny buckles on my knapsack. I pulled the drawstring tight to keep my tuna sandwich safe inside.

"Do you know about Raven?" Frank asked.

"Tapping at my chamber door," I recited. "Only this and nothing more."

Frank scrunched up his face. "What's that?"

The sun warmed the back of my neck, and I noticed how soft his skin looked, like suede or fontanelle. His eyes, dark brown and gentle. "'The Raven,'" I said, poking the sand with my stick. "Edgar Allan Poe."

"Is it a story?"

"It's a very famous one." I nodded.

"Tell it to me." His voice was kind, welcoming. He patted the spot next to him, indicating that I should sit, then he put the seashells on top of my knapsack as if they were gifts in exchange for my story.

"No." I laughed, and remained standing. Around the curve of shoreline, I could see the corner of a red roof poking past the trees—the edge of the Tawakin Reserve. "It's too dreary a story for such a beautiful day."

"Raven is a trickster in our stories," he said. "If you stay here for a while, you might hear about him."

I wasn't sure if he meant it in an immediate sense, like there on that log that afternoon, or more generally. "I'm the new nurse, Bernadette Perkal. I imagine I'll be staying for a good long while."

He smiled. "I doubt it. None of you ever stay for long."

"Maybe I will," I said.

"Maybe." He shrugged, still smiling.

I was insulted by his tone, skeptical and dismissive, as if he knew better than me. I tried to make light of it. "Then I suppose I'll have to prove you wrong, or I'll never get to hear your stories."

"You can hear the stories whenever you want," he said. "You can hear them in the water."

"In the water?"

"They swim in the ocean with the killer whales."

"What do?"

"The stories," he said. "And some of them grow in the cove with the eelgrass. And some fly on the wings of crows. You see that spot over there?" He pointed to the mouth of the cove next to my island. "If you stand on the rocky beach there, you can hear the stories in the wind, and if you get up real early in the morning and kneel down close to the water, you can hear them turning with the tide between the kelp. But you got to be real quiet, and you got to stay still a long time. And if you aren't scared to, you can cross the water to that small island next to yours and listen to the stories that wash up over the shore where the old fossils are, and then if you're really not scared of nothing, you can go into the forest and hear the stories grow with the ferns that bend over the bones of the woman in the box with the baby, but don't ever look for the woman."

"Why not?"

"You'll have bad luck the rest of your life."

I gazed behind him at the ragged arms of cedars waving from the rain forest, fascinated. Enchanted. "Who is the woman?"

"Only a few people know, but they won't tell," he said.

"Do you know?"

He shook his head.

I turned to the rippled Pacific, which dragged glass balls, Japanese bottles, tooth shells, sailors' shoes and animal bones to Tawakin's shores, and I imagined what mysteries must exist beneath its surface. Things in this world were not all they appeared to be, and the idea of that awakened something in me. A sense of possibilities. A belief that what Frank said was more than metaphor.

"Maybe you'll figure out who she is," he suggested, "if you listen for her stories in the silver light that comes through the trees."

Whatever he possessed that enabled him to see the world in this way, I wanted it. For four years prior to this, I'd spent my days and nights writing down medical facts, following clinical procedures, memorizing signs of a sick body. I yearned to experience the sacred. I sat down on the log beside him, and I swore I could feel the energy of his arms, his skin, his breath near me. He was vibrant. He was copper, a conductor of electricity, and as I leaned a little closer, I was wired. And a little off balance. After all, I hadn't come here to meet a man. I had come here to show myself that I could live without one.

That afternoon, we sat for the better part of an hour in silence, and when I finally dared to glance sidelong at his face, I saw that his eyes were closed, and so I closed my eyes as well and tried to hear the stories in the gentle breeze that brushed my cheeks. I would never feel the wind in the same way again.

*   *   *

Back then, I had no clear vision of how long I might stay in Tawakin. My mind was open to possibilities, which was what differentiated me from all those Users who left the community as soon as they'd accumulated whatever they'd come for—be it money or work experience. Maybe I would stay a year, maybe six years. But forty? How many times had I said to myself, just one more season here, just one more, and then it's onward. But there was always something to keep me from leaving. There was Frank, of course. But there were others, too. Like Miranda, whose friendship had promised to be the kind to last a lifetime. Like Chase, the boy who should have been mine. The boy I sometimes pretended *was* mine. I saw now how slippery time was, that four decades could escape my grip so easily. I should have held on more tightly. Squeezed my fist around those years.

Don't think I've been oblivious to the passing of my life. There were many moments when I had wondered what else the world could offer me. By my mid-thirties, I'd saved a good deal of money and had ideas of travelling Europe. But I'd hesitated too many times, I suppose, because one day I found my courage shrunk, and soon I reached a point in my life when I thought it was too late to move and continue my career somewhere else, let alone travel the globe. The world beyond the shores of Tawakin had become unfamiliar to me. Living like a hermit had made me feel obsolete—I didn't know the first thing about working in a hospital anymore, or even what it cost to reside in the city, yet one day, I knew I'd become too old to work and no longer useful, and I'd be forced to leave. The outpost was for the nurse's use only, the Tawakin Reserve too crowded already, and there were simply no other houses to rent or buy in the remote wilderness.

It was the death of my sister, Anne, ten months ago that prompted my decision to retire and leave Tawakin once and for all. Uterine cancer. Anne had been sixty-two, a children's author. I took a short leave to visit her in the Cowichan Valley Hospice. The day before she died, without asking whether I wanted it or not, Anne gave me her apartment in Duncan, a small town an hour north of Victoria. The paperwork was taken care of, she'd said, and the keys in the nightstand next to her. I suspected she knew what I hadn't yet told her: that I'd been starting to dread my inevitable departure, my extraction, from Tawakin one day, and that those keys might be just the thing I needed to ease my uprooting.

I took the keys from the drawer, though it was another eight months before I had the courage to send my official notice of retirement to the health authority, and another two months after my official notice before I had the courage to tell the people of Tawakin. So far, the response had been quiet. Nobody had expressed any opinion about my decision yet, nor shown any disappointment. But I knew that the people of Tawakin saw me as a dedicated nurse: reliable, understanding and filled, like the earth out back where Patty's placenta had been buried, with good intentions. A bit forgetful perhaps, and I had made small mistakes here and there. The underestimation of a broken bone, the overprescription of laxatives, minor difficulties in the delivery of babies. Still, it was my belief that when I retired in two months, I'd be remembered with fondness for my loyal service to the people across the cove.

5

I heaved open the rusted door at the back of Nan Lily's house and entered the dark basement. Through the open crack, the morning sun cast a dim light over the room. Outlines of old junk receded in ever-higher piles to the back of the room. It smelled of fishnets and old rope and desiccated seaweed. I closed the door, shutting out the diffused light of the overcast sky, and called, "Hello?"

Footsteps scraped across the floor overhead. The door opened at the top of the stairs, followed by a click, and a single bulb coloured the windowless basement with a dim halo of yellow. Nan Lily descended the wood stairs in her slippers, clutching the loose banister in one hand and pinching her cardigan closed with the other. She was ninety-five years old, and she came down the stairs sideways, slowly lowering one foot and then the next, bringing both feet together before attempting the next step.

"What's the story today?" Nan Lily asked.

"I need some tea, Nan Lily." I looked on the shelves, which were mostly bare except for cans of minestrone soup and boxes of macaroni and cheese. I took the single box of Red Rose that lay dusty behind the cornflakes. Since the Tawakin Market was only open in the afternoon three days a week, today I would have to make do with whatever was sold in the basement stores on the reserve.

I fingered the chocolate bars and candy bags that lined a foldable card table. Blue and pink hats and mittens crocheted by Nan Lily; one pair of boy's basketball shoes, size eight; and a pair of prescription eyeglasses were also arranged on the table for purchase. I put a bag of butterscotch candies and a pair of large mittens on top of the Red Rose tea.

Nan Lily sat down in a lawn chair and said, "You heard about the dream Loretta Joe had?"

I opened the fridge door and a band of light stretched to Nan Lily's slippers. A lonely jug of milk past its due date, marked $10 with a black felt pen, was the only thing inside. I pulled it off the shelf and let it swing heavily in my hand, balancing the tower of tea and candies and mittens in the crook of my other elbow.

I set my things on the wobbly table next to Nan Lily and handed her some money. "About Chase Charlie." I nodded. "About how he's going to return to Tawakin soon."

"Loretta is wrong." As the oldest elder in Tawakin, Nan Lily was the only person who could get away with saying Loretta Joe was wrong about anything without fear of reprisal. "He can't return soon," Nan Lily wagged her finger, "because he's already here."

"Here?" I glanced up the staircase.

"Not right here," Nan Lily said. "Somewhere here."

"Do you know where?"

Nan Lily wrinkled her nose, no.

It was impolite to ask an elder too many questions. It was okay to request a small point of clarity here and there, but for the most part I was expected to trust that she had told the story in the most useful way, and that if there were things I didn't understand, I needed only to be patient and wait for my understanding to come in due time. So I gazed at the black oil puddled on the floor under a motor boat and hoped that Nan Lily would fill in more details. But she bent to get a rusted coffee tin from under her chair, and as she dug around for my change, she said, "*Chuu*," which meant the story was done.

Believe me, when an elder was done, you did not push your luck. I'd seen enough Savers come into the community and hover around the elders like busy hummingbirds drawing nectar from flowers. *Chuu*, the elders would say. Oh, but how fascinating, the Savers would reply. Tell me more. I'm so intrigued by your history. I really *get* it, you know, what it must have been like for you. What it must have been like to have gone to residential school, or to watch your language disappear, or to... fill in the blank. We must do something about it, they'd say, continuing in that way, those Savers, as if their empathic words were nothing like patronizing, as if their whole mission in life was to demonstrate how singularly different and progressive they were in their thinking than the rest of their fellow white citizens in their uncaring white cities. Before long, the elders would turn away in their seats at bingo night, or up at the school during Friday breakfast, and pretend to sleep, never again offering their flowers to those hummingbirds.

And so I asked nothing more from Nan Lily about Chase, despite my fervent desire to do so. I revered Nan Lily. For her long years on this earth, for her experience and wisdom, for how respectful she was to me, for how she treated me as a part of this community. She made me feel like I belonged, like I always had, and the idea of upsetting her scared me, kept me on my toes.

Fear and respect were not the only reasons for my politeness. To be honest, I'd always held out the hope that one day Nan Lily would tell me the story of the woman in the box with the baby. Living for the past four decades next to Fossil Island, looking upon its thick forest from the outpost, knowing that somewhere in those trees hid the woman in the box with the baby—well, it stirred something deep inside me. I felt an affinity for the woman, as though an invisible thread connected us. Sometimes I hoped that I'd kept her company all these years—for I imagined her to be awfully lonely there in her box—and whenever a newborn baby cried out for the first time in the outpost, I couldn't help but wonder if her baby mistook that distress for his or her own and started to cry as well. At any rate, I yearned to know who she was and why nobody had ever buried her properly after all this time.

"Will you ever tell the story of the woman in the box with the baby?" I once asked Nan Lily. This was some time ago, when I was buying a knitted scarf for Anne's birthday and a fresh loaf of bread for my lunch.

"Over and over and over, I tell the children the stories they like to hear," she replied. "Like the story about the time the Basket Lady stole a boy who'd been very bad. And how his mother loved him real lots and she could not ever forget him, so she would go down to the shore and pray: 'Please bring my son back, oh Creator!' And then she cried so hard that snot came out of her nose. The thick line of snot fell to the ground, and the mother thought, 'Oh, that's nothing, that's only some snot.' But soon, she saw a face in the snot, and the snot grew into a boy. Mucous Boy. And the mother cried with joy." Nan Lily folded her hands on her small belly, round and tight and hard as a soccer ball under her cardigan.

"When I tell the stories to the children, I tell the stories in circles, and each time I go around a circle, I put in a hint of an old secret, like the secret of the woman in the box with the baby." Nan Lily paused for some time. "It is too much for one person to carry old secrets. It builds up inside you, and so you let out small breaths of it, a little at a time. Like unpinching the end of a balloon."

I asked, "Can't you just tell the whole story? Instead of carrying it by yourself?"

Nan Lily shook her head. "If I told the secrets I know all at once in a straight line, real quick like that—zoom, done!—the truth of it would get lost. You have to turn in a circle many times to get the truth, picking up just a little each time, taking it in while you eat, digesting what you learn until you are well fed."

"*Chumiss*," I said, referring to the people's name for dessert, which also meant to be deeply satisfied.

"*Chumiss*." Nan Lily nodded.

6

I drove the boat north along the coast, past the triangle of islands: Toomista Island, with its small cluster of abandoned grey clapboard houses; Rubant Island, where the dead were buried in a grassy clearing marked with wood crosses; and Waas Island, forbidden because of the cave—a single dark eye—on the southwest shore, filled with the bones of enemies from a battle long ago. I knew the route to Miranda's home well enough to steer clear of the giant kelp bed swimming with otters and the ridges of rocks where seals sometimes scrambled away from killer whales. Many times, I'd driven this desolate route with a box of apples or a baked lasagna or a plate of blackberry muffins. But because Miranda had always run away as soon as I got within a hundred steps of her hut, I'd left these things outside, never knowing if she took them, or if a critter got to them first, or if she simply didn't want any more gifts.

Our friendship started with a gift. It was my second week in Tawakin and my first bingo night at the community centre. A few days earlier, I'd learned that my predecessor, a nurse named Penelope Talbot, had quit her job by hopping onto the mail plane with one satchel of belongings and not a word to anybody on the Tawakin Reserve. "Penelope Talbot," people were saying, "her name is a swear word to me." I heard the hurt in their dismissal, how disappointed they were to be abandoned, and so rudely. Did they expect the same from me? I worried. Maybe it would be good, I thought, if I mix socially with people, get to know my patients, show them I want to be a part of the community. Make amends for the previous nurse. When I shared this idea with Frank, he said, "Then you better go to bingo."

Without a nurse to give me an orientation, I had to learn a lot on my own back then. Namely, the boat. Whatever I hadn't figured out by the end of the first week, Frank taught me. Initially, I resisted any help and was determined to learn on my own, but I quickly gave up on that idea after getting nowhere fast. Even with Frank's instructions, I still struggled for months to make a proper knot in rope, and I feared that one day my boat would come untied from the dock and I'd find it cast adrift in a medical emergency.

Everywhere I looked in Tawakin I saw rope—lengths of rope, coils of rope, nets of rope—and within a few days, I'd realized how crucial it was to surviving this place. It tied things down, stopped things from drifting away, kept things from sailing off in the strong gales of wind. Rope helped to catch meals—it pulled up the prawn traps and crab traps, and Frank told me that in the days of his grandfather, rope thicker than my arm was attached to the long harpoons used to hunt whales. Well, anyway, that evening was the first time I managed to make a hitch knot on the first try, leaving the boat securely strapped to the dock, so I headed to bingo figuring I was in for a lucky night.

The entire Tawakin Reserve consisted of a double-looped road, triple if you included the footpath that rimmed the shore. Twenty, maybe twenty-five, houses in total. To get to bingo, I walked up the dirt road between the houses painted in bright colours, reds and blues and greens, and the houses painted in dull browns and greys, some of the walls demarcated by a jagged line where a particular shade had run out and a new one started. Seen this close up, the houses appeared beaten, with large cracks and peeling paint, rotten sections patched with scraps of waterlogged lumber.

It was strange to see this dilapidation in the midst of an ancient rain forest. I was caught off guard by the judgements about the mess and decay that crept into my mind unbidden, and I had to fend them off as I walked through the reserve. Everywhere, dark green grass sprouted tall in ragged patches around the houses, out the cracks of overturned canoes, between the toppled stacks of firewood and rusted propane tanks. Some yards sported mountains of old junk—bent bicycles, foam floats, fishing nets covered in algae, broken laundry baskets, boat motors, tangles and tangles of rope. A layer of grime appeared to coat everything. It was a stark contrast to the street of my childhood, with its trimmed lawns and rounded shrubs, the clean stucco and swept walkways, the pink roses that my father kept along the side of the house.

Across the street from our house lived the Smiths, a middle-aged couple whose yellow roses were the envy of my father. They had no children of their own, until one day in the spring of 1961. Out of the blue, the Smiths had suddenly become parents to two children. A boy, who was ten like me, and a girl, nine, both with complexions noticeably darker than the Smiths. "Maybe they're fostering them," suggested my mother, who mostly kept to herself and her books, and who therefore was not privy to any of the neighbourhood gossip. From Mr. Roberts, who bred rare orchids in his greenhouse two doors down from us, my father learned that the Smiths hadn't said much to anybody about where the children came from, and that when asked, they simply said, "It was something of a rescue mission." Years later, I realized that the two children were most likely victims of the Sixties Scoop, the government program that took thousands of Aboriginal babies and children from their families and placed them with white parents, often hundreds of miles away from their homes.

They went to my school, the boy and the girl, and my classmates said their real parents were probably drunks and that's why the Smiths got them and that they, the boy and the girl, were probably drunks too, even though the oldest was only ten years old, like the rest of us. During recess, I watched from the swings as Marcia Winston and some of the other students formed a tight circle around the boy and the girl and chanted, "Lazy, dirty, drunk Indians." Marcia, who thought she knew more than any of us because her father was a police officer, clarified: "Or if they aren't drunks now, they will be someday for sure. It's a fact."

After all these years, Marcia's words lingered. I used to believe that

I'd never thought these words myself, but now, in my older age, I finally admitted to myself that this wasn't always the case. During my early years in Tawakin, long before the reserve banned alcohol, biases crept into my mind at times, usually as I was tending to alcohol-related injuries. I wished I'd never fallen into the easy trap of thinking the way Marcia Winston and her father thought. As I came to know the people, and as I watched the community reclaim their sobriety and their culture, I realized how wrong I'd been. Eventually, I no longer had to reckon with my own ignorance.

As I walked that evening, children sprinted past, squealing and shouting in a game of tag. A girl, about ten years old, stopped abruptly in front of me and demanded to know who I was. I introduced myself, explaining that I was the new nurse. "Oh. I'm Margaret Sammmmmm!" And she took off like a shot, screaming her name as she ran away from a boy who appeared from behind a shed. I continued up the road. Shapes moved past the windows above my head. Curtains tugged back and then shut again. I had the feeling I was being watched by many pairs of eyes.

A man chopping wood gave me a nod and asked loudly and exuberantly, "Whatcha doing?" This took me by surprise. I stared blankly at him. "Bingo," I finally managed to blurt out. He smiled, and told me to win something nice to put in my pretty blonde hair.

Soon, I spotted the community centre up on the ridge above the north shore, and when I turned the corner, I came upon an elderly man seated in a lopsided lawn chair. I said hello. He reached into his pocket and held out pieces of bubble gum.

He motioned to the gum. "It's cheap," he said.

"No, thank you," I said with a small laugh.

He motioned again, his head pecking like a bird. "It's cheap."

"Oh, okay. How much?"

He stretched his arm out farther. "It's cheap."

I showed him a nickel.

He stared at it. "It's cheap."

I searched my pockets until I found a penny and offered it.

"It's cheap," he said but didn't take the penny.

"He's not speaking English," a woman said from the window above.

She sounded bored. "He doesn't know any English. Only Nuu-chah-nulth. He just wants to give you a piece of gum."

I smiled and took the gum, slipping it into my pocket.

"Ain't you gonna eat it? When we give you something, you eat it," she said, and shut the window but kept watching me.

I unwrapped the gum and popped it into my mouth.

Inside the noisy community centre—a large room about forty feet squared—dozens of people, talking and laughing, sat along five rows of long tables. The room was filled with such a dizzying array of sounds and movements that a shyness rushed through me, and I nearly retreated out the door. At the front of the room, a man cranked the handle of a metal cage, inside which rattled wood balls. As I forced myself to walk to the table where I spotted a stack of bingo cards, I was aware that some people's conversations abruptly shifted gears. There was whispering.

"Who's that?"

"New nurse."

"Her name's Bernadette or something."

"Frank calls her Bernie."

"Yeah, I seen him with her."

"You know what that means."

"She might stay longer than the last one."

"Better tell Frank to be real good to her then."

The gossipers burst into laughter.

I blushed, turning my face away from them. After paying a young man at the table for a bingo card, I found an empty seat near the back next to a woman who would turn out to be Miranda Charlie. She paid no attention to me. She was too busy calculating possibilities. Whispering things like: if G22 then this and this and this, but what if N43, then only this and this. She was about my age, I figured—twenty-four or so—with long black hair and plump cheeks and a burn scar the shape of a scallop shell next to her eye.

"G10," George called out. "G10."

I placed an orange plastic chip on the G10 square of my card.

"You can't play," Miranda said.

Pointing at my card, as if its existence somehow disproved the logic of her claim, I stated the obvious. "I bought a card."

"Don't matter."

Again the balls rattled around the cage.

George called out, "117. 117."

I looked at my card, at the 117 square I also had, and then at the pile of plastic chips in front of me. Out of the corner of my eye, I looked at Miranda and saw that she too was looking at the chips, as if waiting to see if I would keep playing. Elsewhere in the room people checked their cards, or chatted with their neighbours, or threw their heads back in uproars of laughter. Some faces I recognized from the Tawakin Market, some from my walks along the shore. Frank had told me I'd be welcome, and except for the group of gossipers and an occasional nod or smile, nobody in the community centre had taken much notice of me. Miranda crinkled the candy bag in front of her as she took a butterscotch. Turning to me, she popped it into her mouth.

"You got an 117," she said.

I nodded.

"Aren't you going to put a chip on it?"

"You said I can't play."

"I was just teasing you," she stated simply.

She went back to studying her bingo card and whispering various scenarios. Something about her made me feel guarded. It was more than her telling me that I couldn't play. She buzzed with a competitiveness. Later that evening, just before the generator was shut off and the lights in the community centre went out (it would be another twenty-five years before hydroelectricity finally reached the remote community in 2001), I learned that Miranda had given birth two months earlier to a baby boy named Ronnie. He and her four-year-old son, Stan, were home that evening with their father, Jimmy. She was exhausted by the baby waking at all hours of the night, she'd told me when we said good-bye. Even that statement sounded like a challenge, as if to suggest that I could never in my life feel as tired as she.

"B7," George called out. "B7."

"You got that one, too. You're going to win my moccasins," Miranda said, and with a jut of her chin, she indicated the table next to the bingo cage, on which numerous items were laid out: blankets, sweatshirts, beaded jewelry, packs of cigarettes, various kitchen utensils and a pair of moccasins. "You probably won't even wear them. You'll just put them on your windowsill or something."

"N36. N36."

I was doing well. I put another plastic chip on my card and said, "If I win the moccasins, I'll give them to you."

I didn't win the moccasins that night. Miranda did. To my surprise, she returned to our table and gave them to me.

"You won't like wearing them, I know it, it will hurt you to walk for very long in them," she said. "But they'll toughen you up."

"Thank you," I said.

"You say, *klecko*," she explained.

"*Klecko*," I said, and felt my guard drop.

*   *   *

Picking up speed, I followed the ragged Vancouver Island coastline, through the estuaries and their swirling collisions of incoming tides and outflowing rivers, and as the wind whipped against the rectangular windows shielding the cab of the boat, I played out the possibility once more that I was wrong about Chase. What if he was at Miranda's? No, I knew him. He wouldn't ever have gone there. Yet I felt envious at the thought of it. After all the ways I'd helped Chase since he was a little boy, and after how close we'd become, as close as real family, it would be difficult for me to understand why he'd chosen to hide away with a mother who had abandoned him. Why he wouldn't have come to me instead.

As I neared the small inlet where the hut stood, I felt more on edge. Nervous. How could I approach Miranda so that she wouldn't run away this time? So that she wouldn't shoot at me? The boat lifted and dropped over the heaving mounds of water, the ocean moving like a thoracic muscle inhaling and exhaling, and I looked again at the gifts I'd brought.

A jug of milk, tea, wool mittens, plus a bag of butterscotch candies. It only made practical sense to bring a care package when you visited somebody living off the land and so far away from others, but part of me wondered if these gestures meant anything else anymore. Not that long ago—three, four, five years ago—these packages were my gifts of reconciliation. But now? Forgiveness, yes. And a new start, perhaps, but a new start to what exactly? Was there anything more we were still willing or able to give one another than milk and sweets?

Some distance away from Miranda's home, I anchored the boat and hiked along the shore. I hid in the trees next to the hut and set the jug of milk, the tea and the mittens on a springy bed of moss. I took a butterscotch candy from the bag and popped it into my mouth. Moist sweetness filled my dry mouth. Between the branches, I peered at the rocky shore below and crumpled the stiff cellophane wrapper, the noise crackling along with the rustle of the breezy leaves.

How tough it must have been for Miranda to live here alone all these years. Whereas I worried about wildlife coming to my small isle, Miranda had to worry about wildlife coming through her fabric walls. Wolves, bears, cougars. She'd given up the relative safety of life on the Tawakin Reserve to be with the ghost she could feel in this place. She'd given up a life with a son who was alive to be with one who was dead. I had both compassion and disdain for the life she'd chosen, a hermit in her shell on the shore.

✳   ✳   ✳

The day after my first bingo night, Miranda had knocked on the back door of the outpost. "I brought you jarred fish and these," she said, handing me a bag of butterscotch candies. She took off her old moccasins and set them carefully on the mat. She told me that I should get some bread and mayonnaise for the fish so that we could make sandwiches. I put on the kettle for tea, and soon we were eating together at the kitchen table. Miranda said nothing while I gazed out the window at the clouds shifting quickly across the sky and tried to think of things to talk about.

"It's very beautiful here," I commented.

"Mmm," Miranda agreed.

"Have you always lived here?"

Miranda didn't answer. She took a butterscotch candy.

"Don't you get lonely sometimes? It's so far away from everything," I said, unaware at the time that my view of the world was so narrow, so biased. How presumptuous it was of me to see Tawakin as a place removed from the true centre of life. "Do you leave here very often? Go to other places?"

"Town," she said, the candy clicking around her teeth.

"Town?"

"Port." She nodded.

"Port McNeill?"

"Port Hardy."

"Have you ever been to Victoria? That's where I'm from."

"No, I never."

I wanted to grasp a sense of her world, a sense of what it contained, how far it extended. I wanted to correct her grammar.

"Have you ever been anywhere else?" I asked.

"I been to Port Alberni when I was a kid."

"Did you like it?"

"No."

On the windowsill, among the seashells, was a cribbage board, one of the many things left behind by the previous nurses. Miranda's face brightened as she pointed at it.

"You play?" she asked.

I shook my head. "I don't know how."

"I'll teach you."

As she set up the pegs and shuffled the playing cards, she became infused with the same energy I'd sensed in her at bingo night. It was something to behold, this transformation, like the opening of a brilliant purple sea anemone. And the more we played, the more Miranda changed. The game seemed to ignite something inside her. She laughed. She became more talkative, more opinionated, more expressive. She invited me to pull cedar with the women and to search for glass balls on

Toomista Island. She called me "Bernie," and when she looked at me to announce her score, her brown eyes seemed to glow from behind like orbs of sunlit glass.

This light I saw in Miranda, the way it flared suddenly and brightly reminded me of Anne when she thought of a new idea for a story. I watched Miranda shuffle the cards and thought of her as a comfort to the homesickness I expected to feel, somebody to help fill the void left when I moved away from Anne.

Excitedly, Miranda said, "Nobody else likes cribbage. I don't ever have nobody to play with."

I said, "Well, now you do."

*   *   *

The hut was built on a frame of thick fir branches and smooth driftwood. The bottom half of the walls was covered with flimsy sheets of plywood and rows of more driftwood. Smaller branches were jammed between the gaps where the driftwood curved. Sheets of blue and orange tarpaulin covered the upper half of the walls. A large hole ripped through a section of the tarpaulin, and the torn shreds flapped in the wind. There was no sign of anybody. No sounds coming from the hut. Miranda's rowboat was on the shore, but Chase's rowboat was nowhere to be seen.

"Miranda!" I called out. "Miranda Charlie!"

A pair of hands separated the tears in the tarpaulin wall.

"Miranda!" I called out again.

"Stay away or I'll shoot!"

"Don't shoot! It's Bernadette Perkal!"

"It is not!"

"It is so! If I come out and it's me, will you shoot me?"

I waited. The torn slits closed. The door, which was not hinged to the hut, lifted and slid to one side. Miranda stepped out with bare feet and empty hands. She looked in my direction, her eyes squinting and searching the trees for my exact location.

Miranda's appearance shocked me. I barely recognized her. Her flesh was drastically thinner than I remembered, her limbs sharp and bony, her body bent at sharp angles. Her face, too, had changed. Softer, with deep wrinkles pulling her mouth into a sad frown. Some changes were to be expected after all this time, sure, but she looked nothing like the woman I was friends with long ago. So fragile, worn. She hurried around the corner of the hut, out of sight.

I worried she was going to run away again.

I called out, "Is Chase Charlie here?"

"Chase is here?" Miranda yelled back.

I couldn't tell if it was a question or a statement. "Is he?"

"Isn't that wonderful!" Miranda reappeared with her hands clasped together.

I shouted each word slowly. "Is Chase here?"

"Chase is here."

With a small gasp, I quickly bent to pick up the tea and the mittens and the jug of milk. I dropped the tea, and then dropped the mittens trying to pick up the tea, and finally, when I'd gathered everything in my arms with a mitten tucked under my chin, I burst out from the trees. The branches scratched across my face and caught in my hair and my sleeve hooked on a snag, and as I tried to tug at my arm without dropping everything, I heard a tearing sound from my coat, and I nearly stumbled forward when it finally ripped free. I staggered a few steps before hitting my stride, marching towards Miranda, who did not run but only stood and smiled a gummy smile that shocked me. Since the time she moved away, she'd lost all her teeth. I smiled back, my breathing fast and heavy, and I asked, "Where is he?"

Flinching, Miranda stepped back from me. Then she saw the things in my arms. "Tea!" She pulled the Red Rose from my arms and hurried into the hut, exclaiming, "We can have tea!"

I followed her inside, but Chase was not there. I glimpsed the two empty chairs in the corner. In the middle of the small room a tree trunk adorned with pots and pans and small towels held up the cedar roof. I leaned around the tree trunk to look at the narrow cot on the other side. It was also empty. Turning in a circle, I scanned every surface of the room, across the animal hides and the tools and the traps and the fishing poles. I looked out the makeshift window where the tarpaulin was torn.

"Where is he?" I asked.

"Stop playing around that way," Miranda muttered to herself, shaking her head while she filled a kettle with rainwater from a large metal tub. "That's what my grandmother used to tell me, but would I listen? No!"

"Where is he?" I asked again.

"Even when I was grown up, I was real mischief. I still never listened to my grandmother." Miranda set the kettle to boil on top of the potbelly stove. "I'm so ashamed. He knows. He knows what the shame is like. And he knows I know what the shame is like. 'It was all our fault,' he said. But what can you say? It was so long ago, I told him."

"You told who? Chase?"

"I got pregnant with a bastard child."

"I know," I said. "I was there."

"And did you know I gave birth to three babies?"

I nodded impatiently and moved around the perimeter of the room, searching for evidence that Chase had been there.

"Where is Chase, Miranda? You said he was here. So where is he?"

"Did you know they were dogs?" Miranda asked.

"What?"

"My children were dogs," she repeated, pouring the tea into two cups. She handed one to me.

The water was stone cold, and there was no tea in it.

I asked again, "Where is he?"

"For years, I lived alone with my dog babies," Miranda said. "Then one day, I went down to the beach to dig clams and I heard someone singing inside the house. Whenever I got close to the singing, it stopped. So I stuck a stick in the sand down there and hung my coat over it, and I snuck up to the house and looked through the window and I saw them, my dog sons, dancing naked, stripped of their fur, and the two oldest ones were singing, 'Don't cry. Don't cry. Your mother is still on the beach, digging clams. Don't cry.' They were singing it to my youngest, Chase, and I ran inside and I picked up their furs and I threw them in the stove and I set the furs on fire. And then—I couldn't believe my own eyes—I got boys instead of dogs. Boys."

She began to cry.

I had no clue what she was talking about. Her mind didn't seem to be all there. Reaching into my pocket, I held out the open bag of butterscotch candies.

Miranda sniffled, wiped her nose on her sleeve, then stood on her tiptoes to peek inside the bag. At first she seemed mesmerized by the silver-and-gold wrappers, but she eventually reached for a candy with great caution, as if the bag were a trap about to snap her hand. Watching her closely, I wondered whatever happened to the clever woman who used to double skunk me in cribbage and sew the most intricate and dazzling dance shawls in Tawakin.

"Chase isn't here, is he?" I said.

Miranda shook her head and took the candy wrapper to the small table, sat down on one of the rattan chairs and carefully smoothed out the wrapper.

Sitting in the chair opposite Miranda, I set the candies onto the flotsam table. "Was he ever here?" I asked.

"He took some rope to the beach and caught a whale."

I lifted a small flap in the tarpaulin. Large smooth domes of rock made up the empty shore below.

Miranda popped another butterscotch candy into her mouth and rolled it around so that it knocked against the molars she must've had left. "We had to find a way to let everybody else know about the whale, but how could we do that without going back? And neither me or him wanted to go back," she said, leaning forward and smoothing out the candy wrapper and stacking it on top of the other wrapper. "But my son, he's real smart. He cut out a chunk of the skin and the blubber. He threw the skin into the air, but nothing happened. He threw it up again. Nothing happened. He threw it up again. Nothing happened."

I shifted in the frayed chair and looked at the snares, the fishing poles and the shotgun once belonging to Miranda's husband, Jimmy Charlie.

"He threw it up again," continued Miranda, "and it turned into a bird—a crow—and it started to fly. He put the piece of blubber into the crow's mouth and told it to drop it at the feet of one of the women in the village. I don't know who got that piece of blubber. Do you? Was it Sophie Florence? Margaret Sam? Gina Joe? Oh, who knows? But you need to find out, because when they come for the whale, it's going to get really stormy, and they'll never reach it." Miranda sucked noisily on the candy and her eyes grew wide. "They'll all drown."

I sipped my cold water and studied Miranda, measuring her carefully. What were these things she was saying? Delusions? She was clearly not well. Out of touch with reality. Then I remembered the mittens, which I pulled from my pocket and set on the table.

I said, "Those are for you."

Miranda put the mittens on her hands and clapped them together. "Tea and candies and fishing lures—" Miranda pointed a mitten at the smoothed candy wrappers. "And mittens! Who needs a man, when I got mittens to keep me warm at night?" Miranda laughed, her eyes disappearing into wrinkles.

Those deeply buried feelings of hurt rose in my chest once more, just as they had when I heard Frank say Miranda's name. It surprised me after all these years. I pushed them back down and looked again at the shotgun that had killed Miranda's husband when Chase was five years old. I hadn't thought about that night for a long time either, but I thought about it now, how it happened in the dark of winter. How George Sam drove me up the mountain in a rusted pickup truck with one headlight and the passenger door tied on with rope. We'd arrived at Leslie Lake and stumbled through the trees, the path lit by our flashlights, until we found poor Frank holding his brother, Jimmy, on the ground. Jimmy was already dead. His face unrecognizable, sticky with blood and half of it missing. Jimmy had been trying to climb over a fallen snag, Frank explained, and shot himself by accident. A helicopter arrived, landing two miles away on the school soccer field, to take the body to Port Hardy.

When Frank and I broke the news to Miranda that night, she looked up from the silver and gold sequins she was sewing onto a black dance shawl and said, "When I die, you better bury me on the other side of

Rubant Island opposite from him. I talk in my sleep. Who knows what secrets he'll hear." Then she smiled and breathed out a long sigh that sounded like relief. Weeks later, after I wrote to Anne about Jimmy's death, she sent me a seashell as a small token to honour his memory. (Despite the sort of man he was, Anne said that "all life should be acknowledged.") It was a species found off the shores of Japan called a triumphant star, which was strangely fitting, since Miranda seemed to consider her husband's death a victory.

"The apples," Miranda now said as she smoothed yet another wrapper for her fishing lures, "and the lasagna, and the blackberry muffins. I have your dishes if you want them back."

I shook my head. She had received my gifts after all.

"We should play cribbage," Miranda suggested. "I think I got some cards here somewhere. You got a board? I guess not. You bring us one when you come back. Yes, we'll play, and I'll tell you the story of the serpent that pulled the boy's legs in the water."

"What boy?" I asked. "Chase?"

Miranda's eyes grew wide. "We'll play cribbage!"

Later, as I walked along the shore towards my boat, I turned and saw the hut in the distance, a small postage stamp of blue and orange clinging to the edges of the world. Who was that woman living there? Miranda's face was that of a stranger now, nothing more than a shadow on the water. A dark reflection of what lay beneath the surface. All those years of seclusion, plus the haunting memories of two dead sons. Life had done peculiar things to her mind. And what about the tale of the whale? Had Chase actually been there, or had Miranda's sense of reality become distorted?

Hallucinations. Paranoia. Delusions. Misidentification. All possible symptoms of dementia, I knew. Miranda Charlie was sixty-five years old now, making this a distinct possibility. I couldn't ignore what this meant for her. I would need to come back and assess her health thoroughly. As I pulled the boat out of the inlet, I found the ocean flat and calm, but it still took me twice as long as it should have to get back to the outpost. I couldn't help but drive slowly, taking my time to survey the shoreline for a little rowboat and a whale.

7

I stepped onto a flooded kitchen floor, my feet skidding out at different angles like a deer on ice. I tried to grab the counter but crashed onto my knees. The water soaked through my pants, and I flopped down onto my bottom in resignation, stretching my legs out straight and rubbing my sore knees. Not for the first time, I wondered what might happen if I ever suffered a more serious injury. How long would it take for somebody to check this lonely island if I slipped in the bathtub or fell off the ladder?

The old refrigerator had been ready to give up the ghost for some time, the mountains of frost inside the little box freezer now melted and leaking out the loose seal around the door. I sighed and climbed up off the floor. It would cost many hundreds of dollars to fly a repairman into Tawakin, and to buy a new refrigerator meant several weeks of waiting. The new nurse, Wren Featherstone, would be here in a few days for orientation and training, and there would be no refrigerator to store any perishables.

I hung my coat on the back of the door and imagined what it would be like to have a new nurse here. I'd had replacement nurses come before so that I could go on short holidays or visit the dentist, but they were never here long enough to require a thorough orientation. Besides, I was always away during those stints and therefore never had to witness how they filled my shoes. But soon I would have a shadow following me for three weeks. The thought of it made me claustrophobic. Yes, I felt lonely at times, but I'd grown accustomed to having my own space. And really, wasn't the whole thing an impossible task anyway, showing somebody forty years of learning in three weeks?

I mopped up the water and cleaned out the freezer, tossing the three bags of thawed halibut into the sink and extracting a sticky puddle of orange popsicle from the back corner. I emptied the refrigerator of all its contents and unplugged it.

Soon, I was wearing dry clothes and drinking hot tea, surrounded by stalks of wilted celery and a jug of milk and Tupperware containers of leftovers. Dozens of wallet-sized photographs were scotch-taped to the door and sides of the refrigerator. I peeled these off and put them into a shoebox, a jumble of grinning children, elders, aunties and uncles, chubby-cheeked newborns.

The only thing in Tawakin we liked to collect more than tooth shells and glass fishing floats was photographs. They wallpapered the insides of the houses—collages of unframed, sun-faded, corner-curled photographs that covered the cracks. Every year since I could remember, when the photographer travelled to Tawakin to take school pictures, everybody, not just the students, would line up at the gym all day and into the evening to get their picture taken.

When the packages arrived a few months later, the community buzzed with excitement as everybody swapped copies of their portraits, me included. (In fact, if you went into any house on the Tawakin Reserve, you'd see pictures of me throughout the years.) The photographs were handed out with pride and enthusiasm, and, in turn, they were received with appreciation. This went almost without exception. Even Loretta participated. It was as if the giving and receiving of our sunny faces eclipsed, at least for a moment, any hurt and discontent between neighbours.

A number of years back, for example, Teresa Henry had an affair with Margaret Sam's husband, Arthur. Everybody heard about it of course, and Margaret wouldn't come out of her house, no matter how hard Sophie

Florence and I tried. After crying her eyes out for weeks, Margaret finally opened the door to see Teresa standing there, her outstretched arm offering Margaret a newly arrived photograph of herself. Not a small one, either. An eight by twelve. Margaret took it and taped it to the wall. Right there above her kitchen table, among all the others.

It might seem unbelievable that anybody would have the strength to do such a thing, or the capacity to forgive in such a way, or even the willingness to look at a portrait of an adulteress every morning over coffee and fried bread, but it was true, it happened just like that. In a place like this, so tiny and faraway, you often had no choice but either to forgive or pretend not to be angry, unless you wanted to live like Loretta, and the fact was that those annual photographs seemed to do something good to people's spirits. I'd bet that if the devil himself lived in Tawakin, he'd thankfully tape a photograph of Jesus Christ onto his wall if he were given one.

I took the shoebox into the living room, where the wall above the couch was also covered with photographs amassed over the years. Most of the photographs were wallet-sized, with some people—like Sophie Florence and Margaret, for example—repeating themselves year after year so that their lives showed like a time-lapse movie on my wall. Beside the light switch, there was a large photograph I took of Nan Lily last year. The principal of Tawakin School had the students make signs for the Idle No More movement after watching on television how people across Canada were protesting the treatment of First Nations people. The thirty-five students who made up the school gathered at the band office on the reserve and held their posters of protest, despite the fact that there was nobody to see any of it except themselves. A few of the adults joined them, including Nan Lily, who fell asleep in her lawn chair with her cedar hat tipped forward over her eyes and an Idle No More card propped up against her torso. Since I was the only one with a camera, it was up to me to take a picture of what people thought was the funniest thing they'd ever seen. We printed copies at the school. Even Nan Lily put a copy on the wall in her store.

"Idle No More." She laughed. "Real nutty. I fell asleep!"

Among the many other people on my wall were Miranda and Chase. I possessed a photograph from each year of Chase's life, but of course I had none of Miranda from the past twenty years. Looking at her younger pictures, it was impossible to connect them to the frail woman I'd just seen. The photographs themselves, mind you, appeared as worn out as she did. When I received the one of her and an eight-month-old Chase, which she'd put in my mailbox at the post office, I took it back to the outpost and tore it into pieces. I couldn't bring myself to throw it out, though. Why, I'm still not sure. I put the torn shreds in a drawer. The next year, Miranda handed me a photograph in person when Sophie Florence and Gina and I went searching for dentalia on the beach. In front of the other women, I took it thankfully, and when I got home, I crumpled it and threw it into the drawer. But in due time, after I'd grown close to Chase and come to civil terms with Miranda, I brought them out of the drawer, and there they were now, on the wall, crumples smoothed out, pieces scotch-taped together into a mosaic, a picture once as torn as Miranda herself at that time of her life.

"Please, please," she'd whispered to me after giving birth to Chase, her eyes rabid with fear. She grabbed at me from the bed, while scarcely holding on to the wrinkled ball of flesh that wailed and twisted against her bare breast in search of a nipple.

"I can't," I insisted. "I can't knowingly record Jimmy as the father when he is in fact *not*. It is fraud. I could lose my licence."

"But I could lose my life." Miranda grasped my arm so tightly her fingers left a row of button-shaped bruises.

✻   ✻   ✻

At midnight, I woke startled, a sound in the outpost so loud it cranked me into a seated position on my bed. I opened my eyes wide, but it was too dark to see anything at first. My entire head buzzed, and the skin on my arms and across my collar bone prickled, and I perceived the sound to be coming from the kitchen. I rushed to the window, the tiles icy under my bare feet, and I saw through the flailing branches only my boat at the wharf. On the other side of the closed bedroom door, I could hear clattering noises, things falling to the kitchen floor, and I remembered the time a small group of kayakers came to the outpost in the middle of the night, soaking wet and shivering violently, how I found them heating tomato soup on my stove. It hadn't occurred to them that anybody actually lived there year round, they told me as I stood open mouthed in my flannel nightgown that stopped at the knees to show my unshaven legs.

But this noise was something else. Glass—a jar?—thudded on the floor and shattered. I grabbed my VHF radio from the cradle on the nightstand and scrambled to the closet, standing on my tiptoes, stretching for the small box of slugs on the top shelf while whispering "Tawakin, Tawakin" into the radio, half the time listening to the strange clicks across the kitchen linoleum and half the time nudging the corners of the box with my fingertips until I'd inched it within reach. I broke open the breech of the shotgun that I kept leaning in the closet and pushed one slug into the barrel. I was pulling a second slug from the box when there was a loud thump, twice as loud as anything that had come before it, and my limbs flinched, the slugs launching from the box and rattling across the tiles.

Feeling in the dark, I pressed my palm on a cold slug and picked it up, jamming it with shaky hands into the other barrel. Again, I whispered, "Tawakin, Tawakin," but I failed to push the button on the radio, my movements becoming more clumsy. Once I realized that I couldn't hold on to both the radio and the shotgun, I tried to clip the radio onto my nightgown, but it was too heavy, so I dropped it onto the bed. I thought to pull on some pants, and then there was a metallic clank of the kitchen sink and suddenly the tap was on, the rush of water from the faucet on full force. I cracked the bedroom door open.

The rest of my home was dark. The bedroom was separated from the kitchen by the small living room, the open entry to the kitchen only ten steps in front of me, a cool draft blowing from what I presumed was the kitchen door left open at the back of the house. I tried to make out shapes in the dark, but it was as black as the basalt on the beach below. Whoever was there was not trying to move quietly, the footsteps not quite the clunk of heeled shoes but something softer yet heavy. I thought I could feel the largeness of the intruder's movements, the sound of breathing—loud and thick and nasal. I slammed closed the break action, a dense metallic clank and a click as the shotgun straightened into a single lethal shaft. In the kitchen, there was a din of shuffling and scraping and scrambling, the chairs around the table tipping and crashing to the floor, and then the open door at the back banged against the wall and rebounded with a creaking squeal, followed by silence. Nothing except the water rushing out of the faucet, filling the sink and overflowing onto the floor.

After waiting a few moments, I flipped on the light. The kitchen had been ravaged. The table was leaning on its side, all the things on top of it crashed to the floor, the chairs toppled. All the food leftovers looked to be gone, the empty containers thrown one way, the lids another. Half a jar of mouldy tomato paste was shattered near a streak of cheese that had been squished underfoot. I moved across the floor with the shotgun raised and butted against my shoulder. Once I reached the open door, I pointed the barrel out into the dark, sweeping it from side to side, then closed the door and turned the dead bolt, finding it stiff from lack of use. Adrenaline flushed through my whole body to my extremities as I slid my back down the door until I was sitting on floor. I set the shotgun astride my legs.

There was a strong smell in the air. Like wet dog, only ten times worse. A black bear. I'd smelled it before, on the back trail up to the school. On the floor, there were smudges here and there but nothing discernible as tracks. It seemed like the best explanation, but what if it wasn't a bear? After all, not one had ever swam across the channel to my island in the forty years I'd lived here. Never had I seen or smelled one on the island. Never had I spotted any scat on my walks. Adrenaline still coursed through my limbs, mixing with exhaustion. Could it have been one of the dogs from the reserve? No, the smell was too strong. But if it were true, if it had been a dog, it must have come across the cove *with* somebody.

✻   ✻   ✻

The Heaviness of Things That Float

"Sophie Florence," I spoke into the VHF radio. Up all night, wide awake and listening for sounds, I couldn't wait any longer. "Sophie Florence."

Sophie Florence, sixty-five years old, was a pillar in the Tawakin community, a strong maternal figure, a kind of spiritual leader who nurtured the young and the old. She'd been the secretary at the Tawakin School for more than twenty years, which meant she was also the heart of the school. Even after losing her uncle and three cousins in a fire that destroyed her home a few years ago, she remained a source of comfort and laughter to others, especially her fourteen-year-old granddaughter, Odelia. She was also one of my closest friends.

"Go onto our secret channel," I said.

The Tawakin community channel was fourteen. You never said anything personal on that channel, because everybody left their radios turned on at all times, and that meant the whole community listened to every conversation. Sophie Florence and I used channel thirty-eight as our secret line of communication.

"What's the story?" Sophie Florence asked.

"I had an intruder break into the outpost last night," I said.

"Ay-ha! Somebody's been mischief! Was anything stolen?"

"No," I said. "It smelled terrible. I think it was a bear."

"Haw-ess, isn't that something?"

"My fridge broke. I left food out on the counters. Lots of fish."

"That'll get their attention, hey?"

"Still, I've never had one swim across the channel."

"I seen wolves swim from Waas Island to Toomista Island one time," Sophie Florence said.

"What do you think I should do?" I asked.

"Be careful. What else can you do?"

*   *   *

For decades, I'd lived near bears. I'd seen them on the school soccer field, and I'd even startled a few while walking on the logging road. But this felt different. Aggressive. Personal. Far be it from me to suggest that a wild

animal had a vendetta against me—that would have been ridiculous—
but its appearance after forty years, and coinciding so closely with my
departure from Tawakin, made me wonder whether the cosmos, or fate,
or God, or maybe even an ancient ancestor was telling me something.
But what, exactly? I had no clue. All I knew was that the safe sanctuary
of my little island had been broken, and since there was nothing else
here except me to attract the bear's attention, it felt like a showdown, a
game of cat and mouse when I left the outpost that morning. For some
time, I stood in the doorway, listening and watching, before I hurried
down the steps with two garbage bags of spoiling food and my Styrofoam
box. Inside the box were vials from the tiny cube of a refrigerator I kept
in the examination room for biological specimens. I set the box on the
passenger seat and started the motor. There was a new crispness in the
air, a tiny prick of autumn chill.

On the wharf beside the Tawakin Market on Mitchell Island, I tied
up the boat and carried the box up the long ramp to the higher pier built
on tall pilings black with creosote. Docked at the side of this pier was the
Pacific Sojourn II, a large black vessel that brought cargo and sometimes
passengers from the other side of Vancouver Island. Deckhands hooked
pallets of breakfast cereal and cake mixes and cola onto the cables and
lowered them down to the pier, the pulleys squawking along with the
sea gulls.

Standing against a large shed across from the *Pacific Sojourn II*, a
row of Dumpsters spewed out garbage bags ripped and gutted by gulls.
Soiled coffee filters and swollen diapers and empty soup cans were scattered everywhere. In the middle of this mess, looking up at the men on
the *Pacific Sojourn II* as they shouted down to her, was Hannah Charlie.

"No sign of your dad," they said. "Sorry, Hannah."

They promised to radio with any news, but Hannah had already turned
away, kicking at a rotten grapefruit as she headed to the end of the pier.
She perched there, on the ledge facing the south end of the cove, a thin,
solitary figure with a missing father. I followed her, my shoes crunching
the mosaic of clamshells dropped by the gulls. Along the way, I hurled the
garbage bags, filled with all the food from my kitchen, into the garbage

bins. Then I sat on the ledge a few feet away from her. I set the Styrofoam box down on the wharf even farther away, well out of Hannah's reach.

I said hello, and Hannah said nothing. I asked how she was feeling today. Nothing. Finally, I asked, "What are you doing?"

"Looking for my dad, stupid."

"Please don't call me names," I said.

"It wasn't a name," Hannah said. "It was a fact."

I bit my lip, keeping in mind how worried Hannah must be about her father. Her brain wouldn't retain the lesson for long anyway. She was doomed to a life of relearning short procedures, revisiting daily schedules and practising basic behaviours the rest of us took for granted.

"I heard the Basket Lady came for you last night," she said.

"Where'd you hear that?" I was always amazed at how fast news travelled.

"Around." Hannah shrugged. "What'd you do wrong?"

"It wasn't the Basket Lady," I said.

According to the legend, the Basket Lady stole children who didn't listen or who did something they shouldn't have, blinding them by rubbing tree-sap gum over their eyes, and then tossing them into her basket.

"You must have done something bad," Hannah said.

"It wasn't the Basket Lady," I insisted, sighing impatiently.

Our legs dangled over the end of the wharf. The water was fifteen, maybe twenty, feet below us. A long fall. I tried not to let it bother me by fixing my eyes on the narrow strip of white clouds drifting across the blue sky.

"We'll hear from your dad soon, Hannah." My voice sounded confident, and for good reason. It wouldn't be the first time Chase had run away, after all.

Hannah pointed to the sky. "You know what that cloud looks like?"

"Sort of like a dragon's tail."

"No, it doesn't."

"Maybe you're right," I said. "What do you think it looks like?"

"Toilet paper. All ripped up. From wiping your ass."

I drew in a long breath through my nose.

Hannah turned to me. The way her eyelids drooped made her look sleepy, but I knew it was disdain. She scratched hard behind her ear, and in that tone of hers, flat and lifeless, said, "Know how I know? It's so big it's got to be from your ass."

She burst out laughing, her laugh razor sharp.

A strong breeze pushed through the trees and lifted the hair off her eyes. Parts of Hannah's face resembled Patty, but many features were hers alone. Although her eyes would forever have that wide spacing she had at birth, the gap had lessened slightly with growth, as had the abnormally low bridge of her nose and the smooth upper lip with the missing divot. Sometimes I wondered if Patty looked at those features and ever felt guilty for Hannah's fetal alcohol syndrome.

I felt guilty. Never had I forgotten the promise I'd made to myself when Hannah was born, that I would look out for her, do everything I could to help lead her to a bright, happy future. Thank God, I'd never shared this vow with anybody else. I don't think I'd ever done enough to keep it. Sure, I'd shared new medical research with the teachers at the school, though Loretta would never let Patty have anything to do with such nonsense, and I'd taken a seminar once in Port Hardy, but what did that amount to?

Suddenly, Hannah leaned so far over the water that I thought she was going to dive right in. Lurching forward, I tried to snatch at her, but the girl was too far to reach. I steadied myself as she leaned backwards, away from the water, and then forward again, and then backwards again, until she was teetering back and forth like one of those drinking bird toys. I could never guess what troubling things Hannah might suddenly do, not from the moment I delivered her into this world. She was now taunting the old nurse, that much I knew.

"What's in the box?" Hannah asked.

"Cultures."

"I want to see." Hannah lunged for the box, falling sideways.

"You can't." I pushed it farther away. The Styrofoam box was specially designed to transport cultures—samples of urine, blood, feces—on the mail plane to the Port Hardy Hospital.

She gritted her teeth. "Let me see."

"There aren't any needles in there," I assured her.

That was the only thing about me that ever seemed to interest Hannah. When Hannah was in grade one, I went to the Tawakin School one day to give the kindergarten children their immunization shots. Hannah stole a syringe from my case and tried to give the class guinea pig a booster shot of strawberry Kool-Aid. The next year, she burst into the small office where I was bandaging a cotton ball on another child's shoulder. Hannah ran out of the school with a fistful of needles in vacuum-sealed wrappers.

She focussed on the box. "What did you say is in there?"

"Cultures," I repeated. "Specimens. From people."

Hannah was quick. I leaned backwards against the wharf to block her from grabbing the box. She narrowed her eyes at me, and for a moment, she looked like a precise miniature of her grandmother Loretta.

"Let me see," Hannah said. "Or I'll push you off the wharf when you're not looking."

I ignored the threat. "You cannot open this box."

Hannah slapped her hand onto the wharf. "How come?"

"Because the cultures will get ruined. They're delicate things."

"What kinds of things?"

"Blood."

"Blood?"

"And... poo," I said.

"Poo?" Hannah curled her lip. "You got shit in there?"

I nodded, my arms wrapped over the top of the box. A sea gull glided in front of us, landed on a piling and cried out.

Hannah watched the bird for a moment then waved me away with the back of her hand. "Go take your shit somewhere else. Figures you got shit in that box. You're a shitty nurse, that's what my grandma says."

This stung me, even coming from Loretta. Many times after Teddy's death, I'd driven across the cove in the middle of the night to help Loretta, who was hysterical with grief and wailing, back to her house. Sophie Florence and I would take her gently by the arms and guide her along the dark dock. Maybe she never knew that it was me who lifted her feet onto her bed, moved her tear-soaked strands of hair from her cheeks, pulled the blankets over her trembling body. Loretta would drift to sleep, pale and worn out, with her fists curled under her chin. In the candlelight, her mouth, with its fallen lines, had seemed to me to hold some quiet remorse. Her face exposed a profound weariness—perhaps from maintaining the loud resentment that had been present long before Teddy's death and would continue long after. Asleep like that, and without her sharp voice, she was reduced to something else. A child. Soft skin and vulnerable bones, and her broken heart.

One night after putting Loretta to bed, I found Patty in the kitchen. Sophie Florence was in the basement doing the mountains of laundry nobody had done in their enervating grief. It was 2:30 AM, but that didn't faze Sophie Florence. It never did. The women here often baked bread and jarred fish well into the wee hours of the night if the mood struck them.

I dropped into the chair across the table from Patty. She was picking at a carrot cake with her fingers, half of it still covered with cellophane wrap. "Can't sleep?" I asked.

"What do you think? My mom was crying at the top of her lungs." Patty sucked icing off her finger.

"You're welcome to sleep at the outpost anytime," I offered, "if you need some peace and quiet."

"I promised her I wouldn't ever leave."

"Maybe I could talk to her. You really should get some rest."

"I don't want you to talk to her," Patty said flatly. She flopped backwards against her chair and narrowed her eyes at me, as though she were trying to figure me out. She stared like that for a long moment before asking me, "You talk to Chase?"

"About what?"

"He's upset about my brother."

"We all are."

"But Chase is real upset."

Surely, you're more upset, I wanted to say. But I didn't. Patty seemed to be in denial of her own grief, which gave me the impression that she was even more fragile than if she were screaming at the end of the dock every night.

"Well? What'd he say about it?" Patty asked.

"Nothing, really."

"Nothing?"

"Well—" I paused, "he told me he's worried about you."

"What for?" she demanded.

I thought about Chase's concern over her drinking. Somehow, it didn't feel like the right time to bring it up. She'd get defensive most likely, and it was late. I was exhausted. It had taken us an hour to get Loretta back into bed tonight.

"He told me that you're his girlfriend," I said.

She pressed her thumb down on the cellophane until the cream cheese icing oozed out the sides. We both stared at it.

"He's worried what people will say," I said.

Patty's head jerked up. "About what?"

No sooner had she asked this question than she added, "You know, sometimes things get all mixed up inside his head. He says strange things to me sometimes. Things that aren't true. I thought you should know that."

Her thumb had impaled the cake right down to the plate.

"If you ever need someone to talk to, Patty, you know I'm always here for you."

"You?" She looked straight at me and laughed.

As I walked away from Hannah and along the wharf towards the Tawakin Market, I recalled how much Patty's scornful laughter had hurt me that night. It then occurred to me that it was the first time she'd ever spoken to me like that. No look of pity. No hint of compassion. She turned mean that night, plain and simple. I'd let it go, of course. Who wouldn't? She'd just suffered a terrible loss.

But now that I thought about it, things didn't ever change back to how they once were between us. For months after, Patty ignored me at the Tawakin Market. She provided only single-word answers when I asked how she was feeling. I assumed then that her coolness towards me was grief compounded by her pregnancy, which she'd announced not long after that night. And then there was the day on Toomista when Sophie Florence and I tried to stop her drinking. That seemed to drive the wedge between us deeper. If I saw her on the reserve, she'd turn and look the other way. If I said hello at bingo, she'd pretend not to hear me. Admittedly, she became more friendly with me over time, but she never returned fully to the sweet child or the young chatty adolescent who showed only light shades of her mother now and then.

✻   ✻   ✻

"She didn't actually see it, you know. It was dark," Robert said.

Outside the Tawakin Market, the ten-year-old stood in a circle with four other children. As I came around the corner of the wharf, I slowed my stride and listened.

"Might have been a *puukmis* that broke into her place. A big hairy one," said Tyler, who was in grade four and who sometimes cut my grass for five dollars.

"They're always big and hairy, stupid."

"Bigger than bears!"

"No, no." I smiled and approached the children.

They all turned to me.

"It was nothing bigger than a bear," I said. "It *was* a bear."

Robert squinted one eye skeptically.

"Did you see it?" he asked.

"I smelled it," I said.

"I bet a hairy *puukmis* smells real bad," Robert insisted.

"A *puukmis* isn't hairy. An *alth-maa-koa* is hairy," Kim said. She was nine, a budding artist who made me colourful cards every Christmas. She wore thick glasses that enlarged her eyes when she looked up at me.

"Then what's a *puukmis*?" Robert asked.

"A man made out of tree bark," Kim said.

"No, a *puukmis* is a man who got lost at sea and grows lots of hair to stay warm," Robert said.

"It was just a bear." I chuckled, shaking my head.

Kim ignored me and turned to Robert. "That's not a *puukmis*. A *puukmis* is a man who got kicked out of the village for being mean to his wife. He has to live alone in the forest up there. After a real long time he grows tree bark for skin."

"Why would he grow tree bark? Tree bark don't keep you warm," Tyler said.

"He didn't grow it like hair. He just turned into bark."

"Oh, yeah? Well, how'd he break into Nurse's house if he's made of bark?" seven-year-old Olive asked, her tongue slipping between the gap in her front teeth.

"Well, how did he find her island if he's lost at sea?"

"He's got those glowing eyes to see the way."

"Maybe it was the Basket Lady who smashed up her kitchen."

"The Basket Lady don't take bad grown-ups. Just bad kids."

"Real dumb, Kim."

"Plus, Willie said her fridge was broke in half. Right, Willie? No way the Basket Lady is strong enough to break a fridge. She's an old woman."

I laughed. "My fridge wasn't broken in half!"

"So what if she's an old woman?" Willie said, giving me a brief look, as if to say I wasn't qualified to participate in the debate. "She carries all them kids in her basket don't she? She's strong enough."

Waving my hand in playful dismissal of their theories, I left the children and headed inside the empty market. Usually, there'd be a small crowd of people who'd fill the tiny area between the post office counter and the store counter, but not today. The lid of the deep freezer under the front window was dented with the imprint of absent bums. The low-slung deck chair in the middle of the floor also sat unoccupied, and there were no small dogs scurrying under people's feet. The little bells on the door rang out behind me a second time.

"Buy us candy!" the five children shouted, following me inside.

"I don't have any more money," I said. "My piggy bank is empty. I spent it all on candy last week."

"How much money you get for being Nurse?" Olive asked.

"None of your beeswax!" I said, laughing.

Robert said, "Nurse gets the big bucks."

This cued the others to shout, "Big bucks! Buy us candy!"

"All right, go on," I said, rumpling Kim's hair. "You can each get one licorice and tell George to put it on my bill."

As the children raced off to the candy rack, I looked around for George Sam. I took the Styrofoam box across the empty store and put it behind the post office counter on its own special shelf where it would stay until the float plane arrived later to take the mail.

"Hello?" I called out.

"Bernadette!" George came out of the storage area in the back. He often ran the store for the owner, a ruddy-faced Finnish woman who lived upstairs but travelled frequently to town. Like the medical quarters, the Canada Post office, which consisted of a counter wicket and a set of old wood pigeonholes, was situated off the Tawakin Reserve, here on Mitchell Island. "Heard you had a real scare last night," he said.

I rolled my eyes. Since I knew Sophie Florence would never gossip about my intruder, I concluded that our secret channel was not as secret as we'd thought. Somebody had eavesdropped.

"A bear," I admitted.

George nodded. "Must've been hungry to cross the water."

"Must've," I said.

"I have something for you," George said, moving behind the post office counter so that the wicket framed his bushy black hair. He smiled at me with teeth too big for his face, a snow-white wedge against his dark skin. Today, it was his turn with the new teeth he and his wife shared. I'd seen their kitchen calendar, how it was delineated according to denture wear—*Elizabeth-George-Elizabeth-George-Elizabeth-George*—except for Sundays, when they tossed a coin.

He turned to retrieve a package from one of the pigeonholes on the back wall. Sliding the small package across the counter to me, he asked, "Do you like oysters?"

I looked at the package. "These are oysters?"

"No. But I can get you some," he said.

The envelope, one of those puffy things with Bubble-Wrap padding, was addressed to me personally, not the outpost. I never got mail since Anne died. The ink had smudged, and the return address was impossible to make out without my reading glasses.

"Do you want some?" he asked.

"What?"

"Oysters."

The envelope was no larger than my hand, but it contained something as big and round as a tennis ball. I felt its light weight and traced the edges of its slight asymmetry. I was intrigued, but if I opened it now, the whole village would know its contents by supper. I tried to keep some privacy now and then, so I put it in my coat pocket.

"George!" I pressed a palm to my chest.

He'd come out from behind the counter and was standing next to me, smiling that big smile, lifting his hair off his ear and peeling away a thick wad of bandage and cotton swabbing to reveal an earlobe severed at the tip. The freshly scabbed wound was deep crimson and shiny as shellac.

"Caught it on my chainsaw this morning," he said. "I watched a little piece of my ear fly into the air and land on the trunk of the tree I'd cut down. It was easy to spot because my earring was still in it and the sun was starting to come out and it was real sparkly. Elizabeth gave it to me for my birthday last year, so I tried to get it back, plus I was also thinking, who knows? Maybe Bernie can sew it back on. Next thing that happened, *swoop!* It was gone."

"Gone?"

"Gone."

"What do you mean?"

"What I mean is a damn crow swooped down onto the end of the tree. My ear was dead centre to both of us. I froze for a moment, and then whenever I moved, it turned its head kind of sideways like this—" George tilted his head at an angle, "—and the damn thing hopped towards my ear. Finally, it just swooped up and back down and flew off with it. Real mischief crow."

George kept on smiling.

"Can you do anything about this?" he asked. "It stings like a million bees."

I felt a tinge of resentment as I looked closely at the injury. To be the nurse was a small imprisonment, and I sometimes grappled with the constant intrusions on my time. I wasn't on medical duty every minute of every day, yet even when I didn't feel like it, I addressed their needs in order not to disappoint.

"You better come over to the outpost today," I said.

"I can bring you some oysters," he said, as though he had a secret stash, which wasn't far from the truth. George Sam was the hereditary chief of Yellow Cedar, an inlet near Tawakin. A hundred years ago, it was a whaling station. Nowadays, there was nothing except a vast wealth of shellfish and tracts of coastal land. "Do you know what oysters are supposed to do to you?"

Gently, I lifted the remainder of his lobe to look underneath, and then fixed the bandage back onto his ear.

"Do you?" he asked.

"You might get an infection," I noted.

"Depends who you eat the oysters with." He laughed, and danced his eyebrows up and down. "Oysters are supposed to make you... you know."

"George. Stop it." I refused to talk about the aphrodisiac qualities of oysters with George, no matter how harmless his teasing. I warned him, "You better be nice to the new nurse. She's young. You'll make her nervous with all your flirting."

"I like older women," he said.

"Like your wife?" I smirked and took a plastic basket down the first of three short aisles. "You come over to the outpost in an hour. I'll give you some ointment and put a proper bandage on it. You really have to start taking these things seriously, George."

"Who says that I don't?"

I threw a box of crackers into the basket. "Have you ever?"

In George Sam's younger years, before Tawakin banned alcohol and became a dry reserve ten years ago, he was prone to drunken spells of violence. This was back a few decades, when the logging camp still operated in Wharton and the dirt road, now filled with forest, connected Tawakin to the rest of Vancouver Island. By day, George had been a faller, climbing up the trunks of trees to great heights, and by night, he fell. His drunken outbursts had kept me busy in those days, often caring for the injuries he and his wife, Elizabeth, sustained during their many domestic disputes. Back then, Elizabeth drank heavily too, and there were frequent incidents with cast-iron pans and kitchen knives and broken windows and shotguns. Every so often, however, George Sam didn't become enraged after drinking, and these were the times he slept with other women on the reserve. Young mothers told me this secret in confidence, usually right before or after—though sometimes during—the delivery of their fatherless babies at the outpost.

At the end of the aisle, I passed the shelves of gum boots and Tawakin T-shirts, the old greeting cards with faded colours, the dusty cassette tapes of country music and the electric kettle marked with a price tag made from masking tape. Along the back wall under the windows was a row of chest freezers. I lifted the lids and eventually chose two steaks, both white with freezer burn, and a loaf of shrunken bread.

I looked out the windows at the Tawakin Reserve dock across the water. It was not far. A fit person or an animal could swim the distance in a pinch. I walked back to the front of the store, throwing two boxes of Kraft Dinner into my basket along the way, and asked George, who reappeared from the storage area, "Did you see Chase leaving the cove the day he went missing?"

George nodded from behind the cash register and helped me unload my basket onto the counter. "He came in here to buy soup before heading out on the water."

"Soup?"

"And those cans of pasta. Lots. Too many to put into a bag. Too heavy. I gave him a cardboard box to carry them in."

"Did he have any trouble paying you?" I asked.

George squinted up at the baseball caps hanging from a ceiling rafter. "Mmmm, I was going to put it on his tab, but he paid with cash."

"Did he seem confused when he was paying?"

George shrugged. "How do you mean?"

"Did he have trouble figuring out how much to give you?"

"No. He gave me the exact amount. Forty-six dollars and twenty-nine cents. I remember thinking it was exactly my age and my daughter Laurie's age."

"Did he sway?"

"Sway?"

I nodded. The idea of a concussion still jabbed at me. Head injuries could be tricky to pin down with complete confidence.

"No," he said.

"Did you notice anything unusual about him?"

"He was white," George said, poking numbers into the cash register. "Patty dumped a whole tub of flour over his head, furious about something, that's what he said. It was all over his face and his clothes and in his hair. I had to sweep it up after he left."

"Then maybe he just wanted some quiet for a while," I said.

"That sounds about right."

"Hunting, I figure. Don't you?" I asked.

"He said something about whales."

I remembered Miranda's strange story about Chase catching a whale. "What exactly did he say about them? Is that what he's hunting for?"

George burst out laughing. "What? By himself?"

I felt my face flush. "I suppose that is ridiculous."

"Besides," he said, "you know we ain't allowed to do that no more." He wrote down my total bill on a little slip of paper and put the tab inside the cash register. Then he packed my groceries in a cardboard box.

"How did he seem?" I asked. "His mood, I mean. Good? Bad?"

"Oh," he laughed, "he was happy. Real happy."

I smiled with relief as I took the box from the counter. "You come see me later about that ear," I reminded him, fumbling for the door. George was there in a flash to hold it open for me. Outside, I checked with him once more. "You think he's okay, then?"

He nodded, and then his face lit up as if something occurred to him. "Chase was also telling me something else, but I was already real mad about the flour I had to sweep up, so I wasn't listening too good. Something about a story? Returning a story he never wanted in the first place? I don't know, something like that."

✳   ✳   ✳

On a sunny afternoon like this one, the benches outside the Tawakin Market were normally filled with women who tossed back their heads to laugh or swill cola from cans while men pushed baseball caps off their faces to catch the afternoon sun. Neither the women nor the men would let me walk past without teasing me about something. My sex life, more specifically my lack of one, was a perennial target. Innuendoes were often made about my solitude and the mechanical devices I must surely use in the absence of a real man. But today, nobody was sitting on the benches.

Before heading back to my boat, I sat down on an empty bench and considered what George had said about Chase returning a story he never wanted in the first place. I peered between the railings at the mucky beach below. A clapboard box of a structure stood on stilts at the edge of the shoreline. It had only three walls—the side facing the water was open—and a long platform coming out the front. The rotting boards had fallen off in many places, and most of the platform had collapsed into the water. Back in the twenties, it was a whaling station. It startled me to imagine one of those gigantic mammals atop the platform where Chase once nearly drowned.

It happened on a Friday, when the Tawakin Market was packed with people getting their mail and snacks for the weekend. It was the winter after Chase had turned three, and I'd just come out of the noisy market.

I didn't hear his cries because of the pouring rain and because my raincoat squelched loudly as I walked along the wharf towards my boat. Then I heard the dog start up. It was George Sam's mongrel, Skipper. It was running back and forth along the waterline and barking madly. That's when I spotted Chase at the end of the rickety whaling-station platform. He was on his hands and knees, and from where I stood, he looked to be stuck on a plank next to a gaping hole in the rotting structure. The high tidal water sloshed a foot or two below him. Panicking, my first impulse was to run back to the market and get help. But I didn't want to lose sight of him. If he fell, I wanted to be able to keep my eyes on his bright red raincoat. No, I needed to rescue him myself.

On the platform, the wood was slick with algae. Some of the planks sunk slightly under my weight. I stepped carefully over the spaces where the wood had crumbled away. At that point in my life, I was still attempting to bury my anger towards Miranda for the way our friendship had ended, and every so often, this anger reared its bitter head. Maybe part of me embraced the chance to expose her as a bad mother—whether she was or not didn't matter. For heaven's sake, Miranda, I'd say in front of everybody, did you even *know* your son had slipped out of the market? Did I think she was a bad mother? Later, yes, after she abandoned Chase, but not back then. Or maybe part of me saw the opportunity to show Frank, in the lingering hurt of our split, what a great mother I'd have been. The kind of mother who climbs out on rickety platforms for her son. Remembering this, I laughed at myself. That this was my capacity for revenge. Saving a child I'd have helped anyway, while hoping the act would bear subtle messages of guilt and regret. How ruthless of me.

Somehow, Chase made his way to a spot where a chunk of the dilapidated platform was hanging over the deep water like a crooked finger. He was like the child who climbs a tree and can't find his way back down to the ground. One of his red boots had fallen through the hole and was floating on its side in the cold water underneath him. He was frightened to the bone, inconsolably so. Inching my way out to the end of the platform, I told him to stay still. I said, "Everything will be just fine." He sobbed. When I finally reached him, grabbing at his red raincoat and clutching it tightly in my fist, he was shaking.

Truly, I believed then that I'd spared him from drowning, and although it might not have been like that exactly, it was not so farfetched. Drowning, at least the constant threat of it, was a part of life here on the Pacific, so when we safely reached the shore, I felt a surge of relief. I sat down on the pebbles, my rain pants keeping me dry against the

The Heaviness of Things That Float

wet ground, and I cradled him on my lap. He started sobbing even more loudly, his little body lurching and quivering. The sock on his bootless foot was soaked and stretched and dangled heavily off his toes. I wrapped him inside my coat and felt his fingers burrowing into the folds of my sweater. It was, in no small measure, the most tender thing I thought I'd ever felt, these small appendages desperately kneading me. Since slicing him out of the amniotic sac, this was the closet I'd been to Chase.

He'd spent most of his toddler years in their home on Toomista Island, and I'd often seen him only from a distance, as he passed me in the cove on the boat with Jimmy, or from his living room window up on the field above the shore where I combed for treasures with Sophie Florence. When I did speak to him—in the market or on the wharf—I always made it nothing more than a quick hello and a ruffle of his hair. He was Miranda's secret, and he was my secret, too, and I worried that others would see it written across my face whenever I looked at him.

"I seen a gas baw in the water," Chase whispered to me once he'd calmed down. He looked up at me from inside my coat. A film of mucus covered his upper lip.

"A what? A glass ball?"

He nodded and rested his head against my chest.

How obsessed we all were with finding these things that washed up onto our shores. How often we took boats to the small outlying islands to scour the crevices of rocky shores. We spent afternoons on windy banks of driftwood and rustling grasses, collecting blue and green shards of beach glass and iridescent abalone shells. For hours at a time, we sifted through deep beds of sand to find dentalia shells for dance shawls or for keeping in glass jars on our windowsills. And that's when it occurred to me, as I sat there on the beach holding Chase like a newfound treasure I wanted to keep all to myself, that this was how people who know the tragedy of sinking spend much of their lives: in search of those things that find a way to their shores across watery depths and drowned voices.

* * *

Heading back to the outpost, I cut the boat motor halfway across the cove so that I could observe the scene in quiet. The Tawakin Reserve, a few hundred metres away, looked just as colourful with its red and blue and green houses as it did forty years ago, the windows cracked from years of stormy weather, the roofs leaking where black mould crept across the ceilings like a rash.

"How come you don't got any black marks on your walls?"

Chase asked me this once when he was eight.

"The outpost was built carefully," I said. "The seals around the windows and doors are tighter, I think. It's important not to have mould in here when sick people come."

"Is that how come there's no cracks or holes in your walls?"

"I guess so, yes."

"Auntie says it's because you're a *mamulthni*."

A white person. At one time, I wondered if this would always make me an outsider. If I'd always be separated from the reserve by the cove and by the differences in our conditions and our places in this unbalanced world. I had hoped otherwise, believing that if I stayed long enough, I'd eventually become a part of the community. And I had. I couldn't pinpoint the exact moment, but along the way somewhere, they'd come to feel like family.

How terribly I would miss this place. In a way, it felt at times as though I'd already left Tawakin behind. It was my heart working on its own, I suppose, preparing me for this unimaginable change.

I scanned the reserve. Little moved. There were only a few children riding their bikes along the path rimming the shoreline. A pack of dogs tumbled over one another. No aproned women shuttled across the thick grass to and from the fish sheds. No boat crammed with laughing people going to hang out at the Tawakin Market. No faraway whine and grind of a chainsaw. Even the regular ensemble of axes splitting wood had taken an intermission to search for Chase Charlie. The more I thought about it, the more convinced I was that he'd run away again. Although I couldn't imagine what the reason might be this time.

The first time Chase ran away, I found him by accident. It was three months after Jimmy Charlie accidentally shot himself in the face, and Chase had decided to leave the reserve for good. He'd managed to row a small boat—a tiny thing the size of a bathtub—all the way to Rubant Island, even though he was only five years old that summer. It was early evening when I found him. The water was calm and the wind steady yet gentle, and much later, I'd found out that nobody on the reserve had noticed Chase was gone. Why would they? It was the adventurous season, the time when children stayed outside for long hours, jumping off the dock, catching rockfish, paddling canoes, playing hide-and-go-seek. At that time, Miranda and a few others had been living in the houses on the Toomista Reserve, a tiny reserve on Toomista Island now used only for summer picnics, the houses long since abandoned. Immediately after Jimmy's death, however, she and her sons stayed that summer in the church on the Tawakin Reserve so that the people could take care of them, bring them meals, keep them company in their time of grief.

On the day Chase ran away, I'd spent the afternoon on Toomista Island, looking for glass balls and sifting through the deep beds of sand in search of teeth, those small hollow dentalia shells shaped like miniature tusks. After several hours, I'd found nothing except a pocketful of beach glass and an empty plastic bottle that had once contained some type of Japanese beverage. I was getting ready to return to the outpost when I glimpsed neighbouring Rubant Island across the narrow sleeve of water. Through the trees there, I could see a hint of blue and yellow paint up high in the branches. The branches lifted and dropped in the wind, and at first, I could see only the blue ovoid eye carved into wood, and then the hook of a yellow beak as long as a man's arm.

This happened, if I recalled correctly, around the time I suffered from insomnia. The image of Jimmy's bloodied and sunken face haunted my sleep, and I was taking pills to help me rest. Some nights, even these didn't work, however, and I'd developed many symptoms of sleep deprivation. Often, I thought myself unfit for work. I was clumsy from exhaustion, and there was a slight yet constant tremor in my right hand. My memory lapsed now and then, and I had dropped some weight, about ten pounds that I couldn't really afford to lose. And the headaches.

Dull and thudding and ever present. Hallucinations, too. Some were visual, a disturbance in the peripheral field. The smallest movements seen from the corner of my eye—a leaf turning in the yard, the slightest shift in the grass, a change in light as the sun passed partly behind the clouds—caused me to be startled by things that weren't there. Some were auditory, sometimes nothing more than whispers behind my ear. At first, I'd thought it might be those stories that resided, as Frank had insisted, in the wind and the water. But other times, it was only a single word spoken loudly and clearly, buttressed by complete silence, and I then realized it was not a story at all but a sign: I needed respite from my job.

That day, in the grassy clearing of wood crosses on Rubant Island, I found a small mustard-coloured pup tent pitched directly on top of Jimmy Charlie's freshly filled burial plot. In the near distance behind it, standing guard over the dead from the edge of the clearing, was the totem pole with the blue ovoid eyes and the yellow beak. I walked past the older crosses, the names effaced and the wood faded to grey, past the newer plots surrounded by small picket fences and adorned with desiccated flowers, sun-faded teddy bears and photographs, muted and curled. When I reached the tent, a voice cried out.

"Go away! I ain't going home!"

I crouched down and lifted the tent flap. "Chase?"

He was sitting in the middle, his black hair lifting with static electricity against the low ceiling of the tent. His head looked like the fuzzy blowball of a dandelion. He was eating dried salmon, biting it off with the side of his mouth, since his two front baby teeth were already missing after a fall on the cement dock earlier that year. He lowered his chin into his chest as teardrops fell fast onto the photographs spread between his legs. He was blubbering, and I had a hard time making out what he was saying.

"She wouldn't take me to come see him and I asked Uncle to take me to come see him and she said I weren't allowed to come see him and she's been—" He sucked in a breath that shuddered through his small body. Thick mucus rattled his nose. "She's been dancing in the kitchen, I seen her two times, and you're not supposed to dance after somebody dies, and I heard her say his name lots of times to Uncle—*lots* of times—and you're not supposed to say it or else he'll get lost in the other world and—" He wiped his nose with the length of his forearm. "Uncle told her she wasn't supposed to say his name or else he won't make it to the other side, and she laughed and said that she doesn't care." He emphasized this last word by screaming it. "She said she never wants him to get to the other side, and then I got all these out of the garbage." He motioned weakly at the photographs that looked to be covered with food residue, mayonnaise or yogurt. He slammed both fists onto his thighs and his voice undulated with grief. "She's not doing it right!"

I curled myself into a ball and squeezed into the tent beside him. I just sat like that, my head tilted to my shoulder, my bent limbs contorted into a pretzel, without saying a word. And then—I do not remember what possessed me—I started to tell Chase a story. It was a tale about a tribe of Wilde Grannies with silver hair who lived out of sight in the treetops and in ferny nooks. It was the sort of story Anne and I used to make up when we were children, sitting under the Garry oaks in our yard. At the end of each adventurous tale, Chase asked, "Can you tell me another one, Nursema'am?" After some time, he leaned forward so that his head rested on my knee. My heart tugged at the sadness in his face, and my knee warmed under his cheek. He smiled at me—a small, sad smile—and held up his baggie of salmon.

I took a piece, my other hand stroking his thick hair, and I said, "If you make room for me beside you, maybe we both can have a rest."

8

The thing about having your home perched on a stony ridge was that you couldn't see from down below what might be lurking up top. Creatures could easily hide out of sight, surprising the daylights out of you as you ascended. The point was: I carried my box of groceries up the stairs from the dock to the outpost once again on high alert, flinching at every small sound, turning towards the movement of every windblown branch, fully expecting to see the bear. I was aware of something strained and unsure inside me, like a length of frayed rope, and I had a sense *There is something pulling at me*, though I couldn't have said what, because no words rose to describe it, just the horrible feeling of danger. At first, I assumed it was only the threat of wildlife, the prickle on my skin, but then, as I hurried to the door of the outpost, the feeling grew stronger, and an image pushed its way into my mind of Chase wandering alone along the dark shore at night, and a sound filled my ears, like words muffled in the wind, and then it was gone.

I didn't know what to make of the image. Shutting the door safely behind me, I turned my thoughts back to the bear. I needed to be pragmatic. Perhaps somebody could do a reconnaissance of the island for me, confirm that there was in fact a bear lurking around. No point in being afraid if there was nothing out there. I decided I'd call Frank. We needed to talk anyway about my trip to Miranda's—what would he make of her story?

After that first day I met Frank, he showed me all the places in the cove where I could listen for the stories, the ones he said could be heard moving in the water and in the wind and up the tree trunks. I could never hear them, but I would imagine their presence. Whenever I spotted a crow, I envisioned the stories flying on its wings through the clouds of smoke rising from fish sheds, over prawn traps stinking up wood boats, over the restless children jumping into the water, over the gossiping bread bakers, the cedar pullers, the canoe makers, over rubber-booted clam diggers, stone skippers, beachcombers, hat weavers, drum beaters, fish cleaners, urchin eaters, over the wives sewing dance shawls, the husbands splitting wood, the grandmothers beading shells, the aunties stewing jam, over elders picking berries, and uncles singing songs, over the young and the old, over Frank as he kissed me gently on the mouth.

We spent every day together that first summer. We shared hot tea out of a steel thermos on his boat, searched for glass balls on the beach, the wind tangling our hair, his long black hair and my blonde hair. Sometimes we walked for hours and he told me about his time at residential school, the way he was hit with hickory sticks until he bled, until his tender skin split open while he bit his lip in vain, unable to stop the tears as the drops of his blood stained the whitewashed floors that his cousins had to scrub clean after, and the homesickness he'd felt. I told him about the afternoon I stole a *Rand McNally Road Atlas* from the Victoria library at the age of twelve, and the routes I marked with my crayons, how I was homesick for all the places I'd never been. He told me about putting a harbour seal in his mother's bathtub. I told of my plan to never get married. He told me, "I hope you'll marry someday."

I set the box of groceries onto the counter and looked out the window at the forest in the back, searching for breaks in the brambles, and at the patch of grass for any mounds of scat. There were none.

From my coat pocket I took the mail package to the couch in the living room and sliced the top of the envelope open with a filleting knife. Inside, there was a second envelope, with my name on it, written in Anne's handwriting, the mysterious object bulging inside. Paper-clipped to this second envelope was the following note:

Dear Aunt Bernadette:

We have cleaned Mom's apartment in preparation for your arrival. I found this envelope in Mom's desk.

Love, Sarah

Inside the second envelope was a seashell. It was white and painted with black and brown stripes. Collectors always refer to how a seashell was painted, as though they never doubt the existence of a Painter. I'd always liked the certainty of that.

When I put the seashell on the coffee table in front of me, it fell into two perfect halves. It seemed to have been cut like that on purpose, because the severed edges were clean and straight, as if done with a very fine, sharp implement to reveal the elegant architecture inside, the small paper-thin chambers spiralling with measured precision into larger ones. The inside of the shell had a delicate beauty. I loved that I could see its internal cross section, its inner life, its secret self exposed.

I unfolded the accompanying slip of stationery and held it on my lap as I sat on the couch in my living room.

My Dear Sister,

My last gift to you is the most magnificent and mysterious of all seashells, the chambered nautilus. Its insides spin in what mathematicians, those logarithmic lovers, call the miraculous spiral. Each time the creature grows, finding its chamber then too small for its existence, it moves into a bigger chamber and seals off the old one.

If I haven't already asked you by the time I am gone, won't you please step in as grandmother to the children now and then? As Granny. And not one of those dull Housebred Grannies but a real Wilde Granny! I hope you will say yes, because I have already told them you'd arrive with scads of new stories. Also, there are three empty jars in my Pickled Poem Pantry. Please fill them for wintertime.

Until we meet again,

Your Anne

Looking again at my sister's name at the bottom of the letter, an image of Anne lying in the hospice bed bloomed in my head. Anne and her husband, Kevin, had divorced ten years earlier, but the rest of her family was there: her two children, Sarah and Mark, their loving spouses, Tom and Yoland—or was it Yolanda?—I kept forgetting and grew tired of asking. The four young grandchildren were there as well. They ranged in age from five to ten, and I couldn't remember any of their names either. Joshua and Samuel and Leah and Miriam, or something with that Old Testament ring.

In the afternoons, the grandchildren circled Anne's bed. Sometimes they stood and sometimes they sat, bouncing on their haunches in chairs. In the first few days, when she was still often alert, Anne made them daisy chains and told them tales and read them poems she kept on the nightstand—little slips of paper inside glass jars labelled *Pickled Poems*. With one ear to Anne, I kept busy reviewing the nurses' charts, checking the circulation in Anne's hands and feet, replenishing the ice chips in the cup on the bedside tray. As Anne slipped into longer spells of sleep, the children took turns holding her hands—tiny anchors stretching out from the bed along tender chains.

Straightening the intravenous needle in the back of Anne's hand, I had thought of our parents, both dead several years earlier. I was a nurse, and a sister, nothing more, and soon I would not even be a sister. And what had I done with my life except receive patients who shuttled by boat across the windy cove, or foggy cove, or rainy cove, or snowy cove, or when the hail drummed the outpost window from where I watched the passing seasons. I'd been drifting into a new season of my own for some time, alone and aging and without anybody to anchor me in the dark waters of an uncertain future—what *does* one do when retirement finally comes and there is nobody to nurse? Would I ever have loving arms to anchor my bed one day, or would I end up completely alone in the world after all these years?

Or could I become, I now wondered, a Wilde Granny? I hadn't thought often of the Wilde Grannies in years, not since I used to tell Chase the stories when he was young. As children, Anne and I spent our summers under the Garry oaks behind our house with our neighbours, the Riley sisters, Alice and Rebecca, who lived with their grandmother. Sometimes the Riley sisters would bring porcelain figurines and miniature dolls from their grandmother's curio cabinet, which we'd repainted one summer to look like old women. Together, we created the tales of the Wilde Grannies. Creatures with long hair of silver and short hair of black and wavy hair of blue. Ragged dresses made of maple leaves and scarves of reeds, hats of upside-down dandelion tops. We hid them all over the scant forest we named Pothenroth. If you looked carefully, you could spot fifty-five grannies under the ferns, up in the boughs, in little huts made of twigs, between stones, hanging in tangled brambles. I had the best printing of us all, so I wrote down our tales in a black composition book. On the first page it read: *The Legend of the Great Forest of Pothenroth, or How the Ancient Tribe of Wilde Grannies Came to Be So.* We took turns telling the stories.

One day, I started a new story. "It has long been our—"

"Say 'hath,' it sounds more sophisticated," Anne interrupted.

Alice and Rebecca nodded in unison.

"It hath long been our belief—"

"Conviction, maybe?" Anne suggested.

Alice and Rebecca nodded again.

"It hath long been our conviction that great tribes of Wilde Grannies, *Grannica wilde*, once roamed the earth. Sadly, we very much doubt whether many tribes remain. We have, however, caught brief glimpses of these wondrous Creatures within the Great Forest of Pothenroth." I swept my arms around to indicate all the tiny figures watching from the woods. "That's how this story will begin," I said.

"Read it back to us," Rebecca suggested. "The beginning is the most important part of the story, after all."

"Actually, I think the ending is more important," I said.

"But the beginning is like a promise."

"Yes, but the ending is what the story means," I insisted. "How it turns out is everything it ever was."

I now read the letter again, this time aloud. When I reached the end, my eyes swept over her name without me saying it. I knew better than to do that. It was local custom not to speak a deceased person's name for at least one year. If my sister heard her name, she might think she was being called back, and then she might try to return, which was not possible. Disoriented, she would lose her way to the other side, and I couldn't allow myself to risk that. Like so much in this place, the custom had seeped into my own beliefs over time and I could no longer see death in any other way. It was a journey that, once started, took time and attentiveness. Like life, you had to be truly present or risk losing everything.

Next to my new nautilus shell on the coffee table was a case the size of a tea tray and shallow, with a hinged lid and thin slats of pine that walled a hundred tiny rooms lined with red velvet. Most rooms housed a seashell, and of the few empty spaces left, none were big enough for the nautilus. Lifting the lid, I plucked a hat-shaped limpet from the box, turned it upside down in my palm and circled my fingertip around its delicate brim, feeling the tiny chips and cracks. My sister sent this shell to honour elder Candice Joe's departure to the other world. Poor little Candice Joe, her grandmother's namesake, lost her name for a whole year after her grandmother died. I returned the shell to its proper place, took out a triton and touched its fragile tip. My sister sent this shell after Miranda Charlie's oldest son, Stan, died. There was a sundial shell in the room next to it, which she sent after Miranda's second-oldest son, Ronnie, died. It had become a tradition of Anne's to send a seashell for every death in Tawakin.

It was a beautiful gesture of empathy, this tradition, and although it seemed morbid turning a collection of memorial shells into a pastime, I'd become something of an amateur conchologist, one of the few hobbies I'd stuck with over the years, ordering collector's guides in the mail, spending my free time combing the beaches of the outlying islands for local specimens to accompany the more exotic shells my sister bought from a shop in Victoria. The local specimens I stored in jars on my windowsills or in the halves of clamshells, keeping the red-velveted case for my sister's special shells. It was overwhelming at times to see how many my sister had sent—whelks, wentletraps, nutmegs, turbans, ceriths, conches, cowries, periwinkles—yet I could instantly recall every death. Every man, woman, teenager, child, baby: so many deaths in a place that seemed too small to bear even one tragedy.

The tiny room in the top corner of the case held a turritella shell. It was the first shell Anne ever sent. Turning my eyes skyward, I surveyed the treetops out the window and remembered poor Esther Sam, pulled off the swings by her face and dragged into the rain forest behind the reserve. The other children playing on the basketball court screamed in terror. People raced from their houses while Esther's mother and father stood in their yard trying to understand what had happened. Several men chased the cougar into the woods, but it was never found. Esther was discovered up in a tree that same evening, little left of the three-year-old, her body devoured.

That happened during my second summer here, and I nearly resigned and left Tawakin because of it. Nightmares of her ravaged body were haunting my sleep, and I soon decided that life was too raw for me here. Too wild. I kept replaying the last time I'd seen Esther alive. The day before the attack she'd intercepted me as I walked along the dirt road to Frank's house. "Fowers for you," she said, handing me a bouquet of dandelions and wrapping her arms around my legs. On my way back to the outpost, the dandelions blew off the seat and into the water, and were probably, I always imagined, still floating limply somewhere in the cove the moment she was attacked.

I cried whenever I thought of those flowers, cold and lifeless, and in my dreams they morphed into mountain lions, yellow heads with long teeth, and I'd wake wanting to be back in the busy centres of the world where tragedies happened to people I didn't know. My desire to be an independent woman in a wild land was crumbling away and falling to the floor as I wandered around the outpost every morning in a fog of despair. I wanted to hop onto the mail plane with one satchel of belongings and not a word to anybody. I called myself naïve for what I thought I knew about the world, about earning money and bucking conventions and living independently, about Friedan and Greer and Steinem. What I knew amounted to a hill of beans.

I'd phoned Anne that night and sobbed. "I shouldn't have come here.

I thought it would be adventurous, but I don't belong here. I'm not even sure I'm cut out to be a nurse."

"It's a terrible tragedy, Bernie." Anne cried, too. "How is everybody else doing?"

"They cut their hair," I said.

"What do you mean?"

"Even Frank. He cut all his long hair off," I said. "They did it in mourning, to honour her, to show how much her death has changed them, I think. I don't know. I don't really understand. It's a tradition."

"Maybe you just need to find your own way to honour her. I've got an idea. I'm going to send you something in the mail, Bernie. Don't quit until you get it. Will you do that?"

I hesitated. "I suppose."

"Promise?"

I promised, and two weeks later, I received a purple seashell.

Frank stopped by the outpost for lunch the day I received Anne's gift. We sat in the kitchen, eating crackers and cheese and watching the windblown trees sway outside the window. Frank picked up the seashell, long and tapered to a point.

"I never seen one of these," he said.

"It's from the Mediterranean," I explained. "My sister bought it in a store in Victoria. It's a turritella shell. To remember Esther."

"That's a good way to keep her memory. You need things like that. Things that keep you floating when you're heavy." He nodded. "Seashells. I got a good story about Raven and abalone seashells."

"Not now, Frank. I'm tired."

"But this story is a box you can put your tired bones into."

I clutched at the table tightly. I looked at the seashell, and although I deeply appreciated that my sister was trying to help me cope, trying to encourage me to stay here and prove to myself that I could do what I'd set out to do, I didn't think I had the strength. I hadn't told Frank any of this yet, that I was thinking of leaving Tawakin, because I didn't want to think of our love, for that's what it had grown into by this time, coming to an end.

"When you open a story's lid," Frank reached out and pulled my hand gently from the table, "sometimes what's inside the box reminds you of darkness, and it scares you real bad. But sometimes you open the lid and you find room inside the box to store all your fears for a while."

Whatever pain Frank himself felt seemed to shine with hope. This faith he showed—that there were things in this world, such as stories or seashells or the cutting of one's hair, that could keep you from sinking—lifted me up that afternoon. After Esther's death, I'd thought this small faraway world would forever be surrounded by grey walls of grief and despair. But thanks to Frank and Anne, I saw the windows in those walls.

*   *   *

Later that day, after walking around the island and along the paths that crisscrossed the forest, Frank returned to the outpost kitchen and reported to me that he saw no sign of a bear.

"Thanks for doing that, Frank." I handed him a can of cola.

"Probably swam back across, but I can't say for sure," he said, popping the tab and taking a long drink. "I didn't see any tracks or scat. Then again, I've never been real good at that sort of thing. You would have been better to call George."

"I'm still waiting for George to come by about his ear. Said he would, but you know him. Gets distracted easily." And then I broke the news to Frank. "I saw Miranda. Chase wasn't there."

Frank sunk down into a chair at the table.

"But she might have seen him," I added.

His face brightened.

"I really don't know what to believe," I said. "She told me a strange story about having dog children, and how they took their furs off one day and then they were boys. And then she said Chase had caught a whale and that he sent a piece of blubber with a crow to the reserve—like a carrier pigeon with a message. She's not well, Frank. I need to see her again. Examine her. I suspect I'll be trying to coax her back so she can get proper treatment. But really, she needs to go to town for that. There's not much I can do for her."

"When are you going back up there?" He sounded anxious.

"Next week, most likely. The new nurse arrives tomorrow."

"Oh." He frowned.

"What?"

"So you really are leaving?"

"It had to happen someday. There's no room for me here."

Frank cleared his throat. "You could move into my place."

I pulled my head back in surprise.

"You know," he said awkwardly, "as a friend."

"Thank you, but you already have four of your cousins and your great-uncle living in your little house," I said. "I hardly want to spend my twilight years camped on your couch."

"It's a very comfortable couch," he said.

"Oh, I know." I smiled.

"We had some good times on it," he said.

"Yes, I remember."

And I did. But I remembered the bad times, too.

*   *   *

"I seen you lots with Frank," Miranda said, tallying her points on a piece of paper and moving her pegs up the cribbage board.

It was the fifth Saturday in a row that she'd come to visit since that night we met at bingo. She'd brought the boys this time, four-year-old Stan, and Ronnie, who must have been about three months old. At our feet under the table, Stan wrapped gauze around fake wounds on his baby brother's head.

"You better watch yourself with that one," Miranda continued. "Frank's exactly the sort women fall for, all sensitive and playful and real carefree and likely to cause you a world of trouble just because they know you'll cross the cove for their soft touch, the way their eyes shine when they tease you—I bet they do, sure they do, I can see it in your smile right now—the way their voice says your name, and then there's the hope they give you—like if you want to get married or have children someday, which might be exactly what happens if you keep on with Frank. You'll get married and you'll move into his house and you'll think it's a real nice house with only a few dots of mould here and there—that's to be expected in a rain forest—nothing that can't be cleaned and dried out, but then you scrub and you scour until you've worn right through the wall and that's when you see the house is rotten to the core and things were never what they appeared to be."

In a matter of weeks, Miranda and I had grown close, but I didn't know how to respond. If I didn't know better, she sounded jealous. Maybe her own marriage was in trouble, but I didn't know the right way to ask. Miranda didn't talk about Jimmy often. Whatever the reason, she sounded intent on pushing me away all of a sudden. It wasn't only her words but how she spoke them with such resentment that took me aback. There was a tinge of disenchantment, too. As if she were a woman who refused to idealize love, and more than that, as if she were filled with disdain that I would ever dare to. Then, as fast as this more surly version of Miranda appeared, it vanished again.

She counted her points aloud, moving her pegs to the end of the board and pointing it out to me.

"Do you see that there?" she asked cheerfully.

"Yes," I said.

"Double skunk." She smiled. "I beat you real bad."

✻   ✻   ✻

Two slugs, their brassy bottoms shiny as coins, were loaded into the barrels of my shotgun, breached open and angled down from the stock like a broken bone. The VHF radio on the kitchen table was set to the emergency channel. I kept the stereo off—my usual Cole Porter or Oscar Peterson not playing tonight—and I didn't dare turn on the television that evening when it was time for my favourite game show, *Jeopardy!* I'd heard enough stories over the years of how clever a bear could be if it wanted to get inside a house, and one time Chase showed me an Internet video in which a black bear managed to open the doors of a minivan. If the bear from last night returned, I wanted to be alert, though the empty quiet made me feel lonely. Not lonely in that general sense of apartness, which was often moody and curable, but something worse, something bottomless and beyond this night. A cold, naked, endless drifting on a dark and shoreless ocean. It brought death to my mind, as it always did, and I thought of Anne, her last breath at sixty-two, and Frank Charlie, his heart failing at sixty-three, and now Miranda, her mind fading at sixty-five.

In the living room, I tried to busy myself with a new book on seashells I'd ordered in the mail from the library. When that didn't work, I recited one of the poems I'd memorized last year after reading an article about how memorizing poetry could ward off those slips of the aging mind, and I found myself thinking of Miranda again. I paced the living room window and said a line of poetry under my breath, "It was many and many a year ago—" I hadn't slept well last night, and my eyelids were heavy, but I knew I wouldn't be able to sleep. "In a kingdom by the sea—" Out the window, the last slice of sun mounded the horizon and the cove was wrinkled by the gusts of wind that blew through the trees in short bursts. "That a maiden there lived whom you may know—" In the corner of the living room, the greasy window at the front of the wood stove glowed orange and the wood inside crackled, and I tried to remember the next line of the poem as I pulled two more logs from a crate. "By the name of Annabel Lee; and this maiden she lived with no other thought than to love and be loved by me."

Who loved me? I set down the logs. Chase cared about me, I knew that much to be true. But did he love me? And if so, how deeply? Would he hold my hand in a hospice one day, should I ever be so fortunate as to die with the same dignity and comfort as Anne had been given? All I knew for certain was that I never wanted to end up so alone that I lost my mind to delusions of dog children and blubber-carrying birds.

I opened the little door in the wood stove and pushed a log into the fire, spraying orange embers up the stovepipe. In two months, I'd be retired and living in Anne's apartment in Duncan, where I had no friends, only a niece and a nephew and their children I barely knew anything about, except that they liked to make daisy chains and hear make-believe stories and devour poems freshly picked and preserved in jars. "I was a child and she was a child, in this kingdom by the sea—" I wondered: would Anne's grandchildren like to hear this story about Annabel Lee? If I'd told it to Chase as a child, he would never have forgiven me. A girl shut up in a sepulchre by the sea? Its sadness would have sunk him for a month.

"With a love that the winged cherubs—" Cherubs, was that right? No. Guardians, winged guardians? Damn, I hated it when my memory failed me. I went to the bookshelf and searched the spines until I found the right book, fanning the pages to the dog-eared page of Poe's poem. "Seraphs," I whispered. "Of course, of course." And I tapped my temple as though I were nailing a board onto the ramshackle hut of my mind.

I went back to the kitchen, taking with me the VHF radio and the shotgun I'd set on the couch. I sat at the table and read Anne's last letter again. Her words were like warm winds from the past. As we did for everybody who lost a close loved one, the community collected money for me when Anne died, and some of the women gave me a special pen in Anne's honour. "You know," Sophie Florence said, "because she was a writer." It was covered with beautiful beadwork, miniscule beads coloured turquoise and red and white. I got the pen from the window sill and some paper and tried to write a poem to fill the empty jars of the pickled poem pantry, but I hadn't written a poem since my school days and every line came out stilted and dry.

9

Wren Featherstone leaped from the water taxi over a three-foot stretch of icy green water and landed on the wharf next to me with a twirl, her arms stretched out like wings, followed by a curtsey and a wide smile. "Ta-da!" she said, her tight brown curls springing in every direction. "Never fear, I am here!"

I smiled, and guessed the young woman to be about twenty-four years old. I'd never met Wren Featherstone before, had never even spoken to her on the phone. I'd only received a formal email from the health authority announcing that the nursing job in Tawakin had been filled. I stuck out my arm to shake Wren's hand, but she was too busy turning in a circle to notice. Her eyes shifted constantly, moving up to the treetops and then down to the water and then up to a sea gull and then down to the wharf below her feet, as though she were trying to take in everything at once. I stretched my arm out farther and said, "Welcome."

"Oh, honey." Wren stopped moving for a brief moment to wave off my hand. "I was raised by a couple of hippies in the Slocan Valley. Homeschooling, homesteading, homeopathy. Shit, I didn't even wear shoes till I went to university. I don't do handshakes." She wrapped her long thin arms around me and squeezed.

I gasped. My arms were pinned against my ribs, and my hands flapped loosely as Wren swung me from side to side. My upturned chin locked onto Wren's shoulder, and I looked slantwise at George Sam, who'd driven the water taxi and was now lifting a Rubbermaid tote onto the wharf. Breathlessly, I suggested, "Let's help George with your things, shall we?"

"Yes!" Wren pulled away. "Poor Georgie! Doing all the work!"

Georgie? I set the first tote onto an old wood wheelbarrow. Wren crouched at the edge of the wharf, shrieking over a large starfish wrapped around the piling below the water. I smiled and stacked the second tote on top of the first, then waited for George to pull the last of Wren's things out of the cab in the bow.

I asked George, "So how's that ear doing anyway?"

George shifted his feet and turned his head so that the grimy old bandage curling off his earlobe was hidden from my view. "Elizabeth took a look at it this morning. She says it's doing good. Supposably." I tried not to smile when he said it in that way he always did.

"Good, glad to hear it." Then I asked George to bill the outpost for the taxi ride as I lifted the handles of the barrow, turning it around and negotiating the soft wheel over the lip of the ramp. The tide was low, making the ramp steeper than normal, and the totes were heavy and they teetered as I struggled to keep the barrow balanced. The wind pulled wisps of my hair across my face. Halfway up the ramp, I stopped, set the barrow down on its back legs and tugged a thick strand of hair out of my mouth, sweeping the rest from my eyes. I looked down at the wharf, unsure where Wren had got to, but there was only George tossing an untied rope into the hull of his boat.

I waved good-bye to George and steered the barrow along the path rimming the ridge, taking the long way around to avoid the stairs. My nerves about the bear had settled since Frank had found nothing on the island, but I still couldn't help but look around attentively as I walked. Eventually, I set the barrow down at the door and went back to find Wren standing at the top of the wharf ramp. Her eyes were closed, and she seemed to be catching the wind with her large tangled net of brown curls.

"There's a positive energy in this place," she said.

"It's beautiful, yes."

She still had her eyes closed. "It's not just the beauty. There's a vibration, a life force, something unseen but felt. It comes from the people, I bet."

"The people are wonderful," I agreed. "Especially kind. Expect to gain about ten pounds, because they are very generous with food."

"How nice. Only raw vegan for me, though," she said. "No meat, no eggs, no fish—"

"No fish?" I laughed, and looked down at the ocean.

"Fruits and vegetables, mostly. No canned foods, either, and definitely nothing processed."

"Hope you can survive on wilted celery and shrivelled apples then," I said, not bothering to mention how often the *Pacific Sojourn II* failed to reach Tawakin with food supplies in the winter months. Then it was canned soup and jarred salmon for breakfast, lunch, and dinner—unless you were lucky enough to travel to Port Hardy.

Inside the outpost I showed Wren her room, the small bedroom next to mine that once served as a storage area for all the junk I'd collected over the years—books and camping gear, various hobbies left unfinished, old clothes. Wren pulled her tower of totes backwards over the tiles and into her bedroom.

"How about a glass of wine or something?" she suggested. "Wouldn't mind one after that trip. Hell, it was a long way. That logging road is rough."

"I don't keep any alcohol in the outpost," I said.

"None?"

"Didn't you get my email?"

"Which one?"

"The only one I sent."

"Then yes," she said. "I got it."

"I suggested you not bring alcohol."

"Right," Wren said, walking to the window, stretching out into a lanky yawn. "That the reserve over there? Smaller than I thought."

I'd celebrated enough sobriety birthdays with Gina Joe, sober fourteen years, and Sophie Florence, sober twenty-one years, and Margaret

Sam, sober eleven years, to know how much it hurt them whenever alcohol was brought to Tawakin. Even Patty seemed to have a disdain for alcohol now, ever since she also quit drinking years ago. It was the tenth anniversary since Tawakin had created its own bylaw making it illegal to bring alcohol onto the reserve. No doubt the teachers sometimes smuggled it through the reserve on their way up the hill to their homes on government land, but they took certain measures, like buying boxes of wine, which did not clink like bottles and could afterwards be burned in the woodstove rather than put in the community garbage bin. I thought I should share some of these tips with Wren, discreet ways to manage the occasional glass of wine, but not until I got to know her better.

"You do understand about the alcohol, right?"

Wren looked at me. "Of course. Absolutely." Her eyes moved to the photographs on the wall behind me. She went to them, examining them closely.

"Good," I said. "I'll make us some tea. Make yourself at home."

Wren called to me from the living room as I plugged in the kettle. "Who's the elder with the Idle No More sign?"

"That's Nan Lily," I called back.

"I got really involved with the movement myself," she said. "Was there a big protest here?"

"There was a small demonstration, yes. Nobody except ourselves to witness it, mind you."

"Still, it's empowering," Wren said. "Georgie was telling me about the guy who went missing. Did you know him?"

"There are just over a hundred people here. Of course I know him. I know everybody," I called back.

"Georgie said—"

"George," I corrected. "His name is George."

"He said the man's been missing for a week now."

"That's right."

"Not too hopeful, is it? Hard to survive the cold of the ocean for that long."

I took the tea tray out to the living room and poured two steaming cups, then took a seat in the chair next to Wren. A light rain started to fall outside. I then told Wren about the missing rowboat and how skilled Chase was at hunting and fishing and how he knew the land like the back of his hand and how he probably only left to be on his own for a while. As I said all of this, I blew intermittently on my tea while I wondered how to find out what sort of woman sat in my outpost.

"I find it all really fascinating," Wren said.

I stopped cooling my tea. "You find what fascinating?"

Wren pushed aside a tight brown curl hanging in her eye, and I thought how much tighter those curls would get in the endless rain of winter.

"Their faith in visions," she said, pressing her palm against her chest, and tossed her head back with a sigh. "I said to Georgie, 'There's a calm in your eyes, Georgie. Something serene, as if you know in the end everything will be okay, even though your cousin is lost out there somewhere,' and he told me about how the lost man had visited his mother-in-law in her dreams to let everybody know he was okay, and I asked whether everybody believed the dreams were true, that they were real, and he said, yes they did, and I really got that, you know, because I was raised to believe in that sort of thing. I was raised really spiritually."

The VHF radio on the small table buzzed. A static-filled voice asked for me.

I picked up the radio. "Yes?"

"Tell that new nurse there's going to be a lunch on Sunday."

"All right, will do." I put the radio back on the cradle. "You heard? There's a lunch on Sunday for you."

"For me?" Wren smiled.

Nobody had ever stayed at the outpost before, except for Chase when he was young, Anne on a few occasions and Frank when we were together. Nobody I didn't really know. I now felt crowded. I got up and went to the window.

I said, "We start right at nine tomorrow morning. And some nights you'll be on call, so you'll have to be alert and ready to go."

"Of course, of course. So tell me, why have you decided to retire? You don't look all that old. You're what—sixty?"

"Turning sixty-five this year. I'm going to spend time with my grandchildren," I said, smoothing a tattered edge on the arm of my chair and thinking of Anne's letter. Since I hadn't yet given much thought to Anne's request that I step in as grandmother—as a real Wilde Granny—I surprised myself by saying this.

"Good for you. Grandmothers are vital," Wren said. "Who else can make you feel like you so perfectly belong in this world? Your grandmother."

"And what about you?" I asked. "What brings you here?"

"Well, I mentioned being involved with the Idle No More movement, and ever since then I really wanted to work with a First Nations community," she said. "It really inspired me, you know? That chief who fasted, all the flash mobs, the protests. Treaty Rights Not Greedy Whites! Am I right, or am I right? Did you see the big march to Vancouver city hall on TV?"

"No," I said.

"Too bad, you might have seen me. I was there," Wren said, pausing to take a sip of her tea. "I'd love to get involved with the politics here. Help get them their treaty rights, or whatever."

"They already signed their treaty last year," I said, recalling the ceremony up at the school gym when the first independent government was sworn in and everybody followed Ernie Frank and Nan Lily outside where they burned the Indian Act inside a metal barrel. "It gets implemented in phases starting in November."

"Oh." Wren frowned.

"You seem disappointed."

"Well, no," Wren laughed. "I just mean I would have liked to have been a part of it. What do people here think of the TRC?"

"The TRC?"

"Truth and Reconciliation Commission," she said. "The recommendations were just released. Figured it'd be a hot topic here."

Last year, Frank travelled down island to be interviewed about his time in residential school. I sipped my tea and remembered what he had told me about his years there. He said, they gave us these sheets we had to fill out all the time. We had to write down everything we ate, how much, stuff like that. I was eight. I thought we were learning how to print.

Not long after Frank's interviews, it was reported in the news that a researcher had uncovered evidence about these types of biomedical experiments. Experiments in which some children received a dozen vaccinations at once. Experiments in which some children received vitamins and minerals while others did not. Experiments in chronic malnutrition, too. I was always hungry, Frank told me. I ate with one arm wrapped around my plate or else the other boys would steal my food. One time, one of the boys got caught stealing potatoes from the farm beside the school and he got taken into his office. Whose office Frank meant, I didn't need to ask. Harold Slant was convicted almost twenty years ago for thirty-six counts of sexual assault during his time as dormitory supervisor at the Alberni Residential School in the years Frank was a student there. I'd never forget the look of sorrow on Frank's face at the utter disregard for his dignity, for his very life, when he added, "They're saying the experiments were designed by the federal government. A guinea pig, that's all I was."

Nodding, I looked at Wren. "Truth and Reconciliation Commission. Right, of course," I said. "Actually, not a lot of people are talking about it."

Besides Frank, I hadn't heard much about it. I used to think that the people in Tawakin didn't seem too concerned with our country's politics, even when it affected them, and I'd always assumed it was because of our remoteness. Maybe this used to be the case, back before TV and Internet satellite dishes dotted the roofs on the reserve, but in recent years, especially since the start of treaty negotiations, people had become more vocal in their political opinions. Now I wondered why more people weren't talking about the commission.

"Oh, I'll get them talking. It's my specialty," Wren said, her voice full of good cheer.

"You should know," I said, feeling protective, "we've had teachers or band managers come here thinking they're going to somehow save the people here. They'll bring new social programs, or they come to tell the people about their own First Nations history, or they hatch some big entrepreneurial scheme that's going to transform everything. I'm never quite certain how anybody can presume to think that the people here even need saving, or, even if they did, that they'd want help from some stranger, some outsider to do that."

Wren winked. "Point taken. I read you loud and clear. Don't worry, I'm not here to rescue anybody. But if I can be a political ally in any way... " She paused. "Really, I came here because I didn't want to work in a city where my patients are all strangers. I want to get to know the people. Really get to know them."

She sounded genuine, and I was touched by her desire. I said, "That's good. Though really getting to know them takes a very long time. They'll welcome you warmly, and they'll quickly make you feel like you're family, but you have to accept that you'll always be an outsider."

The only way a person became an insider was to stay for forty years, but I left this part out. I didn't expect her to stay more than two, maybe three years tops. Based on the history of teachers in the community, it was a reasonable prediction.

Wren said, "Oh, I don't know. I'm a real 'people' person. It'll take me no time at all to make a good connection here. They won't think of me as an outsider for long."

"Yes, they will," I insisted, my voice firm but friendly. Better she know the reality now rather than feel disappointed later. "That's just the way it is for everybody who comes here. It'll seem like you belong in the community, but ultimately, you're still seen as an outsider. Unless you stay here as long as I have. Then you'll really know them. Then you won't be seen as an outsider."

"When did you know?"

"What do you mean?"

"When did know you weren't still seen as an outsider?" Wren asked. "Like, how did you know for sure?"

It was a question I couldn't answer on the spot.

"We better get ready," I said. "We've got a patient coming."

✻ ✻ ✻

Nan Lily came in for her medical appointment that afternoon an hour late. At ninety-five she was too old to drive herself over in the boat anymore, but she insisted on coming to the outpost rather than receiving a house call. "Need to feel that salt air on my cheeks," she always claimed. One of her great-grandchildren, a young man named Jeremy, dropped her off and said he'd return for her shortly. Nan Lily lowered herself into a chair and closed her eyes halfway, her hands clasped in her lap.

"You the new Bernie?" she asked Wren.

"I suppose I am," Wren said.

Nan Lily turned to me. "Heard you had a visitor. You be careful when he comes back. Don't look at his eyes. Remember Candice Joe? She got blind from looking at one's eyes that time. Out in the vegetable garden at night on Toomista Island. She wanted to see who was stealing their lettuce. And then she saw diamond eyes that glowed real bright and shined in long beams and then she never saw a thing again after that."

I recalled diabetes being the cause of Candice Joe's blindness.

"Nan Lily ," I said, "I'm not sure what you're talking about."

"Your night intruder," she said.

"Intruder?" Wren looked at me.

"You mean the bear," I said to Nan Lily, pushing up her sleeve and wrapping the blood pressure cuff around her arm.

Nan Lily laughed. "Bear? It was no bear."

I pumped the blood pressure monitor.

"What was it?" asked Wren.

"It was Chase." Nan Lily nodded her head of wispy white hair.

"No way!" exclaimed Wren. "The missing guy?"

I stared straight at Nan Lily's clunky black orthopedic shoes. I didn't have a clue what to think. On the one hand, it did surprise me that a bear had finally swum to my island after all these years. But like Sophie Florence said, there had been instances of other animals swimming to islands even farther away than mine. And until the other night, I'd always been careful about storing my food properly, never leaving garbage out or fish guts down on the dock, so maybe a bear simply never had a reason to make the short journey in the past. On the other hand, the idea of it being Chase seemed farfetched to me, and besides that, he would never just mess up my place and take off. I tore the Velcro blood pressure sleeve from Nan Lily's arm.

"I told you he was already here," Nan Lily smiled.

Gently, I pulled down on Nan Lily's earlobe and peered through a lit scope into her ear. "You mean that Chase broke into the outpost?"

Nan Lily made a sound of affirmation.

"Why didn't he just knock?" I asked.

"Or go to his family on the reserve?" Wren added.

"Because he's not quite him anymore," Nan Lily said. "He's a *puukmis* now. Probably confused. Feeling like an outsider, not the man he was before—he's grown a body of hair like a monster to survive the cold of the ocean, eyes that shine like diamonds and glow bright to find the land at night. Worried he won't be welcome."

I remembered only darkness in the kitchen, not bright lights. A sense was rising in me again, the same one I'd had outside, that something was pulling at me, a danger. Once more, my mind filled with the image of Chase wandering alone on a dark shore. I was surprised by the effect it had on me, how strongly it took hold of me, and for a moment I was certain that the dark shore I saw was fringed with the same daffodils as those on my beach below the outpost.

Wren's voice was full of wonder. "Will he always be that way now, a *puukmis*, or will he become himself again?"

"It is not a coat," Nan Lily said. "He can't just take it off."

I asked, "Nan Lily, what's a dog child?"

"A dog child?" She shook her head and touched her hand to her face. "There are all kinds of stories about people who become dogs."

I nodded, slipped the stethoscope under Nan Lily's collar, and we fell silent as I listened to her heart. When I finished, Nan Lily pulled her loose cardigan back up over her bony shoulders.

I said, "Miranda told me a story about her boys being dogs, and then they became boys again."

"Who's Miranda?" Wren asked.

I ignored Wren and waited for Nan Lily to speak.

"We were not allowed to give something to some animals like wolves, cougars," Nan Lily said. "We were not allowed to give them food. A person should only give food to his own dog. Dogs are smart and helpful and they keep evil away, that's what people said. So we are never supposed to kick our dogs, that's the reason. Everybody was kind to their dogs. But then something strange happened. Then there was a man who was mean to his dogs. He kicked them, and nobody knew why. How did one man, out of so many who were kind, become so mean? Nobody knew how this happened. One day, the chief turned into a dog and became the man's dog. After the man kicked his dog every day for many days, he got a funny sense that the dog was a spirit and it made him upset. Four days later, the dog told the man, 'This is not our teaching. Don't hurt your dog. Don't kick it. Feed it. Whatever you eat, you give it to your dog.' Then the chief took off his dog fur, and underneath, his colour was purple. 'Look at how I am now from all your kicking.' And the chief told the other kind people what the mean man did and they could see the chief was purple."

Wren and I exchanged puzzled looks.

Then Nan Lily said, *"Chuu."*

"Klecko," Wren said.

Nan Lily and I turned towards Wren in surprise.

Nan Lily said, *"Klecko, klecko,"* and gave Wren what I thought was a smile of appreciation for knowing something of her language.

✳   ✳   ✳

That evening, while Wren unpacked her things, I sat in the living room and thought of everything Nan Lily had told me. Despite the deep regard I had for Nan Lily, I just couldn't bring myself to believe it was Chase who broke into the outpost, or that he'd turned into a legendary creature.

"What is this anyway?" Wren called.

I followed her voice to the bathroom. The door was open and she stood gazing at the mural, the acrylic rain forest of rich browns and varying shades of green.

"It's quite the dark piece of art, isn't it?" she commented.

"How do you mean?"

"It's like two completely different paintings crashing together. One on top of the other. Like a juxtaposition. Light and darkness. Hope and despair," she said. Then she pointed to the shapes of translucent black, painted with crisp lines, that underscored every object in the painting. "Everything in the picture casts a strange shadow. They go every which way."

"I did paint this with a thirteen-year-old. He might not have been thinking about the science of light," I said, remembering that the shadows were Chase's idea.

"I guess not," she said. "Who are these women?" She pointed at the little old ladies, some with silver hair, some with blue hair, hiding high in the treetops.

"Those are the Wilde Grannies of Pothenroth," I said, feeling a little shy as Wren raised her eyebrows. "An ancient tribe. They're just some silly stories we used to make up when I was a child."

Wren nodded. "Personal mythology. Love it."

We stared at the painting for a little while longer in silence. A patch of blue sky and greyish-green ocean coloured the spaces between the broadly stroked cedars and hemlocks. White lines crested the waves. A pale yellow sun radiated in long spokes. Far below the Wilde Grannies, black snakes slithered in the tall blades of grass. Through the tangles of forest two small figures sat together on the distant shore, a nurse and the boy she loved like a son.

"And who are these two?" Wren asked.

"Just a couple of friends enjoying the ocean," I said.

"Are these cedar trees? I love cedar trees," she said. "Think I'll get a chance to learn some cedar crafts?"

"Sure, I can arrange that," I said. "We'll go cedar pulling with the women."

Wren looked pleased.

I told her about the first time I pulled cedar. Sophie Florence and Gina and I paddled a canoe over to Toomista Island, where Miranda lived with Jimmy and her boys. Ten families lived on Toomista back in the 1970s. Like Tawakin, it was a First Nations reserve, though much smaller. Traditionally, the island served as a summer residence for the people; in the winter, the houses were battered by the ocean winds and rain. Nobody lived there now, not since the water well could no longer support the growing number of residents, but the abandoned houses still stood there. They reminded me of large grey skulls, with eyes of broken glass.

How thrilled I was to have been invited, I explained to Wren. In my first year here, I wasn't sure if the people would include me, as a white person, in their traditional activities, or if there were some unspoken rules prohibiting that. You could say there was a lot I didn't know back then. As an outsider, I was scared of making a mistake, a misstep, perhaps insulting them somehow, and while Frank was a help, I could see how central the women were in the village—how they made many of the decisions on the band council, how they ran the community events, how they chopped wood and skinned fish with incredible skill and strength and stamina. I admired them greatly, I told Wren. They were my Greer, my Steinem, my Friedan.

"Your who?" she asked.

"My role models," I said. "The women in the village had the stuff to survive life at the edge of the world, and I was eager to learn."

After Wren left to unpack the rest of her things, I continued to dwell on that day. Miranda had met us down on the beach, where we hauled the canoe up over the tideline, her husband, Jimmy, waving at us from the front steps of their house. He was a small but wiry man, handsome like his brother, Frank, and here was the thing about Jimmy: he appeared to be the friendliest person in a community of friendly people. To see Jimmy at the Tawakin Market or beachcombing along one of the shores made you feel as if you were bringing water to the middle of the desert. The ecstatic manner in which he greeted you—with an explosive smile and exclamation of your name as he gave your shoulder a squeeze—left you floating inside an orb of kinship. If he'd seemed aware of this effect, I might have warily considered it all a show. But he didn't seem to be aware, and his genuineness was often highlighted by a childlike and self-deprecating sense of humour. Also, he was generous with his time and ready to help anybody in a heartbeat. This part I knew because I often spotted him across the cove helping people run supplies up the Tawakin dock, and several times, he appeared at the outpost with a bag of fresh prawns for me. "You must be real smart to know about all this stuff, Bernie," he'd say, smiling as he looked around the examination room. "Smarter than me, that's for sure."

Except for the grass field where the houses stood and the rim of the rocky beach, Toomista Island was covered by a thick forest. Single file we entered this forest, bending branches out of our way and climbing over the ancient trees that lay covered in moss on the ground. Even though the day was bright, the cloud layer a light gauze across the sky, it was so dark under the canopy of cedars and hemlocks that it was like stepping into another world altogether. Once I was inside, the forest mesmerized my vision with a collage of layers upon layers of wood, moss and foliage, infinite shades of green, all of it bisected here and there by beams of silver, spore-filled light.

After about five minutes of trekking in silence, we stopped next to a cedar. Sophie Florence swung a hatchet into its trunk three times, making an angular U shape. She then pulled on the scored section, popping off a piece of the outer bark, and peeled away a few inches of the softer layer underneath.

"This one is yours," she told me.

"What do I do?" I asked.

Miranda smiled. "We're pulling cedar. You pull."

I took hold of the small tab of inner bark that Sophie Florence had started for me and pulled on it. With some effort, I managed to pull it off the trunk until the narrow strip was a couple of feet above my head. I heard a soft, high-pitched sound, like a whining dog. Then it stopped. Behind me the women chuckled, and when I turned to look at them, they straightened their smiles and pretended to be serious.

"Doesn't this hurt the tree?" I asked. Underneath the soft fibrous layer in my hands was the glossy, smooth bone of the tree.

All three of them shook their heads, little spurts of laughter escaping

The Heaviness of Things That Float

their throats. I didn't know what was so funny until I started to pull again and I could hear them adding little moans of agony to their whining.

"Ha ha. Very funny," I said.

As the strip grew longer, I found myself stepping backwards to get the leverage I needed to force the cedar from the trunk. Once the strip reached a certain height, however, I struggled to pull any further. All three women gathered around me, intertwining their arms around mine as they took hold of the cedar with me.

"Pull!" Sophie Florence said.

We took a step backwards, bumping into one another.

"Pull!"

We took another step backwards, and another, and another. Then Miranda let out a shriek of surprise as we tripped over a small snag hidden in the ferns. Tumbling onto our backs, all four of us, we lay on the ground in a heap of tangled limbs. Gina and Sophie Florence and Miranda erupted into fits of laughter, shrieking and whooping and wiping tears from their eyes, and then I started laughing, too. We stared straight up at the spokes of branches above our heads, our bodies lurching against one another in laughter. Sophie Florence's long black hair spilled across my face, while my leg was hooked over Gina's knee, my head resting on Miranda's wrist. The strip of cedar, which had come off the tree, was draped like a giant ribbon over us.

In the first moment of complete silence after our laughter finally died down, Sophie Florence blurted, "Real nutty!" and we all burst into laughter once again, loud and uncontrollable and twice as long as the first time, with the reckless abandon of children, and I thought in that moment that I'd never felt such joyous camaraderie since I was a young girl.

Miranda sat up so that her back was to us, her T-shirt twisted up above her belly and covered in bits of bark and fern fronds. In the swath of exposed bare skin, I spotted a large red welt in the shape of a curved triangle. Running down along two sides of the triangle was a single row of small circles. Miranda tugged her shirt down as she climbed to her feet.

As we pulled more strips of cedar from the trees that afternoon, a memory rose unbidden in my mind. When I was young, my mother would occasionally take my sister and me to the parliament buildings. My mother was a kind and curious woman who loved history, but there was one thing she never allowed us to see inside the rotunda of the parliament. It was a painting, a mural entitled *Labour*, which adorned the ceiling. She'd give us a dire warning: "Don't look skyward, girls."

But I couldn't stand not knowing what was up there, and so once, when I was ten, I left my mother and sister in the Legislative Library and took a roundabout way to the washroom through the rotunda. The mural depicted five bare-breasted women, and at the time, I assumed that this was the scandalous reason we were not to look. But later, I realized there was something more to my mother's censorship. The bare-breasted women were First Nations, and while they hauled timber and baskets of fish, two white men stood and watched them.

The memory of that mural nagged at me that day on Toomista. As I worked alongside the women, separating the patches of rough bark from the soft, fibrous layer, I started to see Sophie Florence and Gina and Miranda in that mural, and I felt embarrassed, unable to reconcile my close bonds here with my ties to a world that painted my neighbours as nothing more than labour, naked and degraded. Almost a decade ago, Anne mailed me a newspaper clipping, an article in the *Times Colonist* about how the mural was being taken down because of its negative portrayal of First Nations women. In reading it, I was surprised at how much weight lifted off me. "Doesn't surprise me," Anne said during one of our weekly phone calls. "It was unsettling. Apparently, some American visitors said it reminded them of the slave paintings that had been removed from their institutions down South."

We coiled the cedar strips, which would later be used to make baskets and hats and little roses for special occasions, and tied them with a thin piece of cedar around the middle into sweet-smelling loops of infinity. Afterwards, we scattered along the shore, each of us picking a spot several feet away from the others, and sifted quietly through the deep mixture of tiny shells, searching for dentalia. From where I sat, I could see Miranda taking fistfuls of desiccated shards. As I watched the tiny bits of beach pour out between her fingers—the anemone spikes, the crinkled blades of seaweed, the broken shells—I wondered about the mark on her back. Maybe it wasn't an injury at all but a birthmark. A large birthmark possessing an unusual pattern of dots. You never knew. There were people who had birthmarks shaped like crucifixes and hearts and faces. I wanted the mark to be something like this, something benign, but I struggled, knowing it might not be.

Pushing around the sand and shells, I picked up a piece of white coral shaped roughly like a B. Maybe she bumped up against her wood stove. That seemed a real possibility. Wood stoves have grates that might have made the pattern I saw, though I knew it wasn't likely. The pattern of tiny circles were so distinctively from an iron, but I didn't want to imagine how it got there on her back. I put the coral in my pocket. I then spotted a strange shell and turned it over in my palm. It wasn't a shell at all but a piece of a bone. Part of vertebra, from a seal or otter. I tossed it and climbed to my feet.

"I saw your back," I said, sitting next to Miranda. "If you come to the outpost, I can put something soothing on it. Make sure it heals properly."

"It ain't nothing," she snapped.

The way she spoke made me realize, with a sinking feeling, what I had known in my heart to be true. "If it ain't nothing," I said, changing tact, "that means it's something."

She flapped her hand at me. "It was just a stupid accident."

I kept my eyes on the sand as I struggled with this idea.

"You got accidentally burned with an iron?" I asked, not sure I wanted to hear the answer.

Miranda stayed silent for several moments. Then she motioned at the others and said in a low, serious tone, "Don't tell them. They'll tell the elders. Everybody will vote to kick him out."

"Kick him out of what?"

"Out of here," she said impatiently. "They'll send him away. Men who are mean to their wives get sent into the rain forest and they grow bark for skin. It happened to my grandmother's cousin."

"Maybe if he's mean to you he should be sent away," I said, struggling to connect the friendly—no, the positively charismatic—man who brought me prawns with the marks on Miranda's back. I looked more closely at her now, noticing the small mark on the top of her cheekbone, the little one shaped like a scallop shell, with different eyes. "Is that from him, too?"

"Don't you dare tell nobody," Miranda said sharply. "I'll never forgive you. He's good to the boys, and it ain't none of your business."

"If I ever find out he's not good to the boys, I'm not only telling the others, but I'm calling the police."

Miranda laughed and rolled her eyes. "You think the police care what a bunch of Indians do to each other in their house?"

*   *   *

Now, sitting here in my living room, I thought about the chief who disguised himself as a dog to expose how mean one of the men was being to his dogs, and about the purple bruises all over the chief's body. But he was a man, and Miranda's story was about dog children.

After that day of cedar pulling, I kept a close eye on Stan and Ronnie. I never spotted any signs of abuse on their bodies, and I started to concede to myself that it was just excessive worry, there was no abuse of the boys, and eventually my suspicion waned over the years. As for Miranda, she slowly confided in me more and more over the next few years, confessing Jimmy's abuses—the verbal attacks, the small shoves against the kitchen counter—and since I never again saw anything as terrible as that burn mark, I came to believe Miranda when she insisted it was the worst thing he'd ever done, and that he'd never done anything like it ever again. Not to her, and not to the boys.

"What the hell is that doing there?" Wren walked back into the living room and pointed at the shotgun, still bent open on the coffee table from the night before. "A gun? And oh my God, it's loaded. I'm telling you right now, I won't be able to sleep with that thing in the house. Not loaded, at least."

I slid the two slugs out of the gun and put them in my sweater pocket. "There you go." I smiled. "Problem solved."

"Why do you even need it now? You heard Nan Lily. It's not a bear. It's Chase Charlie."

I shook my head. "No, it's not."

"But Nan Lily told us it's him, and she probably has more wisdom about this world than you and I put together."

"That's true," I said. "But I know Chase really well. We are very close. Very close, and I just know he'd never break into my place and wreck things. Even if he's become something else."

"A *puukmis*," Wren clarified. Turning, she headed back towards her bedroom. She sang out cheerfully, "There's truth in mythology!"

I smiled. As an outsider, her instant belief seemed over the top. But I'd take her reverence for the culture over disdain any day. It was only her first day here and already Wren showed passion for the people. She'd come for good, healthy reasons, it seemed. Maybe even commendable reasons. In comparison, my reason for coming to Tawakin was dull, insofar as it was about nothing but myself and my desire to achieve a sense of independence and self-determination. Hearing Wren's enthusiasm for politics made me wish I'd come with the same sense of advocacy. And she showed respect for me, too. Which was exactly what I wanted.

10

An RCMP boat pulled up in front of the outpost. A police officer jumped out and tied the boat to my wharf, the light morning rain stippling the cove. He was alone. I'd never seen him before, but that didn't surprise me. Rookie officers were constantly being transferred turnstile-like to these sort of remote postings, usually assigned to visit Tawakin from the dispatchment in Port Hardy.

"The police?" Wren asked, cup of coffee in her hands. We stood at the living room window and watched the young man. "I don't care much for cops. They caused us a lot of trouble at our protests. Do they come often?"

"Not often, no," I said.

In the aftermath of serious domestic disputes, accidents and deaths, I'd been interviewed by the RCMP several times, but I couldn't even guess what this might be about. I knew it wasn't anything to do with Chase, since I would have heard something long before the officer reached Tawakin. The only thing I could figure is that somebody called the authorities about my intruder. News travelled fast. The officer wasn't going to be pleased to discover that he'd made the long trip on account of wildlife, especially when nobody got hurt and the bear was gone.

"You the nurse?" he asked when I opened the back door.

"What's this about?" I asked.

Behind me, Wren leaned in the doorway between the kitchen and the living room.

"Bernadette..." He riffled through the pages of a small notepad. "Perkal?"

"Yes, that's me."

"Constable Diller," he said. "I've been sent to investigate a matter in which you've been named."

"Well, then," I said. "You better come in for tea."

In the kitchen I put on the kettle, and while the officer sat waiting at the table, I took my time retrieving cups from the cupboard and dropping sugar cubes into a small bowl one at a time.

"Earl Grey okay?" I held up the box.

Constable Diller nodded, setting his hat on the table.

"My apologies for the cup, but several things were broken the other night when the bear broke into the outpost," I said, setting two chipped cups down. "Scared me half to death. Never had a bear come across the channel before. George figures it must have been hungry to swim like that—"

"A bear? Here in the house?"

Wren shook her head. "It wasn't a bear. It was Chase Charlie."

Falling back against his chair, Constable Diller looked back and forth between Wren and me. "Chase Charlie broke into your house?"

"It wasn't Chase," I said. "It was a bear. Woke me from my sleep in the middle of the night. The second I came into the kitchen with my shotgun, I heard it run out the door."

"Heard it? You didn't see it?" Constable Diller asked.

"Well, no. It was pitch black."

"Did you discharge the weapon?" he asked.

I didn't like how official his question sounded. Perhaps I shouldn't have mentioned the shotgun. I didn't have a gun licence.

"Didn't have to," I said.

He looked at Wren. "Did you hear it too?"

"I wasn't here," said Wren.

"Then what makes you think it was Chase?" he asked her.

"One of the elders told me."

"Who?"

"Nan Lily."

He wrote this down in his little notebook, then raked his fingers through his hair, the short spikes stiff and glistening with hair gel. His head reminded me of the sea urchins that the Tawakin people ate raw, cracking them open with screwdrivers and sucking the orange roe from the bottom. The first time I tried one, I drank all the briny insides by mistake and threw up over the end of the dock in front of Frank, who couldn't stop laughing about it for the rest of the day.

In the back of the cupboard I found a box of stale chocolates. It would look tacky that half of them were gone from their slots in the box, so I arranged them on a plate and set them on the table.

"Well," he said, looking at his notebook, "I don't know what to make of this now, but—" He paused and flipped through the pages. He looked up at me. "Ma'am—"

"Bernadette."

"Bernadette, I'm here to investigate a formal complaint lodged against you regarding your actions on the sixteenth of September."

I viewed his notepad with alarm, not quite understanding what he was telling me. I looked at Wren, and her eyebrows lifted high. I blurted, "My actions? I—"

"On the sixteenth of September, you treated a head wound suffered by Chase Charlie, correct?"

"Yes," I said.

The kettle whistled full steam. I yanked the cord from the wall and poured hot water into the pot with a tea bag. "I'm sorry," I said, putting the bowl of sugar on the table. "I've got no milk. Refrigerator is broken."

"A complaint has been filed on behalf of Chase Charlie by his wife," he said, consulting his notepad. "It's not clear yet whether any charges will be pressed, so for now—"

My breath caught. "Charges pressed!" I sat down.

"Nothing will be done unless we see sufficient evidence for Mrs.

Charlie's claim that there was gross negligence in your treatment of Chase Charlie's head wound, and even if that was the case, nothing will be determined until Chase Charlie is located. I've heard from the coast guard that his trawler has been found and that he's believed to be alive, so hopefully this matter will be resolved quickly."

My hands quivered on the table. Believed to be alive. Although I'd been believing it all along, it was an added comfort to hear it reinforced by the authorities. But then, as his other words sunk in, I grew humiliated. Gross negligence?

"I don't understand," said Wren, giving me a sympathetic look as she spoke to the constable. "Even if there is anything to this, which I'm sure there isn't, why are the police involved? Is this a crime?"

"We had a complaint," he explained, his tone casual, as if the whole thing was routine. "I'm here to follow up on it, that's all. It's only a preliminary inquiry, fact-finding. I wouldn't worry at this point."

I fumbled on my words. "What exactly did Patty tell you?"

The officer didn't answer this. Instead he dropped a sugar cube into his tea, stirred it, then clinked the spoon against the side of the cup. "So what was your assessment of his head wound?" he asked, poising his pencil.

I spoke with measured indignation: "Chase Charlie said he cut his head on the kitchen counter in his house. He said he tripped. It wasn't a bad cut. Just a couple of butterfly bandages. I tested him thoroughly for a concussion and found no signs. I told him to go home and rest."

As I watched him scribble something down, I felt a weight inside me, as if a sack of something heavy and wet was spoiling in my stomach. Investigation? I couldn't fathom it. Investigations, at least the ones I'd seen on the news, happened to bad people, selfish people, careless people. Not to me. I'd done nothing wrong. I was the one being wronged. Loretta—because surely she was the one who put Patty up to this—had gone too far this time.

"Did you report all this in his medical record?" he asked.

"Of course."

"Well, if it comes to it, I'll come back with a warrant to take a look at those records." He drummed his notebook with his pencil. "I'll be in contact in another couple of weeks, sooner if Chase is found. I'm still not sure what to make of this whole bear business, but I'll talk to Nan Lily. Either way, I'm sure all this will be cleared up when I have a chance to talk to the patient himself."

He straightened his hat on his head and put his notebook in his pocket, then thanked us and left.

"Do you get many complaints?" Wren asked, her tone still sympathetic.

I thought I might cry. "I've never had a complaint in forty years." I cleared my throat and buttoned my cardigan.

Wren nodded.

Later that morning, I went to my office, closed the door for privacy and pulled Chase's file one more time. Doubt was a menacing creature that crawled around my mind and wreaked havoc on my memory. Once again I couldn't remember—not with complete certainty—which signs of a concussion I'd checked. Had I assessed his pupils? Of course I had. Had I asked about symptoms? Of course I had. At least, I thought I had. Was he nauseated at all? I couldn't recall now. I opened the file, his birth record on the top, and my eyes moved to the top of the page.

Mother: *Miranda Charlie.*

Father: ~~*Jimmy Charlie.*~~ *Frank Charlie.*

I could practically hear Frank shouting that night.

"Oh God, what's wrong with it? What's wrong? What is that? Is it dead? My child! Oh God, my child!" He'd been standing silently in the corner but started to cry out at the strange sight of Chase, slightly premature and inside the amniotic sac.

I turned in disbelief at this sudden confession, but the stark look on Frank's face, his eyes wide with terror, told me beyond a doubt he was the father, not Jimmy. As the pain of his words struck me to the bone, I grasped the edge of the bed like I'd been struck in the back by a heavy stone, my spine curved in anguish, a pair of scissors in my hand, and when I saw the baby's head of black hair through the translucent membrane, with his little fingers and toes suspended in fluid, I despised his existence even more for his rarity. An en caul baby was maybe one in eighty thousand. A small miracle. He continued to receive oxygen through the umbilical cord.

I feared not caring for his wondrous existence, I feared losing my grip on reality, I feared the bite of grief sinking its teeth into my flesh, I feared the depths of truth lying under the surface of this moment, I feared losing my friends, losing my future, my pride and every ounce of my happiness, and I also feared for the price Miranda would pay if Jimmy ever found out the baby was not his. But more than anything, I feared for the bitterness I could feel leeching inside me, spoiling me, turning all my love to hate.

And who would fault me for this bitterness? Frank and I had been together for seven years. Seven years. I loved Frank with all my heart, and I had been shocked that night by a betrayal double edged. Frank *and* Miranda, my best friend. It had taken every ounce of my strength to stay the course the night of Chase's birth, to follow my sense of duty, to uphold my moral obligation of care as my heart fractured along every one of its chambers.

But oh, how I resented that baby. Or rather, I wanted to—and I did for that one moment at his birth—but somehow I never could again. Those moments when his face reminded me so much of Frank would trigger an unexpected spasm of grief. A moment. That was all it ever lasted. Mostly, I was drawn to the child, probably for the same reason he occasionally caused me grief, and from the start, I'd found it difficult not to search his face for features that'd help me pretend he was mine. I wasn't crazy. I knew very well he wasn't mine. But I was lonely, and overspilling with grief and a sense of scarcity that my door had closed; I would never have a child of my own. And then, as the years passed, a funny thing happened: I didn't want a child of my own anymore. I only wanted Chase.

I first realized this one night when he was seven. This was back when I used to go regularly to the community dance practices in the school gym on Monday nights. There'd be the usual half-dozen teenagers, another dozen younger children, plus five or so men and five or so women. In the corner of the gym, the men sat on chairs in a circle clutching the sinew knots on the backs of their large drums. With round-tipped mallets, they pounded the rawhide, which was brightly painted with eagles and killer whales, and they sang in harmony, their voices undulating between a low, haunting hum and a loud, booming call. Frank used to drum, too, but around that time he'd started working with a heli-logging operation just outside of Holberg, and he really wasn't around Tawakin much for about six years. By this point, Chase knew that Frank was really his father. Not from Miranda, who, as far as I could tell, didn't have much to do with Frank anymore. But one day, when he was six, Chase went fishing with Frank.

"Uncle is my dad," he told me shortly after.

"What do you think about that?" I asked.

Chase shrugged. "He's going to teach me to hunt *muwach*."

"That's good," I said.

While the men drummed and sang, all the women, including me, practised our dances and taught the children. As a break, the men would surprise everybody by drumming the bird dance. At the sound of the song's beat, the children would squeal with delight and rush to the centre of the gym. It was a fun dance in which one of the women played the role of the mother bird, who, because of a nearby predator, had to bring the little birds back to the nest one by one.

One night, when it was my turn to be the mother bird, Miranda appeared through the gym doorway. Sophie Florence called her over to join our practice but she shook her head, said she wasn't feeling well and only came to watch. Ever since Jimmy's death, Miranda didn't participate as much in community activities, which I thought was strange, since, if anything, I thought her husband's absence would have given her a newfound freedom.

The drums beat. The children danced all around me, the wax on the wood floor worn away in patches, the black lines of basketball and badminton courts muted. Our circle of sky. The little birds bounced low to the ground with their knees bent deeply, until the men started to beat faster. A predator! Quickly, children! I danced around them in silence, stretching out my wings to scoop them along and into the imaginary nest, taking one child at a time. I returned to the sky to rescue more, but the children did not want to come in from playing, even with the danger of a cougar looming, and so I had to fly around and bring them back home safely.

I always left Chase for last. It was uncanny how much his movements resembled a bird's—many of the elders said he was the best dancer they'd seen in decades. The beat slowed down again as the imminent danger of the predator subsided, and Chase pretended to perch on a treetop, lifting his head rhythmically to the pulse of the drums, his arms spread out wide. The predator returned—*boom, boom, boom, boom, boom, boom*—and Chase lit from the branches and flew in circles with me in pursuit. We danced in swirling arcs around one another, turning and crouching and flapping and brushing our wings as we passed, and I glanced at Miranda, how she watched us, and I grew dizzy as I circled and circled around my baby bird. I felt the drumbeat deep in my chest and in my feet and in my wings, and it brought out something hidden in me, something unused, a desire I'd never felt keenly before, a drive, maternal and undeniable, and I saw in that moment that the sweet boy could have been mine, that the sweet boy should have been mine, and the gym floor opened up underneath us and became the sky, the whole world rendered small and faraway below us as my heart swelled with what felt like love. My eyes filled with tears. Swooping rapidly towards Chase, I tucked him under my wing and led him back to my nest.

He smiled at me. "The cougar almost got me, Nursema'am!"

Nursema'am.

Nursemom.

Mom.

In the corner, the gym door closed. Miranda was gone.

Time did heal. The world spun, sometimes too quickly, and sometimes out of control, but every now and then, it mercifully stopped and gave you time to see everything from a new perspective. A bird's-eye view. Things that once loomed large became smaller. The lines around what once appeared sharp and clear—cruelly so—became blurred. There was a sweetness in what used to taste bitter. I knew more than I'd ever known, thanks to that new view, and I thought: this is what wisdom is, this bright strip of blue sky I see after a long and battering storm, when all living things appear worn and heavy and waterlogged, when the wind finally settles and the last residue of rain rolls down the leaves and patters lightly upon the earth, and all the birds take flight over the fresh new world.

✻   ✻   ✻

I slurped a late dinner of tomato soup with crushed saltines. Outside, it was growing dark and a strong wind clinked the rows of seashell chimes hanging under the eaves, tilting from their fishing lines like ghosts in tattered white sheets.

I got up from the table, checked the dead bolt, sat back down at the table and took a small sip of cold tea. Wren had turned in early, but I wouldn't be able to rest anytime soon. I couldn't silence the words in my mind. Investigation. Negligence. Charges. I didn't care if there was nothing to it, if it was only a routine follow-up to a baseless complaint. I felt as though a black mark had been drawn across my name, my forty years of loyal service tarnished. Over and over, I played back the meeting with Constable Diller, and each time I imagined his voice sounding more disgusted with me, his gaze more disregarding of me; I reinterpreted his every word and every move, from how he tapped his teaspoon exactly three times to how he straightened his hat from front to back, as signs of his obvious suspicion that I was the type of nurse who, because I was posted at an edge of the world that nobody paid attention to, was unskilled and negligent.

What was wrong with me, for heaven's sake? So negative and paranoid. Normally, I prided myself on an ability to see things plainly, to react calmly, to reserve my judgements until after I'd gathered all necessary information, assessed all factors, diagnosed all symptoms. It was the way of any good nurse. Especially one who had depended largely on her own devices.

In the living room, the VHF radio buzzed with static. Somebody reported finding some empty cans and the remains of a beach fire at the north end of Ootanish Inlet near where Chase's trawler was found. Other voices came on with questions.

"Was the fire still warm, or nah?"

"Nah."

A feeling of joy and relief washed over me. Chase, I thought.

Somebody asked, "What sort of cans?"

"SpaghettiOs and Alphagettis."

"Did he spell out something?"

"What?"

"With the Alphagettis." It was Patty. "Did he spell out a message?"

"I don't think so."

"Did you even look?" she asked.

"Yeah." There was a long pause. "I think he ate it all up."

Patty sighed loudly on the radio. "Oprah always says that if you can't spell for help, then you don't really want it."

I rolled my eyes and wondered if there was an all-Oprah, all-day channel.

A resolve grew inside me. I was proud of the work I'd done all these years. It was all I had. I knew the accusation was false. Chase knew the accusation was false. It was nothing but a rumour, an evil one. I was not going to end my time in Tawakin by being part of a story that Loretta Charlie picked for me. I would confront her tomorrow. I would. I had never confronted her before, but I would. Tomorrow.

The thought of confronting Loretta both scared and exhilarated me. It was like a burning that radiated out my chest and down my arms. Why hadn't I confronted her in the past? I should have. She'd talked behind my back before. Many times. Just last year, when I misdiagnosed Olivia's broken collar bone, she went around asking everybody, "Did we ever check that she even has a licence to be a nurse?"

As far as I could remember, Loretta had always been bitter and calculating. At one point or another, she'd made hurtful comments about every person in Tawakin.

I asked both Frank and Sophie Florence: "How come she's so different than everybody else here?"

Frank said: "Because her family was not from Tawakin. They came from up island. After her father died, her mother married Ernie Frank's brother. All the time, her people used to fight with our people. Long before I was born. Big canoe wars over the land. Places like Cougar Point. Sometimes there was kidnapping. Killing. Our peoples hated each other. She feels like an outsider."

Sophie Florence said: "She spent a lot of time in Harold Slant's office at the residential school."

If there was one flaw in how the community handled things it was this: they were too quick to pretend that everything was fine. Too willing to act as though things that happened never actually happened. Too inclined to never mention what was right in front of one's nose. Like Hannah's fetal alcohol syndrome. "That family don't ever listen to the truth anyway." Sophie Florence shrugged. Or like Margaret putting Teresa's photograph on her wall after Teresa slept with Margaret's husband. "What's the point in staying mad?" Margaret said. "She'll never apologize for real."

As the nurse, I could pull no punches, of course. The examination room was a place of truth and consequences. But out in the community, I had followed along with the local ways from the start. It was my desire to fit in, I suppose. If ignoring certain pieces of the past was how the community coped with living so close together, who was I to question it?

Yet people did not always look the other way. Plenty of times, they faced the truth. They apologized. They forgave. The no-alcohol bylaw, for instance. That was debated for months with raw honesty before the band council passed it. And there were many individual cases. When Thomas Joe was caught stealing gasoline from the dock, he had to host a dinner in the community centre and apologize publicly to everybody he harmed. When Fiona Charlie got mad that her teacher was leaving Tawakin and broke her teacher's house windows, the elders held a talking circle with Fiona and all the teachers so that everybody could state their feelings.

And then of course there was the time Sophie Florence and I tried to confront Patty about her drinking, though nothing came of that, and there was the time after that, too, the one and only time I talked to Patty about Hannah.

Patty had come to pick up cough medicine. September that year had been one of the worst for bronchial infections on the reserve.

"So Hannah's started school," I'd said. "Kindergarten. That's exciting."

"Yes," Patty said.

"Was she excited?" I asked.

"Real excited," she said, her face brightening. "We went to town and bought new shoes and a blue backpack. She said it had to be blue. Pretty cute, huh?"

"Yes," I said, laughing. "And her daddy's off to college, too. That's neat, isn't it? They've both started school at the same time."

Patty shrugged.

"I bet you're proud of Chase," I said, thinking of how proud I was of him to be getting a college degree.

"Mother says he should be here at home with us," she said.

I nodded and smiled at the thought of Chase's dream to become a teacher. "It is a sacrifice, that's true. But in the long run it will be great for all of you. It'll be great for the community, too, to have a teacher up at the school from here. What a great role model he'll be for the children."

Patty shrugged again.

"With Hannah starting school," I said, "it would be the perfect time to maybe take her to the doctor the next time you go to town."

Patty looked at the cough medicine in her hand.

"If you get her diagnosed by a doctor," I continued, "then the teachers will be able to get funding from the school board to help her. They'll be able to put her on her own special education plan. It will be so good for her."

Patty said, "Thanks for the medicine."

Then she turned and left.

I'd sat on a chair in the waiting room afterwards. A feeling of accomplishment flooded my head, and, after a few minutes, I started to feel relief for having said what I hadn't before. I patted my knees as if congratulating myself. I wouldn't be reticent to discuss Hannah's condition ever again. Not to Patty, not to anybody. Although at that moment I'd felt bold, honest, empowered, I knew that I was a long way from convincing Patty to see a doctor, that there was Loretta blocking the path—a path on which, if I persevered, Patty would do something important for Hannah—and that part of convincing meant getting over my fear of confronting Loretta, who could make everybody feel wrong, unworthy and ashamed with one of her glares and a few sharp words.

The following week, Loretta sent a rack of chip bags crashing to the floor of the Tawakin Market. There was a *bang!* of metal on the ground and a *pop! pop! pop!* as several bags burst like balloons under the metal bars. Chip bags and loose chips flew everywhere, some skidding across the floor, some hitting the legs of the people gathered between the post office wicket and the store counter.

I watched from the meat freezers at the back of the market. Looking up the short aisle, I could only see a narrow slice of what was happening, but I could hear George Sam's voice loud and clear.

"Ay-ha, Loretta!" he cried out.

From where I stood, Margaret swivelled her head from the overturned rack to the store counter, where George must have been standing. Her brow looked worried, as though she spotted an unexpected windstorm rolling swiftly across the sky and hadn't yet tied down her favourite things.

George accused Loretta, "You did that on purpose."

Gina crouched down to pick up a couple of the bags.

"You don't touch them!" Loretta snapped.

Gina dropped the bags like they were on fire.

"Well, somebody's going to pick those up," George said.

"Not me," Loretta said.

"Why not? It's your fault, ain't it?" George asked.

Quietly, I made my way up the aisle, peeked around the shelves of shampoo and soap. There were about twelve people standing in the front of the market, each one of them standing statuesque and silent as they waited for Loretta to reply. Judging from the tension in the air, I wasn't the only one who sensed something more than a toppled chip rack was going on here.

"It is not my fault," Loretta scoffed. "You know I always squeeze in this way to get my baking goods, my vanilla, my yeast, my sugar, and you don't ever fix nothing in this store. This rack is all rickety, plus you don't keep it pushed over far enough."

George crumpled a small paper into a tight ball.

"You owe me for those busted chips," he said.

Loretta smiled. "You owe some things, too. Don't you, George? What might those things be? Hmm." She tapped her teeth with her finger. "Perhaps there are a couple of children out in town we could ask?"

George's face turned deep scarlet. His head shook until a sound of frustration erupted out of his mouth. Abruptly, he turned and went into the storage area behind him, blurting out, "All right, all right, I'll clean it up!" He returned with a broom and a dustpan and started to sweep up the loose chips while everybody remained fixed to their spots.

Loretta stood over him and said, "Can you believe this? Something ends up broken on account of people not doing their job right and what do they do? They try to blame others. They ask other people to clean up their mess for them." Then she looked straight at me and asked sharply, "Don't you find that?"

In my shock, I said nothing. But later that day, I tried to contemplate the meaning of this. It wasn't easy. Loretta was the grand master of these sort of indirect, ambiguous messages that insinuated just enough to keep you off balance yet never offered quite enough for you to grasp anything for certain. Was she capable of carrying out that whole chip rack fiasco just to make a point to me about Hannah? Was she actually blaming me for Hannah's condition? Was she suggesting that I was trying to get Patty to take Hannah to a doctor in order to clean up after my "mess"?

As my mind began to come apart with outrage, I sought to keep it together by going to the reserve to visit patients the next day, to reach out and reaffirm that everybody else was still friendly to me, to outfit them with smart medical advice that might counter any complaints Loretta might make about me. She could do that to a person, turn them paranoid. I asked people if they had any questions for me about their health, when what I really wanted to do was set the record straight.

"I know there are ways of doing things here," was what I wanted to say to everybody. "I know there are ways of talking about things, and not talking about things. I know there is a delicate balance that is to be maintained. But I thought the timing was right, you see. I thought maybe Patty would realize how reasonable it was to address Hannah's condition now that she was starting school. On top of that, I believed Chase would return from college with new ideas about Hannah, with a new understanding of her condition and the resources available out there in the world, so I figured it was only a matter of time before the subject was raised anyway, and maybe I could help things along by planting the seed in Patty's mind. And yes, I know that this is Loretta's granddaughter we're talking about here, and that if it had been anybody else's granddaughter I probably could have spoke freely about it all along.

"But I care about Patty, that's the thing. I wanted her to take responsibility. Not out of punishment, but because I believed it would empower her. Isn't that what holding somebody accountable does? Empower them? Isn't it a way of saying, it is within your ability to account for this. She deserved to be held accountable. Don't all young women? How else do they ever become independent? It was a way for me to care about both Patty and Hannah. It really was."

But I refrained from saying any of this. Already, I'd seen from Loretta's outburst in the market that my discussion with Patty had threatened to knock off the community's equilibrium. I had invested too many years in maintaining my own respected spot on this balance beam to risk falling off it.

And what about now? Why didn't I feel the same concern this time? All I could imagine, with a sharp and confident determination, was the surprised look on Loretta's face tomorrow when she saw that I wasn't going to let her get away with false accusations, that I wasn't going to shrink away timidly. I supposed the difference this time was simple: lying to the authorities was different than starting rumours around the cove. I would point that out to her. Yes, that would be a good way to put it. And using your own daughter as a puppet—should I mention that, too? Might be a good thing for Patty to hear. Put the idea into her head that she didn't have to live under her mother's thumb.

I touched the spoon lightly to the surface of my tomato soup, right

The Heaviness of Things That Float

at the place where the liquid met the air and I could feel the tension there. I tried to sense the liquid molecules, how they stuck together, more attracted to one another than to the air molecules that pushed against them. It was an inward force, and it coated the soup like a membrane of elastic, barely perceptible. I pushed the spoon a little harder against the surface and broke the tension apart.

11

Loretta lived next door to Patty and Chase and Hannah in a house that looked out over the low-lying ridge onto the mouth of the cove. I climbed the wood steps to the door. Normally, I wouldn't knock—people here just walked straight into a house and hollered—but today I knocked and waited, watching the water down below churn in giant circles between the rocky shores of the reserve and Mitchell Island across the narrow channel. A sea stack—a tower of black rock about twenty feet tall—stood on the end of Mitchell Island. Once upon a time, the rock had been a chief, transformed in death into a loyal guard, a sentry watching all those who entered the cove. From years of tidal weathering, the rock's bottom was thinner than its top, and it appeared as though the old chief might one day fall to his knees with exhaustion.

The door opened, a loud screech of hinges.

It was Patty, not Loretta.

I asked, "What do you think you're doing?"

Her face dropped. She said nothing.

"A complaint to the police? Why?"

She lowered her eyes to the railing that wobbled in my hand.

"Who's at the door, Patty?" Loretta's voice called down from the top of the stairs inside.

Patty didn't answer. She took a quick glimpse of me.

Loretta's slippered feet thumped down each step. She was a short, plump woman who swivelled as she descended the stairs. She saw me and frowned.

"What's this about?" she asked.

I looked at Patty.

"Well?" Loretta folded her arms like she meant business. Between the bun that tugged her hair tightly off her face and the thick hood of her sweater that framed her neck like a royal collar, Loretta reminded me of the Queen of Hearts, all blind fury and decapitation decrees.

There was a slight tremor in my voice. "I want to know why you filed a complaint about me."

"I didn't file no complaint." Loretta blinked slowly, very slowly, as if she were bored and wanted to make sure I knew it.

"I know it was you," I told Loretta. "Because I know *you*"—I paused and craned my neck down to intercept Patty's slantwise gaze—"would never do such a thing to me, would you?"

Patty poked her tongue into the side of her cheek and stretched her gaze straight up at the splintered door frame.

Loretta scoffed. "She's not doing anything to you. She's fighting for justice."

"Justice? That's a bit overblown, don't you think?"

"Don't try to bully me—"

"Bully?" I laughed in disbelief.

"Yes. You're a bully," Loretta said.

I could feel my jaw tighten. Loretta had a way of pushing buttons in people. I wouldn't let her get to me. I took a deep breath and stretched my fists wide open.

"Patty's just standing up for what's right."

Smiling, I spoke through clenched teeth. "This is not right. This is a false accusation." Then I doled out the facts slowly, angrily. "I assessed his cut. It was not deep enough for stitches. I closed the cut with two butterfly bandages. I checked his vital signs and conducted a series of tests to check for signs of a concussion. There were none. I told Chase to stay at home and rest. All of this is recorded in his medical file."

"So what?" Loretta cleaned something out from under her fingernail. "You probably make up stories in them files all the time."

I couldn't believe what I was hearing. "I don't *ever* make up stories in the medical records." Which, with one terrible exception, was true. A single breath of wind pushed at the power lines and ruffled the treetops above the houses across the dirt road. "You phone the police and the health authority and you take the complaint back."

Loretta snorted. She put a hand on her hip and pointed at me. Her voice grew louder. "Why don't you take back what you said about our culture?"

"What?"

"Granddaughter told me what you said on the wharf. You told her our culture was shit."

"I didn't! I said no such thing. I would never—"

"Are you calling my granddaughter a liar?"

"No, but—"

"If my granddaughter's not lying, then you must be lying."

Crows fluttered back and forth between a telephone wire and the ground, pecking at a candy bar wrapper in the long grass, crying out.

"It was just a misunderstanding," I said, remembering the conversation on the wharf. "Hannah wanted to know what was in my Styrofoam box and I told her, cultures, and she asked again, what's in the box, and I told her about the specimens, and she said, shit? And I said, yes, and then I told her there was blood in it, too. I didn't mean—"

"You're lying. Just like you're lying about Chase's head injury."

"I am not lying about Chase. I would never lie about Chase. Patty—" I tried to give her a meaningful look, imploring her with my eyes to believe me. "You know that's true, Patty. You know how much I love Chase. I've always been there for him. I've always been there for both of you. How can you do this to me? Especially now. What's the point? I am leaving Tawakin in less than two months. Nothing will come of it," I said, turning to Loretta again, "if you think you're going to get some money out of it or something."

The door creaked as Patty fiddled with the doorknob.

I raised my outstretched arm towards the rest of the reserve and said, "Nobody's going to believe you."

"Oh? Who do you think they'll believe more? Me or you?" Loretta sighed. "You, an outsider? Or me—family?"

"I'm hardly an outsider," I said.

"But you're not family."

I didn't want to hear this. I turned quiet.

Loretta smiled. "You think you are, don't you?"

"I think forty years counts for something."

"Forty years across the water." Loretta shrugged. "You're not one of us, you're not family, and it's a joke that you think you are."

Hiding my hand behind my back, I pinched a little fold of skin at the back of my thigh. Hard. I focussed on the pain, and it stopped me from getting teary eyed. A little trick I had used since I was a child.

"I'm not the only one on the reserve who thinks it, either," Loretta went on. "Other people also think it's a joke—how you believe you are part of this community in the way you do."

I pinched harder.

Loretta flapped her hand in the direction of the water. "You get to just go off and live in some fancy apartment. Look—" She pointed to a spot behind her. "Look at my house, look at it. There's a big crack in my staircase right there. Nearly tripped and broke my neck this morning. And here you are acting like one of us. Ha! I seen you wearing our treaty T-shirts. *Nuu-Waas-Sus*—'Our Day,' that's what they say on the front, ain't it? *Our* day. Is it your day? No. It's *our* day." Loretta shook her head, gazing steadily at me. "It's real nutty, that's what other people say about you."

I felt wounded by her words, but I steeled myself. "Well," I said, forcing my voice to sound aloof, "I guess none of us can ever really know what people say about us, can we?"

Patty jerked her head towards me. A look of distress crossed her face. She stared at me intensely. "What's that supposed to mean?"

"Just that..." Caught off guard, I stumbled on my words. My comment was meant for Loretta, not Patty. "Just that we all have things that other people might talk about behind our backs."

Patty narrowed her eyes and glared at me.

"Yes, and now you know what your things are," Loretta stated plainly, seeming unfazed by my retort.

My chest ached with sorrow. Was it true? Did some people—any people—think I was a joke? No, it was just Loretta trying to get to me. But if what Loretta said was a lie, what was the truth? Exactly who was I to the people of Tawakin? Without another word, I turned and hurried away, biting my lip. I didn't want them watching me, and I hadn't yet heard the screech of the door hinges shut, so I turned quickly off the dirt road and headed down the footpath to the shore.

Climbing onto the slippery black rocks where the purple and orange starfish gathered, I sat on the edge a few feet above the water and watched how it churned. Along the shores of the Pacific, it was often difficult to tell whether the tide was going out or coming in. This difference could mean life or death if you chose to rest, for instance, on a narrow shore framed by looming walls of stone. In places like this, the water rose in tumultuous waves faster than you could ever hope to escape. But if you knew to first check which way the kelp was leaning in the water, the long ribbons of dark green shifting the strange light of the stories that Frank said hovered there with the flecks of detritus, you could interpret the tides and save your life.

Other times, as you travelled along the shores and in the rain forest, or perhaps in your boat on the water, other signs would not be as easily interpreted. Some signs might mean one thing, and also another thing. Some signs would tell you what would happen next without a shadow of doubt, like knowing that if you chased the brightest star in the sky, you would end up farther north, whereas other signs opened the possibility that many different things could happen. Like how the gathering of black clouds might bring rain, or maybe hail, or maybe no precipitation at all. Only darkness. Neither the sea nor the sky nor the stories can ever be controlled. You can only wait under the dark sky for ambiguity to resolve itself, for there always remains the possibility of more rain, or hail, or terrible winds.

The Heaviness of Things That Float

As I tied the boat to my wharf, I spotted flashes of colour on the outside stairs. Balloons. A dozen or more tied to the railing that led to the medical quarters. When I reached the door to the waiting room, a sign said: *Welcome! Come on in and meet the new nurse!* Red and yellow streamers curled around the door frame. Inside the waiting room, quiet and empty, there were more of the same decorations.

"What do you think?" Wren asked as she strolled in from the examination room tying up a blue balloon. "I found this stuff in a box in the office."

"Very colourful," I said. "What's it for, exactly?"

"I thought it'd be great to have a meet and greet this afternoon," Wren explained. "Maybe you could show me how to use the radio so I could invite everybody?"

"Of course," I said.

"So it's a good idea?"

"Excellent idea. Why not?" I nodded.

"Well then, if I'm meeting new patients this afternoon, then I better get the key from you," she said.

"What key?"

"The key to the filing cabinets," she said. "The medical records. I better start going through them now."

I kept the filing cabinet key, along with the outpost key and the boat key, around my neck on a long strand of deer hide. As I pulled it out from under my cardigan, I felt disquieted. The idea of entrusting all those secrets to a stranger distressed me. Could Wren be trusted? Of course she could. Why should I think otherwise? Still, I wanted to look over Wren's shoulder when she went through the files. Not only did I feel territorial but vigilant also, excessively so, and if I stayed here with Wren, I'd have the overwhelming urge to sugarcoat every suspicious injury, to defend every domestic dispute, to pardon every unknown paternity. But the records had to speak for themselves, no matter how protective I felt. I feared being judged. I feared my friends across the cove being judged.

Not every bad choice ended up with a patient at the outpost, but many did. There among the stomach flus and the outbreaks of scabies was an archive of mistakes and mishaps and violence. Those things were found in any hospital or doctor's office, I knew that, but here, in such a tiny place, they felt magnified—not anonymous but intensely personal.

It wasn't going to be easy, this passing of the guard, and I worried whether Wren would be discreet enough. I didn't have a choice, did I? Soon, Wren would be responsible for the entire outpost, all on her own. Soon, she would be the new secretary of secrets in a place that felt too small for secrets. I unwound the key from the small metal ring and, as I handed it to Wren, I felt strange. After feeling weighed down by these files for so long, I'd have thought the lightness of passing the burden would feel different. I was surprised by this emptiness inside me. Like something had been lost.

✴   ✴   ✴

That afternoon, people came to the outpost in a steady trickle. When the sudden rain turned to hail and the wind picked up to gale force, I thought they'd stop coming, but they didn't. Not many search parties could venture far in this weather, and everybody was eager to catch a glimpse of the new nurse.

At first I hovered like a ghost around the periphery of the room. I wanted to give Wren space, but after some time I felt awkward and useless gawking from the wall where I stood, so I retreated to the dim light of the office and listened from my seat at the desk. As I heard many familiar voices come through the examination room all afternoon, I told myself again and again that Loretta had lied—nobody on the reserve was talking behind my back, saying it was a joke that I thought I was family. Yet the doubt kept creeping in, got me wondering if it was at all true. The community had always made people feel welcome, as if they belonged. I'd thought I was different than all those others. Special. In a class of my own. And maybe I was. But like Wren had asked me, when did I know for sure? Moreover, I now asked myself: *How* did I ever know for sure?

Throughout the day, Wren laughed brightly at the men's corny jokes, she flirted innocently, she told the little boys and girls how strong and smart they were, she pulled magical coins out from behind their ears, she told them jokes rife with toilet humour that sent the children into fits of giggles, she promised the elders that she'd learn to speak Nuu-chah-nulth, she asked the men if the hunting was good this year, she got invited to go fishing, she got invited to bake bread with the women, she agreed to pull cedar with Margaret and Gina, she asked Chief Trudy Henry what she thought of the new treaty, she discovered which elders had gone to residential school, she discussed the biomedical experiments that some of the elders now talked about, how they were conducted and how she could help to document any testimonies the elders might wish to make, she learned that *chumiss* meant "dessert" and that it was considered disrespectful to call a close family member by their first name, she learned that cousins were considered to be brothers and sisters, she started to connect who was married to whom, and whose children were whose, and a couple of times she even learned who'd been unfaithful and with whom, and to every patient Wren expressed her sympathy for Chase Charlie's disappearance, saying things like, "I heard about the young father who went missing recently, my heart goes out to you," or asking questions like, "Was it like him to leave like this?" or "Tell me again about Loretta Joe's dream," and sometimes after, she would say, "You believe the dream, but there is a sadness in you, I can see it," or "You know, I sense the fear in your voice."

In hearing all these questions and comments, I wondered whether Wren was being too pushy, overstepping her bounds as a new arrival to the community. Worse yet, I worried that these questions would prompt somebody to talk about Patty's complaint. Did others already know about it? If so, did they believe Loretta? In the end, though, nobody mentioned the complaint or the RCMP's visit. Normally, it was the sort of news that people couldn't resist gossiping about. Was it possible that they knew nothing about it? Not likely, and while I was confident that the accusation was ridiculous and unfounded, I worried nonetheless. Because once a story got told, there could be no unhearing it.

Wren appeared confident whenever the VHF radio began to crackle with a medical question, or when Carl Henry came to check on his eczema, or Ernie Frank boated over for his insulin, at ease when she felt for mastitis on the swollen breast of Wendy Sam, whose husband brought Wren six bags of dried salmon, genuine when she allied herself with the people, agreeing that, "It certainly *is* an insult that the doctor doesn't fly in more often," or "You bet it's not right that the RCMP boat hardly ever visits, except when there's been a tragedy, and then when they show up they can somehow think they're cozy with the community. *Pfft!*" On a couple of occasions, whomever Wren was speaking to would start to cry and Wren would comfort the person in a tight embrace. In short, the people took to Wren, and Wren responded with the perfect amount of humble curiosity and generous charm, uplifting and cheerful, with a buoyancy that seemed to rise above the undercurrent of despair flowing through the people who were finally growing weary with worry.

✳   ✳   ✳

After dinner, I went back into my office and entered a search term on the computer: "Wren Featherstone."

There was a Facebook page blocked to everybody except her friends, an Instagram account with only a photo of a daisy posted two years earlier and a few references to social activities at UBC's School of Nursing.

I entered: "Wren Featherstone Idle No More."

A list of results appeared on my computer screen. I scanned a couple of newspaper articles, but they seemed to be about the Idle No More movement in general. I surveyed pages and pages of images but saw no sign of Wren. There were photographs of crowds at the federal parliament buildings and in the snowy streets of Manitoba. People carried drums and signs and flags.

I entered: "Wren Featherstone Idle No More Vancouver City Hall."

And there she was. Not one but two photographs of Wren interacting with police officers, presumably during one of the demonstrations. The first photograph was a close-up of Wren staring down an RCMP officer. She

     The Heaviness of Things That Float

wore a short-brimmed hat, under which she'd tucked all her hair, and a scarf, which she'd tied around her face so that it covered from the bridge of her nose down, like a bandit. Her face was only inches away from the officer's, and it immediately brought to mind the iconic photograph of the Mohawk warrior and the armed forces officer during the Oka Crisis. Except that Wren looked much less menacing in her straw hat and pink scarf. There were no captions, and although her face was almost entirely covered, I could see from her eyes that it was Wren, and from the stray curls that had escaped from her hat.

In the second photograph, evidently shot the same day, Wren had lost her hat in the melee. Her scarf was around her neck now, her face fully exposed. An RCMP officer was pulling her backwards. Restrained in handcuffs, Wren wrenched her body towards a second police officer. Although her eyebrows furrowed in what seemed to be intense anger, her lips were formed into a small o. Between her and the officer was a tiny blurred mark I couldn't make out.

I spent several minutes studying the photograph until it occurred to me that Wren was spitting, and that the photograph had managed to capture her spit midair as it flew straight for the officer's face.

Rebel. That's the word that came to my mind. Part of me admired the passion being displayed, the moxy, the boldness, the relentless pursuit for something better. For justice. At the same time, the fact that Wren was belittling the officer in this way suggested that she wasn't as professional as she appeared. Maybe she'd done something to deserve to be in handcuffs; maybe she hadn't. I was eager to know. But I didn't want to ask. I didn't want her to know that I'd been looking her up on the Internet. I shut off the computer, the image of Wren's fiery outrage burning in my mind.

12

Early the next morning, the sun peeked over the bristle of black trees on the mountaintop. I'd been dreaming in flashes, images without action, like a sequence of disconnected sepia photographs. Miranda, the details of her face overexposed, washed out. Frank Charlie as a handsome young man, long hair and a smudge of black on his upper lip. Chase, the child. Patty, the child. Sometimes Anne's face rosy; sometimes Anne's face slack jawed after her very last breath.

Through the window, the morning shone into the bedroom like a movie on a glassy screen, the intense colour of the cloudless sky as purple as a deep bruise, and it startled me out of my monochrome dreams.

Slowly, I became more lucid, and soon I heard a noise—a rattling—coming from the back door in the kitchen. I rubbed my eyes and shuffled out the door and peeked into Wren's room, opening the door a crack. Her form lay sideways under the blankets. Groggy, I went back into my room and checked the wharf below, which was empty except for my own boat, and I then moved towards the noise without thinking, picking up the shotgun along the way. In the doorway of the kitchen, I stood swaying sleepily, my right foot numb with pins and needles, and I called out "Who's there? Who's there?" the sound of my own voice jolting me fully awake. Adrenaline rushed through my arms and my hands, which now pointed the barrels of the shotgun across the room. The dim morning sky left most of the kitchen shrouded in shadows, and the edges of the fridge and the table and the teapot were soft and diffused and tinted indigo. With my eyes, I traced these outlines in the empty room, and I turned my ear to the sounds coming from the back steps outside. Footsteps shuffled, and there was a sharp scratching on the door. My palms felt moist and slippery holding the gun. "Who's there?" I called again.

With the gun butted against my shoulder, I stepped slowly towards the door, then stopped and turned, darting back into the living room to load the gun, hurrying down the short hallway and into the waiting area, where I opened the door and stepped outside, treading across the soft grass and alongside the outpost, keeping close to the wall as I headed towards the back door of the kitchen. My heart walloped against my chest, and I felt a terrible foreboding. "Please God, let it be a patient or a child," I thought, as it wouldn't be the first time somebody stopped by without warning, yet I considered making one of those bargains people sometimes made with God, like promising to become a nun or wash the feet of the poor in return for divine intervention, but I didn't have time. I'd already reached the woodpile, and by then it was too late. There was a huffing sound, and then a snort and the sound of agitated jaws chomping, and in the next instant, just as I changed my mind and decided to retreat to the outpost, I found myself only steps away from a black-haired creature, and without a moment of hesitation, I pulled the trigger and flew backwards into the woodpile, sending a pyramid of split logs rolling to the ground.

✻   ✻   ✻

The first thing I noticed as I opened my eyes to the sky, now a light mauve, was the throbbing ache in my right shoulder. I was flat on my back, and all around me was silence. The blue-needled branches of fir trees radiated high above my head, and for a moment, I watched a crow hop along the eave. From my spot on the ground, I could just see the black feathers of one wing and occasionally its head whenever it stretched over the edge and opened its beak as though calling for something, though no sound came out.

"God, what happened?"

Wren bent over me, her curly hair framing her face. She offered her hand and I struggled to sit upright, wincing at the pain where the butt of the shotgun had kicked back.

"I think you hit him." Wren's voice was solemn, shaky.

Nearby, the gun lay on the ground, and farther away, tucked under a cluster of dense shrubs, there was a patch of black hair. It wasn't moving, and when I climbed to my feet, I could see the whole body there in the long grass.

"You've killed him," Wren said under her breath.

I picked up the gun and moved slowly towards the creature, Wren inching alongside me, clutching my elbow, both of us studying the mound of blackness. It was shapeless, unidentifiable. About eight feet away, we stopped. Lying there, it looked smaller than it had when it approached me from the steps. I didn't know what to do. I was scared to get any closer, in part because I didn't know if the creature was dead, and in part because I feared, as ridiculous as it seemed, that the thing might be Chase Charlie.

From the eave, the crow called out into the stiff morning air, and I also then noticed the gentle slap of the water against the rocks on the beach below. It was as if I'd been trapped inside a big glass jar after the gun fired, and now the jar was lifting and the sounds around me were emerging, one by one. The smell I noticed now, too. Like a wet dog, only much stronger. I took a small step closer, and then another, and soon I was close enough to see that the hair was thick and coarse and wiry. Wren stayed put, watching from farther back. I quivered from head to toe. Long claws, shiny and hooked like bird beaks, extended from one of its appendages. I couldn't tell right away which end was the head because the branches of the shrub concealed it, so I started to lift the branches with the tip of the gun barrel. I gave the creature a poke with the gun and then leaped backwards, my heart racing.

"Is it him? Is he dead?" Wren whispered.

I didn't answer. I poked the creature with the gun barrel again, significantly harder this time. The third time I did it as hard as I could. The creature didn't move, and it felt flaccid under the push of the gun.

It was dead.

The creature did not seem as large as I'd first thought. It was about the size of a small man, only shrunken and deflated in its present condition. Still nervous to see its face, I flitted my eyes to the ocean, and then to the forest in front of me, and finally to the sky above. It soothed my nerves a little to take in the surrounding landscape, the giant trees, the expansive ocean, the slow-shifting clouds.

I tried to lift the branches with the muzzle of the gun once more, and this time I did not leap backwards, though my skin prickled. I saw an ear, not unlike that of some dog breeds, and the broad furry skull. Some of its face was a lighter shade than the rest of its fur, and it too was similar to a dog's, with a black leathery bulb at the end of an elongated snout, and that's when I finally saw it.

I turned to Wren, who chewed on a fingernail.

"It's a black bear," I said.

Wren's shoulders slackened. "Thank God."

I nodded and looked at the channel of water that separated my isle from Vancouver Island, and I wondered: What drove this bear to be the first in forty years to take the plunge?

*   *   *

"Not too big, is it?" Frank pushed the shrub aside and looked down at the black bear. "Looks real old."

Never in my life had I killed anything larger than a beetle. Its blood streaked across the grass.

"Why'd it swim over here?" I asked.

"Couldn't find food. Too old. Too small. Too weak," Frank said.

"Wouldn't it be too weak to swim, then?" Wren asked.

Frank looked in the direction of the narrow channel. "It's not far. Easy enough if it was hungry."

"Berries are gone now. Probably smelled some good cooking over here," said George. Without his teeth in today, the edges of his consonants were soft and rounded. He reached down and took hold of the bear's paw and dragged it out from under the shrub like a large rag doll. He held the bear's front leg high to reveal the blood-soaked patch of fur on its chest. "Female, just shy of a hundred pounds I'd say. Nice clean shot. Not much meat for eating, but I'll take it. Should be good without having been bled out right away. Heart probably hemorrhaged into the lungs."

"You're going to eat it?" Wren looked horrified.

George shrugged. "My wife made a delicious spaghetti meat sauce out of a cougar I shot last year behind the reserve, didn't she?"

"It was very good, yes," I said.

"She'll do something real good with this, I bet," George said.

Wren asked, "Isn't there something else we could do with it?"

Frank looked annoyed. "Like what?"

"I don't know," she said. "Something to honour its life?"

"What's more honourable than making use of it?"

"Maybe I could bury it," Wren suggested.

"No, you just leave it," Frank said firmly. "You let us deal with it. We have our own ways of doing things here."

Wren looked dissatisfied.

"Don't you eat where you come from?" George asked.

"Not meat," Wren said. "Plus, I think you'll end up digesting a lot of negative energy if you eat this—"

"Hold on there!"

We turned to see Patty marching up the path. Down at the outpost wharf, her little kicker was tied up between Frank's boat and George's boat.

"Just wait a minute!" Patty wriggled her shoulders between the two men, scrutinized Wren for a moment, and then looked straight at me. "Mother is furious with you. How dare you get on that radio and ask for our help? You think we got time to help you when my husband is still out there somewhere? Didn't you hear what I said on the radio this morning? Didn't you?" Patty didn't wait for me to answer. "Chase visited my mother in another dream, and this time he said he's going to return, but only after we come find him on account of him being lost. We don't got time for your little problems."

"Haw-ess, bebba," Frank said to Patty. "Calm down."

She was always, I noted, more vocal when she was free of her mother. But today, she seemed more aggressive than normal.

She looked down at the bear. "I want the meat. Chase ain't here to hunt or fish for me. So I should get it."

"Fine." George shrugged. "I get the skin."

"Better take them ears as well," Frank said.

"Real funny." George touched the bandage over his earlobe.

Wren muttered, "I just can't—" and turned around.

Patty nudged the bear with her toe. "What an old and scraggly thing. Skinny, must've been starving. You take the meat," she told George. "We'll take the skin. And the claws."

"Then I get the gallbladder," said Frank. "Nan Lily will want the bile."

Poor Nan Lily, I thought. She'd be disappointed to learn that her *puukmis* theory was wrong.

"Be my guest," I said.

Patty glared at me. "Be *your* guest? This is *our* traditional territory. You're *our* guest here. This is *our* bear. You just leave it there."

"What are you so worked up for?" Frank scowled at Patty.

Patty shook her head and started to walk away. "I don't got time for this now. I'll come back later to skin it."

We watched as she cut the corner of the path at the far side of the outpost, stepping over the patch of dirt where the daffodils sprung to life every April. It was the same patch where Chase and I had buried those three strips of cedar with the placenta from Hannah's birth while Patty recuperated in the examination room. The strips of cedar that promised to turn Hannah into a weaver as good as her mother. I wondered if Patty could sense the presence of what was buried there. Did the earth resonate with good intentions?

*   *   *

Somewhere in the outpost was a cedar headband that Patty had made for my fortieth birthday. It seemed like another lifetime ago, those days when Patty and I would sit at Margaret Sam's kitchen table, or maybe at

Sophie Florence's kitchen table, weaving headbands for dance practice and eating fry bread, the fruit-sweet smell of cedar rising from plastic tubs where the long strips of bark soaked in water. That headband Patty made for my birthday was thin and woven into small squares, the ends knotted in long strands that burst outward like a flower or a star.

No, I remembered: it was a rose, not a headband that Patty made for my birthday, with splits in the cedar where Patty bent the bark into petals.

After Frank and George left, also promising to return later for the bear, I searched the windowsills, the jars of beach glass, the halves of clamshells, around the green glass balls, looking for the cedar rose.

Where had I put it?

Almost everybody had gone to my fortieth birthday party at Sophie Florence's house. Birthdays were always big celebrations in Tawakin. Frank once told me that this was because they never got to celebrate in residential school. There was a large bonfire in Sophie Florence's front yard, and crosses of cedar sticks leaned out of the ground and held slabs of salmon over the flames. On the big deck, people lounged in chairs while children sprinted in and out of the open door, shrieking and laughing. More people filed through the front door with trays of baked fish and pots of fish head soup and jars of tiny translucent fish eggs. Soon, there was a mountain of shoes beside the front door and the table was covered with dishes. Inside the crowded house, every seat was taken, and those who did not have a seat found a spot on the floor, leaning against the walls or against the sides of old couches where elders sat quietly. Children sprawled on their bellies across the dirty floor, with the tiny crabs they'd stolen from the beach scuttling between the walls they made with their hands. I brought devilled eggs. I always brought devilled eggs. Sprinkled with paprika.

Sunlight streamed through the outpost window. I closed my eyes. I could almost hear the fragmented conversations of the women in Sophie Florence's kitchen from that evening more than twenty years ago.

"Are those barnacles cooked, Daughter?"

"Ay-ha, Sister! You're cutting those pieces real *uncy!*"

"Haw-ess, Mother, you didn't get any coffee?"

"Auntie took the last of it."

"Not even!"

"Look at those oysters, you're real *uussiick*, Sister."

This was the birthday party when Sophie Florence had presented me with an unusual gift. But first Nan Lily had said a prayer in Nuu-chah-nulth before dinner, speaking softly as she always did, so that all I could hear were the low, throaty, guttural sounds and the hard glottal stops and the ending of the prayer when Nan Lily said, *"Chuu,"* which meant it was time for the children to fill plates of food for the elders.

Maybe it happened that way. Or maybe it was Ernie Frank who'd said the prayer. I found it hard to rely on my memories sometimes. I was always inserting events into the wrong time or place, or converging two events into one, or erasing events altogether. Memory is funny that way. Was it the natural course of life to reshape events into a new narrative?

Sophie Florence had called everybody's attention to the greyish ball cradled in her palm that evening. She stood in the kitchen doorway with several women gathered behind her, many giggling into the lifted corners of their aprons. In a loud and clear voice, Sophie Florence said, "On behalf of my family, we—" motioning to the other women, "present this gift to you, Bernadette Perkal, for—shush, Sister!—for giving so many years of service to Tawakin."

Sophie Florence had lifted her outstretched hand, encouraging me to take the object. Everybody watched in anticipation. The generosity of the people in Tawakin was as big as the ocean, and a gift offered on their traditional territory was not to be refused, no matter how politely. I moved halfway across the room to Sophie Florence, looked at the round thing with the dark circle in the middle and took it between my fingers. It was a salmon eyeball, moist and slippery. If I pinched it too tightly it would have popped out of my grip. I held it gently.

"Go on," Sophie Florence said, "eat it."

They seemed to have forgotten that they'd already made me eat an eyeball, many years earlier, because the women laughed at their own mischief, as did many of the children, including Chase and Patty. I winked at Chase and then winked at Patty—at least that seemed like something

I'd have done—and popped the eyeball into my mouth and bit down into the cornea, soft like jelly, and down into the middle where it was rubbery and tough. A warm fluid filled my cheeks and coated my tongue with a salty taste. I pretended it was a pickled onion, though my imagination did not stop my eyes from brimming, or my cheeks from reddening, or my throat from clamping tight and jerking upward to retch. But I could feel everybody staring, and so I stopped my face from convulsing and forced the eyeball down in a single swallow, the room erupting into laughter and applause when I smacked my lips and said: "*Chuu.*"

Afterwards, Patty slipped her small hand into mine and said, "Happy Birthday," and pressed the cedar rose into my other hand. Her words spittled through the gap where she'd lost her two front teeth. "I made it myself."

"*Klecko*," I said, hugging her. "*Klecko.*"

In my bedroom, I pulled down the boxes from the top shelf of the closet. From one of the boxes I lifted some newspaper clippings—reviews of my sister's books, mostly—and found the cedar rose underneath. The newspaper had sucked all the moisture from the rose so that the bone-dry cedar crackled when I spread out the flattened petals. I set it on the kitchen table.

Maybe I could give it back to Patty as a gift, a peace offering, and maybe when Patty held it between her fingers she would be overwhelmed with a recollection of the past, and maybe all those memories of our relationship when she was little would surround her like a soft blanket or a warm womb, and she would throw her arms around me and say how sorry she was for filing a complaint, and she would thank me for not forgetting the connection we once shared. And she would say, "I saw how you stood up to mother. I'm going to stand up to her, too. I'm not going to become like her. I am not going to keep blaming everybody the way she does."

*   *   *

From the kitchen, I watched Hannah as she stood on the grass over the dead bear. I looked around for Patty, assuming she'd brought Hannah to help her skin the bear, but after a while, I realized Hannah was alone.

The Heaviness of Things That Float

In the summers, Hannah often came to my island and walked along the beach and around the outpost. Never did she stay long, wandering up and down the side steps until I opened the door and asked if she wanted to come inside. No, she'd say, with a tone of disgust that I'd dared to ask.

I pulled back the translucent sheers. Hannah kept approaching the bear and then retreating. She hunched forward, a thin branch in one hand, the other hand to her mouth, chewing those fingernails like crazy. I thought she was going to poke the bear with the stick, but instead she waved it in the air near the carcass. Then she looked around, and I saw the distress in her face.

I went out back and stood beside her.

A few bluebottles buzzed around the carcass now. Hannah swung the stick at them, then she bent over and tilted her head to one side. She took a long look at the bear's face. She sniffled.

"What's wrong, Hannah?"

She swiped her eyes with the back of her hand.

"Tyler told me you shot the *puukmis*," she said.

Her voice was unusually quiet, almost gentle.

"Oh, Hannah," I said softly. "This isn't your father."

"Duh. I know that. This is a bear."

She continued to examine the dead animal closely.

"Your dad will come home soon, Hannah," I said.

"You think I'm stupid? I know that."

She turned, threw herself into my body and wrapped her arms around me.

I could scarcely believe what was happening. The only time Hannah had ever touched me was when she once shoved me away from the last apple in the Tawakin Market. She hadn't even wanted it. She just didn't want anybody else to have it. "Oh, Hannah, everything's going to be okay," I soothed, and wrapped my arms around her shoulders.

She cried, drenching the shoulder of my shirt with saliva.

Behind us, the door opened and I heard footsteps.

"Sorry," Wren said. "I'm interrupting."

Hannah pushed me hard and turned away. She rubbed her cheeks vigorously with her sleeve.

"It's all right," I said, even though it was terrible timing. Who knew when Hannah would ever reach out to me again? "Hannah, this is the new nurse. Wren Featherstone."

"What kind of stupid name is that?" Hannah asked.

Wren laughed. "My parents were hippies."

Hannah squinted an eye. "Whatever, When."

"Wren."

"*When*," Hannah repeated. She stepped up into Wren's face. "*When* you going to go away and leave me alone?"

"Hannah—" I warned.

"Gross, you smell," Hannah told Wren. Scowling, she plugged her nose. "You smell like old feet."

"It's the bear you're smelling, Hannah," I offered.

"No, it's her breath," Hannah said.

Wren laughed, took an awkward step back from Hannah, but Hannah, relentless, closed the gap again.

"You smell like rotting berries."

"Hannah—" I tried again.

Wren chuckled. "It's all right, she's only testing me," she said, then turned and hurried back through the kitchen door.

Hannah faced me. "I don't like her."

Then she, too, hurried away, leaving me alone in the yard, trying to make sense of what had just happened. I was surprised at Hannah's harsh reaction to Wren, but that was the lesser of the two things on my mind. Never before had Hannah reached out to me like that, and I was left wondering what might have transpired if our embrace hadn't been interrupted. Could it have been a turning point for us, or was I making too much of it? Maybe she would have suddenly pushed me away anyhow. Katarina, the counsellor who flew in on the mail plane once a month to help people in the community, once told me how some children had trouble forming attachments with others.

"It can happen," she'd said in her Dutch accent, "for any number of reasons—certain developmental disorders, traumatic events, general neglect—and for many, it continues through adulthood. In some, it manifests into pursuits of perfectionism, in others into socially poor behaviour. And because they do not trust relationships, the moment they sense you getting close, even if they like it in their hearts—*bam!*—they will push you away before you can leave them or hurt them, yah? Before you can ever get a chance to reject them. They will not let you get the chance, and so their brains trick themselves into thinking they are being clever like this, protecting themselves. Like Fiona, this is true?"

Nodding, I remembered the time Fiona broke her favourite teacher's windows.

Was Hannah only throwing stones at me? If so, didn't it mean that she saw me as somebody she could feel close to? In light of Loretta's claim that I was not family to the people here, Hannah's moment of reaching out to me lifted my spirits. For the time being, I didn't want to try to explain it to myself. I wanted to simply savour it. Embrace it. Enjoy it for what it was, a sweet mystery.

13

I got on the VHF radio several more times to ask the two men when they were coming. Soon, the meat would start to rot. I reminded Frank of this, and in response he promised to get the bear off the island no matter what. Even after forty years, the glacial pace at which things were done in Tawakin still frustrated me at times.

The trouble was this: even indoors, the bear had started to haunt me. Whenever I made tea or heated another can of soup for lunch, I could see it, though not clearly, out the kitchen window. Through the sheer curtains, it appeared as a black spectre, its soft-edged shape shifting between the pleats. The curtains had yellowed slightly with age, and it gave everything outside a sickly hue that I hadn't noticed previously.

When I went out back to get more wood for the stove, I tried not to look at it. Instead, I lifted my eyes to the poplar leaves, which were starting to sound as dry as paper blowing in the wind. Soon, they'd brown and fall to the yard and decompose in rain-soaked layers. The smell of the bear, however, was unavoidable: it was awash with the pungency of death. Why was it troubling me so? Surely I wasn't repulsed by the carcass, not in a purely physical sense anyway. I was a nurse. And an emotional reaction also seemed unlikely. After all, I had witnessed the tragic deaths of people—some children—I knew personally. Esther and Teddy, not to mention many others. In comparison, an old bear should've hardly bothered me.

Standing next to the woodpile, I put on a pair of oversized garden gloves and stacked triangular logs into a plastic milk crate, trying to ignore the foul odour. I could see the bear out of the corner of my eye. Twice, I took a quick glance. Its limp mouth gave me the shivers, how it twisted open at a dislocated angle. I could feel its eyes, two amber marbles set deep and close together in its head, staring at me while I split kindling with a hatchet. As I hurried back into the house with the wood, nudging the door open with my shoulder and slamming it closed again with my heel, I decided to gather less wood until the bear was gone, and although the house was starting to turn cold at night, I was perfectly happy to wear thicker sweaters.

In the office, I sat at the computer and read an email from Saul Finkler, an American who divided his time between Tacoma, Washington, and Mitchell Island, where he operated a small bed and breakfast. Often, he brought items for the people in Tawakin, finding great deals at American outlet stores. Turned out he was arriving tomorrow with my new frost-free refrigerator.

Leaning back, I looked out the window at the floating junkyard in the distance. It stretched in a narrow line from a densely forested strip of the Vancouver Island shoreline. There were window frames from old houses and planks from the old whaling station, cracked buoys and fishing nets, crab traps and wood pallets angled this way and that. A sapling grew out of a half-sunk fibreglass boat. The makeshift junkyard was not there when I first moved to Tawakin, and I'd watched it spread slowly, a constant reminder of how hard it was to get rid of unwanted things in a remote community. There were no places designated just for junk, no garbage trucks to haul stuff away. If you wanted to dispose of something, you had to take care of it yourself.

At suppertime, I entered the kitchen with my face turned from the window. Wren had eaten early and was in her room reading, or maybe she was taking a nap. The whole outpost was quiet. I stood at the counter and watched the kettle, waiting for it to shriek, and as I did, I could feel the bear tug at my gaze. Look at me, it seemed to say. Look at me. You cannot ignore me. I turned my concentration to the spinning can opener as it popped open the minestrone, and then to the empty cupboards, and then to the unwashed soup bowls submerged in red dishwater, but that black heap of death was like a magnet my eyes couldn't resist. Look at me. Look at me. And the next thing I knew, I was staring at the body through the window with the curtains pulled apart tightly in my fists. I stared intensely, as though the harder I looked, the less hold it would have on me. Its rotting body rankled me, and I imagined its dissolving flesh and its gaseous spirit seeping into the soil and creeping outward in all directions, like a dye or a poison networking through veins and capillaries, tinting the ground black, a stain that would never stop spreading until it had darkened everything.

That night, the stain spread into my dreams, and it woke me in the dark. I stood on the cold tiles, and in that strange state between sleeping and waking, I felt I'd figured out something important, something about why a dead bear was haunting me so much—me, a nurse who'd seen things much worse than an animal carcass—and I even thought, wasn't that always the way, that something important got figured out after a death, but by the time I stumbled to the couch, where I sat and fumbled with the wood case of seashells that lay on the coffee table, I'd forgotten the thing I'd realized. And wasn't that also, I lamented, always the way?

I lifted the lid of the case. Whatever I'd figured out in my dream, the seashells must have factored into it somehow. Why else had I gone straight to the case in my sleepy state?

The seashells clicked lightly against the thin pine slats. I fingered each of the shells in the dark and felt a momentary chill seeing some of the faces of people who'd died over the years, as if they were in the room. Esther Sam, three. Cougar attack. David Frank, thirteen. Drowned. George Sam, Sr., forty-five. Drowned. Henry Joe, two. Choked on a bone. Julie Charlie, seventeen. Car accident. June Charlie, eighteen. Car accident. Kenny Henry, fifteen. Suicide by hanging. Thomas Joe, twenty-eight. House fire. Verne Joe, forty-eight. House fire. Sam Joe, thirty-six. House fire. Martin Joe, forty-one. House fire. Candice Joe, seventy-five. Heart attack. Theodore Joe, seven. Drowned. Francine Jimmy, eighty. Pneumonia. Bradley Joe, two months. Unknown causes. Sarah Henry, nineteen. Fall. Barbara Joe, seventy-three. Stroke. Justin Jimmy, twenty-five. Motorbike accident. Derek Charlie, forty-four. Drowned. Fiona Henry, nineteen. Suicide by hanging. Paul Jimmy, ninety-two. Heart failure. Ronny Henry, ten. Cougar attack. Jeffrey Jimmy, forty-four. Heart attack. Jimmy Charlie, thirty-eight. Shooting accident.

Jimmy Charlie. I couldn't conjure his face without reliving the shock of pointing my flashlight beam first at Frank Charlie, kneeling under the trees in a crowd of ferns the night of the hunting accident twenty-eight years ago, and then at Jimmy Charlie, his chest and head propped on Frank's blood-soaked arms. I'd been unprepared for what I saw that night, and I later tried to mask it with clinical language: it was simply a matter of the zygomatic bone detaching from the partially shattered frontal bone, as well as the smashed maxilla and temporal bones, releasing the left eyeball from its socket and discharging a fatal quantity of brain matter from the temporal lobe. The mandible was fractured in several places, with all but two teeth ripped out by their roots on the left side, plus eight teeth on the right side broken from the projectiles of bone fragments. The absence of skin on the left side of the face contorted the patient's mouth into what looked like an exaggerated smile.

It was always that word—"smile"—that tore away my protective mask of scientific terminology. For months after, that smile made sleep impossible for me. I always claimed to believe Frank that it was an accident, and part of my mind truly supported this notion. Yet another part of my mind, the deeper part that took over during sleep, suggested something else, because that smile appeared in my dreams, taut as a fully drawn bow, vengeful and bitter and nocked with a poison-tipped arrow.

Jimmy Charlie, always smiling. Did he smile when he shoved Miranda around? Or when he took the hot iron she used on her dance shawls and put it to the bare skin on her back? Or when he called her an "ugly dog," like she once told me he had?

One day, Jimmy came to the outpost with a large fishhook in the heel of his hand. He seemed almost the way he always seemed, because his smile was big and he laughed a lot, but he winced whenever he moved too quickly, and I could tell he was hiding significant pain. The hook was buried deep in his hand, and the barb at the end of the hook made it impossible to slide the hook back out without tearing the flesh.

I got some special pliers and a small wire cutter.

Under my breath, I said, "It hurts your wife when you are so mean to her," as I laid his hand flat and open on the counter.

"What did you say?" he asked.

"Others know it, too." I pushed the hook forward through his skin so that the barb poked out, then I clipped the barb off with the wire cutters. I was not entirely careful or gentle. "Some of the other women, at least. We know what you're really like."

"There's something you should know about Miranda," he said, wincing as I pulled out the hook. "She lies lots."

I cleaned his wound. "I saw the burns on her back."

"Like I said, she lies. She probably lies to you about all sorts of stuff. Maybe you shouldn't hang around her no more."

He smiled, as always.

The next day, Miranda showed up at the outpost, furious.

"Who asked you to do that? I don't need you to save me."

*   *   *

It was hard work hauling a bear, even a small old female. The carcass was floppy, the joints loose and coming apart, there were stairs to drag it down. At first, I tried to hoist it onto the wheelbarrow, but it was easier to pull it along the ground. At five in the morning, I'd snuck out of the outpost long before Wren awoke. It was mostly dark still, with a hint of light appearing at the eastern edge of the mountains, which made the task even more daunting. Confronting death in the dark added to the horror of it, the surprise of it. The bear's fur was wiry, and, like its joints, the skin sagged and slipped over the flesh. What other choice did I have? It was true that Frank told us to let them dispose of the bear, but normally I would respect this wish, but I was not feeling especially patient or even tolerant. There was Loretta's suggestion that I did not belong in the community. There were whale stories. There were stories of dogs slipping off their furs. Nothing was what it appeared to be.

On the dock, I rolled the bear over the edge so that it landed on a platform of totes I'd stacked level with the boat's gunwale. Then I covered it with a sheet of blue tarpaulin and searched the outpost windows for any movement. I didn't want Wren to know anything about this. There was no room here for her sentimentality. For her ideas of honouring the dead. I knew that I shouldn't dispose of the bear the way I planned. I knew the community would get upset. I could have tried to drag it onto another island, perhaps even along the coast of Vancouver Island, but that would only attract more scavengers, and I couldn't imagine getting it from the boat onto the shore.

Instead, I motored slowly and quietly out of the cove. I stopped about a half mile offshore. The sun was just about to peek over the tree-bristled mountaintops. Bluebottles swirled into the air when I uncovered the bear and wriggled my forearms underneath its body. The stench was caustic. Holding my breath, I heaved it into the ocean, the provider of life for the Tawakin people, where it smacked the surface of the water with a great splash.

I felt buoyant, as though a weight had lifted. Perhaps I had grown weary of death. I missed Chase. I missed my sister. I believed that one day I'd see her again. It was not one of those springy beliefs either, the type you volley back and forth in your mind between dream and logic. No, this was the type of belief as real and central as marrow, and so far, it had kept me warm on the stormy waters of grief, though I worried the day may come in which, for a brief flicker of time, I'd falter and ask myself that shattering question: But what if I do not see her again? And in that moment of perceived finality and eternal darkness, I'd flail and gasp, the torment a wall across my throat, and I'd suck in the cold, dark waters and suffocate with the sudden realization that the end was inevitable. But for now, as I bobbed at the edge of the Pacific, where the world spread out above me and beneath me and before me, I chose to believe that a sister waited for me in a sunny room full of books and seashells with a pot of steeping tea. Maybe this was preposterous and escapist of me to think, but when you've seen as many deaths as I had, you had to accept solace in whatever way your imagination offered it to you. Often, I thought about all those years we spent in our backyard forest, our mythological Great Forest of Pothenroth, with Rebecca and Alice and fifty-five Wilde Grannies, and I imagined Anne adding more mythology to our composition book.

Sometimes people returned home to escape their troubles, and sometimes people returned home to face their troubles. The reasons might be different, but everybody returned eventually, even if only in their imaginations. Fragments of an idea swam inside my head, and although it wasn't likely, I decided to visit Chase's old house, his first childhood home on Toomista, for any sign that he'd been there recently.

I headed towards the back of Mitchell Island. A stone cliff striped black and green with tidelines stood tall at the far end. Gnarled trees grew out the side, the mossy branches hosting a murder of perched crows. The way they cocked their heads had an eerie effect on me. It was exactly how Chase always looked at me when he brought those bags of halibut, tilting his head to one side. At the farthest tip of the longest branch, the largest crow stretched out and cawed into the brightening sky. I called back, "See you later but preferably sooner," which was what I always said to Chase at the end of every visit. I did not actually believe that he was costumed as a crow, though the winds of the Pacific were known for bringing about extraordinary transformations since as far back as anyone could remember. There were stories of Raven trying to become Eagle, Mother turning into Blue Jay, Mucous Boy growing out of his mother's snot. And in Chase's family, everybody turned into killer whales when they died, he'd told me this more than once.

Miranda said that Chase had caught a whale. She'd said that clearly, that he'd *caught* a whale, not turned into one. She couldn't have meant he was dead. After all, she'd explained that afterwards he'd sent a message made of blubber. I didn't know what her story meant, but this was a place filled with incredible stories, stories that could be heard in the wind and in the water. Was it so strange then to think of Chase finding a whale or turning into a crow, some sort of temporary transformation as he hid in peace and quiet for a while? This was a place where old friends turned into hermit crabs. Old lovers into broken hearts. Old nurses into—

Into what?

Grandmothers?

Maybe. At least then I'd belong to a family of my own. Except it felt as though there was no going home for me, really. I was leaving the only home I'd known in my adult life. And my sister was dead, her apartment resonating with nothing but her essence. I was starting to get the awful sense that there was nowhere I belonged, and it felt unfair that after forty years of living here, I couldn't stay.

I anchored the boat beside a finger of black rocks that jutted out from the beach at a perpendicular angle, then climbed ashore. Sea gulls soared low above the rolling waves near the Toomista shore and wailed. One of them dropped a clam on the rocks, the shell smashing into white shards. I walked around the corner and along the strip of pebbled sand below the grass field. Between the clusters of shrubs and brambles and tall weeds, there were small paths leading up to the field. I hiked up one of these paths and onto the low ridge. The field was a verdant, thick carpet of grass with an underlay of moss where nests of snakes lived. I knew this because every summer, on Toomista Day, the children dug into the grass and pulled out fistfuls of wriggling snakes. In the middle of the field were the remnants of a concrete building foundation, a small square that was once the schoolhouse for the children living on Toomista Island in the late 1970s, after the residential school closed. Four houses stood in various spots around the field, the only houses left. Behind the schoolhouse there used to be a large vegetable garden. This was where elder Candice Joe said she went blind after looking at the bright diamond eyes of a hairy *puukmis* that was stealing her family's lettuce at night. Beyond that was the dense forest that filled most of the island.

Chase's childhood home nestled at the edge of the trees. The stairs leading to the front door rotted in places. I climbed slowly, holding the rickety railing, testing each waterlogged step before fully putting my weight down. Somebody had taken the doorknob, so I only had to push the door open to enter. Inside, the house smelled faintly of mildew.

Black stains of mould splotched the white carpet in the living room, which made the floor look like cowhide. I entered carefully, the floor soft and spongy in some places. In other places it had already caved in, leaving splintered holes through which I could fall into the black basement below.

"Hello?" I called out. "Are you here?"

Had Chase returned home?

I went into the kitchen. Many things had been left behind when Miranda and Chase and his two older brothers moved into a house on the Tawakin Reserve. On the table where Miranda sewed sequins onto a shawl the night Jimmy Charlie died, there was a swollen Sears catalogue displaying the fashions from more than two decades ago, plus a rusted cookie sheet and a child's pair of mismatched mittens. So many things were left behind in each of the crumbling houses on this island. Perhaps it was only a matter of economy, only those things most wanted and needed making their way onto the boats and over the stretch of water to the Tawakin Reserve. Or perhaps some things were left as a sign of hope that they would one day be able to live again on this beautiful island the people loved so dearly. It was, for many of the elders at least, a nostalgic reminder of simpler times.

I called hello again, then headed down the hallway towards the bedrooms. Something scurried along the wall as I passed the bathroom.

In Miranda's bedroom, the carpet had been stripped, exposing the sheets of plywood underneath. With my toe, I poked one of the floorboards. It bent like a bow, nearly as soft as cardboard, coming off the nails like paper torn from the rings of a binder. I walked to the window along the seams between the boards, staying on the support beams. Out the window, I could see a hint of the totem pole that guarded the burial plots on Rubant Island. Pinned to the wall beside the window, a few sun-faded photographs showed a very young Chase and his older brothers. On the sill was an abalone shell, its iridescent pink and blue inside lustrous in the warm sun. Beside it were several loose beads, tiny ones hardly bigger than sesame seeds, a needle and a long length of thread. Somebody—Miranda—was going to cover the ugly outside of the abalone shell with beads but never got around to it. Had Miranda intended it to be another gift for me?

She'd given me numerous gifts in an attempt to reconcile after Chase's birth. For the first six months, I didn't see Miranda at all, not once, which wasn't surprising given that it was wintertime, she had a newborn baby at home and she still lived here on Toomista Island. Then one day, she started to show up alone at the outpost, each time with a different gift. A cedar rose. A small cedar basket. A beaded abalone shell. A glass ball the size of a grapefruit. A beaded bracelet. Jars of salmon. A bag of halibut. A necklace with two cobalt blue beads—Russian trade beads. Highly coveted by the people in Tawakin, they were made of glass, tubular with flat outer edges like a pentagon.

Standing at my back door, Miranda dropped the necklace into my palm, said quietly, "For you, Sister," and looked into the kitchen with the hope that I might finally let her inside. She saw how her words touched me—that she would call me, a *mamulthni*, her sister—I knew she saw it in my face because three more times she repeated it. Emphasized it. "I'm sorry, *Sister*," she said to me. "I don't know how it happened between me and him, *Sister*, I really don't. But we ain't together now and we never will be and he loves you. We love you, *Sister*."

I handed the necklace back to her.

"You could never find a way to pay me back for what you did to me," I said, my voice full of anger. "There is no gift big enough."

The fact that Frank had also tried to reconcile with me might have led me to have faith in Miranda's words. But it wasn't a matter of belief. I was simply too sad and angry to forgive anybody yet, and I said as much to both of them.

"Please," Frank said to me, "my sadness is sinking me."

"Then why don't you tell yourself a story," I replied coolly, hiding my grief from him as a way to keep my pride, and to protect myself from my own desire to stay with him. "Stories are like boxes you can put your sadness into."

Over the course of the following year, Frank tried several more times to reconcile with me. Remembering it now, I couldn't imagine where my willpower came from, how I managed to set aside my deep feelings of love for Frank and stand my ground. Was it the right decision? I wasn't sure, but Anne insisted it was.

"He wants to marry me," I explained.

"So he says," Anne said.

"He seems to mean it. He cried today."

"Seven years. You two were together a long time. Why didn't you get married before? Suddenly it's a big deal to him now?"

"Not only now. He's asked me to marry him before, too."

"You never told me that. When?"

"A couple of times. A few years ago. I said no. Not yet."

"I thought you loved him."

"I did. I do. I wasn't sure I wanted to get married."

"Right," Anne said. "The life of servitude for women."

"No offence, Anne."

She'd been Mrs. Kevin Marsh for six years at this point, though her books were published under Anne Perkal. A small gesture of independence.

"Do you think you'll ever forgive him, then?" Anne asked.

"I do miss him."

"How do you know they aren't—" Anne paused. "Are they still together?"

"No," I said.

"How do you know for sure?"

"I don't, I guess."

After Jimmy died, I watched tentatively to see if Miranda and Frank would become a couple. As far as I could tell, they didn't. But Frank did confess openly to being Chase's real father. A few eyebrows were raised, but on the whole not much was said around the cove. This led me to believe that many people knew all along, which in turn led me to believe that their relationship had been going on for longer than either Miranda or Frank would ever admit to me. I was too humiliated to ask anybody if any of this were true, not even Sophie Florence. Many people in my circumstance might have wanted the full truth, I suppose, but I preferred ignorance. I didn't want to know any more than what I already contended with.

Things mended slowly for me, over the course of years. But time was felt differently in Tawakin than elsewhere. Here, time was a fine mist we moved through, scarcely feeling it, hardly noticing how it fell upon our coats, slowly accumulating, until it eventually, once heavy enough, soaked through to our skin and chilled our bones.

Carefully, I now walked to the closet in Miranda's bedroom. The doors to the closet had been ripped off, and inside empty coat hangers were pushed to one end of the rod. A man's belt, slung over the middle of the rod, was tied to the handle of a plastic pail, and behind it, stuck on the wall of the closet, was a row of objects. Long things that looked like shrivelled banana peels.

I leaned forward to get a closer look.

Shocked, I jerked back. Somebody had nailed a row of garter snakes to the wall. Seven of them. Not the empty shed skins of snakes either, but the entire creatures. Their triangular heads punctured with a tiny pin. And on the floor underneath, dead grasshoppers, as if those executed had been given a last supper. Somebody had done this recently. Inside the pail the wilted blades of grass were still verdant with chlorophyll, and the flesh of the reptiles was still in the process of decaying.

I looked around the rest of the house, trying to find any more grisly evidence. I found nothing. No sign of Chase. No sign of anybody else. But I couldn't bring myself to leave until I returned to the closet and untied the belt from the rod. I dropped it on Miranda's bedroom floor. The light clank of metal. I thought of her son Ronnie's death nineteen years ago. He had hanged himself with a belt in his Port Hardy apartment—that was the report from the coroner. Twenty-one years old. Ronnie's death was difficult to bear after his brother Stanley's the year before, though nothing could ever compare to the shock of that first death, Stanley's death. Nothing could have ever prepared Chase for the change Stanley's death brought to his life.

Stanley Charlie was born in 1971. I met him when I arrived in Tawakin in 1975, when he was four. He was always a quiet boy who preferred to play under low-lying shelters: the kitchen table of the outpost, the front porch of his house, the spot where the wharf met the shore on Mitchell Island. He loved to go hunting and fishing with his father, Jimmy, and often followed Jimmy everywhere around the cove. He had the same large smile and used it as generously as his father, though he was shy to speak. From the moment Chase was born, eleven-year-old Stan protected him, adored him, teased him. "Your name is Chase, so you ought to get chased," Stan would say as he started to run after his squealing little brother.

At the time of Jimmy's death, Stan was sixteen. Afterwards, Stan did not speak for nearly two years. People went out of their way to strike up a conversation with him, but he'd only nod and smile—a small smile with tightly closed lips, as if he were trying to hold in something that might otherwise erupt and leave him emptied.

And then one day, eight years later, Stan drove his trawler out of the cove to go fishing. Often, he took Chase, who was thirteen at the time, but on this day he went alone. It was a beautiful April morning. He anchored his boat near Ootanish Inlet. Who knows how long he bobbed there on the ocean before he shot himself. He must have sat on the edge of the stern because his body fell overboard and was never recovered. The only things left were his shotgun on the deck and the spray of his blood.

It was Margaret who telephoned the outpost a week after Stan's death. "Miranda's making no sense. It was my turn to sit with her and I'd only stepped out onto the porch when she locked me out."

"What's she saying?" I asked.

"Whenever we knock on the door," Margaret explained, "she tells us that she's packing up to go be with her son."

The actual work of reconciling with Miranda had taken many years, through Jimmy's death and a few years afterwards. By the time of Stanley's death, we were friendly with one another and I held no bitterness towards her, no grudge, though we never returned to our Saturday cribbage games. We all seemed to be left damaged. Hearts broken. Friendships, too. I'm not sure forgiveness was the right word to describe what came to pass. I'm not even certain reconciliation took place. After all, we'd never spoken openly about the truth of their betrayal, and without knowing the truth, could there ever be a genuine reconciliation?

Perhaps that was precisely what we agreed upon, to move on without ever discussing the truth. A kind of restart button, only the slate wasn't wiped clean. Like words printed on a chalkboard, the previous words only partly erased underneath. True, Miranda's annual photographs started to make their way straight onto my walls instead of into the drawer. And yes, we began to laugh again when we pulled cedar with Sophie Florence and Gina and Margaret on Toomista. From out of nowhere, I'd patched together a life again, and it was because of that sweet boy—that's how I saw it, and I think that's how Miranda saw it too, because by the time Stanley died, she had made room for my relationship with Chase, though of course neither of us ever acknowledged it. It was an unspoken agreement between us that we shared him, and as I now thought back to this time, it was impossible to trace how or when exactly this came to be.

After Margaret's phone call, several women accompanied me to Miranda's house that afternoon. The door was still locked. When I knocked, it was just like Margaret had reported.

"I'm busy," Miranda said. "I got to be with Stan."

"Somebody get an axe," I said, worried Miranda was going to take her own life. "We've got to get this door open now. Where's Chase?"

"Safe at Nan Lily's house," Gina said, as Sophie Florence hurried around the corner to retrieve an axe.

Within minutes, we broke through Miranda's front door. Although she was stunned by our entrance, Miranda was docile and too preoccupied with the things strewn all over the floor to protest. Pots and pans, knives, clothes, rope. It was not a euphemism. She was, in reality, packing to move closer to Stan's place of rest.

This packing, which seemed to require much deliberation and planning by Miranda, continued for the next week. Then one day, Chase appeared at my door with a satchel of his belongings and a note, written in Miranda's handwriting, that read: *I hope this gift is big enough.*

Racing past Chase and down the outside stairs, I caught a glimpse of Miranda as she pulled away. I shouted. She didn't hear me. The gunwale of her boat was barely above the water, the weight of her supplies heavy. Stacks of rubber totes, planks of wood, fishing rods, tools of various shapes and sizes. As I watched her drive across the cove, I had no idea she would never return.

When they realized that Miranda had left, Sophie Florence and Gina drove up to see her, returning with a message that she was never coming back.

"She's building a house of some sort," Gina said.

"What about Chase?" I asked.

"In six months the heli-logging operation is all done," Sophie Florence said. "Then Frank will be back for good and Chase can move in with him."

"Maybe he can move in with Nan Lily until then," Gina said.

"He could just stay here." I shrugged to conceal my shyness in making the suggestion. "If that's easier for everybody."

And so it had been settled. The six months that followed—the happiest months of my life? I've often wondered if they were, even knowing that poor Miranda was grieving over Stan's suicide. Poor Miranda? Was that entirely accurate? She had, after all, abandoned Chase, who was suffering his own grief at the loss of his brother. Anger, too. Directed straight at his mother.

He told me this one night when we were painting. It was at the end of his first month in the outpost, and the endless downpour of rain had started to give us cabin fever. Most days he was sad and quiet in his grief, and some days I could hear him crying in the bedroom I'd set up for him. Sometimes I'd go and hold him, and other times I'd keep him distracted with activities. Through the mail, I'd ordered various things to pass the time—a checkers/chess set, Monopoly, a plastic model of the *Lusitania* that came without any glue, and a set of acrylic paints and brushes, along with several small canvases. We were each painting on a canvas at the kitchen table one afternoon, when I suggested it would be more thrilling to paint a mural on the wall.

Chase lifted his eyebrows. "Won't you get in trouble?"

I shrugged. "Let's start somewhere small. The bathroom."

We decided on a forest theme. It took us two hours to paint the trees. I added little Wilde Grannies in the branches, while Chase started to paint grass and ferns along the ground. Then he added several thick black squiggles.

"Worms?" I asked.

"They're shadows," he said.

"Of what?"

"Snakes," he said.

"Like on Toomista," I nodded.

"Like at home," he said.

"How come they're just the shadows?" I asked.

"That's what they look like in my dreams."

I dabbed little circles of grey on one of the grannies.

"I hate the snakes," he said.

"Me too," I said, dabbing.

"They're all my mother's fault."

I stopped, my brush in midair. "What do you mean?"

"I hate her," was all he'd say.

The angry pull of his eyes, at once glaring and searching. And I thought, this was what it was like to be needed by a child. This was what a mother felt. I felt complete but also disassembled. Bliss wrapped inside dreadful uncertainty. It was rapture while standing on a crumbling precipice. The inevitability of heartbreak.

What was it like to lose two children to suicide?

I tried to imagine it for a second. Even one second was too much.

✻   ✻   ✻

It was just before seven when I returned to the outpost. There was still a chance that Wren was asleep, so I tied up the boat and took the long way around the ridge. That way, if she hadn't seen the boat gone, I could claim to be returning from a morning walk around the island. I didn't know yet how I planned to answer any questions she'd surely have about the bear, but I really didn't care. I was just glad to be rid of it.

As I walked along the ridge, something glinted in the middle of the swordferns. After years of combing the beaches for glass balls, my eyes were quick to pick out any hint of lustrous reflection on the ground. I waded through the knee-high ferns and picked up the bottle. Johnson Little Pinot Grigio. White wine. Empty. I put it to my nose and smelled it. Still a hint of alcohol odour. Sour, I thought, recalling Hannah's scowling face as she insulted Wren's breath. I carried it back to the outpost and put it in the bottom cupboard in the kitchen for the time being.

In the bathroom, I cranked the bathtub faucets on full and poured an entire bottle of liquid soap under the cascading stream. Bubbles grew and gathered like storm clouds while I wriggled out of my clothes and kicked them into the corner. Steam rose from the water and clouded the mirror and the small window above the toilet. My foot reddened from the heat when I stepped into the tub.

I reclined, the water rising to the top, and hoped the heat was killing any bacteria that may have rubbed off the bear and onto my skin. With a stiff brush and a bar of soap, I scrubbed every inch of my arms until the skin was raw and red. I dropped the soap and it sunk slowly to the bottom. Feeling around until my fingers wrapped around the slippery bar, it popped out from my grip and I fumbled blindly for it once more. I washed my face and my neck and shampooed my hair. I then shampooed it a second time as I thought about Miranda and how I'd promised to visit again. When I'd told her that, I'd honestly believed that Chase would've returned by now, and since he hadn't, I started to feel eager to go back and press her harder for answers about his whereabouts.

In my heart, I still believed he was alive, but now I had the sense that maybe he wasn't off hunting. A gut feeling told me there were undercurrents swirling beneath the surface of the community. I suspected Miranda knew something about it, if only I could decipher the meaning of her stories. But like Frank, I was anxious to confirm that he was safe, and I started to envision my next visit to Miranda's, puzzling out how I might access that brain of hers.

First, though, I promised to show Wren the daily routine, including a trip to the Tawakin Market and a tour of the reserve. That way, she could operate the outpost solo while I headed back up the coast tomorrow to check on Miranda by myself and see what I could find out.

After soaking for a long time, the bubbles disappeared and the water cooled. I stared at the water while thinking about buoyancy, how the pressure on the object increases the deeper it sinks, and how, if the object is less dense than water, it will accelerate back to the surface.

I held my breath and lowered my face under the surface.

* * *

Outside the kitchen window, the dry leaves of the cottonwoods were turning in the early morning light. I rubbed the towel over my damp hair and smelled the season shifting in the air. Past the grassy ridge, the water was gunmetal grey and chopping into small crests, while farther out, past the tail end of Mitchell Island, it was erupting and frothing over the jagged rocks. There were no oystercatchers foraging the crevices with their bright-orange beaks today, though the sea gulls had gathered in large skyward groups, sailing and twisting in the wind. Under the turning leaves in the yard, a crow walked the perimeter of the discoloured, flattened patch of grass and pecked one of the leftover maggots. Soon, it would get dark earlier in the evenings. Less time for searching.

I remembered an evening twenty years ago, in the early fall, when Chase came back to the outpost late for dinner. This was during the six months he lived with me, back when he was thirteen and our days were closely knitted together. I could picture the cluttered table that evening: an extra workbook on polynomials I'd purchased online, and beside it, a diagram of a plant cell that Chase had coloured the evening before, as his homework, chloroplasts and mitochondria and a large vacuole, and beside that, three paperback novels we were slowly making our way through. *The Phantom Tollbooth; Charlie and the Chocolate Factory; Danny, the Champion of the World.* Chase struggled with reading, and his literacy, like many of the students in Tawakin, was below grade average. When he moved in with me, I'd made it my goal to improve his skills. I was determined to see him succeed, to see him have choices in life. Maybe college.

"Where were you?" I'd asked, hands on hips, as he walked through the door late that evening.

"Me and Henry went up to Leslie Lake," he said.

"Your supper is cold now," I said.

"I ain't hungry," he said. "Me and Henry got fish sandwiches from his place."

"I asked over the radio for you and nobody had seen you."

"Sorry," he grumbled. "I forgot."

Instead of getting upset over his insincere apology, I was elated by how normal it felt, how domestic, how much like a real family it was to suffer the moodiness of a teenaged child.

I said, "What about your homework?

"I don't got none."

I corrected, "You don't have any."

"I know. That's what I just said."

I explained, "No, you say: 'I don't have any,' or 'I've got none,' not 'I don't got none.' It's a double negative. It means you have some."

"But I don't got none," he said.

I sighed. "You always have homework, Chase."

"Real dumb." He flopped down into a chair. "Henry's grandpa says our land teaches us lots, you know."

"What? By throwing stones into the lake? Homework's not real dumb, it's smart. Get a good education and you can be anything you want."

He'd just entered the high school side of the hallway, grade eight, and now, as I'd told him so many times already, he had to be thinking seriously of his grades and his academic future.

"I want to go heli-logging like my dad."

"But you'll have the whole world open to you with an education," I reasoned.

He stared at me blankly.

"Or I'll be a fisher," he said. "Like my dad Jimmy."

It was strange to hear him refer to Jimmy in this way, but even after learning at the age of six that Frank was his real father, Chase had always continued to call both men "Dad."

"Or I'll work in the bush," he said. "That's what Henry's gonna do."

"You can become those things if you want, but you should go to college first," I said. "Then you'll have lots of choices."

Chase looked at the books waiting for him on the table. "I choose to not do homework."

"That's not one of the choices." I smiled.

He rolled his eyes.

"One day you'll thank me," I said.

And he did thank me, though not in so many words, at his high school graduation ceremony. Chase and Patty were the only two graduates that year. They sat together on a small makeshift stage made of plywood and painted black. The women, me included, spent two days decorating the school gym and preparing a huge feast for the entire community. Patty had given birth to Hannah three months earlier, and Hannah rested quietly in a basket on the stage between Chase and Patty. Margaret and Gina made three graduate caps out of cedar strips, including a tiny one for Hannah. Cousins from all around Vancouver Island made the long journey, as they did every year for graduation, and the gym was packed.

My influence over Chase's schooling had continued throughout high school. Often, he brought his homework to the outpost so that I could give him extra help. For hours, I helped him study for his provincial exams, and one day in grade twelve, just before Hannah was born, he told me that he wasn't sure he wanted to keep fishing. Not as a job, and not for fun either.

"I just don't like the ocean no more," he said.

At the time, I wondered if it was because of Teddy's death.

But then he said, "I think I want to be a teacher."

"That's wonderful," I said. "You'll be a great teacher."

Patty received her leaving certificate that day, awarded to students who completed enough years of high school but not enough academic requirements. Chase, on the other hand, was the first student in years to graduate with a full Dogwood Diploma.

Far off to Chase's left, I sat along the gym wall on a bench and held back tears. I didn't think he knew where I was sitting, yet he turned during the ceremony and looked straight at me and waved. He did not wave at anybody else. I know, because I watched carefully for it. He singled me out, was all I could think, in front of everybody, and it was all the thanks I needed, to be acknowledged.

14

An hour later, Wren was up and ready to learn the routine, or so she claimed. She appeared half awake, occasionally rubbing her temples and scrubbing her palms over her whole face. She was dressed like a hiker, wearing some sort of water-resistant pants, a fleecy pullover with a thermal waffle undershirt sticking out the bottom and chunky boots. Her unruly hair was pulled back into a stubby ponytail and a wide wool headband, the kind people often wear when skiing, covered her hairline. I felt old and sedentary in my pilled cardigan and navy slacks.

When Wren saw that I was waiting for her, she quickly nibbled a pinch of granola from a little plastic baggie, put the baggie inside the pocket of her cargo pants and gave a Japanese-like bow. "Your student awaits, oh wise Teacher."

In the waiting room, I unlocked the main door and went around flipping on the lights and the computer in the office, Wren's nylon pants shushing two steps behind. I took an inventory sheet out of the binder and surveyed the medical equipment, counting the analgesics, the tubes of ointments, the plastic syringes, the tongue depressors. I confirmed that my travel kit was still stocked with scissors and splints and rolls of gauze, checking the little boxes beside the list of medical supplies on the sheet while Wren watched.

"You're the only nurse here. Is it really necessary to take inventory like that?" she asked, motioning to the sheet in my hand.

I hesitated. "I don't know. I've just always done it this way."

Wren was right. This part of my routine was unnecessary, unless you figured that an outpost perched on the brink of a vast and largely unsettled rain forest was a target for thieves who happened to be passing through, or if you believed it was a locus of supernatural activity where mischievous apparitions congregated to steal my syringes or to simply move them from one place to another so that I'd start to question my aging mind. But this was how I'd signalled a new day for the past forty years, and I wasn't sure what I'd do without this routine. When I tried to imagine my new life I could only ever see myself drinking tea, and more tea, and reading books, and more books, and staring out the window of Anne's apartment at the parking lot where the elm trees blocked the view of the Cowichan River. It hardly seemed enough to get me out of bed in the mornings.

"I see they took the bear away," Wren said.

"Huh?" I pretended that a line of text caught my attention.

"This morning, when I was having coffee. I noticed the bear's gone."

"Oh, yes. It's gone."

"They must have come early."

"I don't know," I said.

"You don't know?"

I tried to change the subject.

"I found a wine bottle in the bush out back," I said.

"Oh?"

"Do you know where it came from?"

"No," she said. "You were supposed to wait."

"Wait for what?"

"For them to come and get the bear."

I asked, "Was it yours? The wine bottle?"

"Of course not," she said. "So what did you do with it?"

The assumption in her question threw me off. I hesitated a moment too long. I felt caught, and so I said, "I took it away."

"Where?"

"A peaceful spot."

Wren nodded, though she looked unsure, and left it at that.

"What about the bottle?" I asked.

She shrugged. "I told you. It's not mine."

❅   ❅   ❅

Later that afternoon, Wren and I locked up the outpost and took the boat to Mitchell Island and walked along the wharf with the slanted rain pecking at our cheeks. Outside the market, the light from inside filled the glass door. Under the small awning, we shook the rain from our jackets and went inside, where we found a small crowd, five or six people, plus a handful of children, who, as usual, begged me to buy them candy.

"Did you all work hard at school today?" Wren asked the children.

"Yes!" said the seven children in unison.

A small girl pointed at her brother and said, "Kenny never does."

"I will tomorrow," said the boy called Kenny.

"Promise?" Wren narrowed her eyes at Kenny.

He raised his eyebrows. "Promise."

But the children's faces dropped when Wren bought each child a carrot stick and a juice box. "Healthy eating!" she said.

"Quit spilling juice on my clean floor," George told the kids.

"Whatever," said little Kenny. "The floor's real dirty."

Standing at the post office wicket, I glanced at the floor. Muddy boot treads everywhere. I shuffled through a stack of mail addressed to the outpost. It was mostly junk, except for a couple of medical supply catalogues.

"Go on, go eat your *chumiss* outside," George said, and when the children skipped towards the door, he called after them from his spot behind the post office wicket, "What do you say to Nurse?"

"But it's not even *chumiss!*" Kenny said.

Still, the children screeched to a stop and Willie even said, "*Errrch!*" and then they turned and called out, "*Klecko klecko klecko!*"

Wren looked through the wicket. "*Chumiss* means dessert, right?"

George stood at the special post office computer. "Sort of," he said as he typed something on the keyboard.

"It also means to be deeply satisfied," I said.

Wren nodded slowly, as though giving this serious thought, and as she leaned over the counter and rested her hand on the wicket frame, I noticed that her fingers partially covered a small heart drawn with blue ink. Other bits of graffiti—hearts and statements like *Frank was here*, and *Gina stinks*, and *Ernie is real nutty*—covered the frame of the wicket, some drawn with pen and some carved right into the wood. It was an archival record of sorts, evidencing the names of people and the dates they visited the store and even some of the romances they'd had.

At that moment, George stopping typing.

"Do you like oysters?" he asked Wren.

"Who doesn't?" Wren smiled.

George lit up. "I can bring you some."

"That would be wonderful, Georgie."

George flashed his large white teeth. "Cooked my special way or raw?"

"Well, how about half of each? You have to have some raw, you know."

"You know what raw oysters are supposed to do to you, right?"

"Why, yes I do." Wren smiled and winked at George.

"Is it true?" asked George, now beaming. "Do they do what they say?"

Wren said, "Give a few to that lucky wife of yours and see for yourself."

Wren and I left the market, and as I started the boat, a silver punt moved across the middle of the cove. It was crowded with several adults and children heading back to the reserve. All of them waved excitedly and shouted, "Hello, hello!" Wren waved, and I waved too, and suddenly I felt enveloped by a brightness, a hopeful mood. I felt a hint of peace to know that the people I loved might be left in good hands after all. It fed me like *chumiss*.

✳ ✳ ✳

Once we reached the dock at the bottom of the reserve, I explained which parking spots were off limits and which of the loitering dogs Wren should kick in the ribs if it got too close.

To start Wren's tour of the Tawakin Reserve, I pointed at the white house in front of the dock and told her that's where Shelly and her teen-aged daughter, Marjorie, live with Shelly's mother, Julia Henry. Julia, who now gave me a nod from the big window on the second floor, hardly ever left the house. Shelly and Marjorie slept together on a mattress in the basement, between old fishing nets and traps that stink of prawns. There were rats, too.

"How come the daughter doesn't move somewhere else?" Wren asked.

"Look around. There are maybe twenty-five houses on the reserve, and a lot of these houses are already crowded with six, seven, eight people. Nowhere else for them to live."

A group of children shouted hello from one of the nearby yards. They circled a trampoline. There was the squeak of rusted springs as little Kenny bounced from his feet to his bottom and back up again. I waved and gave Kenny a thumbs-up.

"Anyhow," I said, "you need to keep a close eye on Marjorie when she comes to the outpost. She steals things."

"Will do." Wren nodded. "And who is her father?"

"Marjorie's father was sent away for molesting her."

"Sent away by who?"

"The whole village. They voted."

"So where'd he go?"

"Don't know. Port Hardy, probably. A long time ago it used to be that bad men were sent away into the rain forest up the mountain, where their skin supposedly turned to tree bark as a punishment for what they did."

A light drizzle started to fall from the ash-grey sky. The children beside the trampoline broke into peels of laughter. A television show murmured out the crack of an open window. The rising breeze pushed the shallow tide into long folds and rustled the brambles growing out the side of the ridge. Otherwise, the reserve had an eerie quietness, a strange emptiness. I looked to the edges of the sky for any sign of rough weather, but there was only the usual grey. People often headed indoors when they smelled a storm coming.

We walked past the contaminated house, as people called it, an especially dilapidated place that was boarded up and spray-painted with red graffiti: a pot leaf, a raven, a giant penis. We waved at Ernie Frank, who was out chopping his wood in the next yard. I pointed out Nan Lily's house off to the right and explained that there was a store in the basement. "In case you need something and the Tawakin Market is closed, just go through the basement door and call out. Wait a bit, though, because it takes her a long while to collect her slippers and put on her sweater and get down the stairs." I pointed out two more houses at the opposite corner of the reserve where there were also stores in the basements. "And at that blue house over there, you can buy fresh-baked bread and all kinds of *chumiss* on Fridays."

I showed Wren the community centre where the dinner for her would be held. Then I cut across the asphalt basketball court, its cracks and blisters filled with dandelions and thistles, and squeezed sideways through a mucky trail between the blackberry brambles. On the other side was a large blackened square of earth. Ashes, two feet deep, and chunks of charred debris filled the low-lying cement foundation like a giant sandbox. This, I told her, was Sophie Florence's house. It burned down three years ago. Her uncle and three of her cousins died in the fire. We walked the rest of the loop around the back of the reserve. I pointed out Chief Trudy Henry's house and explained how I was called there ten years ago after her teenaged daughter hanged herself. "Trudy's a good woman," I added. "If you have any concerns about the reserve, talk to her."

It was not easy to tell these stories. So much sadness was bound up in their lives, yet their lives were so much more than just their sorrows. How should the reserve be explained to an outsider? I didn't want to turn each home into a simple tale or reduce each family to a single tragedy. At the same time, I didn't want to ignore the realities. Though of course, there was so much that Wren would need to learn for herself.

On our way back down to the dock, I showed Wren the house that once belonged to Candice Joe, an elder who started raising her eleven-year-old granddaughter, whose name was also Candice Joe, after the girl's mother left for a party in Port Hardy and never came back.

"Elder Candice died one night while she was beading a shawl with her granddaughter. She had diabetes," I said, "and had been blind from it for years. I'll warn you, some of the other elders, including Candice herself when she was alive, have always insisted that Candice going blind had nothing to do with diabetes. They claim she went blind after looking at the glowing eyes of a *puukmis*, and there's no point in trying to argue otherwise."

"Who knows? Maybe they're right," Wren said.

Before I had a chance to say anything more, a man's voice called out from behind us. We turned on the dock to see George coming down the road.

"Hey! That bear you shot—where'd it go?"

"It's gone," I called back.

"Did Patty take it?" he asked.

"No! She never even came for the skin and claws."

"Be spoiled by now anyways. Did Frank take the gallbladder?"

"No!"

"What about Saul? Did he come take the foreskin?"

I untied one of the ropes from the dock. "What?"

"I seen Saul at the market. He said him and his son were going to deliver your new fridge, and I told him he could take the foreskin."

It was true, Saul Finkler and his son Woodrow had delivered my frost-free refrigerator after Wren and I had finished going through the morning routine. I couldn't wait to stock it with milk and fresh vegetables, scheduled to arrive this week on the *Pacific Sojourn II*. It'd be a long time before I'd have to stomach another can of soup.

"Get it? Foreskin?" George shouted. "On account of him being Jewish?"

"I get it," I called back. Rolling my eyes, I glanced across the water to Saul Finkler's place on Mitchell Island. The only thing worse than an inappropriate joke was one shouted inside the cove where the surrounding bowl of trees reverberated all kinds of sounds and voices. How often had I heard nearby conversations from my yard only to discover that the voices actually came from halfway across the cove. Sometimes the wind silenced words in the cove, whereas other times it carried words, whipping them into the air and swirling them like autumn leaves. Indiscriminately dropping them into ears that shouldn't hear them.

The wind whistled under the door, and there was the smell of a storm coming. Across the table, in the pale flicker of the dying fluorescent light, Wren stared at her supper. Her elbow was propped on the table and her hand, which held a spoon, moved in a constant slow arc from the bowl to her mouth like a mechanical lever. Each time the soup reached her mouth she slid it off the spoon with her teeth, pulling her lips back and scraping the metal, which gave the impression that tonight she found the whole process of eating tedious. She'd had to give up, at least temporarily, her raw vegan diet, or else starve. Every now and then, she broke this rhythm to take a gulp of water from her cup, an ornate teacup with an Emily Carr sketch reproduced on the front, my favourite teacup, now with a chip in its brim from the bear.

"I got that cup years ago at the Royal British Columbia Museum," I said. "Have you been? You should go during one of your debushing breaks if you haven't. They had this special exhibit on Emily Carr when I went. It was quite something. They even had the trailer where she lived and painted alone in the woods. Boy, was it tiny. About as small as a bathroom. Well, I don't think it was the actual trailer, probably a reproduction, but still it really gave a sense of—"

"Doesn't it make you want to pull your hair out?" Wren interrupted.

"What do you mean?"

She pointed her spoon in my direction. "Our government should be strung up by their balls. Look at their houses over there, it's disgraceful, it looks like a shanty town, and their lives—"

"Their lives aren't terrible," I said.

Wren gave me a look of baffled anger. She snorted. "What was that you just showed me, then?"

"Sure, things aren't always roses and laughter here, but there's plenty of good, too. Life is beautiful here. Sad and happy, and beautiful. Besides, it's not like they have a monopoly on bad stuff. It's not like any of that stuff doesn't happen elsewhere. It just all happens in a tiny space here," I said, not entirely convinced of everything I was saying.

"Don't you care about how everything's affected them? Residential schools, reserves, institutionalized racism? *Colonialism?*" She pronounced every syllable of the last word as though it were obvious and shouldn't even need mentioning.

"These people are my friends, they're my family. Of course I care," I said.

She rolled her eyes, almost imperceptibly. She looked up at the ceiling and motioned around the kitchen with her spoon. "Do you see the difference?"

"Of course I see the difference."

"Doesn't it embarrass you?"

"Why should it? It's not my fault the outpost was built so sturdy."

"We've taken away their language, their culture, their identity. We've said, 'You're going to be this, not this, and here's the proof, this little status card with a number that says you're an Indian.' Pieces of paper, that's how we define them. That's how we're all defined. Social insurance cards, birth certificates, bank records, criminal records." She paused and stirred her soup around. "Take those medical records, for example. Those things don't define a person, and yet there they are, labelling people, keeping them trapped by their past. He punched this person and broke his nose. She got herpes from some guy in Port Hardy. He was a drunk for twenty-five years and now his liver's giving out. Doesn't it bother you? Storing all those private things about people?"

Did it bother me? Of course it did. I hated it. I hated knowing what was in those records. I never had anybody except Anne to share this part of my job with, and I had to carry this burden by myself, yet here was somebody who understood. Somebody with whom I could share the burden.

"But those records hold crucial information for some people," I said.

"But they're so often negative labels. This is how you were once broken, and this piece of paper will make sure it's never forgotten. Doesn't *that* bother you?"

"It does," I admitted. "It weighs on me. I feel like I know too much, and people have treated me differently now and then because I know too much. Sometimes I've just wanted to be free of it all. It's like a private piece of each person's past is in those files, and I'm trapped in there with them. I guess that sounds a bit pitiful."

"Nobody should ever be trapped by their past or by another person's past," Wren said, her tone softening, but she was no less fired up. "Nobody should ever be trapped by the things people say, or by little black marks typed onto a piece of paper, or by little blue scribbles handwritten on a piece of paper."

She slurped her soup.

I remembered watching Nan Lily and Ernie Frank burn the Indian Act in a rusted metal barrel behind the school to mark the signing of their treaty. My heart wrenched at the sight of Nan Lily's face as she dropped the pieces of paper, one at a time, into the orange flames, rivulets of tears glistening on her cheeks.

"Records are like ghosts that never stop haunting your identity," Wren said.

There was a strain in what she said, a faint undercurrent of something else, and I couldn't help but feel as though she wasn't only talking about the people on the reserve. I thought about the photos I'd seen of Wren online.

"You're really passionate about these issues, I admire that," I said, as I got up from the table and scraped the residue off my plate into the trash bin by the wall.

"You have to do more than admire it," she said, "you have to take action."

"Protest, you mean?"

"Not just protest," she said. "Revolution. Through actions that change everything. Actions that can't be undone. That's the goal of the true revolutionary."

"The revolutionary?"

Wren nodded. She stood up. Her chair let out a low screech across the linoleum. There was the clatter of metal on porcelain as she picked up her bowl and dumped the last chunks of her soup into the trash bin. Then she rinsed the bowl and left it unwashed on the counter beside me.

Listening to Wren's fervour for changing the world left me feeling small and obsolete and, quite frankly, old. As she walked towards the living room, I saw the teacup, the solitary figure of Emily Carr—the lonely woman wearing a long coat and floppy hat, with an umbrella in one hand and a folding stool in the other, and a satchel over her shoulder, a furry dog underfoot—the spinster dangling from Wren's fingers.

15

That evening, I went to my bedroom, closed the door and stretched out on my bed. On the nightstand was a miniature oar Chase gave me shortly after living with me in the outpost. I reached over, and as I picked it up, I remembered the night Frank returned from his heli-logging job. He had stood in the doorway of my kitchen with rain streaming off the hood of his jacket. Every loss in my life had fallen like rain, I thought then. Fallen like rain and eroded deep holes I had to watch out for, or plummet.

"You're back," I'd said to Frank. I remembered feeling my face splitting open with joy at the sight of him, and although I made every effort to keep it in check, including rubbing my hand across my mouth, I couldn't contain myself.

"I am," Frank smiled.

He looked very much like a man out of the bush. His hair hung down to his shoulders, though it was still not quite as long as it was in his younger years. His skin had a patina of dirt, as if he might never get fully clean again, and his wiry beard was an unruly patch of black and silver. He was as handsome as ever, and part of me still loved him.

"Dad!" Chase exclaimed, looking up from his schoolwork on the table, his grin stretched wide. He pushed his chair away from the table and ran into Frank's arms.

Frank laughed. "You're getting wet, Son."

"I don't even care," Chase said.

"How long you here for?" I asked, thinking of his two-week visit the previous winter.

"For good," he said.

My stomach lurched. Would he want Chase back?

After shaking off his wet gear, Frank sat at the table next to Chase. I stood at the window.

"Thanks for taking care of him, Bernie."

I bit my lip. When Chase came to live with me, I'd known that Frank was returning for good in six months. Secretly, I'd hoped he'd get another extension on his contract. But here he was, and now here I was, at this moment of inevitable loss. I clutched the curtains and stared out into the dark night.

"You miss being back home, Son?" Frank asked.

"Home?" I laughed. "What are you talking about, Frank? The reserve is right there across the water."

Frank shrugged. "His family's over there is all."

I frowned. Frank didn't realize how close Chase and I had grown. "Still," I said. "*Over there?* You make it sound like it's in Japan. I could swim to it if I had to."

Frank turned to Chase. "So how's school, Son?"

"Real good," Chase said, turning his worksheets for Frank to see. "I finished my math homework."

"Ay-ha, you're smart," Frank said.

Chase held up a paperback novel. "And we finished reading *Lord of the Flies* for my book report. I tried to read some of it, but Nursema'am read most of it to me out loud."

"Was it good?"

"I picked it from the library, but I wish I picked a different one," Chase explained. "I didn't like it much. Too many people are mean in it, and I could hunt better than Jack's whole hunting party. They don't know nothing about living on an island."

Frank laughed heartily. "Not like you, huh?"

Chased grinned, his eyes lit up.

Frank said, "You got your own little island here."

"Just don't say I'm Piggy," I joked.

"Piggy?" Frank looked puzzled.

Chase laughed and told me, "You can be Ralph."

"No, you're Ralph." I smiled.

"Well, I've come to rescue you and bring you back home," Frank said, tussling Chase's hair.

I clutched the curtains tighter, twisting them in my fists.

"Go pack whatever you need for school tomorrow," Frank instructed Chase.

I said, "He could stay the night. He doesn't have to go now."

"It's no big deal. Might as well get him out of your hair."

"He's not in my hair," I said, moving to the table and restacking Chase's math textbook on top of his worksheets. "Do you have a bed for him? He might prefer to sleep in a bed tonight."

"I'll take the couch tonight. He can have my bed."

Sitting, I put Chase's coloured pencils inside his pencil box one at a time. "You sure your cousins won't be too loud tonight? He's got school tomorrow."

"Don't worry, he'll sleep good," Frank said.

"What about his homework?" I asked. "Who's going to help him with his homework?"

"Bernie," Frank said sternly, "don't worry so much."

"I just want him to keep his learning up," I said.

"He has lots of teachers at home, Bernie."

To my surprise, I found myself contemplating a farfetched proposal. Why not ask Frank to stay, move into the outpost instead of that crowded old house, and we could care for Chase together? He could move into my bedroom and I could take the couch. I could become the heart of the house and their lives, caring every bit as much as a real mother.

"How is he doing?" Frank lowered his voice.

"Good, I think."

"About Stan, I mean."

"He used to wake up screaming," I said. "Doesn't happen anymore. At least, not often. Once in a while. He misses Stan. He doesn't understand why this happened."

Frank said, "Well, he can get some healing at home now."

"I've given him a lot of comfort."

Frank gave me a sympathetic look. "I know. Thank you. But healing is through our culture."

"I'm ready, Dad." Chase entered the kitchen holding a small duffel bag. He slid his schoolwork off the table and into the bag.

"We'll come back for the rest tomorrow," Frank said as he pulled on his boots. "You say thank you, Son."

"*Klecko, klecko,*" Chase said.

"See you later," my voice cracked, "but preferably sooner."

That night, after Chase and Frank left, I sat next to a table lamp in the living room and folded some of Chase's clothes that had been left in the dryer. Every once in a while, I'd burst into heaving sobs. It was an expected change, but it hurt nonetheless, and in the days that followed, I imagined what Frank and Chase might talk about when they were together. Maybe it was true, that healing was through culture, but did he share with his father the private feelings he shared with me? About how much he hated his mother? About how much he missed his brother? About how he'd never know why a person would kill himself? They spent their time talking about fishing, I guessed, or reminiscing about the hunting trips they went on when Chase was younger, before Frank left for logging camp, or sharing their predictions on the Vancouver Canucks' hockey season. Then, one day, I spotted the two of them on Toomista Island, and I saw they weren't discussing anything at all. Without a word, Frank was showing Chase how to carve a miniature oar.

Chase visited me the Saturday after I saw him on Toomista. He brought the oar, smooth and shaped with perfect symmetry, and in that moment I was relieved to see that my relationship with Chase wasn't going to change with Frank's return. I was as important to him as ever. He handed the oar to me and said, beaming with pride:

"I made this for you."

Outside, the rain now started to fall. Within moments, it turned into a downpour. It pinged off the metal roof, hurried and irregular and relentless, like a steel drum played by a child. In the far distance, a low rumble of thunder unfurled from the north. Two small prongs of lightning sparked the edges of the horizon. The first hint of autumn's early dusk dimmed the sky. Across the cove the dogs scurried along the dock and took shelter under overturned boats. The thunder rattled again, loudly. It was getting closer. A long white branch of lightning tore across the sky and the cove flashed like a camera bulb. I sucked in a small breath of awe, then waited and listened and started to truly worry about Chase for the first time as I watched the Pacific darken.

After a while, I took a long tube of paper from the closet and unrolled it onto my bed. It was a map of the entire northwest coast of Vancouver Island. Beside the bed, I knelt with a pencil in my hand and scanned the pale green and blue patches, the relief contours representing the rising mountains of the ancient rain forest where the Basket Lady, and the men with tree bark for skin, and the *alth-maa-koa* creatures slipped through shadows and silver streams of sunlight. In some places, such as the mountains above Cougar Point, the hair-thin topographical lines squiggled into intricate patterns like swirling grains of wood. In other places, such as domes of land near Ootanish Inlet, the lines expanded into simpler patterns like pond ripples around a dropped stone, only more twisted and asymmetrical. These contour lines, as well as the shorelines, conveyed nothing of the place's true nature. Like those MRI maps of the brain: the squiggles of tissue and the brightly coloured patches of thought showed none of the intimate memories or dreams or fears contained within the landscape of the secret self.

This land hid Chase Charlie.

And hiding he was, I was sure of it. It only made sense. If he were no longer alive, the rowboat would have been discovered by now. It might have sunk, but Chase's trawler was found anchored near the shore in Ootanish Inlet, and he would never be foolish enough to leave the trawler and take a rowboat out to deep waters. He would have stayed near the shores, in which case, if it had sunk, the searchers would have discovered it washed up somewhere. Everything washed onto these shores eventually.

Where would Chase go? It was my private hope that somehow, after everything we'd been through together and all our talks over the years, I would be able to puzzle out where he'd hide. I looked at the contours and the islands, all those jigsaw pieces, and I tried to resurrect old memories in search of clues, but I was growing tired, and I soon realized that I'd never complete the puzzle without first deciphering Miranda's bizarre story about Chase and his whale.

16

In the morning, I took the wine bottle out of the cupboard and rinsed it thoroughly. Then, dousing the outside of the bottle in hot water, I scraped off the label with a butter knife until the glass was bare except for the tacky remnants of glue. I didn't know whether to believe Wren, and I kept my mind open to the possibility that the bottle was perhaps tossed there in the summer by the kayakers who often stopped on my shores. I wondered what to do with it. I could bury it in the garbage I boated over to the bins at the end of the wharf on Mitchell Island. But I worried the sea gulls would rip the bag apart and people would see it and somehow know the bottle came from the outpost. This wasn't the message I wanted to send to the people of Tawakin, especially right before I left them for good. I thought of burying it in the sand down on the beach. Instead, I got the idea that something better could be made of the glass vessel.

I took a paper from the drawer and ripped it in half, and then in half again, and sat at the table with a pen. On the ragged square of paper, I wrote a short note. I extracted the words from deep within me, the truth wriggling out like a loose tooth. A single sentence. And then another. I rolled the paper up and slipped it inside the bottle. I tore a strip of cloth from an old dish towel and stuffed it into the top of the bottle, sealing it. On one of the other pieces of paper, I left Wren a note reminding her that she was in charge of the outpost today.

The rain came down in drops the size of marbles, and it pinged off the aluminum hull and smacked my rain jacket. I drove out of the cove and steered the boat towards the grey horizon, past the small islands that dotted the coastline, past the outer ridge where the waves rose and washed sudsy foam over the rocky outcrops. A little ways off the coast, I tossed the bottle into the ocean. It splashed and plummeted and popped back up to the surface where it spent a short moment righting onto its side, the curled sentences cradled in the curve of the glass.

I carried on, hugging the coast as I drove north. This time, I brought a jar of instant coffee and a bunch of green bananas, plus my cribbage board and a deck of cards. When I reached Ootanish Inlet, I anchored the boat and hiked along the shoreline, carrying everything sealed tight inside a large orange Tupperware bowl. The medical kit was looped around my neck so that it crossed my chest, and in one of the large pockets of my mac coat was the map, folded to the size and thickness of a book.

The rain showed no signs of stopping. The large mounds of smooth stone along the beach were wet and slick, and I traversed them carefully, skirting my steps around the slippery layers of green: the algae and kelp and sea lettuce and small sacs bundled like grapes.

Soon, the hut came into view. The tarpaulin walls snapped like orange and blue sails in the wind. Smoke curled from the roof pipe. I crossed the scrubby patch of grass, my rubber boots squelching. As I drew close to the hut, I called out, "Hello, Miranda! Hello! It's Bernadette coming," not wishing to startle her. There was no answer. I called out again, knocked on the door and waited, then put my eye to the star-shaped tear in the tarp and peered inside. The hut appeared empty.

I put the medical kit and the orange bowl beside the door and ascended the low-lying ridge to survey the northern stretch of shoreline. A short distance away, there was a long branch stuck upright in the hard-packed sand, draped with Miranda's tattered coat. Miranda herself was nowhere to be seen. I cupped my hands around my mouth and hollered, but only the rain responded, pattering on the rocks all around me, and the wind, brushing through the hemlocks and cedars in its heartless way. I returned to the hut and, after calling out into the adjacent forest, slid the unhinged door open.

Inside, I put the Tupperware bowl and the medical kit on the small table between the rattan chairs and then immediately slid the door back into place, shutting in the rosy warmth that radiated from the potbelly stove. Not sure what to do with myself, I browsed the things on the countertop. Two plates and a few jars, a bloodied knife, three tin cannisters. I opened a tin of something sweet smelling, and then a tin of something bitter, almost pungent. I felt awkward for snooping, so I set the tins back on the counter exactly as I'd found them, slantwise and with the lids slightly askew. Through the wall beside the counter, a plastic pipe emptied rainwater into a large barrel that stood on the floor. I crouched beside the barrel in front of a long wood crate. At first, I lifted the lid just a little and then opened it fully when I saw it was only food, dried and canned goods. I'd read a study once that suggested there was a correlation between dementia and eating foods heavy in nitrites and nitrates. Perhaps it should be my duty, then, to assess the eating habits and living conditions of my patient. This thought brought me comfort as I went through Miranda's things, and many minutes passed before I went to the torn holes in the tarpaulin wall and saw that Miranda was not yet returning.

I moved quickly to the bed in the corner, first searching the tree stump that served as a bedside table. It was cluttered with trinkets: seashells, a glass ball, a broken watch. I spotted another wood crate under the bed and pulled it out and lifted the hinged lid.

It was a mess of old photographs and scraps of paper scribbled with chicken-scratch writing, all covered with little dots of black mould. Kneeling on the floor, I pushed around the photographs, catching glimpses of familiar faces, including several of Chase as a child. Under the photographs, I found a book without a title. I pulled it out and flipped it open somewhere in the middle, reading only a few words before realizing

The Heaviness of Things That Float

it was a diary. I slammed it shut. It would be despicable to read another person's diary, and I knew I'd think less of myself afterwards.

Somewhere in the distance, somebody was singing. The sound was so faint, I thought maybe I was mistaken. It might only be the whine of the wind. But slowly, as it grew louder, it emerged clearly as a person's voice. I shoved the diary back under the photographs, closed the lid of the crate and pushed it under the bed. I lowered my head close to the floor, checking that the crate looked the same as I'd found it, and as I wriggled it so that it lined up with the darkened patch of floor, something beside the wall caught my eye. Stretching my arm as far as I could under the bed, I grabbed hold of it and pulled it out.

It was Chase's greasy green cap.

"Don't cry, don't cry. Your mother is still on the beach digging clams. Don't cry." It was Miranda's voice, singing loudly some distance away.

I rushed to my coat and squished the cap into one of the pockets. Then I kicked the coat under the rattan chair in the corner and searched for Miranda through the hole in the wall there.

"Don't cry, don't cry." Miranda was another couple of minutes away. Only the top of her head was visible above the low ridge as she walked along the shore below. "Your mother is still on the beach digging clams. Don't cry."

I took the bananas and the coffee out of the Tupperware bowl and displayed them on the flotsam table. Next, I put together the cribbage board, two small pieces of cedar that slotted together with a tongue and groove joint. I stood the pegs, four thin dentalia shells, into the roughly formed holes snaking up and down the board. Pulling the elastic off the playing cards, I put the deck on the table ready to be cut.

Miranda's singing was close now.

"It's Bernadette in here. Hello, Miranda!" I called.

She stopped singing.

The rain kept knocking on the roof. I waited a moment before calling out again. "Hello Miranda! It's just Bernadette in here, waiting for you."

Something moved beside me, I could see it from the corner of my eye. Little fingers spread apart one of the smaller holes in the tarpaulin. A single eye peered inside. The hole in the wall whispered.

"Who's there?"

I jumped out of my seat, bumping into the table and knocking over the jar of coffee. The dentalia shells popped out of their holes on the cribbage board, and the deck of cards spread sideways.

"Miranda," I said, breathless. "It's Bernadette."

The eye disappeared from the hole, footsteps swished through the grass around back of the hut and, after some fumbling, the door slid open. Miranda stepped inside, wearing the tattered coat that I'd seen draped on the stick stuck in the sand. When she spotted the contents of the table, her face cracked into a wide smile.

"How good to see you again, Bernadette! Aren't I the lucky one?" She went to the rain barrel to fill the kettle, the sleeves of her coat dripping water onto the floor and onto the hot potbelly stove, where it hissed and evaporated. "You brought me coffee. I haven't had coffee in ages."

She crossed the small hut and reached for the jar.

I shook my head and clamped my hand on the jar. "It's not a gift. It's a trade." With my other hand I lifted my medical kit onto the table beside the cribbage board. "Bananas and coffee if you let me check on you. I want to see how your heart is doing nowadays."

Miranda looked at the coffee and then the medical kit, biting her lip. "Do you got to poke me with anything?"

I opened the kit and stuck the stethoscope tips into my ears. I shook my head and pointed at the chair, requesting her to sit.

She asked, "Can't we have the coffee first? I'm so wet."

I pointed again at the empty chair.

She sat down. "Will you hurt me?"

"I won't hurt you, I promise."

"Because we're friends," Miranda smiled.

"Yes," I said. "Because we're friends."

I wasn't sure how I came to say these words, but they sounded and felt like a gift, and my part in giving it was a relief. It was as though an incomplete circle drawn around us had finally closed with the uttering of those words of friendship, and it dawned on me then how much I had been wanting, not only with Miranda but with Frank and Chase, too, the sense of ending. So that I could leave this place feeling that the time had come, that there was a natural order to my painful extraction.

I slipped the cold circle of the stethoscope under the neck of Miranda's shirt and pressed it gently in various spots on her bony chest until I could hear her heart pound straight into my ears. I listened to the strong beat, the regular rhythm, the moderate pace.

Miranda asked, "Now is it time for coffee?"

"Almost." I opened the arm cuff to take Miranda's blood pressure. "This first. And I'll take some tea, please. No coffee for me."

"I think I'm all out."

"Out? Already? But I brought you a big box last week."

"Sorry," Miranda said. "We drank it all."

I looked at Miranda. "We?"

She looked at me blankly, as though I hadn't spoken.

٭   ٭   ٭

Miranda took a bite of a banana and looked at her cards. My plan had been to assess her cognitive functioning and memory recall through the game we played so often on rainy days such as this one when we were young. Back then, Miranda had been a sharp player, and so far she was winning our first game.

"Where is this whale you told me about?" I asked her, putting down my cards. From the pocket of my coat under my chair, I took out the book-sized fold of paper and dropped to my knees on the floor, spreading the map for Miranda to see. I smoothed my hands over the creases of islands. "Can you show me?"

Sinking slowly to the floor, Miranda touched the flat symbols of land as if the picture itself were a real world she could enter. Her finger travelled across the pale blue, moving from island to island, and as she landed on the various shores she whispered indiscernible words under her breath. When her finger reached Waas Island, she tapped the map.

"Are the bones still there?" she asked.

"They are," I said. "Chase went there once."

Her eyes grew wide. "He did?"

"He wanted to see the bones in the cave and he didn't care if it was forbidden, he just rowed there and climbed down into that dark cave all by himself. He was fifteen and not a bit scared."

"Isn't that something? What a boy," she said.

At that moment, watching her eyes search for a memory that she did not ever possess because she was not there, I felt profound sadness for Miranda. I continued the story, filling in the memory for her.

"After we found out—George had spotted him there that day—the elders talked to him all evening long. He could barely stay still. He kept fidgeting under the table." I chuckled softly, and Miranda chuckled, too. "When the elders told him he'd have to host a dinner for the whole community and apologize to everybody for going to the island, he went hunting with Frank and shot a *muwach* to feed the community. He didn't have to do that. Everybody would've helped him with the meal. Frank told me that every morning he'd jump out of bed and run straight to the shed to see if all the meat had fallen off the *muwach* skull. He was so excited for it to be time to feed the community, I think he forgot it was supposed to be a punishment. It sure was a tasty deer, though."

There was more to the story than that, but that was enough. It was a pleasant memory this way, without bringing up the real reason Chase went into the cave. There was no need to bring up Ronnie's suicide.

I asked Miranda, "Do you know where Chase is?"

"He's with the whale. Because of the shadows," said Miranda. "You get scared of the shame, you know, and you don't know what you remember right. He knows I know lots about shame. Like that night up at the lake. It wasn't easy biking up that logging road. He was so shocked to see me."

"Who? What night up at the lake?" I asked.

She said nothing.

"What night are you talking about, Miranda? Who was shocked?" I asked again, my mind scrambling through memory.

Miranda sighed. "I don't like to tell it too much, and I already told it just the other day."

"Who did you tell it to, Miranda? Chase?"

"Frank. He knows."

"What does Frank have to do with this?" I asked.

"He knows is all," she said.

I retrieved the green cap from the pocket of my coat. Along the sweatband inside the cap there was a smudge of brown, dark and rusty. Blood from his head wound. I held it up for Miranda to see. "Why did he come here?" I asked.

She didn't answer.

"George told me that Chase had a story he needed to return. Is that why?" I asked.

"When you got to tell somebody the truth, got to get it off your chest, and you don't want to disappoint nobody with what you got to say, you tell somebody who already disappointed you bad," she said.

"Who are you talking about? You, or Chase?" I asked, getting frustrated.

"Both him and me. We got stories to tell each other."

"And what did he tell you?"

She put her cup back on the table. She took the banana, peeling it to the bottom. Her head hung low.

With her nearly toothless gums Miranda mashed the last of the banana, smacking her mouth open and closed. When she finished, she spread the banana peel over the top of her head and smiled.

"Do you like my hat?" she asked.

"What did he tell you?" I asked.

She fluttered her eyelashes. "Do you like my hat?"

I pointed at the map. "Will you at least show me where Chase is now?"

"It's a lovely hat." She smiled.

"Where is this whale?"

Miranda didn't answer. She adjusted the peel on her head.

I climbed up from the floor and organized the things in my medical kit, zipping it closed with trembling fingers. Then I put the green cap into the Tupperware bowl and set both the kit and the bowl by the door. "I think you should come with me for some proper medical care."

Miranda shook her head and the banana peel slid down onto her shoulder.

I was too frustrated to ask again. Too tired. Too numb from what I'd learned. I said, "Then I'll come back to check on you in a couple of days. Maybe you'll change your mind and come back to Tawakin with me then."

Miranda stood and opened the potbelly stove, the little black door screeching loudly. The banana peel fell off her shoulder and onto the floor and she flinched as though it were a giant spider. In an instant, she picked it up and flung it onto the bed.

I slid the door open and said good-bye.

Miranda had already turned away, piling wood onto the glowing embers inside the stove, singing under her breath. As I stepped outside and slid the door closed, I could hear her singing grow louder.

"Don't cry. Don't cry. Your mother is still on the beach digging clams. Don't cry, don't cry, don't cry..."

*   *   *

As I thought about the memory I'd given to Miranda, the story of the time Chase went inside the forbidden cave, the skull of the deer Chase killed kept appearing in my mind. Once the skull had lost all its flesh, he'd explained to me, it would be time to feed the community. Each day, the flesh rotted a little more, some of it pecked at by birds, so that for a while it draped the bones like strips of torn rags.

"You do remember that this a punishment, right?" I asked him one day, after he'd reported the latest skull status to me with a proud smile.

"I know, I know." He smiled sheepishly.

On Waas Island, there was a cave in a low cliff on the southwest shore. The cave was forbidden on account of all the bones buried inside it. Enemies from a battle long ago. Elders warned the young: you are never to enter.

A few days before the community dinner Chase was hosting to give a proper public apology for entering the forbidden cave, I asked him about it. "Weren't you scared to go inside?"

"Real scared," he said. "It was dark, like black."

"Why did you do it, then?"

He went quiet.

I waited patiently.

Finally, he said, "I wanted to find Truth."

"The truth about what?"

"No," he said, "Truth. A person."

I was confused. "A person named Truth?"

He raised his eyebrows.

"And this person lives inside the cave?" I asked.

"Ronnie told me about her."

At the mention of Ronnie's name, I checked Chase's face for signs of distress. Ronnie had committed suicide the year before, when Chase was fourteen, and although Chase had been upset and mourned his loss, I was still waiting for a bigger fallout. It seemed impossible to me that this sensitive boy had managed to cope with the suicides of his two older brothers, both within a span of two years, on top of his mother's departure.

But if Chase was struggling, I couldn't tell from his expression. He went on to explain in a carefree tone. "Ronnie told me that he found Truth in the cave when he was my age. She was painting shadows on the walls with a brush and some paint. Her hair looked all dirty and tangled, and her face was covered in warts and wrinkles and scars. He said her skin reminded him of a crumpled brown bag. Her dress was all ripped up and covered with soot from the fire burning in the middle of the cave. Her teeth were yellow and splintered like wood."

"She sounds scary," I said.

"She was," he said. "Ronnie said he could feel things moving past the fire. He couldn't see what they were, but he could see their shadows painted on the wall."

"When was this?" I asked.

"He went there when he was about the same age as me now. But he never told no one and no one ever caught him. He told it to me when Dad Frank and I went out to town last year."

Hearing this put Chase's transgression into a whole new light. I considered the possibility that his desire to visit the cave was a tribute to Ronnie in some way, or an attempt to connect with his dead brother through a shared experience. A moment of seeing the world through his eyes.

Still, I asked, "Why would you want to find her?"

"I wanted to see what she looked like," he said.

"But you already knew what she looked like. You just told me," I said.

"She told Ronnie that she looks different to each person. And Ronnie said that when he left the cave, she asked him to do her a favour. She said: 'If you tell anybody about me, tell them that I have shiny hair and skin as smooth as a drum. Tell them that I am young and beautiful. No,' she said, 'tell them I am a man. Tall. And strong, like an oak tree. A tall, old man with one of those long beards. Tell them that,' she said. 'Or don't. It don't matter. I look different to each person anyway.'"

"Did you find her?" I asked.

"No," he said, "but it's a lot bigger in there than I thought. I think I gave up too quick."

"But you're not going to ever try again right?"

He didn't answer.

"Right, Chase?"

He looked at me and smiled. "Right."

Over the years, I'd forgotten about this conversation. I'd never heard anyone in Tawakin refer to the cave as anything but a forbidden burial site, and I'd dismissed Chase's story as one of those fanciful yarns of childhood. A story of exaggerated adventure and mystery between brothers. But now I wondered if he ever went back to the cave. He wanted to tell the truth. But what truth? Patty had tried to warn me not to listen to Chase. That night in Loretta's kitchen, shortly after Teddy's death, she'd told me, he says strange things to me sometimes, she'd said, things that aren't true.

As if waking from a dream, my mind tried to grasp at the words dropping here and there, pooling like rainwater in my mind. Chase had gone to see Miranda. He returned a story he didn't want, but what was it about? Moving with the sway of the boat, I felt as though I were turning in circles, unsure which direction to go in. Nan Lily said it was best to listen to a story go around and around, picking up a bit more knowledge on each rotation. I'd try to take comfort in that. I'd hope that if I was patient enough, understanding would come in due time.

I looked at Chase's green cap on the seat next to me and smacked myself on the forehead. The map. I'd left it on the floor in Miranda's hut. In a day or two, I'd head back to the hut for the map, and I'd try once more to get Miranda to circle Chase's location. Because the truth, as Nan Lily said, was found in circles.

17

I found Wren bent over Frank in the outpost. His shirt was off and his arms were stretched diagonally over the sides of the examination bed like two cedar planks. He talked quietly to Wren, whose head was lowered so that her curls nearly brushed his bare shoulders. Wren said something, and giggled.

I stood in the doorway of the examination room with rain dripping off my hair, my jacket, the end of my nose. Although the pale fluorescent lights glowed overhead, the dark clouds outside the windows bathed the room in a grey wash. It was cozy, not dismal, the rain on the panes turning the room into a warm cocoon, a haven.

I felt a small stab of jealousy. "Never realized a checkup could be such a party," I said with a smile.

Wren swivelled her face towards Frank and said, "We can turn anything into a party." Then, staying in her bent posture with the stethoscope plugged in her ears, she turned to me. "It's my first checkup on my own. I think it went quite well."

I looked at the clock. It was late in the afternoon. "Didn't we book your appointment for ten this morning, Frank?"

Wren laughed. "He came on Tawakin time."

"Of course he did," I said, and smiled at how quickly Wren was picking up the local ways. I removed my sopping coat and hung it on the rack. For a moment, I listened to Frank's chuckling and the crinkle of the paper sheet as he shifted on the bed, but then I saw that his face looked uneasy, unfriendly. And Frank was never unfriendly.

Wren reported, "Heartbeat sounds regular, strong. Blood pressure's good. Frank's been a good boy, eating healthy. Haven't you?"

Frank was buttoning his shirt. He muttered something agreeable, but his mouth pulled down. His eyes flickered at me. "Heard you went up north to see a patient again," he said.

I waited until Wren turned towards the counter. Then I nodded and signalled to Frank in the direction of the wharf, declaring cheerfully, "Looks like it's going to blow hard again tonight. I better get another rope or two tied on that boat."

A few minutes later, when Frank met me down at the wharf, he got straight to the point. "What's the story? Any news?"

"I need to get Miranda proper care, Frank. I can't do much for her by checking on her every few days. I might need your help to convince her to come back here," I said. "Plus, she's saying stuff..."

"Like what?"

"Something about the night at the lake and how hard it was biking up the logging road. 'He was shocked to see me,' she said."

Frank folded his arms across his chest, and I could see that he was pressing hard against his rib cage as if to contain himself. He closed his lips and swallowed, his Adam's apple sliding up and down while his eyes shifted from the reserve to water to sky to his feet.

"She said you should tell me the story," I added.

"She said that?" He rubbed his chin hard.

"She did."

The light rain was soaking through my shirt. I squeezed my fists to get the blood flowing through my cold fingers and waited for Frank to speak. As he gazed at the reserve across the cove, everything around us was quiet, except our boats bouncing quietly against the old tires on the side of the dock.

"Frank?" I prompted.

He turned and, as if lost in thought, looked at me blankly. I got the impression he'd forgotten for a moment that I was there. Bending his head a little, he stared at the dock planks.

"The night Jimmy died," he said quietly, "me and him were coming down the trail to the lake He's walking ahead of me, it's pitch dark, and all of a sudden he stops. She's just standing there, with his shotgun."

I wanted to sit down. Instead, I took a few steps across the dock as my mind filled with broken images, like a mosaic that had been pieced together all wrong. An image of the night that George drove me to the lake, the five-mile climb up the steep logging road. An image of Miranda biking in the dark, a shotgun strapped to her back, or maybe held across the handlebars. Jimmy's shattered face. Miranda back in her kitchen when we delivered the news. How callous her response. What she said about being buried far from him.

"You told me it was an accident."

He tilted his face to the sky. "We didn't want nobody to find out."

"But she killed him, Frank."

"She had the boys to look after."

"The boys loved Jimmy."

"Jimmy." Frank shook his head vigorously. Under his breath he said scornfully, "We should've kicked him off the reserve when we had the chance years ago. Should've sent him away, far into the mountains to live by himself. Until he grew tree bark for skin. Until he wasn't even a man no more. Jimmy deserved what he got."

"How can you say that about your own brother?"

Frank didn't answer. He kicked shards of clamshells into the water.

"Nobody kills a person for getting shoved occasionally against the kitchen counter," I said angrily. "Nobody kills their children's father for being called an ugly dog."

"She did it for the boys. It was for them," he said. I heard a tremor in his voice. It sounded like something was coming undone, like the confession loosened what he had been holding tightly all these years.

"What do you mean?"

"You don't know the things that man done. You think you know all

The Heaviness of Things That Float

the secrets of this place, but you don't, Bernie," he said. "You don't. Some things stay on the reserve."

It felt like another betrayal—another secret that Miranda and Frank shared together, leaving me outside of their little circle once more. I said, "You could've told me."

"I promised Miranda I would never tell a soul," he said. "She was so scared. She hoped Chase was too young to remember."

I was puzzled. "Chase was only five. Of course he remembered his father's death."

Frank shook his head. "I mean the things Jimmy did."

My voice quivered. "What? I never saw a single mark on any of the boys."

Frank faced me. "Not that kind of abuse."

My stomach hollowed out. "No, that's not true," I said, shaking my head, but when I looked back at Frank, whose eyes had filled with tears, I knew that it was. He'd carried that truth all these years, and I could see the awful burden this must have been for him, for Miranda, too. It is too much for one person to carry old secrets, that's what Nan Lily had always told me. I leaned into Frank and wrapped my arms around him.

For a long time, we stood like that, motionless except for our shallow breathing, and watched the rain stipple the grey water. Finally, Frank pulled back and looked at me with the same uneasy look on his face that he'd had earlier in the examination room.

"That new nurse is not good for here," he said.

"Why not?"

"I don't like how she smells."

*   *   *

I returned to the examination room slowly, taking my time to climb the wharf ramp and the stairs. The balloons still decorated the railing, and their bright colours appeared as a startling contrast to what I'd just learned. Reaching the top of the stairs, I grasped the doorknob and took a deep breath. I really didn't feel like dealing with Frank's complaint right now, but it was my duty to not ignore it.

Wren was tidying the counter when I entered the room. She smiled.

I smiled back. I walked up to her and leaned in close, taking a long sniff as she looked at me with a friendly but puzzled expression. I stepped away. Maybe Frank was wrong, I couldn't tell for sure. I wanted him to be wrong. But I knew it wasn't likely. Not about this.

"Have you been drinking?"

Wren flinched. She jerked her head back, at once incredulous and embarrassed, caught off guard.

"Have you?" I repeated.

"No," Wren said acidly.

Her complexion flushed with pink splotches, her shoulders tensed and raised into a shrug. She fidgeted with the edges of her pockets.

I appraised her, trying to be fair: not too suspicious, not too naïve.

"It's three o'clock in the afternoon," she said. "I was just with a patient. And now I'm cleaning up." She listed these facts as if they made the whole inquiry preposterous.

"Frank smelled it on you," I said, feeling more concerned than angry. "Is that what Hannah smelled on you that day she was here?"

Wren huffed and shook her head rapidly. "This is ridiculous," she muttered. She turned and picked up some loose papers on top of Frank's file and squared them on the counter, tapping the bottom edges repeatedly. Abruptly she stopped and looked out the window. "I had a couple of glasses of wine last night while reading in my room," she admitted. "I suppose if Frank smelled something, that's what he was smelling."

I took a deep breath, frustrated as I realized she must have had the wine in her bedroom. "Then that *was* your bottle I found tossed in the ferns?"

"I already told you it wasn't."

I said, "You can't be drinking here."

Wren's face pulled back into an ugly scowl, as though she were peeling her skin like a banana, revealing something different inside. Something spoiled and rotten and bruised. "You don't seriously think they're not ever drinking over there?"

I felt torn. I liked Wren. She showed great promise as a nurse, and I wanted her to succeed, for her sake and for the community's. But at the same time I had to be firm. "If this happens again, I'll have to file a report with the health authority."

Wren pushed away the file on the counter and walked towards the waiting room, her head shaking vigorously. In the doorway she turned. "Seems a bit patronizing of you, treating them like children who can't handle themselves. You're acting like they need you to look out for them."

She shut the door behind her.

I felt stunned. Was she right? Was I handling the people across the cove like children? I found the idea distasteful. Maybe it was possible, subconsciously, that I was viewing them as if they were somehow deficient. "Ideas of deficiency," that's what my friend Molleigh Royston had called them, these negative biases. The idea that First Nations students couldn't ever achieve high grades because they came from broken homes, or because they came from broken cultures. The idea that a First Nations woman like Miranda couldn't ever be a good mother because she'd grown up in a residential school. The idea that the Tawakin Reserve couldn't deal with a negligent nurse because of their own history with alcohol. Was I acting as if they needed saving? It saddened me to think that such biases could be so deeply and inextricably woven into my mind. Was I acting out of duty and respect, or was I patronizing the people I loved?

As I thought about Frank's complaint, I remembered the letters I used to get from my old university classmates and comforted myself knowing that this was not as bad as some others I'd heard about. The most entertaining tales always came from the nurses stationed in the remote towns of the North, in British Columbia, the Yukon and the Northwest Territories.

One letter described how the principal of a northern school knocked over the toilet-paper pyramid display in the town's grocery store, and then slept on the fallen rolls of two-ply softness, drunk and half-naked, as students and parents strolled by. A teacher in another northern town ran away the night before the school's Christmas concert. When the school board cleaned out her rental house, they found ten porn magazines, two tablespoons used to cook heroin and a hypodermic needle under her bed.

Welcome to the farthest edges of the true north strong and free, my classmate Michelle had written, *where some of the country's most dysfunctional teachers, nurses, doctors, police officers and social workers come to work, and where even the functional ones turn, in the emptiness of the land and in the darkness of winter, into shadows of their former selves.*

Surely there were troubled nurses and teachers everywhere, but the city, with its crowds and its congestion, concealed them. Here everything was on display, magnified. Here the people wore their dysfunctions like hats, for everybody to see. How long would it take before people spotted the crumpled shape of Wren's hat?

I sat at my desk and opened the word processing program on my computer. I had to document this incident in case it happened again. How did I know she was telling the truth and that the smell was leftover from the night before? What if she was drinking while on shift? Or if there was an emergency at night and she had to hop in the boat? How much did she drink, and how often? Clearly, she didn't understand. I'd told her how much it would upset everybody. I'd told her about the struggles people overcame to stay sober here. Should that not be respected? Honoured?

I typed a report that briefly outlined Frank's complaint. I printed two copies and put one in Wren's personnel file. I put the other one in the desk drawer.

✳　　✳　　✳

A skinless face floated through my dreams that night, its zygomatic bone detached, its maxilla smashed and temporal bones broken, its mandible fractured and missing several teeth. The mouth, pulling into a gruesome and taut smile, whispered: "I deserved it."

I woke with a sharp intake of breath. I looked at the faint glow of the clock on the bedside table. It was two in the morning. The outpost was silent, except for the waves below my window raking the small stones at the edge of the shore.

I opened the drawer in the office filing cabinet marked *Deceased*, then walked my fingers over the file tabs until I reached Jimmy's file. I read the report of his death. I'd read it many times before, always believing his death to be a terrible accident. Now I knew otherwise. But why had Frank been so emotionless that night he held his dead brother? Did he know about Miranda's plans to kill Jimmy? His voice was strangely flat as he reported how the gun had fired accidently when Jimmy tripped. Back then, I attributed it to shock. But he didn't ever pause in confusion, never once got stuck on his words. Almost as if the story were rehearsed. Now I understood Miranda's reaction to Jimmy's death. Cold. Bitter. Celebratory. Jimmy's death did, after all, finally free her from his abuse. Whether Frank knew her plans or not, I decided that I didn't want to know. It didn't matter now, anyway.

Frank's words echoed in my head: You think you know all the secrets of this place, but you don't. You don't. Some secrets stay on the reserve.

His remark pushed me to the outside yet again. Just like Loretta said. He spoke about me as if I wasn't a part of the community. What exactly then had I been a part of all these years? I placed my palms on top of the cold metal filing cabinets and thought of the secrets they held. Maybe it was true that I didn't know everybody's secrets on the reserve, but everybody on the reserve didn't know all the secrets in these cabinets. These files had been a burden on me, but for forty years I'd guarded them, the only person with the key to the cabinet, and now the guard was changing. Truth was, I didn't like the change one bit.

18

Regular phones were rarely used in Tawakin, most people communicating over the VHF radio, except in matters of the utmost privacy, so when I received a phone call in the morning from Frank, I supposed another secret was about to ooze out the cracks of the community.

"Can you come over?" Frank asked.

"Is something wrong?"

There was silence on the other end of the line.

"Is it your heart?"

"Nah, it's fine. I got to show you something."

I left straight away for the reserve. I docked the boat near a small group of children who were bobbing fishing poles over the oil-sheened water. One of the children twisted around and unhooked a tiny rockfish from her line and flung the wriggle of silver into a bucket. She gave me a little wave before returning her attention to the water. I waved back and tied my boat to the reserve dock, watching the stooped backs of the children, and I listened to their chatter as they recounted their favourite movie scenes and how little Danny Joe totally nailed that jump with his bike two weeks ago.

Occasionally, there were troubling incidents like the stealing of needles and fistfights, but otherwise, many of the children in Tawakin were caring and gentle. But even these gentle ones, the ones who skipped along the dock and who sometimes drew me cards at Christmas, seemed older than their age, and I often wondered if all children on reserves grew up too quickly, if by living like fish in this small bowl they learned adult truths sooner than other children, if by living in a place of so many losses—the loss of history, of culture, of language, of lives—they learned that some adult truths could slice sharper than barnacles on the dock pilings, and I wondered, too, about the innocence of Anne's grandchildren in Duncan.

I walked on, past the church with its planks the colour of dried mud and past the little community centre where they sometimes played bingo. Somebody in one of the houses at the back of the reserve slowly pounded a rawhide drum.

"What's the story?" Sophie Florence emerged from her fish shed, toothless.

"Heading to Frank's for a house call," I said.

Sophie Florence wiped her greasy hands on the front of her apron. "If I'd known you were coming for a visit, I'd have put on my bra and my teeth," she said, and shimmied her shoulders so that her large breasts wobbled. She laughed. "Want to come in for a fish sandwich?"

Gina came out the front door of her house and said hello. She also wiped her hands on an apron, but hers was covered with flour. Beads of sweat trickled down from her gel-spiked hairline. "How's things?" she asked.

I smiled. "Good, good."

"You lie." Gina looked at Sophie Florence. "She lies."

"Mmm," Sophie Florence agreed.

"So how's the young hotshot nurse doing?" Gina asked. "We better get her a husband so she'll stay. Get a couple of the men cleaned up nice for her."

I laughed. "I'm sure they're excited to have a new woman in the community who's not related."

"Except the new nurse is *mamulthni*," Gina said. Then she jabbed her thumb at Sophie Florence. "This one here only wants beautiful brown-skinned princesses for her nephews."

"Ay-ha!" said Sophie Florence. "I never said—"

"Whatever, Sister! That's what you said, no *mamulthni* women."

"Sister! Shush! Quit your teasing." Sophie Florence glared at Gina, and then turned to me, putting her hands on her hips. "So are you all ready for retirement? Just what are we going to do without you?"

"What are you going to do without *us*?" Gina asked.

"She's moving to her family," Sophie Florence said.

Gina flapped her hand. "We're your family."

It warmed my heart to hear this, and it gave me a reason to believe that Loretta was dead wrong. I belonged. I looked up the dirt road that looped the small reserve. Poking out from behind a woodpile was George Sam's rusted Chevy truck, the same one he used more than twenty years ago to drive me to the lake the night Jimmy died. Just as it was that night, the passenger door was tied on with yellow rope and the headlight was smashed. It was as though time had stood still.

"I'm going to spend time with my grandnieces and grandnephews," I explained.

Gina shrieked with laughter. "Grandma Bernadette!"

"Let's celebrate with fish sandwiches!" Sophie Florence threw up her arms.

"I'd love to, but I can't. Frank's expecting me. House call."

"It's not his heart, is it?" Sophie Florence asked.

"Or is it his *heart*?" Gina asked, fluttering her eyelashes.

The two women laughed.

"Very funny," I said.

Gina patted her pockets. "Too bad. Don't have any minty-fresh gum left for you to chew on the way to Frank's. I wouldn't have even charged you that much. It's cheap."

I laughed. The memory of that day so long ago, when I took the piece of gum from her grandfather, misunderstanding his words until Gina, just a young woman like me then, explained from the window above, filled my heart with so much feeling that I nearly burst into tears.

✳   ✳   ✳

Inside Frank's living room, I sat on the couch with a cup of coffee. Frank went to the stove and unlatched the iron door, then added more wood. When he stood upright again, he fingered the socks that hung from a line over the stove. Dark rings circled his eyes.

"You look exhausted, Frank. You all right?" I asked.

"Haven't slept much. Been thinking too much. Plus, bad dreams."

"About what?" I asked, expecting he had more to tell me about Jimmy.

After a few moments of silence, he asked, "Do you think suicide can run in the family? Can it get in the genes or whatever?"

I was taken aback by the question. I took a moment to collect my thoughts. "Depression might be genetic, and impulsive behaviours might be genetic. But I don't know about suicidal tendencies."

"Have you ever worried that Chase might?" Frank asked.

"Might what?"

"You know."

"Kill himself? Geez, Frank! Heavens, no."

"Why not? His brothers did."

I shook my head. "Chase is different."

"Different, how?"

"For starters, you were his father. Not Jimmy."

"Jimmy was there long enough to damage him."

"But Chase was so young," I said.

"Why are you closing your eyes on purpose?"

"Closing my eyes?"

"Refusing to consider it," he said.

"What? I'm not." I could hear resentment in my voice, but I didn't care. I insisted, "He's special. He's got a light inside of him."

"Enough to keep out the darkness?"

"Enough to light up the whole moon."

"The moon?"

"Yes, the moon," I said.

"That don't seem enough reason to think he wouldn't."

"There were no signs. I'd have known," I said.

Green glass fishing floats filled a cedar basket on the floor next to the couch. Drifting onto their shores from Japan, these balls were revered in Tawakin. Some were as large as basketballs. Frank had one of these large ones hanging from his ceiling in a net. I remembered the time that Frank and George found dozens of these big ones on a beach up north. Never before had so many washed ashore together, especially ones so large. They loaded what they could into their backpacks, and then, instead of leaving the rest for somebody else, they smashed them on the rocks, destroying them for good.

Frank stared out the window, thoughtfully. "But how could you know? How could you know what's in another person's heart?"

"You can see what a person thinks of life by how they live it," I said. "When Chase was twenty-three and he went to college, for example. How many of the young people here try to do that, Frank? Almost none. Over the past couple of decades, you could count them on one hand. But Chase? Chase was different. He had a vision for himself. He wanted to become a teacher. Don't you remember?"

"I remember he came home after a month," Frank said.

I became scornful. "Probably because Loretta was so critical of the whole thing, saying how he wasn't being the man he should've been by staying home and fishing for his family." I recalled the day Chase returned from college. "Don't worry," I reassured him, "lots of people have doubts the first time they try college. It's a big adjustment. You were just homesick. You missed Hannah. You can try again when she's older."

"At any rate, that's not the point," I said to Frank. "He had a vision, he saw something for himself. People with a vision for their future don't commit suicide."

"Why won't you consider that it might be true?" Frank sounded frustrated. "Suicide happens a lot. And it happens a lot more on reserves, you know that. People struggle."

"Chase's vision for life went beyond his circumstance," I said. "Who knows? Maybe he'll even try college again someday."

Frank shook his head.

"You never know," I said.

"He won't ever go back to college. It made him sad."

"He was homesick is all. He was young then."

"He didn't feel like he belonged there," Frank said. "He didn't feel he belonged anywhere except here. That place wasn't made to fit people like him, that's what he told me when he came back."

Out the window, down on the shore, the tide was out, leaving a wide band of muddy beach exposed. I watched the gulls soar.

"He never mentioned anything of this to me," I said.

"He probably thought you wouldn't understand."

My heart filled with sand, with stones. I knew exactly what Frank meant, because it was what Loretta had meant. I was not First Nations; I was white, and the world beyond the shores of Tawakin was made to fit people like me. It was a world built upon ways of knowing and ways of being, ways of seeing, that had been bred in my bones. It favoured people like me, I'd come to believe that, and although I would never give up my own past, I hated how it had continually threatened to set me apart from others here.

Despite this, I believed my bond with Chase was strong. To say it was special was an understatement. After Frank's betrayal had broken my heart, Chase became my connection to life. He'd offered me a chance to rebuild myself. I could never be his mother, but I'd solved that problem with sheer desire. I'd given him years of my time and energy and love. I'd never acknowledged it to myself before, but the truth now became clear. I believed that I'd made a crucial impact on his life. I believed that I was one of the positive influences, one of the few, that floated Chase above the conditions of his life. Was I so wrong to believe that?

19

Wren and I strode up the dirt road in the middle of the reserve, clutching small platters of food wrapped in layers of cellophane like large cocoons. Small children bombarded us, running at us from all directions and crashing into our hips with greetings of giggles.

The lunch was held at the community centre, a small one-storey building that stood low above the shore on the northwest side of the reserve. Outside the community centre, several adults leaned on the wobbly railing of the wood-planked wheelchair ramp. Some smoked, some talked, some did nothing but look out at the water, blinking in the wind. Dogs paced the ramp, and every few seconds, a child burst out the door at the top. I nodded hello at the people and climbed the ramp to the door with Wren following close behind, and as I walked past the adults leaning on the ramp railing, I listened to them predict the weather and Chase's return.

"It's going to blow real hard this week."

"Be real cold for anybody out there."

"Haw-ess."

"He'll be coming home soon with a surprise."

"He said that to Loretta."

"I never heard that. When he say that?"

"Other night. She dreamed about him again."

"She seen him coming into shore. But he didn't have no boat. And she says, 'How come you got no boat, Chase?' And he says he don't need one. And she says, 'But ain't it cold there in the water?'"

"What'd he say? Was it cold?"

"He didn't need to say nothing. He was thick with fur."

The adults fell silent again and returned to their smoking and blinking.

Inside, people crowded the main room, all of them squawking loudly, flocking around the tables like gulls on tidal rocks. The folding wood tables, which were lined end to end in three long rows, filled the space. Along the back wall, five square windows framed a view of the shore below. On the opposite side of the room were three more tables filled with food. I carried my platter in this direction, squeezing between the chairs and the wall where the light-grey paint was battered with small chips and scrapes and holes drilled with ballpoint pens. Occasionally, somebody looked up from their playing cards and nodded, or stopped their conversation long enough to holler, "Hey there," and as I nodded back, I felt a new kind of uncertainty. It clouded my mind as I wondered which of my neighbours laughed behind my back. Who among them thought it was a joke that I believed I belonged. Frank's words echoed in my head: "Some secrets stay on the reserve." He'd said it as if it were a place I was not a part of, as if the cove were something that separated me from everybody else.

Next to a pot of gooseneck barnacles, I set my platter on the table and peeled the cellophane off my paprika-dusted devilled eggs. Wren also found a spot for her platter, and as she removed the cellophane from her dish of celery and carrot sticks, she wrinkled her nose and pointed at a cast-iron pot filled with small slabs of flesh. Some of the slabs resembled tongues, whereas others sported plump, labia-like folds.

"What are those?" she asked.

"Chitons—mollusks. They're good. Sort of like big escargot," I explained, forgetting for a moment that Wren didn't eat creatures of any sort. So I then suggested, "When it's time to eat, fill your plate with lots of salad and cooked vegetables—like mountains of it—that way they can't see that you haven't taken any fish or meat. Otherwise, they'll try to give you some, and you're not supposed to turn away food given on their territory."

The people of Tawakin greeted newcomers with open arms and large feasts. It was done this way for everybody—every User, every Runner, every Saver. Everybody was welcomed, though I noticed long ago that when people left the community, there were no dinners, no commemorations. Nobody ever walked down to the dock to send anybody off, not even the most loved teachers over the years. They were all hellos and no good-byes.

"I should warn you, they'll probably make you eat the fish eyeball today," I told Wren.

Shelly Henry snatched Wren's arm before she could reply. She wrapped a braided-string bracelet around Wren's wrist, then tied it in a small knot. She whispered, "They voted to kick my husband out of the village, but—"

"This is Shelly," I interrupted, making a mental note to later explain to Wren that Shelly gave the same colourful bracelet to every newcomer, telling the same story about her husband every time.

Two children darted past and called out: "Smelly Shelly. Shelly Belly."

Shelly blushed and looked at Wren.

I clapped my hands. "Well. I'll leave you two to chat."

Leaving Wren to hear Shelly's long story about the husband who grew tree bark for skin, I headed into the kitchen to join Sophie Florence, Gina, Margaret and the other women.

The women bustled along the counters and around the large island in the middle of the kitchen, icing cakes and slicing vegetables. Sophie Florence playfully threw an apron into my face and said the carrots needed doing. I got a paring knife and started to peel a carrot over a large stainless steel bowl. Steam rose from giant stock pots on the stove. There was the sound of knives chopping rapidly and ladles clanging on the edge of pots, the screech of the old oven door opening and banging shut again. The other women moved past me, weaving in and out of one another like an elaborately choreographed number. They laughed and teased and called one another "Sister," and as their hips jostled against mine in passing, I knew that Loretta was wrong. The community was generous and kind and warmhearted, and they all saw me as family, just as Sophie Florence and Gina did.

Eventually, the women emerged from the kitchen, sweaty and pink faced from the steam and the oven heat. They stood side by side facing the tables. I took a seat beside Ernie Frank.

"Okay, everybody. Attention, everybody," Sophie Florence addressed the room. Everybody found their seats, or stood against the walls. Slowly, the room fell quiet. People hushed the small children who crawled under the tables and tickled people's legs. I surveyed the room and saw that almost everybody was there. Frank, Nan Lily, George and Elizabeth. On the opposite side of the room, Loretta sat with Patty and Hannah, all three stony faced. Altogether there must have been about a hundred people squeezed into the small community centre.

Sophie Florence said, "We're here today to welcome our nurse, Wren Featherstone, and to thank her for coming to work in our community." Next to Sophie Florence the other women stood quietly, mostly looking down at the floor. "We were going to drum songs and have some dances, but we can't dance while one of our own is still lost." Sophie Florence went on to thank everybody for their hard work in searching for Chase, calling each person up to the front to receive small gifts: cedar roses, beaded eagle feathers, glass balls. When I was called up, Sophie Florence thanked me for my assistance and for having the outpost ready for a medical emergency that night he went missing. When she said this, handing me an eagle feather, I heard a loud cough from the side of the room where Loretta sat. I looked at Loretta, and she stared hard at me in return.

After I sat down again, Sophie Florence called up four men at once. The women wrapped blankets around the men's shoulders. The men stood draped like that while Sophie Florence thanked them for being auxiliary members of the coast guard and for staying out on the water searching until morning the first night Chase disappeared. Afterwards, Sophie Florence said *klecko, klecko* for all the food everybody brought, and then she explained to Wren, who sat in the back corner by the door, that there was no word in their language for "welcome." Sophie Florence said, "We say it with food instead."

I looked at the faces around the tables, identifying those older ones who had attended the Alberni Residential School. When they were at the school, hungry and homesick, did they dream of all this—the gooseneck barnacles, the salmon, the halibut, the chitons, the geoducks that they could practically scoop from the water back home in Tawakin? My own childhood was so safe, so privileged. I'd had advantages that my neighbours here hadn't. The boundaries of this community were so porous, so open and welcoming that I'd allowed myself to seep into it over the years. But had I forgotten what made me different? Was it a joke that I thought I belonged so completely?

"Nan Lily will say a prayer for us now," Sophie Florence said.

I suspected that Nan Lily was still asleep, but she promptly lifted her head. She spoke softly and quickly in Nuu-chah-nulth, the sounds throaty and punctuated with glottal stops. Her voice rolled like a stone down a hill, rumbling quietly, bumping now and then over something sharp. Partway through the prayer, she paused for a long spell, staring at the table. Everybody waited patiently, silently for her to say, *"Chuu."* People shifted in their seats, faint squiggles of steam rising from a few of the pans on the tables. Two children started to whisper. Somebody shushed them loudly, a forceful rush of air. Outside, the dogs could be heard trotting up and down the wood ramp. At last, Nan Lily started up again, presumably thanking the Creator for providing them with a bounty of food from the ocean. She sucked in a small gasp between words and licked her dry lips and spoke in creaky murmurs. Then, out of the sombre stillness, somebody in the back corner shouted. It was nine-year-old Danny Joe, bike jumper extraordinaire. At the sound of Danny's loud cry, people turned and looked. Pointing out the window, he shouted again, "It's him! Chase Charlie's swimming to the shore!"

*   *   *

People rushed to see. Chairs scraped backwards, some tipping to the floor. "Is it him?" Women knocked the tables with their hips as they hurried to the windows, and when they looked outside, they gasped and fluttered their hands to their mouths. One woman screamed. The people gathered in squished layers, those in the back pushing off the shoulders of those in front, jumping and peeking over their heads. "It's just a log," a man said. "No, Danny's right! It's a man!" another replied. Children wriggled between the jostling legs, trying to make their way to the front. "No, it's not!" Another woman screamed. "It is! It is!"

Behind the clamouring crowd, I stood on a chair from where I could see him swimming in the water—was it him? My heart pounded as loud as drums. At times he seemed to be floating, motionless, and then he'd move his arms and kick his legs, though from this distance it was difficult to tell whether he was moving by his own muscle power or the waves were moving him. He was too far away to rush down to the shore and call out to him, yet he was close enough that by the time they untied their boats and drove from the dock around the protruding corner of shoreline he'd have reached the water's edge.

Women squealed and grabbed onto one another, gasping and crying out, "Praise Jesus!" From somewhere in the sandwich of people, Loretta's voice exclaimed, "I told you this day would come! My dreams are gifts from the ancestors!" Hannah burst out of the crowd and doubled over with her hands on her knees. She struggled for air, wheezing. I steered Hannah by her shoulders and sat her in a chair, pushing her head between her knees and telling her to breathe slowly. When Hannah finally stopped hyperventilating, she lifted her head and the tears streamed down her cheeks. Her shoulders heaved and shuddered with sobbing. She pulled her mouth open into a gaping cry, her lips soaked with spit and tears. She squinted at me and clutched at my hands. "My daddy. My daddy. My daddy's back." She stretched the last word out so that it hung in the air and undulated with rapturous joy. Then she threw her head back and began to wail. Others were wailing now, too, and near the far end of the windows, Frank leaned against the wall and sunk to a low crouch, the stunned look of relief in his eyes obscured only by his tears. Arms raised out of the crowd as some people thanked the Creator for answering their prayers, while others praised the ocean. "Our giver of life is good!" A woman declared that she could feel the presence of ancestors in the room, then another woman cried out that she could see their ghostly faces in the windows, causing several more people to cry out, "They are smiling upon us!" and "They've guided Chase home to us!" and "They could feel our pain and they've made everything right again!" Voices gasped in tandem and a path was cleared for a woman who had fainted. Two men carried her to a chair and I moved quickly to help, but by the time I reached the woman, she was already fully alert and fanning her face with her hand.

A child yelled, "He's a hairy *puukmis!*" Then several children yelled, "He's a hairy *puukmis!*" More gasps and shrieks erupted from the crowd. Another child warned, "Don't look into his eyes, he'll blind you!" Frightened children bawled and some called out questions. Would Chase hurt them? Was he a monster now? One of the teenaged boys suggested they get a gun. "We don't need no gun, it's Chase—only different!" But how, somebody wondered aloud, did they know he wouldn't hurt them with those blinding eyes and a body like a beast? "We just know!" a group of teenaged girls shrieked, "It's our uncle Chase, and our uncle Chase wouldn't even hurt a fly!" Nan Lily leaned on her cane behind the crowd, shaking her head as she repeated, "I knew it. I knew it. I knew he was a hairy *puukmis.*" I stood on the chair again. He was swimming closer now, and I could see that his body was covered from head to foot with a coat of thick black hair.

Somebody shouted, "Let's go!" and the crowd bumped and jostled and squeezed through the door. A few people rushed back inside to grab the pot of oysters for Chase, and a carafe of hot coffee, plus the four blankets that had been draped over the honoured search party of men. They stampeded down the wood ramp and moved in a long file along the snaky path that wound through the long grasses down to the shore, the younger ones running on ahead, the hobbling elders trailing behind. Some of the men were shouting Chase's name out to the water. Sophie Florence and Margaret and Gina were clinging tightly to one another as they walked the last length of the path. Once on the shore, everybody gathered at the edge where the incoming tide, fast and foamy, washed over the speckled stones and over their feet. Patty wrapped her arm around Hannah's shoulder and pulled her close, stroking her wind-blown hair. Even icy Loretta put her hand on Patty and stroked her back gently. Children moved back and forth in short sprints along the water, like dogs unable to contain their excitement. Wren stood with George, while nearby Frank rubbed his face with his hands. When Chase passed the tiny isle where the wood cross tilted out of the black rocks, he came into clearer view. Several of the men started to wade into the cold water towards him. Some of the women took hold of the restless children, burying the children's faces into their bellies and breasts, shielding their eyes, anticipating the blinding glare of the *puukmis*'s diamond irises. Others turned away when Chase came closer, the waves now pushing him quickly towards the shoreline. And that's when I could finally see him for what he really was.

I watched from the window in the community centre, alone. I tried not to cry, but the ache in my chest was more than I could stand, and I let the tears spill from my eyes and down my cheeks. Everything looked blurred now. But I didn't need to see any more. I didn't need to go down to the shore and look any closer. I knew what they were going to find. It was not Chase Charlie. It was not a hairy *puukmis*. It was a dead bear.

⚹　　⚹　　⚹

On the south side of my island was a sea stack, a tall pillar of rock eroded into the shape of an old woman's crooked finger with gnarled knuckles, hooking slightly as it pointed to something in the sky. I climbed to the top and perched in the wet grass there. The midafternoon sun, a diffused circle of bone white behind the clouds, hit this part of my island with a wide wash of soft light. I shut off my VHF radio for the first time in four long decades. Nobody in the community would want to speak to me anyway.

Around the sea stack, about fifteen feet below, hilly stretches of black basalt covered the narrow beach. Small tidal pools of serene water filled the rain-carved bowls in this basalt, gentle basins of blossoming colours. From my spot, I could see them: purple urchins, orange starfish, green anemones, olive kelp. In the warmer seasons, I often came here, climbing the knuckles of the sea stack like a ladder to ride the lofty patch of grass as if it were a magic carpet. Sometimes I'd bring a book to read, or some paper to write a letter to Anne.

I ripped tufts of grass from the rock and threw them to the mercy of the wind. It was my fault the community had risen to such a fevered pitch of ecstasy this afternoon. It was only the bear I'd dumped in the ocean, but to them, for a moment, it had been a miracle. The return of Chase Charlie. The resurrection of Chase Charlie.

I would never be forgiven.

Jesus wept.

Anne's favourite line from her favourite story.

"Think of it, Bernie," she'd said one day when we were teenagers. "For God so loved the world that he gave His only begotten Son. No matter what you believe in, there's no denying the magnificence of that story. It's sublime. It's transcendent. And how perfectly told that everything culminates in the moment of just two simple words: *Jesus wept.*"

I wished for Anne right now. I watched the meadows of eelgrass swaying with the incoming tide. The water that rushed to fill the basalt valleys was a soup of detritus, speck-sized dead plants and animals that, when alive, lived near the surface in the full glory of the light. Soon, their dead husks would sink and feed those creatures that prefer the darkness.

I had left the community centre before anybody returned, driving the boat quickly across the cove. Most likely I was seen leaving, but I didn't know for sure. I hadn't dared to look back. Never before had I run away from anything in that way. I was so ashamed of my mistake I couldn't stand the thought of facing everybody.

I climbed down the sea stack, the rock cool under my skin, and trekked across the beach. I thought about how I'd never heard the stories in the wind and in the water as Frank claimed to, and I wondered if it was because they were not my stories to hear. I reached the north corner of the island, where the rock turned into a patch of sand. My rubber boots cracked on the long hollow tails of bull kelp as I walked to the metal ring filled with blackened wood. Beside it was a thick log of driftwood, smooth as velvet. In the summers, I used the log as a bench whenever I relaxed by an evening bonfire. I'd miss my bonfires, which I'd sometimes enjoy alone and sometimes with Frank, or Chase, or Sophie Florence and Gina, and I wished I could have one more before leaving Tawakin. But at this time of year, the wind often whipped around the end of Mitchell Island and funnelled through the mouth of the cove before crossing my triangle of beach at speeds too dangerous for a bonfire. The gusts of flames would catch on the ragged branches drooping low off the ridge.

I sat on the log and pushed a chunk of charred wood around the inside of the metal ring with a branch. The wind wrinkled the water and tugged half-buried bits of seaweed out of the sand, scattering them around me like scraps of old paper. I tilted my head upward and let the cool air wash over my face as I took in my surroundings: the wharf behind me, the outpost on the ridge above, the reserve across the way, Saul Finkler's B&B and the Tawakin Market on Mitchell Island.

I heard a noise come down the ridge. Footsteps. It was Wren.

"Frank and George blamed me," she said, furious.

I poked at the charred wood.

"They thought I was the one who dumped the bear in the ocean," she said, seething. "They said it must've been me because I was the one who didn't want them to skin it or eat it. They told me how disrespectful I'd been to their culture. They were so mad. They called me a stupid *mamulthni*."

"I'm sorry," I said, my voice as small and pathetic as I felt. "I will tell them the truth."

"Oh, I already did. I told everybody it was you."

I swallowed hard. "What did they say?"

"Nan Lily said you should have known better. She was very disappointed in you."

My heart broke. The idea that I'd disappointed Nan Lily was one of the worst things I could imagine.

"She said you should've respected the ocean. She said it's like when they make their big fire on Toomista, and they cook the salmon over it, how they always teach the children not to throw their garbage onto the flames while the salmon's still cooking. It's like poison to the food. She said what you did was like poisoning the ocean. 'Our ocean is a giver of life,' she said. 'It provides us with a bounty of food, it gives us our nutrition and our medicine—'"

I nodded sadly yet thought of the long narrow float of junk in the cove and of all the broken juice bottles and rusted bicycles that lay underwater near the reserve dock.

"I suppose everybody's mad, then?" I asked.

"Furious."

"Even Margaret and Gina?" I asked.

"Even Sophie Florence," Wren said.

My heavy heart sunk. "It was just a mistake."

"They really believed it was him. They were faint when they saw the bear wasn't Chase. Hannah got sick all over the beach, throwing up and screaming and crying."

I started to sob uncontrollably.

Wren put her hand on the space between my shoulder blades and stroked soothing circles. She spoke in a soft voice now. "Frank said you'd better feed everybody dinner soon and stand up and give an apology. I think everything will be okay then." She rubbed my back for a while longer and then hiked back up the ridge, leaving me alone with my thoughts.

I felt weary and confused. My loneliness, my legacy of work, my childless home that wasn't even a home but a few rooms slapped onto a cold, sterile examination area. I'd served my time here dutifully and competently and compassionately. And I'd been respectful, nothing like those stories of dysfunction and abandonment that often poison the tiny towns along the faraway edges of Canada. Was it that people always remembered what was done wrong more than they remembered what was done right? The return of Chase Charlie who was not Chase Charlie. I feared it would be the last thing people would recall about me.

20

The VHF radio scratched with static at 8:31 AM. "Tawakin outpost. Bernadette, are you on? Are you on, Bernadette?" It was Margaret Sam. Her words burst out of heavy breaths.

I put down the cold boiled egg I was peeling at the kitchen table. This morning, I'd gone for a walk around the island, listening for the stories in the wind and in the water, but all I found was another empty wine bottle tucked into the roots of a cedar tree above the east shore. After yesterday, I didn't have the gumption to confront Wren about it. Once again, I cleaned it and placed another message inside it, this time tossing the bottle beside Toomista Island. It had been a tricky navigation across the water. Fog like grey wool swathed the ocean, slipping between the nearby trees on Rubant Island and over the rocky spines that hunched offshore above the black surface. In the grey distance, neither the horizon nor the small yellow circle to the east had been visible. It was the kind of weather that preyed upon travellers, capturing the careless in its sticky web of grey. I'd not journeyed far, and I'd stopped only for a moment to throw the bottle, glancing quickly at the splash it made. For a brief instant, it disappeared as the mouth of the Pacific swallowed it whole, sucking it down into the icy darkness before spitting it back out. Like a seed or a pit worked away from the fruit and discarded, too hard to digest.

"It's Bernadette. I'm on. What's the matter?"

"There's been an accident. A dog bite. It's bad. Can you come quick?"

"Yes. Where?"

"Patty's house. It's Hannah."

"Where did she get bit?"

"Her face. Hurry."

I clipped the radio onto my belt and scrambled down the hallway to the examination room, shouting to Wren through the bathroom door on the way. I hooked the medical kit onto my shoulder and rushed out the door and down to the wharf and into the boat, where I cranked the key, the engine chugging and rumbling and spewing blue-grey smoke into the air. I bent over the side of the boat, my heart pounding and flooding heat into my face and my ears, my fingers fumbling with the knotted rope. By the time I untied the last rope from the pilings, Wren came flying down the ramp in long strides, leaping into the boat and shoving it off the row of old tires nailed to the wharf. Teetering from the motion of the sharply turning boat, Wren stumbled her way to the front seat and slammed down into it as I sped away as fast I could across the cove. In less than two minutes, we reached the reserve dock, bumped against it with a heavy thud, then tied up and immediately started to run up the dirt road with the medical kit swinging between us, each holding one of the straps. Everything around me slipped into silence, except the sound of our footsteps scratching against the wet stones on the dirt road. I gulped at the cool air and climbed quickly up the sloping hill towards the back of the reserve and across the thick wet grass of Patty's front yard. Margaret Sam waited in the open doorway.

"She's upstairs on the couch."

I led the way up the stairs with the medical kit. In the living room, Patty sat on the edge of the couch, leaning over the small figure swaddled in a grey wool blanket. Patty lifted her head as I approached, and although she scowled for a brief second at the sight of me, her face softened as she couldn't conceal her obvious relief. She stood and moved to the big window beside the couch without a word.

Against the left side of Hannah's face a thickly folded hand towel was soaked with blood. A pinkish-grey tensor bandage wrapped diagonally around her head and held the towel in place. I sat on the edge of the couch. Quiet and motionless, Hannah stared blankly. Her pupils were dilated and her face was pale, her skin cool and clammy. I checked her pulse, weak and rapid. She was in shock.

Patty pointed across the room at Margaret Sam, who now stood at the top of the stairs beside Wren. "It was her big stupid dog, Trucker. I'm going to blow that fucking mutt's head clear off."

"Your daughter was sticking Trucker's litter with needles," said Margaret.

"Not even." Patty pulled the half-open drapes farther apart.

A long rectangle of pearl-grey light crossed Hannah's head. I gently moved the fallen strands of black hair out of her eyes, then turned and pushed aside some papers and old magazines and two half-filled coffee cups on the coffee table. I lifted the medical kit onto the table and opened it. As I pulled on a pair of latex gloves, I moved close to Hannah and said gently, "Good morning, Hannah. I hear you had a little run-in with one of the dogs."

"Stupid fucking mutt," Patty said.

"Maybe if your daughter wasn't so—"

"Should've been chained up."

Margaret scowled. "Who? The dog or your daughter?"

I shot each of the women a stern look but kept my voice soft. I said, "I'm going to take the towel off and have a little look-see now, Hannah."

A silence fell upon the room as I located the end of the tensor and started to unravel it, gently lifting Hannah's head off the pillow. I peeled away the towel carefully, slowly, unsticking it from the thick syrup of blood underneath. The area around the eye was swelling like a purple balloon, the apple of her cheek a mess of ragged tissue. The bite had pulled the flesh from the cheekbone, a narrow hinge of skin the only thing holding it to her face. I took the flap of flesh between my finger and thumb and lifted it, exposing a patch of stark white bone the size of a dime. I laid the flesh back in place, then smiled at Hannah, whose eyes looked lost, faraway. "You're going to be just fine."

I nodded at Patty.

Patty looked at Margaret through angry slits. "How could you let this happen at a time like this? You don't think I got enough to worry about what with Chase still missing? You go put down that dog now. I'm giving you a chance to do it yourself on account of you and us being related. But if you don't do it, I will."

"I ain't putting down our dog. Trucker was being protective is all. Hannah was torturing her puppies. I seen her this morning under our porch."

I watched Patty's face as I set the saline on the table. There was the thunder of footsteps down the stairs as Margaret stormed out of the room. Patty left as well, and from somewhere at the end of the upstairs hallway there was the sound of Patty's voice as she complained to herself.

Wren kneeled down on the other side of the coffee table, put on a pair of gloves and helped prepare the dressing. She said nothing of the women's fight. After I finished cleaning the wound, Wren handed me the butterfly bandages one at a time.

"It's going to leave a terrible scar," she whispered.

I nodded and attached another thin bandage, pulling the skin together. There would forever be a thick crescent-shaped reminder on Hannah's cheek, like a slice of the moon.

Looking around the living room, I spotted a photograph of Chase in a red plastic frame on the fireplace mantel. His face was pulled open into a gaping smile, his eyes crinkled tight, as if somebody had told him a great joke seconds before the camera snapped the shot. I'd never seen that picture before. It captured a moment of pure joy, and it made me miss him deeply.

The door crashed open downstairs and there was a racket of women's voices arguing, followed by footsteps coming up the stairs. Margaret appeared again, holding something in her cupped hand. Behind her was Loretta. As she waddled across the living room towards her granddaughter on the couch, she shook her head at Margaret. "Look what your dog did."

"I already told Patty—" Margaret turned as Patty came back into the room. She held out her hand. "I had to pull these out of the puppies.

She'd put them in their bellies, one through an ear, one up a nostril, and one—I don't want to say where it was."

Both Loretta and Wren had moved closer to Margaret to examine what was in her hand. I stayed on the couch, attaching a soft pad over the bandages. I stroked Hannah's forehead and rubbed her shoulder.

"Couldn't have been Granddaughter," Loretta said definitively. "Daughter's only got sewing needles in this house. These ain't needles my little bebba would've got hold of, ain't that right, Daughter?"

"But I seen her," Margaret said.

"They're medical needles," said Wren.

"Just how did she get ahold of those?" asked Loretta.

"So you're admitting it was her then?"

"Don't you get smart with me, Margaret Sam," said Loretta.

I tried to ignore the women and took Hannah's vital signs. Her pulse was still weak, but it was stronger than before, and it had slowed to a normal rate. I tucked the blanket under Hannah's chin to keep her warm and asked her how she was feeling, but Hannah only stared blankly.

"Are you done?" Loretta asked me. "I got something to say."

"Yes. But she'll have to be taken to town today," I said, turning to face the women. "She needs to be looked at by a doctor. I've done all I can to stop the bleeding and make her comfortable for the ride."

The needles in Margaret's palm pointed in all directions like a sparkler on a birthday cake spraying silver light. Loretta took one of the needles from Margaret's hand and held it out towards me.

"Medical needles." Loretta's tone was sharp, accusatory.

"Yes," I said.

"Well. You better be to able explain this."

"I can. Hannah stole a handful of needles from me," I said. "At the school. You might not remember it, but I told you. I told you that I saw her grab them out of my bag right in front of me. You said she didn't take them."

"I guess you should have kept them somewhere more safe," scolded Loretta.

Margaret huffed. "What about my puppies? What you got to say about that? They're under the porch right now if you want to go see for yourself. Whimpering bad, real scared, they ain't even moving nowhere. My dog is not getting put down on account of what she did."

"Then I'm going to put it down myself," Patty told Margaret. "I'm going to get my gun and shoot that dog, and I'm going to borrow George's truck and I'm going to tie that dog to the bumper, and I'm going to drag that dog up to Dog Ditch, and I'm going to dump it there, and I'm not going to care one bit."

"If you do," said Margaret, taking a step towards Patty. "I'll press charges."

"Maybe I should press charges first," said Patty.

Margaret narrowed her eyes at Patty. "Maybe I should press charges against Hannah. It's her fault in the first place."

"It is not her fault."

"It *is* her fault."

"It is not."

"It is so."

"Stop it, you're both right!" Wren said.

Everybody turned and stared at Wren.

Wren said, "It is Hannah's fault, but it's also not. She shouldn't have done what she did, but she can't help it. She can't help how she was born."

I felt as though the floor fell out from under me. Nobody moved at first in the silence that descended. Then Loretta sat down in a chair and strummed her fingers over the wood arm. She strummed slowly, but soon the strumming grew faster, though it made no sound. Her fingers never once made contact with the chair. Margaret stepped back away from Patty, slipping over to the top of the stairs where she stood looking down at the door. Patty backed into the corner of the room behind her mother's chair. Wren looked from face to face, clearly unsure what was happening, what this pantomime meant.

"Wren's right," I said, taking a deep breath. I stood and through the window I could see children walking in scattered groups towards the logging road that led to the school. "You need to get Hannah some help."

Outside, the children's laughter pierced the tension in the living room. It was followed by an explosive sound in the corner—like a sneeze, but it wasn't.

Patty was sobbing angrily.

"You," Loretta glared at me, "you been telling her lies!"

I started to pack up the medical kit.

"She's not told me anything." Wren shrugged, and I realized then that she truly had no idea what sort of vicious cat she had just let out of the bag. She didn't understand that some things on the reserve were never talked about.

"She did," Loretta said. "Or you wouldn't have said nothing."

Wren looked puzzled. "That Hannah has fetal alcohol syndrome? It's hardly a lie. Surely you know that, right? Are you telling me you think it's not true? You think your granddaughter doesn't have FAS?"

Patty's face scrunched up in outrage, but she appeared to be speechless for the moment. Loretta stopped strumming.

Wren continued. "Why would you ever pretend such a thing? For starters, look at her. It's written all over her facial features. It's plain as day. I hate those damn medical files. Even so, I read them, but even if I hadn't I would've known. Second, what does your pretending do for Hannah? I bet you she struggles a lot with learning at school, doesn't she? How can she get the help she deserves if you pretend she doesn't need it? I don't understand you." Wren shook her head then looked at me, appealing for support.

I stared straight at Patty. "She's your child, Patty."

Patty's eyes grew wide, but she still said nothing.

Neither did Loretta.

I slung the medical kit onto my shoulder and took one last look at Hannah, who seemed to be breathing more calmly now, then walked to the top of the stairs. Margaret had left already. As I headed down the stairs, I heard nothing but the strange sound of silence. But I didn't stop. I didn't turn around to see what was happening behind me. I was so grateful to Wren for speaking the unspeakable. It emboldened me to take some actions of my own.

I meandered along the small trails between the houses and the sheds with the *muwach* skulls hanging under the roofs and the rows of red jerry cans smelling of gasoline. Occasionally, I heard the murmur of a television or snippets of a conversation—"You want toast or you want mush for breakfast?"—coming from the houses, or the brush of sea gull wings against the rain gutters above my head.

A community as small as Tawakin required a careful navigation of local personalities and delicate politics, so interrelated they were, so rife with old hurts and open secrets, yet I couldn't now help but think that maybe this was what Loretta and Patty needed. A person like Wren to shake things up. Everybody knew what was wrong with Hannah. Wren was right. You could see it in her face. That hadn't meant, however, that you could talk about it.

In a private file, the teachers had documented Hannah's behaviour: her poor impulse control, her lack of empathy, her inability to read social cues, her misunderstanding of consequences, her weak memory, her learning difficulties. One time, it was discussed with Patty. Afterwards, Loretta sent the school a letter, which said: *Stop requesting that we take Hannah to a doctor or I'll sue the teacher, the school and the school board for your lies.*

Although the teachers ignored this empty threat, there was nothing anybody could do without Patty's permission, and Loretta would not allow Patty to give permission. And since Chase believed that Hannah was only testing, and that she'd stop testing once she found something to trust, he'd always stayed out of it and followed his own method of waiting and seeing instead.

I found Trucker with her litter of puppies under Margaret's porch. Margaret had already pulled the needles out of the poor things, and they seemed to be finding comfort by snuggling into one another. I picked up a broken piece of needle off the ground. I recognized the flat, snapped-off end as being the same headless "pins" used to nail the snakes to the closet wall. I should have suspected Hannah, but it never occurred to me that she'd go to her father's old house on Toomista.

I removed all the medical supplies from my duffel bag and gently placed each of the puppies inside. Then I unrolled a long tensor bandage and tied it around Trucker's neck like a leash. I called up to Margaret several times, but she didn't seem to be home, so I wrote a note on one of the bandage packets explaining that I'd taken the dogs to safety. Then I stuck the note into the dirt with the broken needle.

*   *   *

On the way back to the boat, I stopped by Nan Lily's house and stood outside her basement door, trying to work up the nerve to go inside. Trucker poked her nose into the open bag and nuzzled her puppies. She must have sensed my nervousness, because she then rubbed her large black head against my thighs. "Thanks, girl," I said, and stroked the middle of her forehead until her eyes fluttered gently in relaxation. Crouching down, I kept petting Trucker and whispered, as she licked my face, "What should I say, girl? I'm scared to see how angry she is at me."

I opened the door and stepped into the darkness, leaving the dogs outside. I called out, hello. I could hear Nan Lily's footsteps padding gently overhead, and soon the door at the top of the stairs opened. My heart quickened. Halfway down the stairs, Nan Lily stopped and held onto the railing and stared at me in the pale circle of yellow light. Her gaze was so piercing that I wondered if she was going to turn right around without a word.

My lip quivered. I tried to steady it. I wanted to tell her how much her respect meant to me, how much I revered her and how ashamed I felt. Instead, I heard myself saying, "I guess now I'll never get to hear who the woman in the box with the baby is."

Nan Lily descended the remainder of the steps and sat in her lawn chair in the middle of the basement, her hands clutching a crumpled tissue. She tucked the tissue under the cuff of her sweater.

"Did you hope I would tell you someday?" she asked.

"Yes."

"Why do you want to know?"

"She's a mystery."

"What is it you feel for her?"

I thought for a moment.

"Sadness," I said.

Nan Lily waited.

"Empathy," I said.

She smiled a little. "You put yourself in her moccasins?"

"Yes."

"Why?"

"She's alone."

"No, she's with her baby."

I shook my head. "She never got to be with her baby for long."

"She's with him for eternity."

"I don't think she's at peace, though."

"Why?"

"Nobody cared enough to bury her."

Nan Lily straightened her sweater and clasped her hands on her lap. "What does it matter if you know who she is?"

"It just feels like people should know who she was."

"But what does it matter if *you* know?"

"Maybe I'll understand things better."

"Like what?" Nan Lily asked.

"I don't know. Life."

"Because you think her story is your story."

I stared at Nan Lily.

"It is good that you try to know her," she said. "Because then you might know some of her truths."

I nodded.

"But you cannot know her. Not fully," she said. "And it is dangerous to ever think you can. Because then you will mistake your own truths for hers."

I felt foolish, humbled. "I'm so sorry, Nan Lily."

She smiled. "I know."

The Heaviness of Things That Float

When I left Nan Lily's, I'd found Wren waiting for me down at the dock. She saw the dogs and didn't even ask, only jumped up to help me load them onto the boat. Now I could hear them running around the kitchen floor, their nails scratching across the linoleum, as I sat on the rim of the tub, and drew myself a hot bath. I smelled like dog. As I lowered myself into the fluid heat, my body pushed the water out of its way and lifted it higher in the tub. I slid down until the water reached my chin and pushed a loofah away from my face. It drifted towards my upturned knees. I thought about displacement. When an object sunk, the amount of water displaced was equal to the volume of the object. And when an object floated, the amount of water displaced was equal to the weight of the object.

But just how much did shame weigh?

And what exactly was the volume of grief?

21

That night, I awoke to a crash in the living room.

"I'm so sorry," Wren said when I shuffled into the room. She crawled beside the coffee table on her hands and knees. All the seashells from the pine case had crashed to the floor, strewn everywhere. Dozens of books also lay across the couch and the coffee table, many spread open like fallen butterflies. "I was looking for the story of Theseus's ship, and then I got up to use the washroom and the shells got knocked over."

"The story of what?" I picked up one of my poetry books.

"The story of Theseus's ship. How many planks did they change before it became a different ship? I need to know."

I put the poetry back on the empty shelf. "Why are my books everywhere?"

"I told you. I was looking for Theseus's ship." Only this time she pronounced it, "Seesee's ship."

Wren lowered her cheek to the floor and swept seashells out from under the couch. Beside her, the wood case stood upended and bent open like the corner of a wall. She tried to fit a periwinkle into three different spots, each one obviously too small, the shell knocking against the pine slats. She then turned it sideways to make it fit into the same small compartments, though even a child of two could see it was clearly too large.

I studied Wren closely. "Are you okay?"

"Yes, of course. Why wouldn't I be?"

Wren climbed to her feet and hurried to the washroom, looking a little unsteady. The door slammed shut. Several times the knob rattled as Wren struggled with the lock, and then there was silence, followed by the muffled sound of the faucet and the closing of drawers. I started to pick up the rest of my books. On the small table beside the chair was the Emily Carr cup, half full of liquid. I smelled it. Whiskey. When the door finally opened again several minutes later, Wren continued on her mission searching for something in one of the books, and for a moment, I thought I saw her sway off balance.

"Have you found it yet?" she asked me.

"Found what?"

Wren sighed, sounding exasperated. "Theseus's ship. I got thinking about it after talking about those damn medical records."

"You shouldn't be doing this," I said.

Wren ignored me. She leafed through a book.

"You're drunk," I said.

Wren laughed. "I'm not."

"Well, you're certainly not sober," I said.

"Lighten up. It's no big deal."

"Soon, you're going to be the only nurse here."

"But I'm not yet."

"What if you're on call?"

"I'm not on call right now, am I?"

I bent to pick up my old *Oxford Dictionary of Philosophy* from the couch, stopping for a moment to examine the small red pieces that had fallen into the crack of the open book. I slid my fingernail along the binding to extract the debris and smelled a small sample. Dried salmon. A residue of fish oil had soaked through several of the thin translucent pages. I pursed my lips and looked around, spying the empty plastic baggie on the table beside the couch.

"You dropped food on my good book."

"I'm sorry," she said. "I truly am."

"I thought you didn't eat fish, anyway."

"Couldn't help myself. It smelled so good. Besides, it was a gift."

I sighed. I crawled around the floor and returned the rest of the seashells to the wood case, which I clasped shut and put on the dresser in my bedroom. When I sat back on the couch, Wren was sitting in the chair and staring at the ceiling as though the story she wanted to tell was written up there.

"Theseus killed the Minotaur and then he made the city of Athens, and he kept his big ship there. My grandma told me. We took the bus to Vancouver together every Saturday when I was a child, and she told me. That's why I was looking for Theseus's ship. It tells us a lot about how people change, and how others might see that change," she said.

"I thought you grew up in the Slocan Valley. No shoes and acting in harmony with nature and all that," I said.

"I did live there." She stumbled on her words, slurring slightly. "Sort of. Most of the time. But I lived with my grandma whenever my parents were in jail."

My hand stopped mid-motion.

"Mmm," Wren said, nodding, as if she were answering a question I hadn't asked. Her eyelids fluttered heavily. She leaned sideways and took the teacup from the side table and drank a gulp.

"Don't you think you've had enough?" I asked.

Wren wiped something white from the corner of her mouth, and I guessed it was toothpaste, and that Wren had gone to the bathroom to freshen her sour breath. "This is my personal time," she said. "What I do in my private life is nobody's business."

"How about I make us some coffee?"

"Pass me that book, would you?" She pointed at the fish-stained book.

"Did I find the ship in that book? I can't remember." Wren looked at the window. Then she shook her head and mumbled something to herself. "No, see the people in Athens preserved Seesee's ship by getting rid of the old planks whenever they rotted, and they replaced them with new planks. They did that until all the old planks had been replaced with new ones.

So the question is," Wren took another drink, then leaned forward and rested her elbows on her knees, "after all that switching around with the planks, was it the same ship or a different ship? It's about identity, you see. It's about politics. It's about who gets to define the ship. It's about who gets to say if it's a different ship or the same old ship."

What was I going to do about her? I'd become so hopeful that I was leaving my patients in good hands. Wren had made such a positive impression on nearly everybody. She had appeared to be a competent and caring nurse. I'd hoped the incident with Frank was a one-time thing. It clearly wasn't, and now I didn't know what to do.

Wren leaned back again, her eyelids half sinking. "It's the same ship. But how could it be the same ship when every single plank is different? Fine then, it's a different ship. But then if it's different, when exactly did it become different? Which plank was the one to make it different? Plus, it looks identical. It seems identical, right? Right. I don't know. It's a very important question. I know, I know. I'm tired of this riddle."

Me too, I thought. I picked up the last of the books from the table and slid them on the shelf. I noticed there was still an empty space left over.

"A person can change all her planks over the years," Wren said, "but those damn records will insist she's the same ship. See the problem now?"

"Not really." I yawned.

Wren leaned forward in her chair and looked at me intently. "Haven't you ever watched something or somebody—maybe even yourself in the mirror—change slowly over time, and even though you might sense that their planks are being replaced one by one, you don't know for certain what remains of the old or which of the planks are new, because the changes are subtle, and yet one day you wonder if the person is at all the same, or completely different now?"

I scratched my jaw. Something in Wren's question worried me. It was a feeling, foggy and difficult to grasp, and as I dwelled on it, standing there beside the bookcase, I could not trace its origin. I did not know what, besides Wren's rambling, had caused this feeling, but what worried me was this: maybe Chase had changed so much over the years that he was a completely different ship now, and I was a fool for insisting that he was still the same old ship I'd always known, no matter how many old planks had been switched out for new ones.

Wren didn't seem to be waiting for an answer from me. She nestled in the wing of the chair and turned on the TV with the remote. I left the room shortly after. In the kitchen, I found a stack of children's novels on the table. My prized collection of Anne's publications, and I felt a splotch of dampness on one of the covers. I lifted the book to my nose. Alcohol. I patted it with a dish towel. On the counter beside the oven was a tall bottle of rye whiskey, nearly a quarter of it gone. I unscrewed the cap and poured the remainder into the sink, then rinsed the bottle and hid it in the cupboard.

The Heaviness of Things That Float

22

The wind was wild, tossing the boat over swells that rose like the slowly rousing shoulders of a sleepy giant. Many times, I considered turning back. Instead, I kept as close to the coastline as I could, the waves lifting into crests so white that the ocean looked peaked with snowdrifts. It was impossible to anchor my boat in the same place I'd left it during my last two trips to the hut: the small pocket of coastline was a frothing, churning cauldron of unnavigable waters. I found a spot north of the hut sheltered by a low cliff face. Thick clusters of leafless cottonwoods bent stiffly in the wind, while the tops of cedars and hemlocks curved into enormous bows. Arrows of small branches shot in swirling arcs all around me as I mounted the banks above the shoreline. The ocean attacked the land, clacking its jaws and chomping the beach in large bites. It would devour me if I went that way, so I took a path through the forest where the trees wore a shroud of soft green moss. The shroud coated every bit of branch and bark and exposed root. Even the loose scraps of death and decay that lay forgotten were covered with the same swath of verdant fabric that joined everything, the dead to the living, so that there was no difference in appearance from one to the other, only mysterious contours of green seamlessly melding everything together. It showed the world in its true form, where everything sooner or later became one.

Halfway to the hut, the forest opened into a small clearing of lush grass. At the corners of the clearing were four jagged stones, natural formations roughly the shape of obelisks and about eight feet tall. It was almost as if the Creator knew this was going to be the memorial and burial site for Miranda's sons. Marking the site were two wood crosses, each etched in angular lettering. *Stanley Charlie* and *Ronald Charlie.* Under the crosses, dozens of cedar roses stood in the ground as though they'd bloomed there. About the length of my hand, the roses varied in shades from a very light brown to a deep, dark, reddish brown, depending on how many seasons they'd weathered the sun and wind and rain.

Next to these two spots there was a new cross. It had been stabbed into the grass and held in place with a firmly packed pile of sandy soil. Because it was not stuck into the ground very deep, it tilted at an angle without much care taken to finish the job properly. There were five words on the cross, the wood freshly and roughly carved with thin lines that exposed the lighter, brighter wood underneath. It read:

Mother of the Dog Children.

A darkness moved through me. The earth marked by the cross hadn't been turned yet. At the edge of the clearing, a long branch was also stuck upright in the ground. Draped over it was Miranda's tattered coat, billowing in the wind. A coat had been set upon a stick in Miranda's story, too. As a decoy to trick her dog children into believing she was still on the beach digging clams when she was in fact with them, watching them.

I continued along the path through the forest until I reached the shore near Miranda's home. Just ahead, up on the low ridge, shreds of blue waved from the top of the hut, fraying and pulling into quivering strands, barely hanging on, sorrowful flags of surrender.

"Miranda?" I knocked on the door of the hut. When there was no response, I slid the door sideways and entered. Nothing stirred inside. The light was dim and dreary, the tarpaulin walls shivering madly in the wind.

An odd odour filled the room. Like a jar of old pennies, or the iron nails I sometimes found in flotsam on the beach. Rain sprayed the outside of the tarpaulin walls across the room. The part of my mind that automatically turned the world into patterns detected something wrong with this image of the rain. The outsides of the other walls were dry, and when I looked again, I saw how dark the rain appeared.

I took a step past the thick tree trunk that held up the roof in the middle of the room, where Miranda kept all her pots and pans and a jumble of clothing hanging from hooks. The trunk and everything stored on it had been partially blocking my view of the far corner, but now I could see my map spread out on the floor near the bed. Something dark was splattered on it. Paint, or mud. Blood. I lifted my gaze to the tiny droplets sprayed not on the outside but the inside of the walls above the bed. Below, a grisly figure was lying contorted.

I tightened. I moved towards the figure on the bed, the metallic smells of copper and iron overpowering me. The hills and valleys of the thick woolen fabric partly concealed the thin body, crumpled and sunken. An arm hung from under the blanket, and I at once recognized Miranda's small gnarled hand. Her index finger was obviously broken, as it bent at an unnatural angle. Positioned on her legs was Jimmy Charlie's gun, the muzzle aimed at the head of the bed.

My skin bristled as I glimpsed the pillow, and how the wool blanket concealed the head. I reached for the edge of the blanket, which was drenched in dark wetness, and pinched it between my fingertips. I felt faraway, as though I were watching myself unstick the blanket adhering to the face with viscous blood, and I retreated even further into my mind when I saw how the shotgun had split the head into two halves, each side of the skull bending apart like a flower opening to take in the sun.

My entire body released a violent shudder.

There was not enough left of the face to know for certain that it was Miranda Charlie, but when I peeled away the blanket further, I could see that it was Miranda's small bony frame and her clothes. Although most of Miranda's hair was matted to the bed with blood, I could make out a few silver-streaked black tresses. At the sight of Miranda's broken finger, most likely the result of trying to fire the gun with an outstretched arm, something switched off inside me, like a light.

I stripped the blanket off Miranda. Burn marks from firing at close range surrounded the hole in the blanket. Miranda must have covered her head with it, only to have it fall away during the impact. I folded it and set it aside, then searched the hut for a clean blanket. I found one in a wood crate beside the rattan chairs. Before draping the blanket respectfully over the body, I removed Miranda's clothes—everything including her underpants, which were worn thin and full of holes. As I lifted the torso to remove her shirt, I discovered her notebook wedged under her rib cage. I set it aside on the bloodied wool blanket and then slipped a clean pair of pants over Miranda's cold feet and tugged them up her legs and over her bony hips. I found a button shirt and carefully guided her hands into each sleeve, lifting her torso once more to bring it around her back. As I buttoned each hole and covered her wrinkled body, I felt a deep sorrow and a tenderness for my friend.

Why had Miranda committed suicide now? I used to worry about her doing this after Ronnie's suicide almost twenty years ago. For Miranda to have survived the intense grief for so long only to end her life now seemed strange. Had Chase's visit stirred up old ghosts in her?

But then again, what did I know? I pictured the burn mark on her back from so long ago, as if she'd been branded. Even though she'd tried as a young woman to conceal her fears—her anger and sadness, too—I'd always sensed them lurking deep within her. Why had she been so compelled to hide this part of her away from me? I did not ever know how she saw the world. I had tried to know. But how much of her truth had I ever really understood?

Unclipping the VHF radio from my belt, I put out a call to Tawakin. "Frank Charlie. Frank Charlie, you there? Frank Charlie."

When Frank came on, we switched to a different channel, though anybody could eavesdrop on any channel. I then told him that he needed to come up north right away.

"Is it Chase?"

"No."

"Is it blowing hard up there?"

"Yes, but you can make it. You have to."

It would take Frank at least forty-five minutes to walk down to the dock and drive his boat up to the hut. While I waited, I went down to the beach and started a small fire. The wind was blowing even harder now, so it took me several tries before I got the flames blazing big enough to burn Miranda's clothes. I sat on a large piece of driftwood and looked at the book I found under Miranda on the bed. It was Miranda's diary, the same one I had found in the wood crate last time. It was a very thick book with hundreds of pages stuck together with blood. When I pried them apart, I saw that the blood had seeped between and across the paper. The pencilled words were stained, but their imprint on the page was readable.

I skimmed the recent entries, many no longer than a sentence or two, looking only for any reference to Chase's whereabouts. Mostly, Miranda's diary was a type of almanac, with references to the weather and tide tables and full moons. Occasionally, she wrote cryptic sentences about people from the reserve, but I couldn't make any sense of them, and they seemed like entries from long ago. Things like: *Last night I tried to take my coat off but it was stuck. It was sewed right into me tight with sinew and bone. It's shame.*

Nothing that would help me find Chase Charlie.

I reached the last entry, and my breath caught when I saw that it was dated only a week ago.

No ghost of the woman in the box with the baby.
   Chase and her naked in the trees. Like Adam and Eve. Damn
Serpent out in the water pulling the boy's legs.
   He said it this much.
   It was our fault, Mother.
   It was our fault, Mother.
   It was our fault, Mother.
   He's going to tell the truth.

I felt as if I were being tossed around in a gust of wind, a small leaf, unsure of where I might land. It was incomprehensible. I knew about the woman in the box with the baby—everyone did. But the only time I'd ever heard of the ghost of the woman was when Teddy drowned. It was Patty's story about what kept her from reaching her younger brother in time. *It was our fault, mother*—is this what Chase had come to tell Miranda? Was this the story he was returning, the one he didn't want in the first place? Why would he bring it to Miranda of all people? Why not me? I remembered how upset Chase was after Teddy's death, how he sat in my kitchen shortly after and confessed that Patty was sort of his girlfriend. *Him and her naked in the trees. Like Adam and Eve.*

I felt ill as I realized what it meant. Patty wasn't peeing in the forest. Chase was there. Two infatuated hormonal teenagers. In the bushes together. Not watching Teddy. For how long before they realized he'd gone out into the water? Chase had been carrying the guilt all these years. He'd wanted to confess. To tell the truth, that's what Miranda's diary had said. But why, after fifteen years, had Chase decided to clear his conscience now, and why couldn't he tell the truth to me, or to Frank? Because he hadn't wanted to disappoint us, I figured. And because of Patty, too. She would've been doing everything she could to stop him from telling. She'd be the one looking to keep the secret all these years. Out of fear, not wanting Loretta to ever know that her son died because Patty wasn't paying attention. Patty would never find a moment's peace in her life ever again if Loretta knew the truth.

I threw the diary into the fire. Some secrets, when they could no longer be guarded, were best burned. But then, as I watched the flames curl around its corners, turning blue and white along its canvas-covered binding, a different feeling came over me. I regretted tossing it. What did it matter that Patty would've faced her mother's wrath if the truth came out? When she was young, I felt sorry for her—for how desperately she wanted to please her mother. It couldn't have been easy growing up with such a bitter woman. But Patty was an adult now, and she should have rectified the past, like Chase wanted.

I bolted to the tree line in anger. Retrieving a long branch from the ground, I hurried back and tried to pull the diary back out of the fire. But the flames were intensely hot, and instead of quickly flicking it out of the small inferno, I managed only to flip it wide open. Instantly, the pages rolled into arcs of flame and crumbled into ash, the whole thing gone. It didn't matter. I'd seen it with my own eyes. I knew the truth.

When the clothes turned to flakes and ashes, I hiked back up the ridge just as Frank Charlie was crossing the grass to the hut. He was wide eyed at the sight of the blood on my jacket, and his breathing was quick and hot, expelling white smears of cold mist. He hurried towards the door, which I had closed to keep out any curious animals, and I begged him, "No, Frank. Please. You don't want to go in there. Let me—" but he'd already slid the door open and rushed into the hut, and in the next instant, as I stood motionless on the grass, a long, loud howl rose from the hut into the air and carried off into the wind like a message of grief sent out to the world, and I wondered how far this wind travelled and how long this message would endure before it thinned and frayed and disappeared.

I entered the hut and sat in one of the rattan chairs. Frank remained standing over the bed. His howling descended into moaning, and then into crying, and then into occasional sobbing. While I waited, I tidied the things on the flotsam table, and when I was finished that, I started to clean the hut. In an old tote, I found my lasagna pan and my pie plate from the times I'd left food on the driftwood for Miranda. I thought about how wonderfully surprising it must have been for Miranda to spy something delicious and colourful on the desolate beach. Such a luxury in the midst of a rough life. I hoped it brought her at least a moment of joy.

I piled Miranda's tattered clothes into a small mound beside the front door.

I peeked out the hole in the wall. The clouds were gathering overhead like a ceiling of black smoke. It would be raining very hard soon. If only the rain could cleanse everything inside, washing away all the grief, all the pain, all the death. Somebody once said that the most humane thing was to help people with their shame. And the people on the Tawakin Reserve knew this, didn't they? I thought of the dinner I was now expected to feed the community and how I would have to stand in front of everybody and apologize for what I did wrong. How this would lead to forgiveness. How it was meant to help them, and to help me, too.

Frank had quieted now, though he still had not moved from his spot, towering over Miranda like a totem pole, holding up one corner of the blanket.

"Her finger's all crooked," he said, and lowered the blanket over Miranda again. He sat down on the edge of the bed, gingerly, and laid his hand on her legs. He looked down at her, and in that moment, his were the saddest eyes I'd ever seen.

"We'll have to burn her clothes."

"I already did."

"Good. That's good."

"I'll have to contact the coroner when I get back," I said. "And I don't know what the procedure is—how we can get permission to bury her here—but I know that's what she wants. She even made her own cross. It's already stuck in the ground beside Stan and Ronnie."

"Procedure?" Frank snorted. "This is our traditional territory. We'll just do it. Who'll ever know or care that some old woman is buried beside a shore nobody even knows about?"

As I looked around and wondered who would take care of the things in Miranda's hut, I noticed the map again. Crouching, I saw the circle she'd drawn around Waas Island, though a translucent layer of blood covered it. But there was another circle on the map now. It was marked to the north of the hut, drawn around a northern section of Cougar Point. Over the small circle, Miranda had written: WHALE.

With a towel I quickly dabbed the map, soaking the excess blood out of the paper, then folded it roughly. Was the whale real? The west coast of Vancouver Island was a migration route for many species of whales, so it was possible that Chase had found a beached whale. Or was it nothing more than another metaphor, like the dog children? My mind led down an awful path that ended with Chase using a rope, in the same way that his brother Ronnie had used a belt, but I couldn't ever believe he would do that. At this moment, I had to believe he was alive, and now I could finally find out, thanks to Miranda's last message.

I took one last look at the blanketed outline of my old friend lying there on the bed in her tarpaulin sepluchre by the sea. Words arose quietly in my mind. It was many and many a year ago, in a kingdom by the sea, that a maiden there lived whom you may know, by the name of Annabel Lee. And this maiden she lived with no other thought than to love and be loved by me.

I whispered to myself, "*I* was a child and *she* was a child, in this kingdom by the sea."

23

"We'll have to stay here tonight," Frank said.

The wind had turned into a powerful gale, beating furiously on the tarpaulin walls. The rain fell fast and hard and as sharp as needles from the darkened afternoon sky, storm clouds black and sinister. The passage home would be rough, deadly.

I nodded. "I don't want to stay here in the hut, though. I can't. It's too—"

"You can't stay in your boat. There'll be lightning tonight," he said. "I can smell it."

He stabbed a knife into the bottom of a wall and pulled it towards the corner of the hut, cutting the tarpaulin free from the wood planks. As he sliced upward and back across, rain blew inside. The wind snapped and whipped the large rectangular piece that he was trying to remove. I helped, pinning it down.

With the tarpaulin and some loosened driftwood beams from the hut, we built a sturdy lean-to between two jagged boulders halfway up the ridge above the shoreline. Frank secured another wall of tarpaulin on the ground and covered it with a bed of wool blankets.

The wind through the gaping holes left in the hut walls pushed and pulled at everything: the fishing poles, the pots and pans on the hooks, the small tins on the counter. The wool blanket covering Miranda. I set four large stones on the corners of the bed to keep the blanket in place. The encroaching rain had soaked through it already, forming it to the contours of Miranda's small body.

Cleansing her spirit, I hoped, as I started a fire in the stove and boiled hot water. Inside the coffee container I'd brought for Miranda, there were a few teaspoons left. I made my way out to the shelter on the shore below, but Frank was nowhere to be seen. "Hello?"

"I'm in here, Bernie."

Setting the coffee cups on the boulder, I crouched beside the lean-to and cocked my head to have a look. I found him lying inside, on his back and staring at the slanted ceiling of blue tarpaulin.

"It's real good you came here," he said.

"Is it warm?" I asked.

He nodded and wriggled over to make room for me. The rain smacked against my coat and the back of my neck, my ponytail a sopping rope down my spine. The ceiling was too low for us to sit up and drink coffee, so I left the steaming cups outside as I crawled inside and stretched out on my back. It was a narrow shelter and our shoulders pressed together.

"It's the bluest of skies." I nodded at the blue tarpaulin ceiling.

"It's turning dark soon," he said.

"How is your heart?" I rolled onto my side and placed my palm flat on his chest.

He didn't speak.

I laid my head on his chest to listen to his heartbeat, but it was difficult to pick out in the relentless chaos of rain on the tarpaulin. I thought of telling Frank about the diary and the day Teddy died, but I decided to wait until we found Chase. It was his story to tell, not mine.

After a short while, we both drifted to sleep in our exhaustion and grief, and when I awoke, Frank was shifting into an unsettling dream. I stroked his hair to soothe him, and through the gap in our makeshift tent, I looked out at the ramshackle hut. The bottom half was a patchwork of wood, and in some places it appeared as though newer planks had replaced older ones. I thought of Wren and her riddle about Theseus's ship. I looked again at Frank, and at my own hand gently pushing the hair off his forehead, and I considered all those old skin cells and muscle tissues and hair strands replaced by new ones over the years, exchanged like the tiny planks of a ship. We'd changed so much after all these years. Was he the same Frank or a different Frank? And what about me? How much had I changed over the years? How much needed to transform before something took on a new life of its own? I remembered some of the stories I knew. Mother Turned into a Blue Jay. Man Turned into Son of Deer. Sisters Turned into Yellow Cedars. Stories of transformation, stories of dogs turning into children. How impermanent the world was, I thought.

When Frank finally woke, we stayed motionless and silent for some time, listening to the rain. I didn't want to leave Tawakin, and I wanted Frank to know that, but I couldn't bring myself to say a thing about it. It was too sad, too futile, too hopeless to dwell on what could not be changed.

"I can't leave Wren in charge of the outpost," I said.

"How come it matters? You won't even be here soon."

"She won't be good to this place," I said.

"You don't got to worry about that. We'll outlast her."

I cast a sideways look at Frank and realized he was right. The Tawakin people had carried on all these years, despite losing their childhoods at residential school and despite having their homes displaced to reserves, despite losing pieces of their language and their culture, despite losing so many to substances and sorrow. I thought of their survival, and I felt embarrassed. I'd lived a life on the outside of such hardships.

Frank blinked, his eyes still watching a spot on the ceiling, and a tear rolled down his temple.

"Bernie," Frank said.

"Yes?"

"I am sorry."

"I am sorry, too, Frank."

*   *   *

That night, as Frank slept, I stared into the darkness and remembered the time I drove Chase to college. I'd taken a three-day personal leave. It was just the two of us. We packed the boat and drove along the shore to the harbour parking lot where I kept my van. We drove for almost two hours along the gravel logging road before we hit the highway. We stopped for lunch at a roadside café.

During the long drive, Chase kept saying, "I'm so excited, Nursema'am. Can you believe it? Me, at college."

"I sure can believe it," I said, my eyes on the highway.

"I'm going to be a teacher someday," he said, his face beaming. "And one day I'll teach at Tawakin School, and I'll show all the kids how they can go to college, too, if they want, and when they come to school every morning, they'll see a face at the front of the class that looks just like theirs, and I'll teach them how to be great students and we'll have lots of culture in our class, too. Drumming and dancing, even carving. And math, I love math. I'll miss Hannah a lot, though. She's real cute right now starting school."

"It'll be worth it in the end," I said.

"And Patty, too. I'll miss her."

When he'd returned home from college barely a month later, my heart now ached for how he must have felt. How he'd left with such excitement and hope, only to feel that he didn't belong there. It must have been so deflating for him after all his joyful anticipation. What had happened exactly? Was it one sharp wound or many small paper cuts? If he'd wanted to talk about it when he returned, I never gave him the chance. In my worry that he was embarrassed to have returned so early, I thrust a half-dozen excuses upon him. I thought I was saving him from having to explain, but now I regretted it. I wished I had not talked so much. I wished I had made room for him to talk. I wished I had left space for me to listen.

24

Cougar Point was a long edge of dangerous beauty. The wind here, Captain Cook had once noted in his logs, blew even stronger in this place, and so Frank and I drove our own boats the next morning in the event that one capsized. Unlike the rocky shores to the south, Cougar Point was fringed with smooth sand the colour of bone. When we neared these beaches, we turned into a small channel and followed it around to a gentler cove sheltered by large trees. We anchored beside a narrow outcrop, which we traversed from our boats to the shore. We hiked around a narrow strip of trees to the ocean side, where the waves rolled and crashed like roars of applause and the sand was stippled with a line of fresh cougar tracks. Keeping our eyes on the trees, we leaned into the scouring winds as we walked.

Miranda's circle on the map led us to a small bay. Because of the map's scale, the circle didn't pinpoint Chase's exact location. As far as I could figure, we had a searching distance up to five miles along the shoreline—more if Chase had trekked far into the rain forest, though this was unlikely, since we were, I hoped with every fibre of my being, looking for a whale. Several species were a possibility: the friendly grey whales, hardy travellers who migrated thousands of miles each year and who were known for snuggling up to boats and allowing themselves to be touched by humans; the minkes, the smallest of the baleen whales, who could swim as fast as the wind; the orcas, the wolves of the sea, with their jet-black bodies and their white-patched eyes; and the humpback whales, the graceful giants known for their enchanting ballads.

I could barely keep myself from running down the beach as we walked briskly, marching forward in long strides. Maybe it was the brutality of Miranda's death, but I was now torn between doubt and belief more than ever. No longer did I feel certain that Chase was alive. It was easier to imagine whatever I wanted when I was tucked away in the outpost and not on a desolate and violent beach. At the same time, the thought of finding him alive filled me with an energy I could not contain. It seemed meant to be, that I should be the one to find him. Again. Just like on Rubant Island when he was five. I started to imagine a joyous reunion. I stopped myself from getting carried away with positive thoughts. Not everything would be rosy. We'd need to tell him of his mother's death. How would he take the news? He had hardly spoken to Miranda over the years, but he might have reconnected with her during his recent visit.

Although I'd thought I shared the intimate details of the people's lives, there was in fact a great deal I now acknowledged I knew nothing about. And that even included Chase. My sense now was that I'd been living on the periphery of their lives. From my vantage point, I may have witnessed many private matters, but I had only ever been an onlooker from another world.

Still, I loved Chase Charlie with all my heart, and I couldn't wait to see him again—to feel his arms around me and to look at his smiling face as he pulled back and cocked his head sideways and said, "Got you a present, Nursema'am." Nursema'am. As if it were one word. As if it were actually my name. And we'd all laugh when he said, "It's a whale."

I envisioned a grand scene in which I drove Chase back to the shores of the Tawakin Reserve, people sprinting out of the houses in rapturous joy to greet us both. Who would care about a bear after that? Nobody. It would be redemption. It would be enough.

*   *   *

The wind started to whip the sand up into our faces, and I soon had to walk with my arm wrapped around my forehead. Frequently, I turned and checked that there were no cougars sneaking up behind us. Visitors to this area, though they were few in number since outsiders needed permission from the band, were warned not to bring small pets or children because of the cougars along this stretch, and those who didn't listen often returned to Tawakin devastated by the loss of their beloved terrier or their adorable papillon, pink bowed and perfectly groomed and snatched right off the sand before their eyes. To which locals at the Tawakin Market would say, "Lucky your dog was there to feed the cougar, or it would've been your son."

We walked on without a word. With the sand in my eyes, it was difficult to see very far down the shore. I kept my squint on the edge of the forest for any hint of colour—a tent or clothing or a blue rowboat. The black clouds cracked open and the rain fell hard and sudden, flattening the sand to the ground. The relief from the gritty onslaught was short lived: an instant later, a barrage of raindrops flew into our faces like tiny pellets of lead. I was shivering violently.

In what condition would Chase be? I had asked myself this question many times during the boat ride. He could be weak with hunger. He might be starving. Unless there really was a whale, in which case he'd have eaten like a king. But he might be injured or in a state of mild hypothermia. He could be suffering from delusions. Memory loss. He might become panicked, scared, confused upon seeing us. We should approach him carefully, slowly, taking the time to talk to him every step of our way, settling him into the recollection of who we were and that we were there to help him. Yet what if he didn't want to be helped? He had run away, after all.

After another half hour, we reached an area where thousands of driftwood pieces scattered the beach like giant matchsticks. Frank tapped me on the shoulder and pointed to something in the distance. A spot of blue among the pale tan logs of driftwood. We hurried closer and I saw the curve of a wood gunwale and soon the thin boards of a hull about eight feet long. We clambered over the wet driftwood until we reached the rowboat. Much of it was covered with driftwood, though as far as I

The Heaviness of Things That Float

could tell, it was not damaged. The driftwood had been set there carefully. To keep the boat hidden. Inside, between the planked seats, there were totes of camping supplies: a tent, a sleeping bag, a hatchet, a hunting rifle and boxes of ammunition, warm winter clothing, cooking utensils and several cans of Campbell's soup, Alphagettis and SpaghettiOs.

I smiled with joyful relief. "He's here. He's alive."

We both surveyed the perimeter from where we stood, but there was no sign of Chase, and certainly no whale.

"Chase!" Frank shouted. "Chase Charlie!"

I touched his arm. "Don't startle him."

"He's not a deer," Frank said, shaking his head.

"No," I said, "but he might be disoriented."

Hiking the short distance to the tree line, we looked for trails into the forest. Normally, trails were marked with whale ribs because of their size and because their curved, tapered shape and white colour made them stand out from all the fallen branches. The ribs usually leaned against a tree trunk or a piece of driftwood. Finally, Frank spotted one, and we pushed the branches aside and entered the chamber of moss and hanging gardens of lichen and endless columns of bark. The light was much dimmer inside the forest, and the sounds of the wind and waves, muffled by the foliage, softer, quieter. Weaving between the trees, we walked slowly, taking our time to scan the layers of life and decay, our boots snapping twigs.

It was not long before we found him. He was off to our left, near the tree line, in a spot where the cedars were spread apart enough for him to see out to the ocean. If the sky were clear that night, it would have been the perfect spot to watch the moon and the stars, which always sparkled like diamond eyes in the blackness over the water.

At the sight of him, I fell to my knees.

25

The rain entered the forest at a sharp angle. It slanted under the canopy of green and pelted the spot near the edge of the tree line where the three of us gazed silently out to the ocean. I hung my head. I was kneeling on two large green eyes. I rocked back onto my feet. Crouching, I looked at the face. It was a broken piece of an ancient totem pole, the partial face of a wolf staring straight up at the heavens. The wood was cracked and grey, and moss filled some of the edges of its ovoid eyes. Next to me, I could see Chase's legs. A tremendous gust of wind pushed the branches every which way. The long thick swooping boughs above our heads bounced.

His legs swayed.

I kicked away the fish bucket that lay on the ground and wrapped my arms around his knees. I could feel his skin through his pants. Ice cold. My whole body trembled uncontrollably. Everything around me bloated and puckered, pushed and turned, and I squeezed my eyes shut, trying to block out the space around me. Frank crouched at the base of a cedar tree, his face in his hands, his sounds of grief like the low moan of a large cat.

I steadied myself as best I could, the immense volume of my grief sinking into the bottom of an unknown darkness, displacing the entire world I'd known. I looked up at him, hanging limply from a rope, and then I immediately looked away, but not before I caught a glimpse of his face, pale and puffy, his tongue swollen and poking out the toothless gap in his gaping mouth. I bolted out of the trees and scrambled towards the ocean, slipping and knocking my shinbones against the driftwood logs, the rain smacking my uplifted face and mixing with my tears. I sprinted for the white crests of the waves, crying out, and then my throat opened into an unintelligible, rattling cry of anguish, and when I reached the water's edge, I stopped and doubled over, my whole body cramping with sorrowed pain. I fell onto my hands and knees and moaned, low and primal and from somewhere deep inside the well of my soul. I clutched at the sand, squeezing fistfuls as hard as I could, as if I could grind the grains with my bare hands into glass.

Miranda was right. He had caught something with a rope, but it was not a whale. And while I didn't know what the crow and the piece of blubber meant, Miranda was right about another thing: "When they come for the whale, it's going to get really stormy, and they'll never reach it. They'll all drown."

We *would* all drown.

In grief.

The water rolled over onto itself and pounded against the shore, rhythmically, like the drums struck by men at potlatches in the school gym, rawhide pulled tight over wood circles, echoes of beats hollow and haunting, men's voices singing together, wailing and whooping and crying out, women appearing one by one through doors like phantoms through walls, wearing long black dance shawls and pulling wood paddles through an invisible ocean, short movements in tandem with the beats, spreading slowly in a large circle, circles of truth, stopping whenever voices fall silent and drums thunder, moving forward once more when voices sing once more, dancing and turning and tilting their heads majestically to the sky and then lowering their heads reverently to the water, the large animal shapes sewn onto shawls with sequins that glitter like the Pacific in morning sunlight, moving and dancing around the woman in the middle, the one with the honour of wearing the wood mask with the painted eyes and the painted beak and the tufts of fur perched high on her head, and the people in the chairs, watching and lifting their upturned hands in thanks, bouncing their palms like they're offering invisible platters of gratitude to relatives who've travelled over land and water from far elsewhere so that they can eat salmon dipped into clamshells of oil prepared by fingers that are straight and good and not crooked, cooked over fires that will one day burn the furs of dog children who suffer at the hands of those who hurt before them, and coats, too, they will burn, coats of shame made from pages of the Indian Act, and suddenly the beating of the drums grows louder and the children fill the floor sprinkled white with baby powder to let their bare feet slide freely, and I stand in the middle, the mother bird, while my babies dance, crouching and bouncing and flapping their wings, turning and spinning and flying away, little crows with pieces of whale skin in their mouths—but wait—a predator is coming, says mother bird, and it is strong and vicious and malevolent, and it will fill you with sorrow and shame, and you should all know that the whale is not a whale but a trick that Raven is playing. Do not copy the trick my little birds or the fires that cook your meals and light your skies will burn your fingers and curl them into crooked hooks, and so you must listen carefully, you must get back to your nests quickly—there we go, good little birds—but who's that now? Little Chase, my little Chase, why won't you come back to the nest? If you don't come back I'll take you in my wings and guide you home, though I am not your mother bird, I am only pretending and you are only pretending, but the pretending feels good and right and beautiful in a world where nothing is as it seems—listen now!—the drum beats are getting louder and faster, and louder and faster, and louder and faster, like a frightened heartbeat heard from the womb, but don't be hesitant to come out, my little Chase, come out and come forth into a world where things are never what they appear, come out and I will guide you home with heliographic messages bounced with sunlight off the cracked windows of crying clapboard houses, where the drums beat louder and faster, and louder and faster, and louder and faster...

Icy water washed over my hands and around my knees, soaking into my pants and shocking my skin and shaking me back into this world I was now hesitant to enter, where the boy I wanted for a son was a man hanging from a tree.

When I returned, Frank was sitting with a catatonic stare. I touched his arm. "We need to get him down."

Frank wrapped his arms around his son's hips while I stood on the fish bucket and sawed through the rope with Frank's pocketknife. The rope was stained with algae and the frayed end was black with sludge. It was the type of rope you might find washed onto the rocks. We reclined him gently onto the soft moss. Frank took off his coat and used it to cover Chase's head and torso.

For an hour, we sat on the moss beside Chase. Now and then, Frank sobbed, and the rain and the wind cried through the trees around us. I held my head in my hands tightly, and sometimes I wailed so hard it felt as though I would tear into two halves right down my middle.

Other times we both fell silent.

I loved Chase Charlie, loved him as fervently as a mother loves her son. In him, I saw all that was good and all that was promising. Despite the terrible turns he faced at times, he'd always smiled and kept paddling across the ocean of life with a joyous buoyancy. But now I knew there'd been an undercurrent tugging him down into the darkness. I had never sensed the magnitude of it, and even if I had, I might not have been able to help. The problem with undercurrents was that they flowed beneath the surface, beyond the reach of external influences. Not even the strong winds of the Pacific Ocean could change an undercurrent. Although I rationally understood this to be true, my heart was convinced I could have helped him, could have prevented this from happening, and every cell in my body ached to bring him back.

The night Chase was born, Frank went out back and buried a knife with the placenta so that he would become a good carver. It didn't work. He never was very good, though he never stopped trying. He carved feathers and paddles and masks, and he gave many of them to me. "You're going to become famous one day," I'd always say, encouraging him beyond his ability, "like Charles Edenshaw or Bill Reid." And he would smile at me, with that toothless gap, and say, "You're real nutty, Nursema'am."

Looking up at the ragged circle of grey between the branches overhead, I wept. I had wanted to end my time here without grief. But grief was a constant part of life here. It flowed through the people like Stannani River.

Eventually, we lifted Chase and carried him to the rowboat, and then dragged the boat down to the sand. Frank stayed with him while I hiked back and drove my boat around the peninsula, anchoring it as close to the shore as possible. Frank rowed Chase's rowboat out to me, and we tied it to the stern of my boat. The outpost boat was designed for running the nurse around Tawakin. It was not intended to transport any patients, living or dead, so there was not enough room to lay Chase inside. Instead, we rearranged the totes of camping supplies in the rowboat. Then we wrapped Chase's body in a tarp and secured it to the rowboat with ropes. Frank added some stones to the hull. That way, it would sit low and stable in the choppy waters. I drove Frank to his boat, towing the rowboat with Chase in it.

"Do you want to tow him back?" I asked. "Maybe you should be the one to bring him home."

Frank shook his head. "You tow him. I want to follow from behind and make sure he is all right the whole way. I don't ever want to have to take my eyes off him right now." He stepped onto his boat. "Besides, you were like a mother to him. He told me that."

Hearing this, my chest felt as though my heart had split and spilled out its warm contents.

Nursema'am, I thought.

Nursemom.

Mom.

Mother.

We drove slowly along the coastline, a watery funeral procession: me in the front, then Chase in the rowboat attached to the outpost boat with a long yellow rope, and trailing close behind, Frank. The ocean swells had subsided, as if the Pacific had decided to make a safe passage for us. The wind, however, continued to howl and swirl violently, so I drove slowly, keeping close to the coastline. My heart lay heavy in my chest, and every once in a while, I glanced back at the rowboat, washing my eyes over the figure wrapped in blue tarpaulin. Another sob spat out of my mouth, and, as I remembered that bear, I cried out into the wind, "I'm sorry. I'm so sorry," picturing how it washed ashore, all the people's hopes rising to the glistening surface. Now Chase was truly coming back to their shores, and not in the way anybody hoped.

*   *   *

Patty waited alone for us on the dock after getting Frank's call on the radio. Frank docked his boat and gave Patty a hug that lasted for several minutes while I tied up my boat, then he walked up the dirt road with the dreadful task of telling the others. Danny Joe and a few of the other children straddled their bicycles on the grassy ridge above the shoreline, but they didn't come any closer. They would have recognized his rowboat. Perhaps they could also see the sadness in our bodies. Julia Henry sat in her usual spot in her window, except now instead of scrutinizing, she hung her head, and I then knew that she knew.

Patty turned to face me. She stared at me so intently that I thought she was about to insult me or accuse me, but as I rested my gaze upon her, I saw fear in her eyes. With her arms hanging so limply and her shoulders slackened, she looked like the child who used to cling to me in the forest when we pulled cedar. Something about her had loosened and jarred open. For the first time in years, she appeared vulnerable, her face softening but not yet giving way to grief.

I stepped towards her and slipped my hand into hers. I guided her to his rowboat and crouched over the edge of the dock. Still holding her hand, I looked up at her and pulled her down gently, imploring her to come close to him.

She looked nervously at the shape under the tarp.

The rowboat, tied to my boat, drifted away from the dock and I had to lean far over to grab hold of the gunwale and bring it back to us. Slowly, I unwrapped one end of the tarp.

Together, we gazed at his face.

"I shouldn't have—"

Patty's quivering voice trailed quickly into silence.

I wondered if she'd ever experienced forgiveness. Had she ever forgiven herself? For Teddy's death? For Hannah's fetal alcohol syndrome? If a person was never forgiven for their mistakes, could they ever fully heal?

Footsteps crunched down the road and stormed along the dock.

Hannah stopped about twenty feet away from us.

"Is that my dad? Is that him, fuck faces?"

Patty started to climb to her feet.

"This is all your fault," Hannah told her mother. "You never listened to him. You never listened to nobody."

Hannah turned and ran back up the road, her shoes twisting up the dirt and spitting out small stones. We watched her disappear down the trail between the brambles.

"She's just upset," I said.

Patty shook her head. "It is my fault."

"It's not," I said.

Patty looked up at the sky, closed her eyes and leaned towards me so close she nearly pressed her shoulder against me, but she didn't. Suddenly, I knew how much Chase really loved Patty. The real reason Chase held that secret so long, and why, when he'd finally unburdened himself, it was to the one person who didn't live here in the cove. He loved Patty, and he would have done almost anything to protect her.

As I glanced back up the road at the people who'd gathered outside their doors, I knew then that I'd keep this secret, too. I would do it for both of them. I turned my gaze back to the water. I knew no one would disturb us. I knew they would wait, giving Patty time with her husband. But they were there nonetheless, and that was a comfort, close by and ready to help as always. Because whenever somebody died in Tawakin, the people took turns sitting with the one who'd lost their loved one.

They sat with us while Patty and I sat with each other.

26

From my bathroom, I listened to the helicopter leave with Chase. As the thundering *wop-wop* faded into the distance, the outpost fell silent again. I hadn't seen Wren when I returned, and I had no clue where she might have gone. I locked the door. In the mirror, I could see the mural on the wall behind me. I pulled the elastic from my ponytail and shook my long hair so that it spilled freely, the ends dangling over the small of my back. Nothing would ever be the same, I thought, and I took a long tress of silver hair. I cut it off just above my ear, and I dropped it to the floor. Happiness was a thing, a little bobble, like a glass ball that resided inside of me. I grabbed another thick swath of hair and cut it off at the nape of my neck. My glass ball, once clean and shiny, felt scarred and discoloured now. It felt as if it were stained so black by my sweet boy's death that it could never again shine as bright, never again reflect any light whatsoever, only absorb it, suck it up and offer nothing illuminating in return. I cut my hair until there was nothing but a cap of short tufts. I looked in the mirror, hardly recognizing the woman standing there.

I went to my bed and fell, weeping, into my despair.

* * *

I must have fallen asleep, because some time later, I awoke to see Wren standing at my door. Rolling onto my side, I pressed my cheek into my tear-soaked pillow.

"Your hair—" she started, her face stony and pale.

I touched the short tufts above my ear.

"You don't even know how angry this makes me," she said.

My eyelids felt swollen. Barely moving my head, I looked more closely at her but said nothing.

She was breathing forcefully through her nostrils. "Who's going to take responsibility for this?"

I didn't know what she meant, and my mind, numb and exhausted, didn't care to make sense of anything. I shook my head, so very slightly.

"Nobody, that's who." Wren punched the door frame and clenched her jaw. "Nobody." She punched again, moving her face closer to the spot she'd struck. "Nobody." She punched again. "Nobody."

I got the sense she didn't expect a response. I just watched her.

"All those dreams they were having of him," Wren leaned her forehead against the door frame and spoke through gritted teeth, "they were all true. They were. They're attuned to the world in ways we aren't—this world *and* the spirit world, the dreamworld—we just don't get that. That's who they are. Why can't we let them be who they are? We can't. We have to control. We have to wield power. We have to say, no, you're not going to be this, you're going to be this. We will define you. We will make you be like us, but then we say that you'll never be like us. We will make you live with us, but then we say that you'll never belong like us. We will take away your identity so that you don't know who you are. And we will do this until it kills you, and when it kills you, we will turn our back and wave our hands dismissively and say, doesn't that figure? And we say, look at that—you see that?—that's who they are, they're like that." With her head still pressed against the door frame, she swivelled her face toward me. "If I could I'd take our brains and wipe them clean, I'd do it. Erase every single piece of history from our books and from our archives and from our minds. Maybe then things will change."

She bolted from the doorway and went into her own room, slamming

The Heaviness of Things That Float

the door shut. Through the wall I could hear her moving around, clinking glass, getting herself a mug of wine or whiskey, I supposed. I was tempted to get up and ask for one myself, but I didn't. The heartache in my chest hurt so badly—a deep, tearing pain—but I decided not to dull it right now. It was there for a reason.

✲   ✲   ✲

Around suppertime, Patty came on the radio and asked if anybody had seen Hannah. Her voice was shaky. Nobody had seen the girl, or her little kicker, since she took off angrily two hours earlier, and soon it would be getting dark and the wind was bending the cedars sideways.

"She was real upset when she left," Patty explained. "We're worried. We can't find her anywhere."

I headed down to the wharf and left in the boat, heading across the cove and out into the ocean towards Toomista. On the shores there was no sign of her kicker. I anchored and walked up the ridge to the field where the houses stood, and as I passed the tall grasses that fringed the beach, I spotted Hannah's small white kicker with the tiny outboard motor hidden behind a pile of driftwood.

In Miranda's bedroom, I found Hannah in the closet. She was sitting on the floor among the dead grasshoppers, the snakes still pinned to the wall above her head. When she looked up, she did not seem at all surprised to find me standing there. She punched the wall so hard the snakes wriggled. The poor things were probably preparing for hibernation when she captured them. Moments away from a safe rest before their world was torn away.

I walked along the beams of the sagging floor and stepped into the closet. Pinching the needle with my fingernails, I freed a snake, which I then dropped inside the bucket on the floor next to Hannah. She watched me take the other snakes down without uttering a word. As I put the last of the stiff carcasses inside the bucket, I then thought that this was the great dilemma of life: to gain wisdom too late, and at too high a cost.

Hannah said, "I'll just put them up again, you know."

I opened the window and dumped the bucket out into the tall grass far below.

She shrugged. "Don't matter. They'll come back."

I looked at her, puzzled.

"I heard him. He said they don't never go away."

After that, Hannah wouldn't say anything more. So I sat on the floor under the window for nearly an hour. Sometimes I was silent, and other times I spoke to Hannah, expecting nothing in return. I told her how the months that her father lived with me as a boy were the happiest of my life. I told her how he taught me to fish. I told her how much he loved to dance like a bird and how a book about a spider and a pig made him cry. I told her how he dreamed of becoming a teacher. I told her how happy he was when he found out he was going to be a father. I told her how she looked just like him, especially when she cocked her head to one side like that.

"You smile just like him, too," I said.

"I do?" she asked, looking at me finally.

"Like father like daughter," I said.

*   *   *

When I saw how much the wind had picked up outside and how the sky threatened a terrible storm, I convinced Hannah that she and her little kicker would be stuck here overnight if she didn't hitch a ride back to the reserve with me. When we finally left the house, it was nearly dusk. We passed Rubant Island and entered the open ocean. The swells were high and rolling. I wondered if we should turn back, but it was not far to the cove. As we passed Waas Island, I was about to radio the community, to let them know I'd found Hannah, but I was startled by voices on my VHF, the words from the Tawakin Reserve clouded with static:

"There's something falling out of the sky!"

"It's snow!"

"It ain't snow!"

"Some of the flakes are bigger than my head!"

"It ain't snow."

"Then what is it?"

"It's all over the water!"

"Is it coming from the sky, yeah or nah?"

"Nah. I think it's coming from the outpost."

People stood on the reserve dock and along the shore below the houses and at the end of the wharf on Mitchell Island. The *Pacific Sojourn II* was stationed at the wharf, but rather than unloading its cargo, the men leaned over the port side and stared at the sky. As I motored slowly through the narrow channel between the Tawakin Reserve and Mitchell Island, I estimated more than a hundred people—the entire population of Tawakin—watched the strange sight over the cove.

"What is it?" Hannah asked.

"I'm... not sure."

The wind was like a tornado. It whipped around in great arcs, taking branches and the last remaining leaves of summer with it. The boats tied to the docks rocked and crashed against the pilings, while the water was pulled into long ruffles. Everywhere the cedars and hemlocks and cottonwoods strained at sharp angles. It was the type of wind that split tree trunks down the middle, each splintered side spreading apart like arms to God.

I put the motor into neutral, stopping in the mouth of the cove where my boat was partially concealed from the wind by the small isle of rock and trees that divided the channel. I looked long and hard at the flurry of white across the cove. At first, it appeared to be snowing, but that was impossible, since I felt no precipitation falling on me—not a drop of rain—and the pieces of white were much too big to be snowflakes. I rummaged through the storage compartments, looking for my binoculars, but soon gave up and squinted instead, trying to make out the falling white objects.

"Are they birds?" Hannah asked.

"Maybe."

A flock of sea gulls maybe, hundreds and hundreds of them, all rising and twisting and flipping and spinning and drifting through the air. Some in the branches of the trees on the tiny island in the middle of the cove. But then I saw a number of them—hundreds, maybe even thousands—lying flat on the water, spreading across the half mile of cove from one side to the other. It looked as though an underwater mine had exploded and torpedoed all the fish out of the water. Or maybe it was a massive drift of cargo from a ship, some type of foam, but then why was so much of it in the sky and in the trees?

I drove forward and instead of turning left to the dock on the reserve to drop Hannah off, I made my way to the first cluster of white. Slowly, the sharp nose of the boat cut through the water, separating the debris. Then I stopped, surrounded by flat rectangles, and leaned over the edge of the boat and pulled one of them out of the ice-cold water. It was a piece of paper. I laid it across both palms, its corners drooping heavily off my fingertips, dripping down my sleeves and onto the deck. Some of the ink was smudged, but the words that had been printed from a computer were still legible.

At the top it said: *Health History and Physical Examination Report: Ernie Frank.* I retrieved another from the water. *Colonoscopy Report, Port Hardy Hospital: Sarah Henry.*

My mouth dropped open as the scene became clear to me. The thousands of white things rising and twisting and flipping and spinning in the wind and drifting across the cove and landing in the trees and in the water and on the shores were not snowflakes or birds or fish or cargo. I scooped several more from the water, slapping them down onto the deck and then peeling them apart.

Hannah's eyes were wide with astonishment.

I pulled more papers from the water. How did the records get out of the filing cabinets? Where was Wren? Behind the maelstrom of paper I could see drifts of smoke coming from the direction of the outpost. The smoke wasn't coming from the outpost but from the far end of Hospital Island, though I couldn't see where exactly. I didn't know what to do. I needed to retrieve these documents, all this confidential information strewn around for anybody to pick up and read. Records of suspected illnesses, psychological symptoms, the naming of those who fathered fatherless children.

Slowly, I picked up more paper. My hands were freezing, the wind battering my ears. All around me, the wind spun a vortex of white paper. Pieces landed on the mucky shore of the small island in the middle of the cove, hooked onto the tree branches and drifted towards the reserve. A few pieces even smacked the windshield of my boat. As I continued across the cove, fishing paper out of the water and throwing it onto the deck, I spotted the giant bonfire. It was in the metal ring on the corner of the beach below the outpost. The wind tugged at the tall flames and sent large flakes of ash swirling into the air. The heat made everything behind the fire—the trees, the grasses on the top of the ridge—ripple as though underwater. Next to the fire was my wheelbarrow stacked with a tower of files, papers blowing out of the folders. There was no sign of Wren.

The wind pushed at the water and the tide pulled into the shore, swiftly dragging the papers towards the reserve. Finally, I headed towards the dock. I panicked at the idea of the people scooping all this private information out of the water. When I reached the dock, the silence was solemn. Patty looked at Hannah and smiled, the look in her eyes suggesting sympathy.

Little Kenny Joe and his brother, Danny, crouched at the edge of the dock and reached for the papers as I drew close. Loretta tapped the boys on the shoulder and shook her head sternly. I pulled the boat alongside the dock, bumping it slightly. Without even glancing at the sopping papers, the two boys held them out to me.

"We didn't look. Promise," they said earnestly. "It's not right to look, huh Nursema'am?"

I made an explosive sound—half a cry, half a laugh. "No, it's not right to look." I held up the dripping documents. "Does anybody know what's happened?"

It seemed that nobody knew.

Just then a voice called out from above. "You hold on a minute."

Everybody turned and looked up at the window on the second floor of the white house beside the dock. It was Julia Henry, Shelly's mother, the woman who sat in the window all day watching the boats and counting the catches.

"I'll come and tell you exactly what happened," Julia said.

Everyone gave each other looks of surprise. Julia Henry never left her house. Ever.

She closed the window and disappeared briefly, exiting a few moments later from the door. Stomping with an air of outrage.

"She was drunk," Julia said, as people cleared a path for her. "Stinking drunk! I seen her through my binoculars. She spent a good two hours hauling files down to the beach in a wheelbarrow, piling big stones on them to keep them from blowing away. She fell at least four times coming down the trail, that's how drunk she was. She had a thermos with her, so I figured she was drinking something because, I swear, she got drunker and drunker. I didn't know that them were our papers, or I would've called somebody on the radio. She burned plenty, and then she started losing the files to the wind."

I tried to say, "I don't know—" I choked back tears. "I don't know how I'm going to pick them all up. I'm so sorry."

"I'll help you," Hannah said, still sitting in the passenger seat of my boat. "I promise I won't read nothing."

Not once did I see any sign of Wren as we scooped the sopping records out of the cold water. On the beach below the outpost, the bonfire grew smaller and smaller, until by the time we'd finally picked up all the paper we could from the boat, it had died. The last wafts of smoke streaked across the shoreline of my island, and then faded. Without a word, we floated in the middle of the cove, the wind whipping all around, spinning us in a slow circle, around and around. For a moment, it mesmerized me. Soothed me. After a while, I looked over at Hannah and she, too, seemed entranced by our slow turning. I also saw how she shivered, so I steered the boat towards the dock, the people now gone back to their houses, except for her mother, who sat alone, waiting for her.

27

Two months later, I stood alone in the clearing on Rubant Island. The November skies hadn't stopped raining once in two weeks. Although it was mid-afternoon, the light was thin and grey, making the burial plots and their wood crosses seem especially sombre. I set my wooden case and a small satchel on the wet grass and opened the hinged lid of the case, revealing the little rooms filled with seashells.

With a pocketknife, I stabbed the ground above elder Candice Joe's burial plot and twisted up the grass. Then I pressed the limpet into the hole and pressed the grass back into place. I took a nutmeg, a turban and a cerith to the plots of David Frank, Henry Joe and Verne Joe and buried the shells in front of their crosses. As I continued to plant more shells like seeds in the soil, I thought about all the articles Anne used to send me in the mail. Articles from newspapers or magazines about First Nations' issues, which Anne cut out and often annotated with little comments. There were articles on the conditions of houses on reserves, on which she'd written: "Deplorable! They deserve better! I've written a letter to the government! Shame!" There was a report on the high rate of house fires on reserves and another on the high rate of suicides. Over the years, I'd accumulated a thick file of articles from Anne. Between the seashells and these articles, Anne had shown a genuine concern for Tawakin—a place many people didn't even know existed—and for its people.

"I would have never known about this beautiful place, Bernie, if it wasn't for you coming to work here."

"Don't say that."

"Why not? It's true."

"It sounds so self-congratulatory. We should hardly pat ourselves on the back for such things."

"You devoted decades here, Bernie."

"But I always had the option of another existence."

"Don't they?"

"Yes, and no. No, and yes."

Eventually, the case was empty, each memorial shell pressed into the earth of each burial plot, a piece of Anne left behind. And where those pieces lay, I thought, the earth would resonate with good intentions.

I pulled the two halves of the chambered nautilus from the satchel. The good half I buried in front of Chase's cross. I'd come to accept that I'd never entirely know why he committed suicide. I'd never know what the shadows meant, not exactly, nor the snakes, nor Miranda's inscrutable story of the dog children. I'd never truly know the myriad of factors that contributed to his downfall, in part because I was a *mamulthni*, and as such I could never wholly know what life for Chase was like, to feel discarded and disenfranchised, and in part because nobody could ever wholly know the heart of another, no matter which side of the unbalanced world they lived on. I'd mistaken my truths for his own. I hadn't known that Chase was somebody who didn't see himself belonging to places like college. It was good to imagine what life was like for another. It was the route to empathy. But it was also dangerous to overestimate what I thought I knew about another. Who knew what signs I'd missed during my time with Chase, signs that I might have seen if I weren't so convinced that I had known him so perfectly.

Like the mural—were the shadows of the snakes a metaphor for Jimmy? Or were they something less precise—something dark and haunting and unidentifiable to the thirteen-year-old boy who'd painted them? Which was why I didn't paint over the mural in the end. I had intended to. Digging out my old art supplies, I'd filled a brush with green paint and carefully formed a large circle of green, like the glass balls that washed upon our shores, covering one of the serpentine shadows. When I stepped back to view my work, the haunting image was still visible underneath, like a picture embossed on a green coin. It was not so easy, I realized, to erase the past. Maybe because it shouldn't be erased. I tossed the paintbrush into the trash bin and left the rest of Chase's world as he saw it.

Inside my satchel, I put the other half of the chambered nautilus. This was the half I would keep. I thought again why Anne had sent it as her last shell, as the shell to memorialize her own death. The chambered nautilus lived in a chamber that was the perfect size for itself, no smaller, no bigger than what it needed. Then, when the creature grew, it built another perfect chamber, closing off the entry to the last one. It did this as often as necessary, a new chamber for each phase of growth until it had spun its existence into a spiral of logarithmic beauty.

The geometry of a life recreated.

Shortly after the bonfire, Constable Diller arrived with another officer that same day to take Wren away at the request of Chief Trudy Henry. Wren was still slightly drunk when the police came to escort her out of the community. As she boarded the RCMP boat, she looked up at me standing on the wharf.

"You're welcome," she said.

"For what?"

"The files."

I stared at her in disbelief.

"Think of it as an exorcism," she said, throwing her fist into the air. "Actions that change everything. Actions that can't be undone. That's the goal of the true revolutionary."

Now that the files were all gone, sixty years of births and deaths and information about which families tended to carry which illnesses, I fully appreciated, as I always had deep down, that the burden of being the secretary of secrets had been a necessary one to carry. "You and your symbolic act of rebellion have thrown the baby out with the bath water," I told her, shaking my head in disgust.

"You don't get it," she scoffed.

"No, you don't get it," I said. "Nobody asked you to rebel for them. They didn't want a revolutionary. They wanted a nurse."

As for Patty's complaint, it was quickly dismissed after the RCMP and the health authority found no evidence of negligence. Patty never spoke of it to me again, and her silence over the matter whenever I saw her at the Tawakin Market was the closest thing I'd ever get to a reconciliation.

One day, I left a small package behind the postal wicket with George, who agreed to deliver it to Patty once I'd left Tawakin. Inside was the cedar rose and a note that said: *When you were a child, Patty, you helped me to weave me a beautiful life in Tawakin. Thank you.*

The week before I left, Hannah's teacher, my good friend Molleigh Royston, phoned me. "You'll never believe what's happened at school," she said. "Patty came to see me. She's taking Hannah to Port Hardy for a doctor's diagnosis. We're getting her special education plan all set up—the school board is even sending us an expert who's going to do a full psychological evaluation. I can hardly believe it, can you?"

I could.

Death, I had come to realize, was the ultimate intervention. It cut you off at the knees, stopping you in your tracks, and from down there on the ground, you had little choice than to accept it was no longer possible to continue along your usual path. It humbled you. I don't know if Patty was forgiving herself, but she was letting herself be accountable for Hannah, and that was something.

As for my own search for forgiveness, the elders cancelled the community dinner because of everything that had happened. One day, I took a large platter over to the reserve and knocked on each door. I gave everybody a devilled egg sprinkled with paprika. And I told each of them how truly sorry I was. *Klecko*, they said. Even Loretta.

The new nurse started a few weeks after Wren left. She was a shy woman named Ursa Stapleton, who didn't drink and who said she only wanted to do her part in the community, and maybe kayak a little. She seemed honest and humble, and she gobbled the fish eyeball at the welcome dinner. Although I could never know for certain, this newcomer was not a Runner or a Saver or a User. She was simply Ursa, and when

I changed the guard by giving her the key to the filing cabinets, she declared that she'd guard the cabinets with her life.

I smiled. "There's not much left in there to guard."

Now, standing beneath the totem pole that watched over the dead, I took one last look at Chase's cross. "I'll miss you. You will always be in my heart." Over my shoulder I looped the satchel with my half of the nautilus shell inside. I walked away, my legs and my heart heavy, and I left Rubant Island for the last time.

*   *   *

George Sam was the one to drive me and my things to the uninhabited harbour where the people in Tawakin kept their cars. The tires of my old car would be nestled in weeds. I took very little: my clothes and my books and a special gift from Frank. Three days ago, he'd called me over to his house one last time.

"Look here," he'd said, pointing to the floor where a blanket draped over a large object.

"What's that?" I asked.

He pulled away the blanket. Underneath was a large wood box about the size of an old steamer trunk. Carvings of a deer and a pack of wolves decorated the sides and the lid.

"It's beautiful," I said.

"I made it for you."

Crouching beside the box, I ran my fingers along the ovoid shapes etched into the surface. A fine dust of yellow cedar filled the curves of the deer's dance skirt. I blew at the dust and swept the remaining particles away with the back of my hand.

"You recognize it?" Frank asked.

I looked more closely at the pictures until I saw the scene: it was the moment that Son of Deer stole fire from the wolf village. This happened a long time ago, when humans didn't have fire to cook their meals, and Son of Deer told the humans he could get fire for them from the only place where there was fire, the wolf village, the place every creature feared.

Son of Deer dressed in a dance skirt and a headband and wrist- and kneebands. Behind the kneebands, he hid bundles of cedar twigs. He danced in front of the wolf village, and the wolves allowed Son of Deer to stay because they thought he was just a silly dancing creature. Son of Deer moved closer and closer to the big fire. The wolves didn't see the bundles of twigs behind his kneebands. Around the fire there were big wood stakes so that no one could get near it, but Son of Deer's legs were long and skinny and he could dance-step between the stakes without getting hurt. "I'm going to get a spark of the fire. I'm going to get a spark of that fire," Son of Deer sang as he danced and jumped over the fire. When the flames caught on the cedar twigs behind his legs, Son of Deer ran back to the village. The people were very happy when he brought them fire because they could cook and have light and heat.

"It's beautiful, Frank."

"It's a retirement gift."

I remembered how Frank used to tell me the story of Son of Deer while we kept each other warm on wet winter nights. Nestled in blankets, we would sit in front of his wood stove, and he'd explain that I was like Son of Deer because I had brought fire and light and heat to his life.

He lifted the lid and looked inside the empty box. "It's where I store all the things you gave me from your heart."

*   *   *

As I waited for George to untie the boat from the outpost wharf, I leaned over and lifted the box lid. Inside I'd put all the gifts Chase had carved for me over the years, the feathers and paddles and masks with the abalone shell eyes. I smiled, and almost laughed out loud. The carvings—I'd lied to Chase all these years—they really weren't very good. But I would treasure them for the rest of my life.

As George and I exited the cove, I watched the Tawakin Reserve, its twenty-five houses the colours of sky and salmon and eelgrass, grow smaller in the distance. The boat left behind a white line of foamy water that pointed straight at the reserve. On the ridge above, I saw the outpost's metal roof and the kitchen window and Ursa Stapleton waving from inside, and for a moment, I could imagine myself standing there forty years ago as a young woman who had no sense of the joys and the devastating heartbreak to come. I waved back at Ursa, and as I glanced farther upward, I spotted an eagle's nest from earlier in the autumn, and although I couldn't be certain, I thought I could see a long strip of white paper, a piece of somebody's medical record perhaps, woven into the nest.

As we left the cove and passed Fossil Island, I said goodbye to the woman in the box with the baby, and I listened one last time for her story in the silver light but heard nothing except the rush of ocean air in my ears. In my mind, I thanked her and wished her an eternity of peace.

We picked up speed and made our way across the stretch of open ocean. Suddenly, George slowed down, almost coming to a stop.

"What's the matter?" I asked.

He pointed towards the horizon. It was a pod of killer whales. He cut the engine and let the boat bob in the water. For several moments, we both watched in silence as the killer whales disappeared in the distance.

"See you later," I said, remembering that everybody in Chase's family turned into killer whales when they died, "but preferably sooner."

I thought of Frank's belief that the stories grew in the wind and in the water, life upon life. I thought about how the wind had blown seeds of stories across the soil and sand and between the fractures of rock.

In the woods and in the water, all these seeds had grown together into a matrix of roots and stems and leaves, sometimes becoming so entangled that I could not easily unravel their tendrils, wound together yet profoundly separate. But when I'd paid attention—really paid attention, with my eyes and my ears and whatever other senses I had at my disposal—I had been given the chance to say, if only for a fleeting moment, *I see you, I truly see you now.*

Acknowledgements

I raise my hands to the First Nations friends and family I have been honoured to know in my life, especially to the Ktunaxa, the Tahltan and the Nuu-chah-nulth peoples, whose generosity, humour and resilience overwhelm me.

I am especially indebted to the bright spirit who was Kelly John. Since the first story I ever published, he was wholly supportive of my writing, and I was honoured to be adopted by him in 2010. As a Kyuquot elder, he was a pillar in his community and, since passing away during the editing of this novel, is missed deeply. Missed, too, are my friends Arlene Smith-Titian and Edward John, both of whom also passed away during the novel's creation. May they never be forgotten.

I am grateful for the writers who have personally lifted me with their encouragement and insight. Zsuzsi Gartner, Betsy Warland, Gail Anderson-Dargatz, David Adams Richards, Sarah Selecky and all my friends in the Story Is a State of Mind community.

Special thanks to Barbara Berson, a gifted editor whose grasp of the human condition and what I was trying to say about it still astounds me. To Anna Comfort O'Keeffe whose boldness and open-minded spirit created a space for this novel. To Shirarose Wilensky for her copyediting excellence. To all the wonderful people at Douglas & McIntyre for their hard work. And to my agent, Carolyn Forde, who kept the faith.

All my love to my children, Ben, Emma (NKBK) and Maddy, who are three of the kindest, funniest, smartest people I know. Katherine, Isabella and Alexandra, whose enthusiastic response at every stage has been appreciated more than they may know. Diamond, Sheldon, N.B. and Patrick, who never once said they didn't like it. My brother, David, and my father, John, whose never-ending support has always made it easier to try anything. And Nick, who makes everything special and possible.

Most of all, I owe this book to my late mother, Lynn Manuel, the best writer and kindest person I have ever known, the originator of the Wilde Grannies tales and the greatest of all Wilde Grannies herself. Every day, I miss her. Every day, I write to feel near her.

Nick Caumanns photo

Jennifer Manuel has achieved acclaim for her short fiction, including the Storyteller's Award at the Surrey International Writer's Conference in 2013. She has also published short fiction in *PRISM International*, *The Fiddlehead*, *Room Magazine* and *Little Fiction*. A long-time activist in Aboriginal issues, Manuel taught elementary and high school in the lands of the Tahltan and Nuu-chah-nulth peoples. She lives on Vancouver Island, BC.